She takes the little wisps of daydreams I had as a teenager, and turns them into great novels with plot twists galore, great characters, and good spiritual content to top it all off! I like the fact that characters you meet in one book will keep popping up in later books. I also like the fact that couples learn to really communicate with each other, so relationships are built on trust, not on sexual attraction alone. "Prince from Her Past" fills in gaps, drops hints for the future, leaves me gasping on the sofa with yet another cliff hanging plot twist, and reminds me of what makes a good marriage.

— MARGARET N

Everything about the book is exciting, all the pomp and circumstance, the heart stopping romance and the edge of your seat suspense. Carol paints a pretty picture of three small kingdoms in Europe with their Royal Families. We see the Lord 's protection of the family throughout the book.

— LINDA R

I LOVED the entire book! There wasn't anything I didn't just fall in love with....from Yvette's preparation for a wedding without a groom to the introductions and OH, the suspense throughout! It was just edge of your seat love and romance, with that suspense that only Moncado can add to this series. Just when you think you know where this story is going...guess again because she throws in a zinger that just blows you away! This series is awesome, but this book tops them all....but I say that about every book this author releases...just keeps getting better! A must read!

— RH

Prince from her Past

Carol Moncado
USA Today Bestselling Author

CANDID
Publications

P ounding on the door to her bedroom woke Princess Yvette Alexandra Charlotte Abigail of Mevendia from a dead sleep.

"What?" she yelled, praying it wasn't either of her parents. She'd be read the riot act for replying that way, though she had no way of knowing it was them and - she checked - she didn't have to be up for another hour.

"Your highness? Your father needs you to meet him in the throne room in an hour." Melinda, her personal assistant, walked over to the windows and pressed the button to open all of the curtains. Pinkish light from the dawn filled the room. And it was her birthday. No one should have to be up so early on her birthday. "He gave specific instructions."

"What's this about?" Yvette covered her head with her pillow.

"I don't know, miss. I believe the queen of Ravenzario is here on business, and he wants the whole family there."

Right. Yvette wanted to harbor feelings of snark toward her distant cousin, but found herself unable to. Orphaned by the car accident that took the life of Yvette's fiancé, Christiana had grown up with their mutual distant family members in Montevaro. At eighteen, she'd gained full control of the throne, hers only because of the death of her brother. The old rules of primogeniture still applied in Ravenzario, which meant Yvette would have been queen had Nicklaus lived. But Christiana had survived and should have been her sister-in-law in a week.

A national holiday had been declared in two countries.

The dress designed. The flowers ordered. Cake tasted. Invitations sent.

Nearly eighteen years earlier, her father had signed her life away. A marriage contract with the Crown Prince of Ravenzario. The wedding date had been set long before her first birthday and the contract had been written in such a way that it wasn't officially "broken" until two weeks after her birthday, a week after the wedding.

She'd asked about it a few times in the last few years. Why was she still engaged to a prince who died in a car accident in the last century? Her father had been terribly closed mouthed about it. And in five days, they'd head to Ravenzario where she'd get ready for the wedding, wait in an ante room, and when the groom failed to appear, head home in humiliation.

Yvette sat cross-legged on her bed, covers still pulled onto her lap.

If only she didn't love the dress so much. And the flowers. And everything else. She'd been able to choose whatever she wanted without a groom to interfere. Only her mother, the queen. And the protocol office. And a bunch of other stuffed shirts who wouldn't let her play a dirge as a wedding march, even though everyone knew this wedding wasn't actually going to happen.

And Lizbeth Bence. Really, Lizbeth had planned much of Yvette's wedding for her.

"Is the prince consort with her?" Yvette yawned as she swung her feet over the side of the bed.

"I don't know."

She'd met Duke Alexander several times and liked him. He'd even been her escort a time or two for official events in Ravenzario. However, Yvette hadn't seen him since the revelation of his teenage foray into acting became public. She'd binge watched 2 Cool 4 School, a teen comedy starring Alexander and his twin brother, Christopher, after the news came out.

"Here we go." Melinda walked back into the bedroom carrying one of the dresses Yvette loathed. Midnight blue, cinched waist, short train. Heels were a must. Yvette hated heels. Whoever invented them should have been banished to Antarctica for life. "You need to take a quick shower, miss. Wash your hair, and Belinda will be in shortly to do it for you."

Belinda and Melinda. Twin sisters Yvette didn't know what she'd do without. "Thanks, Melinda." It wasn't her fault the king was obnoxious this early in the morning. A quick shower, a longer hair session, and quick bite to eat later - an hour after the pounding on the door - Yvette was ready to go. As much as she hated dressing up in general, she had to admit, she felt nice wearing it.

Her heels clicked along the stone floor as she made her way to the throne room. Her father rarely conducted business in there, so why was he doing it now? Something to do with the wedding? Maybe they'd call the whole farce of a thing off.

"You're here." Before she fully entered the throne room, her father's voice boomed her direction. "The rest of the family is on their way."

Because of where they were and the staff watching, Yvette dropped a slight curtsy toward her father before kissing his cheek. "Everyone is coming?" If both of her older brothers, her sister-in-law, and her mother would be there, this was big. Whatever it was.

"Yes. Christiana called in the middle of the night and asked for an immediate audience with the entire family. Her plane arrived a few moments ago."

The door behind her opened again and the rest of the family

3

entered. Her brothers looked especially handsome in their uniforms, complete with swords and sashes. Jessabelle, her sister-in-law, looked more uncomfortable than Yvette had seen her in a long time. That wedding had been planned in less than two weeks, and Jessabelle had met Malachi at the altar. Yvette still didn't quite understand the forces behind the suddenness of that arranged marriage, though it was indirectly responsible for a turnaround in her father.

The protocol minister bustled in behind her mother. "They have arrived. Please take your places."

Her father was already seated on the throne. Her mother sat next to him. The children all had assigned spots. Yvette moved to hers as Malachi whispered to his wife, kissing her temple in a move that made Yvette long to be loved like her brother obviously loved his wife, no matter their beginning.

The exceptionally large double doors at the other end of the room were opened by white-gloved doormen. A voice boomed from somewhere unseen.

"Christiana, Queen of Ravenzario, and Alexander, Duke of Testudines, and guest."

Christiana, with her gorgeous blond curls falling around her shoulders, led the way with Alexander just behind. Yvette couldn't see the guest.

Christiana stopped a few feet in front of the throne. "Thank you for agreeing to see us on such short notice, King Antonio."

He waved her off. "My pleasure. But it is early, and I don't believe my family has eaten, so can we get down to business? We would be honored if you would join us for a meal afterward."

"It would be our pleasure." Christiana stepped forward just a bit, and Alexander seemed to fade into the background, giving Yvette the first glimpse of the guest.

Wavy brown hair, lips that threatened to twitch into an easy grin at any moment, and twinkling eyes captivated her. He was easily the most handsome man she'd ever seen.

4

Bar none.

Including her very handsome brothers and Alexander in his teen heartthrob days.

"King Antonio, Queen Alicia, Prince William, Prince Malachi, Princess Jessabelle, and..." Christiana turned to look straight at her. "Princess Yvette. There is someone I would like you to meet."

She stepped to the side, and the guest moved forward.

"My brother. Prince Nicklaus of Ravenzario."

Nick stared at the young woman he was supposed to marry. All the color had drained from her face, and she looked like she might faint.

Definitely not his goal for this first meeting.

The woman standing on the other side of the room moved unobtrusively behind the throne until she was at the younger woman's side. She slid an arm around Yvette's waist. At least he presumed the pretty, suddenly-pale, girl was Yvette. She matched the pictures Michaela kept around the house, though the most recent one had been several years old. The deep blue of her dress didn't help her skin tone any. In fact, the word "alabaster" came to mind.

The king drew Nick's attention back to the chair dominating the end of the long room. "Excuse me?"

Nick's new-found sister stared down the king. "You heard me, Antonio."

The king didn't look too pleased at the use of his name without the title in front of it. But Christiana was a queen in her own right. She may have been the younger generation, but she didn't let the king intimidate her.

Nick kept his eyes on the slip of a girl who seemed to be struggling to stand. Had she not been told there was even a possibility he was still alive? He didn't quite understand all of the dynamics that led to his escape with Michelle...Michaela. Would he ever get her real name straight in his head?

King Antonio ran his hand down his face. "Why don't we go have breakfast? This isn't the official conversation I thought it would be."

"What did you think it would be?" Christiana rested her hands on her expanding stomach. "That I was going to tell you no trace had been found?"

She was bluffing. Nick knew his sister had no idea where Tony had been. She truly believed her head of security had been on vacation, not tracking down the long-missing heir to the throne and his nanny.

"To be honest? Yes. I think all of us who knew of the escape plan believed contact would have been made long ago if the plan had been successful."

"You knew?" The whisper came from the girl to the side. "You knew he might be alive and you never told me? You didn't think I had a right to know?"

Antonio stood and walked toward her, enveloping her in a hug when he reached her. "Why don't we go change into something more comfortable. We'll have breakfast? And we'll talk it through then."

Princess Yvette nodded. "Okay," she whispered, the sound echoing through the large room. She turned and froze as his eyes met hers.

Nick smiled his best smile. He didn't want to scare her any more than she probably already was. He was also sure she didn't know what would happen if the wedding didn't take place. The only reason he still even considered going through with a wedding to someone he'd never met. That the three of them would be exiled if they didn't.

The Mevendian royal family all left with Nick, his sister, and brother-in-law trailing behind.

They were ushered into a formal dining room unlike any Nick had ever seen. He amended the thought. Not since he was a very young child. He'd been born Crown Prince Nicklaus, but he'd been raised solidly middle class American. This kind of dining room didn't exist in his world until a few days earlier.

It took nearly half an hour, filled mostly with uncomfortable silence between him and the family he didn't really know, for the Mevendian family to come back in. By then, food was being brought in as well.

"I suppose introductions are in order." King Antonio started as a plate was delivered. He pointed to the queen, seated to his right. Then his oldest son, William, and so on around the table until he got to the teenage girl, now dressed in nice slacks and a filmy top of some kind. "And, of course, my daughter, Princess Yvette. Your fiancée."

Nick smiled and nodded at her. "A pleasure to meet you."

She looked like she was going to cry and didn't say anything.

Before anyone else could, the door opened behind Nicklaus.

"I heard there was a family breakfast going on."

He turned to see an older woman, not very tall, walking in like she owned the place. Come to think of it, she likely had at one point, if she was a member of this royal family.

She came to a stop next to him, and before he realized what she was doing, her cool hands were on either side of his face. "Welcome home, Prince Nicklaus. We've been waiting for you."

He blinked as a servant pulled out the chair next to him, and she took a seat. "You've been waiting for me? You knew I was alive? *I* didn't even know I was alive." Well, that came out wrong.

But she just chuckled. "Oh, yes. I knew." She waved a hand toward the king. "Not in any official capacity, but I did know, in my heart of hearts, that Prince Nicklaus would be found."

"Why didn't you tell me, Nana Yvette?"

Nick could see the tender look on Nana Yvette's face. "It

7

wasn't time yet, my dear one. Just like it wasn't time for anyone to know about Malachi or Jessabelle until last year."

Who? Right. The king's second son and his wife, both now staring at their plates. That was a thread to be pulled at later.

Then Nana Yvette turned to him. "Why don't you tell us your story, Nicklaus? How did you manage to survive the accident, and where have you been all these years?"

Nick put down his fork and used his napkin to wipe his mouth. "I don't remember much of it," he admitted. "Just what my mother and Tony told me this week."

"Your mother?" The question came from the king.

Right. He needed to be more careful. A glance at his sister showed her studying her plate very carefully, her lips in a tight line.

"Michelle, that is. Michaela." Would he ever get it right? He reached over and squeezed his sister's hand. "Michaela, our nanny, went by Michelle. She never made it a secret that I wasn't her child, but I believed she was my aunt, raising me after the death of my parents. I hated not having a mother, and it kept up our pretense for me to call her mom most of the time. We rarely corrected those who didn't know any better. Those who knew us well enough knew what I believed to be the truth about the relationship."

He squeezed Christiana's hand again before letting it go. "I didn't know my sister was still living until a few weeks ago. I don't remember the escape or the journey to the United States. I just found out about the wedding this week. I always knew there was this girl, Eve, that my parents had hoped I'd marry, but I didn't know about the contract or the exiles until very recently."

"Exiles?" Princess Yvette looked at him then her father. "Who's being exiled?"

King Antonio set down his fork. "If this wedding does not happen, both of you and Michaela will be exiled from the Commonwealth."

Yvette felt the fork slip from her fingers and clatter onto the plate. "What?" she whispered.

Her father folded his hands on top of the table. "The contract is written in such a way that if the wedding doesn't take place, you, Nicklaus, and Michaela will be exiled from the Commonwealth countries."

"Why?" she whispered. "How could you do that to me? How could you sign a contract that would send me away when I turned eighteen?"

"Let's finish breakfast, and I will fill in more details about the circumstances under which the contract was signed and the reasons for some of them."

"Henry Eit." Queen Christiana stared at her plate. "He claimed to be our uncle, succeeded in killing my parents, was going to have me removed from the throne for reasons of insanity, positioned a man in my life to marry me and kill me on our honeymoon, then tried to kill me himself when he got out of prison. I would imagine my father's suspicions had something to do with the outlandish stipulations."

"You imagine correctly." The king took another bite.

Conversation remained stilted, but all Yvette could do was push her food around the plate.

Eventually, they went into the apartment where she still lived with her parents. Both of her brothers had moved eighteen months earlier to their own apartments in the palace. Now, despite the disapproving look from her mother, she sat in her favorite chair with her legs pulled to her chest.

Some eighteenth birthday this was turning out to be.

"Christiana was right," her father started. "King Richard suspected something was not quite right with Henry, though he could not prove it. He wanted safeguards in place in case anything happened to him and the children. If Henry had ever succeeded in killing or removing all of you, Yvette would have become queen."

Her head snapped up. "What? Me?"

Her father nodded. "You would have been queen, and I would have been the regent until you were of age." His eyes softened. "Until today."

"It's your birthday?" The unfamiliar male voice caught her attention.

She looked at him, comforted by the kind look in his eyes. "Yes."

"Happy birthday." His smile seemed genuine.

"Thank you."

"Regardless," her father went on. "Henry never would have taken the throne. Without the clause making Yvette queen, Ravenzario would have been absorbed into Mevendia and Montevaro. That was no one's top choice. Allowing Yvette as a member of Commonwealth royalty and the betrothed of the Crown Prince to take the throne would keep Henry out. Very few people knew all of the details of the contract. It was never made public. Richard and I did, both of our wives, the Prime Ministers and Minority Leaders of both countries at the time. King Jedidiah was the only one in Montevaro who knew anything until recently, but I am not certain if Adeline knows much."

Christiana nodded. "Tony, my head of security, told me bits and pieces over the last couple of years, but I don't know of anyone else who knew everything."

"Tony was very young for the job of head of security. Richard knew he was trustworthy, and he knew that, even if Henry managed to become regent somehow, Tony couldn't be fired or killed without suspicion."

Yvette still hadn't heard the answer she wanted. "None of that explains why you'd let them exile me."

"It was all part of it. Richard was afraid of what would happen if Henry had too much power over Nicklaus. It was part of the insurance that Henry would never have the complete control he wanted. Nicklaus would never have married someone else knowing what would happen to his nanny, even if he was raised not to care for you." Her father's voice was as gentle as she'd ever heard it. "Michaela would have been as difficult to get rid of as Tony. The clauses about the exiles was added to prevent Henry from trying to pass someone else off as Nicklaus who would refuse to marry Yvette. The imposter would have been exiled, too."

"So why is that part still in force? Why can't we get rid of the exile clauses, and let us both go on our merry way?" Tears blurred her vision.

"I am sorry, sweetheart, but it is the way it has to be."

Yvette pushed up from her seat. "I can't do this." She ran from the room, out of the apartment, down two flights of stairs then up several more, through multiple hallways and more stairs until she reached her favorite place in the palace.

The solarium, on the roof of the palace and overlooking the forest beyond, offered solitude she could rarely find. It was here she often came, though taking a much more direct route when she wasn't trying to keep people from following her.

She sank to her knees near the glass wall, her hands supporting her. Sobs shook her shoulders as the information she'd gained in the last hour rolled over her in waves.

"They told me you'd probably be up here."

She was already starting to recognize his voice. Or, perhaps, it was the only male voice out of those who would follow her that she didn't recognize.

"What do you want?" she managed to ask between sobs.

"I wanted to make sure you were all right." She heard his footsteps and the creak of the bench as he sat down. "I've been where you are and rather recently."

Yvette swiped the back of her hand across her face. "How so?"

"I've always known Michaela wasn't my mother. I believed she was my aunt who managed to get me away from a powerful businessman bent on destroying my family. I always knew there was potential danger out there, though it rarely came close enough to us to really make me afraid. Then, less than a week ago, Tony and Michaela told me the truth about who I was and this whole wedding thing and all of that." He let out a bark of laughter. "Of course, I was being chased by an assassin at the time, so I didn't have as much luxury to freak out. By the time we were safe, the initial shock had passed."

She shifted until she sat on the floor. "I'm glad you didn't die."

"Which time?" The smile in his voice surprised her, and she looked over to see the ready grin she'd suspected he had.

And he had a point. "Both, I guess."

"Can we start over?" He was close enough that he held out his hand for her to shake. "I'm Nicklaus, though I've gone by Nick or Nicky or Nicholas most of my life."

She managed to give him a weak smile. "Yvette. That's what I've always gone by unless someone tacks 'Your Royal Highness' or 'Princess' onto it."

Her hand slid into his to shake it, but Yvette found herself completely unprepared for the warmth of his skin on hers or for the shock wave it sent through her. She couldn't tell if he was affected the same way.

"It's a pleasure to meet you, Your Royal Highness, Princess Yvette." He turned her hand over and kissed the back of it. "Would you do me the honor of allowing me to escort you to dinner this evening? It will be a private affair, here on the property. Just you and me, unless you'd rather have someone else there with us."

Yvette blinked the remainder of the tears back. She surprised herself by saying, "I would like that. I would like that a lot."

Nick - no, Nicklaus. He had to start thinking of himself that way. Nicklaus knew he was projecting an image of himself he didn't necessarily believe. Confident and secure in his identity. He wasn't. Not in the least. But he didn't want Princess Yvette to know that. Not right now. His world was being turned upside down, but so was hers. If they didn't get married, he'd go back to the States and pick up his old life. But Yvette?

She'd lose everything.

Her family. Her friends. Her home. Even her country.

And she'd never be able to return.

He'd bet good money she wished he'd stayed dead.

He also had to figure out how to pull off a great dinner in a strange castle.

On her birthday, no less.

"You don't already have plans tonight?" he asked suddenly. Who didn't have plans on their eighteenth birthday?

Yvette shook her head. "No. My family might have had something planned, but if so, they didn't tell me about it."

He gave her his best smile. "Then it's you and me." Nicklaus glanced around, rubbing his hands together nervously. "Um, so who would I talk to about making dinner for you?"

She did something unexpected. Yvette laughed. With the fingers of one hand she wiped first under one eye and then the other. "I guess showing up at a strange palace and not knowing your way around makes it kind of hard to fulfill that dinner promise."

"It's not just the strange palace." He leaned forward and rested his forearms on his knees. "I'm still having a hard time coming to grips with all of it."

Yvette stared straight out the window for a long minute, not saying anything before her phone beeped. She pulled it out of her pocket and swiped across the screen. "My father wants us downstairs now."

He stood and held out a hand to help her up. Did she feel the same jolt of electricity he did when her hand gripped his? And what did it mean, if anything?

Nicklaus followed a couple of steps behind her as she headed for the same door he entered through. She stopped and looked up at him.

"Did you come this way? Or did you follow me?"

He gave her a half-grin. "I came this way. Your mother seemed awfully certain this was where you'd be despite your circuitous route." He didn't know how her mother knew she'd take a long way, but she'd seemed very certain.

Yvette didn't say anything else but turned back to the door. In minutes, they stood in her father's private office.

The dark wood elegance suited the king. Several portraits were hung on the walls with pictures of his children on the credenza. The piece of furniture probably had a fancier name, but that's what Nicklaus would call it.

"Have a seat." The king's voice surprised Nicklaus. Despite having heard him speak before, in here, it took on a James Earl Jones-Darth Vader tone. Nicklaus didn't dare not do as he was asked. After Yvette took one of the leather wingback chairs, he took the other. "There are many things we need to discuss." The king shuffled some papers on his desk. "First, the wedding is in seven days." He stared directly into Nicklaus's eyes. "Do you plan to attend?"

Cuts right to the chase, doesn't he? Nicklaus wanted to give him the answer he knew they both wanted, but something in him told Nicklaus they would both appreciate the truth even more. "I don't know," he answered, as honest as he could be. "I've been thrown into this as much, or more, than the princess has been the last few hours. I want to be there, but I also want to make certain it is the right choice, what God wants for all of us, rather than selfish motives on my part."

King Antonio's eyes seemed to see right into his soul. Nicklaus wanted to squirm under the intense glare, but managed to keep from doing so. "That is a good answer," the monarch finally said. "Yvette, give us some time?"

The princess nodded, but didn't say anything as she left the room.

When it was just the two of them, the king spoke again. "The last thing I want is for my daughter to be exiled. The next to last thing I want is for her to end up in a marriage like her mother's was for many years."

Nicklaus tried to assimilate his meaning, but failed. "I'm sorry, sir. I don't follow."

The king stood and walked to a window, his hands clasped behind his back. "I was not the husband I should have been for many years of our marriage. I was unfaithful to my wife, with a poorly-hidden mistress on the side until Malachi was around three years old." His shoulders slumped for a moment then straightened. "Those I hold most dear have paid a steep cost for my repeated infidelities."

He turned and once again those eyes seemed to see straight through Nicklaus. "If you marry my daughter, it is for better or worse, in sickness and in health, love-honor-cherish, until death parts you. But especially you will abide by the keeping yourself only unto her part. Am I quite clear?"

Nicklaus stood and dug deep inside, trying to find the vestiges of his proud, royal lineage. He walked toward the king, stopping just two feet in front of him. "Sir, when I take vows to love, honor, to cherish, and to keep myself only for my wife, no threats from you will be necessary for me to keep those vows."

"And if you marry my daughter, how will you treat her when the doors close behind you? You will have known her a week, but we all know the Ravenzarian laws. Will you take more than she's willing to give?"

When he stood as tall as he could, Nicklaus had an inch or two on the older man. He wasn't nearly as intimidating as the monarch, but he'd hold his own. "Sir, you don't know me, and I may not remember anything of my royal heritage, but do you really think so little of Michaela Engel, who gave her *entire life* to save mine? Do you think she would raise me to be a man who would take advantage of a lady?"

The stare down lasted several seconds before the king gave a single nod. He didn't say anything else, but Nicklaus sensed he'd passed the test. Following the king's lead, Nicklaus took his seat again. "And for the record, sir, I have no idea what Ravenzarian law you're referring to. I have spent less than thirty-six hours in the country since I was a toddler."

King Antonio sighed. "Ravenzarian law requires the monarch or heir to begin attempting to conceive an heir as soon as possible."

Nicklaus didn't know what to do with that piece of information. "I'm not the monarch."

"No. But you were supposed to be. I am not certain what will happen to the Ravenzarian throne now that you have returned. I would imagine the resolutions passed not long after the accident would remain in effect, and Christiana will retain her position. If you wanted to challenge her on that, you would have a very strong case, despite those resolutions. DNA tests have already proven your relationship to Christiana beyond any doubt. That said, if something were to happen to Christiana before the birth of her child, you or Yvette would be next in line. You, if the resolutions are vacated. Yvette, if not. Unless, of course, she's exiled. Then all bets are off, and Ravenzario would likely be absorbed into Mevendia and Montevaro."

Right.

No pressure.

Yvette sat in the outer office and wondered what her father and Nicklaus could be talking about. It had been nearly an hour since she had been asked to leave. She debated going to find something else to do, but stayed where she was.

"Miss?"

She looked up to see Melinda standing in the doorway. "Yes?"

"Ms. Bence is here to see you."

Right. A last minute wedding planning meeting. "I will be there momentarily."

"I will let her know."

Melinda left, and Yvette took another long look at the door to her father's office. She followed in her assistant's footsteps, exiting the apartment and heading for a conference room on the first floor.

"Hello, Lizbeth. How are you?"

Lizbeth looked up from the binder they'd received from Alexander Bayfield when the planning first started. "Hey. We're almost done. This will be all over before you know it."

Right. Yvette debated telling her everything, that Nicklaus had been found, but decided she should wait until a final determination had been made. If he decided not to go through with the wedding, maybe they would just not tell anyone he'd shown back up. It would be far less humiliating to be stood up by a dead man than by one back from the dead who chose to leave her at the altar.

Lizbeth turned back to the table. "We need to go over the seating chart one more time."

Yvette collapsed in a chair. "Why?" Her eyes filled with tears. "Why do we need a seating chart for a reception that will never happen?"

Lizbeth looked up at her. "Your father didn't tell you?"

"Tell me what?"

"He plans to turn the reception into a belated celebration of life for all four of those lost in the car accident."

A good plan. If Nicklaus and Michaela were actually dead. Michaela's parents knew she was alive. Word would leak out eventually.

But if Nicklaus decided to go through with the wedding, they would need the seating chart.

Yvette had no choice. If he said yes, she *could* back out, but only at the cost of everything she'd ever known.

"Yvette."

She looked up to see an annoyed look on Lizbeth's face. "Sorry. I'm preoccupied."

Lizbeth's face softened. "It's okay. You've got a lot going on. I just said I think we're done until Thursday."

Yvette sighed. "We leave Wednesday, right? But we don't have anything scheduled that day?"

Lizbeth checked. "You're right. You have your fitting that day, but that's it. You'll be staying at the Ravenzarian palace for the duration. You..." Lizbeth shifted uncomfortably. "The cabin on the Baicampo property is reserved for two nights, but Alexander knows the whole story. If you wanted to hide out for a couple of days after this is all over, you could stay there, but you don't have to."

She didn't respond. Yvette didn't know how to. So much hinged on the dinner later this evening.

Once Lizbeth left, Yvette went back to her father's office. The door was closed, but his assistant was nowhere to be seen. She had no way of knowing if Nicklaus was still in there.

After staring for a couple of minutes, she decided it was time to be somewhere else. If Nicklaus walked out he'd find her staring, and she didn't want that.

Instead she went back to her room and into her closet. The wedding trunk used by several brides before her was already open and being packed. Belinda and Melinda would take care of it for her, assisted by several others, most likely. The wedding dress was already in Ravenzario, along with quite a bit of other wedding paraphernalia.

"Are you all right, miss?"

Melinda's voice didn't surprise Yvette as she stared into the partially-filled chest. "I suppose."

"I heard what happened. Not all of the details, but I happened to hear Queen Christiana and Duke Alexander say something to the young man who arrived with them. They used his name. Belinda and I put two and two together."

"Please don't say anything to anyone else." She didn't even need to ask, but she did anyway.

"Are you going to marry him?"

"I don't know." She turned to the dresses in every color of the rainbow. Some looked better on her than others, both in color and cut. Tonight she needed to look her very best. Did she have any new ones she hadn't worn yet? Maybe a green? "We're having dinner tonight. I need to look fabulous." A tear snuck down her cheek.

"You always look fabulous, miss." Yvette felt Melinda's hand on her shoulder. "What is it?"

Yvette took a deep breath and willed the rest of the tears back inside. "I am just nervous. If this night goes poorly..." She wouldn't tell anyone about the exile. Not yet. Maybe she wouldn't have to.

"It will be fine. He's already in your parents' kitchen with Cook. I think they were going to the main kitchen for the actual preparations."

Yvette turned to look at her assistant. "Is he making it? Or just helping Cook plan?"

"I'm not sure, miss."

She pulled one dress then another out for a look. "I don't like any of them." It was too important. Her dress, her hair, everything had to be perfect. "Is it too late to get a manicure and pedicure today?"

"We can arrange it. Would you like me to see if Stefan is available to do your hair?"

And there was one reason she loved Melinda. She understood, even if she didn't understand. Melinda moved to the side. Belinda was technically her stylist, but both had great taste.

"What about this one, miss?" Melinda pulled out an emerald green dress with a bit of sparkle on it. "You haven't worn it in public yet, and you look fantastic in it."

Yvette took it, holding it up in front of her as she looked in the mirror. "Yes. I think this is perfect."

Fifteen minutes before she was to meet Nicklaus, Yvette stared into the mirror again. The dress fit exceptionally well. The strappy silver sandals didn't have a heel. They weren't going *out*. When she left the palace dressed up - or when there was an event held inside the palace - she had to wear the heels. At least she didn't need to bother with a handbag.

"You look lovely."

Yvette turned to see her father leaning against the door jamb. "Thanks."

"I mean it. I don't think you've ever looked more beautiful." He came to stand in front of her, his hands resting on her shoulders. "I wish you were not forced into the position, but it must be this way. I talked with Nicklaus for some time today, and I believe he will be a good husband to you." He held out a velvet box. "Happy birthday."

She'd nearly forgotten, but took it from him. Snapping it open, she gasped. "It's beautiful." The whisper caught on the lump in her throat.

"Allow me?"

Yvette nodded and turned. The elegant sapphire and diamond necklace nestled in the hollow of her neck as he fastened it. She faced her father again.

"I love you, Yvette. I am incredibly proud of the young woman you've become. Tonight will go well."

"I pray you are right."

He pressed a kiss to her forehead. "He's waiting for you."

Yvette took a deep breath and walked toward the main entrance to the apartment.

Here went nothing.

Nicklaus looked around the balcony. Things were as perfect as he could make them. So much hinged on how this evening went. If it went poorly, it would affect all of them. But if it didn't go well...

Could he marry Yvette in a week, if tonight was awful, knowing divorce wasn't even an option?

Nicklaus sighed. Would he be able to trust that the Yvette he got to know tonight was the real Yvette? She had far more riding on this than he did and might put on a good front, trying to get him to like her rather than being herself.

A glance at his watch told him he still had a few minutes, so he leaned against the balcony railing and looked out over the vast forest beyond. He didn't close his eyes, but spent those moments in prayer, asking God to be with them, and to help them both make the right decisions. Though they were just outside the capitol city, it was dark enough here on a hill, on the other side of the palace from the street lights, to see the millions of stars hung in the distance.

"'The heavens declare the glory of God; the skies proclaim the work of his hands.'" He spoke quietly, but with only himself around, it seemed much louder.

"Prince Richard of Montevaro says that all the time."

Nicklaus started at the voice then turned. Yvette still stood in the shadows closer to the palace. He couldn't really see her. "Pardon?"

"I didn't mean to startle you. I heard you quote Psalm 19:1. Prince Richard, from Montevaro, says it all the time when he sees a beautiful landscape. One of his goals in life is to yell it from the top of Mt. Everest."

"Prince Richard?" He should know this. Michaela had made certain he knew all about the three countries in the Commonwealth of Belles Montagnes, though she'd never mentioned Yvette by name.

"Second in line for the throne of Montevaro." She still hadn't moved. "His older sister is Queen Adeline. She has a son. Richard is next in line after him. He's praying Addie and Charlie, her husband, have another child soon. Perhaps then the security teams will allow him to climb that mountain. Until then he has to settle for views like this one." She gestured to the view.

Nicklaus turned back to contemplate it for another moment. "It is pretty gorgeous."

Yvette came to stand next to him, but he didn't turn her direction. Instead, he focused on the stars.

She broke the silence after a long moment. "I took a picture of Saturn once."

"You did?" Did this place have a telescope? That would be cool.

"Saturn and Venus were very close together in the sky a couple of years ago. Summer 2015, I think. I tried to take a picture with my phone. When I looked at it later, it hit me. I took a picture of a planet. I took a picture of *Saturn*. With. My. *Phone*. It's not much more than a lightish half circle next to a brighter circle, but it's a planet nearly 1.2 *billion* kilometers away."

Right. They used the metric system in Europe. Nicklaus mentally thanked Michaela for pounding the conversions into his head. "That's pretty spectacular," he admitted. "I'd like to see it sometime."

"I'll pull it up later. I posted it on my official Facebook page." She paused. "Along with the verse you just quoted. It seemed fitting."

"It would be." They stood for another minute. "Mom didn't want me to have Facebook or other social media accounts. I guess now I understand why, but I'm not sure if she even has one."

"Your mom?"

"Michaela." He needed to stop referring to her as his mother. "I've called her 'mom' for so long that it will be hard to stop. I need to. I know that. And she never really encouraged me to, but even though I knew she wasn't my mom, it was easier than explaining the situation to everyone." He sighed, a bit surprised at how he was pouring his heart out to a virtual stranger. "When you're six, and you tell the class you're being raised by your aunt because your parents were killed by a madman..."

"I can't imagine that went well."

"Not really. It became much easier just to refer to Michaela as my mom. Even when I didn't, she was Michelle. I have to constantly remind myself she's not. She's not my aunt. Not the person I thought I knew." He lowered his eyes until he looked out at the road leading into the palace. From the other side, it sat on top of a cliff with an imposing gate blocking the drive.

But here, it almost seemed unguarded, though he knew that

wasn't the case. The land beyond the road, extending as far as he could see, was also part of the palace property. Out there some-where was a rock wall, a fortress wall, protecting those inside.

"I can't imagine what that was like." Yvette's voice almost seemed to be full of tears. "I still don't even know how you and Michaela survived. I cannot begin to fathom what *that* must have been like."

"I don't remember it." He thanked God for that. "I don't even know how we survived, to be honest. I wasn't even four yet, and I never even thought to ask when I got older. I guess I wondered earlier this week when Tony and Michaela told me the truth, but it kind of got lost in the whole 'you're a prince and getting married next week' thing."

Yvette didn't reply. Nicklaus wanted to look over at her, standing just a few inches away, but he didn't dare. He feared she was crying, and he didn't know how to deal with a crying woman.

"I've known about the wedding my whole life. I spent the last eight months planning a wedding with no groom. Now that you're alive, I have no idea what I feel about the whole 'getting married in a week' thing." Her voice broke. "I'll even admit to you that I wondered what it would be like to suddenly find out you weren't dead after all and find you waiting at the end of the aisle for me. I find the reality of that dream is not quite as I'd hoped."

Nicklaus wasn't sure how to take that. "I'm sorry." He didn't know what else to say.

"It's not your fault. Daydreams and reality are often far different."

He finally turned to look at her. Even with her head hanging down, she took his breath away. "Tell me about your daydream?" He reached out and tipped her chin up.

When her eyes finally met his, he knew.

He would do anything to keep them from showing the pain he now saw.

In seven days, he would marry her.

4

Yvette stared into his eyes and struggled to keep the tears from falling. She'd known this guy less than eighteen hours, and she was about to cry for the second time.

"Tell me about it," Nicklaus repeated.

About her daydream? The one where he waited for her at the end of the aisle, swept her up onto his white horse, and they rode off into the sunset to live happily ever after.

No matter that their wedding was scheduled for two in the afternoon.

She shook her head and turned back to look over the forest. "It doesn't matter. Daydreams are idealistic at best. Reality can never match up. It's just the way it is."

"I don't think that's necessarily true," he countered.

"Have you ever had reality measure up to a daydream? Where your speech went better than you'd hoped? Or you didn't come off looking like you didn't know what you were talking about in that interview? Or where your groom showed up like your knight in shining armor to sweep you off your feet and take you away from it all for a while?" Her voice cracked no matter how much she tried to keep it from doing so.

"Do you need a knight in shining armor, princess?" Nicklaus's soft voice gave her some hope. "Or do you just need an ordinary guy who will do his best to love you no matter what?"

She shook her head, a single tear falling out of one eye. "It doesn't matter what I need. My life has been planned since before I was born. It's part of being born into the Van Rensselaer dynasty." One more tear leaked out of that eye, followed by one from the other.

No! She had to get herself under control. Bawling like a little girl in front of this man twice on the first day of their acquaintance would only send him running for the hills. And she needed him to stay.

Yvette drew in a deep breath and willed the tears to stay put. She blew it out slowly. "It's fine. I've known my whole life what was about to happen. The exile part is new, but I can work around that, I'm sure. My family wouldn't desert me completely, even if they had to come visit me instead of the other way around."

Out of the corner of her eye, she could see Nicklaus start to say something at least once. Then he turned all the way around and offered her his arm. "I'm sure we will have plenty of time to discuss all of it at some point, but right now, why don't we eat? I'd hate for the food to get cold or gross waiting on us."

Yvette didn't look him straight in the eye, but turned and took his arm. "I doubt Cook has ever served anything that wasn't perfection."

He covered her hand with his other one, the warmth sending a thrill through her. "But Cook didn't make dinner tonight. I did. I hope that's okay." She heard uncertainty in his voice. "I mean, I hope you like it. It's not fancy. Doesn't have six courses or anything."

"I am sure it will be fine, Nicklaus."

He stopped at the table and let go of her hand to hold the chair for her as she sat down. A few seconds later, he sat near her. Not across from her. No. She'd known from the moment she'd seen the table that this meal was designed to be an intimate dinner for two. The chairs were only inches apart. She wouldn't be able to see him without both of them turning their heads, but it was better, she supposed, than looking straight at each other the whole time.

Silver domes covered the plates, but Nicklaus held out his hand to her. "Shall we pray?"

Yvette slid her hand into his once more, doing her best to focus on his words and thanking God herself. Instead, she found most of her focus on her hand in his.

"Amen," she whispered when he let go.

A member of the seemingly ubiquitous household staff appeared to take the domes and fill their drinks. They all knew what she liked, but they must have asked Nicklaus. Or he was polite enough to drink what they brought no matter his own preference.

She didn't recognize the meal, but tried it anyway.

Different.

Not bad, but definitely different than anything she'd ever had before.

"The first place we lived when we moved to the United States was Louisiana. Michaela fell in love with the cuisine. We often ate Cajun food, even after we moved."

Interesting. "How many different places did you live?" She had never lived outside the palace walls.

"Five, I think. Six, I guess if you count our last move to Minnesota, but that's because Tony was on our tail. We didn't know who might have been coming after us, so we packed up and left. We left less than an hour after she got a call that someone had been looking for us in Louisiana. Michaela rarely had many clothes in her go bags. Just enough for a couple of days. She mostly brought pictures and a few things from the safe she always bought when we got to a new house."

She looked over at him. "Pictures? Why didn't she scan them and keep them on a thumb drive? Then she could have accessed them and reprinted them later."

"You know, I don't know why she didn't. Part of it, knowing what I know now, was to keep them out of the hands of whoever was following us. I'd guess the rest would be knowing it was a reproduction and not the actual photograph?"

"What kinds of pictures did she have?" Yvette found herself fascinated by the woman who'd given up so much to raise Nicklaus and keep him safe.

"Mostly ones of the two of us. Mine from school, things like that." He hesitated and seemed to stare at his food for a long moment. "There was always a picture of Eve. The girl my parents wanted me to marry."

"Eve?" Could it be that Michaela had been preparing him for this all along? Yvette barely dared hope.

"Yes. There was always a picture in the house, and now I know who it really was." He looked at her with those milk chocolate eyes. "You. The pictures were of you."

NICKLAUS SHOULDN'T HAVE TOLD HER. NOW SHE'D ASK QUESTIONS about what he'd thought about her growing up and who knew what else.

But Yvette surprised him. Instead of bombarding him with any number of questions, she stared at her plate. With her fork, she pushed some of the dirty rice and andouille around. He'd been momentarily surprised to find the andouille locally, then Cook reminded him it was originally a French sausage. It didn't taste quite the same, but close enough.

Time to change the subject.

"Tell me what it was like growing up in a palace?" Nicklaus leaned a little closer as though he didn't want anyone to overhear. Not that there was anyone around. "What's one thing you loved to do that you knew you weren't supposed to?"

She took another bite, but seemed to be thinking. "When I was little, Malachi would sneak me out to the ballroom. We'd put on socks so no one would hear us and go sliding around the ballroom floor." A hint of a smile showed on her face. "After we slid around for a while, he'd teach me how to dance. He's not that much older than me, but he was already taking lessons."

"Did Prince William ever do anything like that with you?"

"No. He's much more of a stuffed shirt than Kai is. He never did anything fun."

"What else?"

She poked at her food for another minute. "Promise not to tell?"

"Maybe."

Yvette looked at him, surprised.

"I mean," he went on. "Even if I promised not to say something, but then I found out there was a safety issue..."

"Nothing like that." Her brows pulled together. "I don't think so anyway. There's a bunch of secret passages around here. I'd guess most castles have some. Anyway, one leads to a spot overlooking the ballroom. Sometimes, when we were too young to go to the balls, Kai and I would sneak up there to watch for a little while." She sighed. A little wistful sigh. "The ladies were always so elegant and the men so handsome in their tuxedos. Some of them would wear swords and sashes, depending on any titles they might have." Color stole into her cheeks.

What was that about? "When was the last time you snuck up there?"

"Um..." She seemed to be debating, then decided. "Christmas Eve. I begged off going to the ball. I hate going to them. Always alone. I told them I was sick. I guess I really meant heartsick. Malachi tried to talk me into being his date because Jessabelle wasn't feeling well. In fact, it was only a couple of days before Catherine was born, but I didn't want to go. Instead, I went up there and watched. I guess she felt better because Jessabelle was there for a little while at least."

"Why were you heartsick?" Would she trust him enough to tell him?

Yvette pushed her plate away and wiped her mouth on her napkin. "I was planning a wedding to a dead man."

Ouch. Nicklaus winced, but she didn't notice.

"I've never had an escort to a ball or wedding or other function. At least not one I wasn't related to. No. I take that back. Alexander was my escort a time or two before he married Christiana. But at Christmas, I sat there in the little nook and saw my parents dancing together. Not the waltz they danced first, but later when he surprised her by having them play her favorite song, and they slow danced together. I mean, they're the king and queen. They don't dance too closely, even during a slow song." She stopped and stared at her hands where they were clenched on her lap.

"And?" he prompted after a minute.

"And I wondered if anyone would ever look at me that way." Her quiet voice crackled with emotion. "The way Malachi and Jessabelle look at each other. Or any of my Montevarian cousins with their spouses. Or Christiana and Alexander. But..." She took a deep, shuddering breath. "None of them have been through what my parents have. To see them so very much in love after everything they've been through in the last eighteen months... I wanted that, and I didn't think I'd ever get it. Who would want to marry a princess and all the responsibilities and pressures that come with being part of the royal family, especially after she was stood up at the altar by a dead man?"

"But I'm not dead." He stood up and held out a hand, bowing slightly at the waist. "May I have the pleasure of this dance, Your Highness?"

When she looked up, he could see the sheen of tears in her eyes, but she blinked them away. "That would be lovely."

She put her hand in his, and he led her to an open space near the table. The music that had been playing softly in the background was louder. They must be closer to a speaker.

Nicklaus bowed again before reaching for her, taking her right hand in his left. His right hand rested on her hip, but he pulled her closer to him. Not too close, but not so far away the *Titanic* could sail through unnoticed.

"You still don't think anyone will ever look at you like that." It was a statement of fact, not a question. "You're afraid that, if we don't get married in a week, you'll still be seen as damaged goods somehow. That no one will want to marry you and everything that goes along with being a royal in exile. You're afraid if we get married, it'll be little more than a marriage of convenience, and I would never look at you like that."

Yvette continued to stare at him, somewhere around the knot of his tie, if he had to guess.

"Am I right?" he asked softly.

She finally gave a single nod.

Nicklaus pulled her closer until the side of his chin rested next to her temple. "I promise you, Yvette Van Rensselaer, some lucky man is going to spend the rest of his life looking at you that way."

Yvette moved away from him just enough to look up into his

eyes. "Are you going to be that man?" Her soft breath teased his skin as a single tear streaked down her cheek.

He released her hand and cradled the side of her face in his palm. With his thumb he swiped the tear away.

Then he did something he'd never done before.

Kissed a girl the day he met her.

5

T he kiss caught Yvette by surprise.

Her heart caught in her throat as her mind frantically scrambled for what to do next.

How to respond.

Should she respond?

But then Nicklaus pulled her closer, and she melted into him, returning his kiss. The hand that had rested on his shoulder while they danced slid around to the back of his neck. And then...

He was gone.

Yvette's eyes stayed closed, not sure she wanted to open them and see the regret on his face.

"I'm sorry," he whispered. "I shouldn't have done that when we barely know each other."

"It's okay," she whispered back. But he didn't let her go. If anything his hold on her tightened.

She could feel him breathing in and out. Feel his heartbeat under her hand. Feel the goosebumps on the back of his neck under her fingers.

But something shifted as he breathed in deeply then

exhaled, his breath teasing the hair near her temple. "We should talk, and I don't think we'll be able to have the kind of conversation we need to have while we're this close to each other. At least, I know my thoughts are kind of muddled this close to you."

Oh, yeah. Her thoughts were all muddled, too. "Okay." She apparently couldn't talk any louder than a whisper with him this close. Her eyes were still closed as she felt him press a tender kiss to her forehead.

He moved away but took her hand. "Where would you like to talk? Here? Somewhere else?"

"It doesn't matter to me." She wasn't sure here was the right place, but she didn't know where else to go either. She thought of several places and discarded them all. None of them seemed right for this conversation.

"Maybe a garden? Some place besides the solarium that you like to go?"

Finally, Yvette shook her head. "Here is fine." She didn't let go of him but walked toward a couple of chairs tucked off to the side. Once there, she dropped his hands, tucking the skirt of her dress underneath her as she sat down. Nicklaus sat in the other chair. "What should we talk about?"

Nicklaus chuckled under his breath. "I suppose we have a lot to talk about."

"I suppose that is an understatement." She stared over the railing toward the trees beyond.

After a minute, he spoke. "I don't want you to be exiled, Yvette. You or Michaela."

She turned that over in her head for a minute. "You don't want *me* to be exiled, or you don't want *Michaela* to be exiled, and we're a package deal?"

Yvette expected a knee-jerk answer assuring her that she mattered to him as much as the woman who raised him. Instead, he took his time thinking it over. "I owe you complete honesty. I owe my life to Michaela several times over. I couldn't stand to see her exiled."

"So you would marry me to make sure she's not?"

He turned to her, and she could see sincerity on his face. "I don't know you, Princess Yvette. I want to get to know you, but I don't yet. I don't want to see you exiled, but in the same way I wouldn't want to see *anyone* kicked out of their homeland for no good reason." He reached for her hand but apparently decided better of it. "I *want* to care about you enough that I don't want to see *you* exiled when I can stop it from happening, but we've known each other maybe twelve hours and most of that we weren't even in the same place."

She turned her head, this time staring at the stars. "I appreciate your honesty."

"I wish I could give you the answer you want."

Yvette believed him. Believed he wanted to say he wanted to marry her.

"When do you need a final answer?"

Now! part of her screamed. She needed an answer *now* for her own peace of mind. Should she be packing for a wedding trip? Or to move to a whole other country?

"Would you do something for me?" she whispered.

"If I can," he replied instantly.

"Take me with you."

"What?"

"If you decide not to go through with this wedding, take me to the States with you. I have nowhere to go outside of the Commonwealth. Please don't leave me to do this on my own."

He didn't actually answer, but did nod. At least he seemed to be considering it.

"I think I'm going to turn in. It's been a long day. Thank you for dinner." Maybe a good cry and strict instructions to only be woken up in case of World War III would help. If she slept half of the next day away, it would be one day she wouldn't have to live through this week.

Yvette stood, said good night, and started for the door. As she reached for the ornate handle, she heard him behind her.

"Wait."

She stopped but didn't turn around.

"I have a birthday present for you."

No one else had given her anything, except the necklace from her father, which she wore. When she faced Nicklaus again, he held a small gift bag. Inside, she found a velvet jewelry box. Not a ring box, but flat and about fifteen centimeters by twenty.

"Michaela had this for many years. She protected it almost as well as she protected me." He shrugged. "I never really understood why, but she told me it was for Eve."

"So it's something from Ravenzario?"

"I would presume so."

Yvette opened the box to find an ornate choker. Diamonds and sapphires. Emeralds and purple sapphires.

And he had no idea what it meant.

"I never thought it was real," she heard Nicklaus say, though she wasn't really paying attention. "But I guess it is. Not cubic zirconia or whatever."

"No. It's very real." Yvette gently ran her fingers over the heirloom. "But I can't accept this."

"Why not? Is it something the queen, my sister that is, should keep?"

She shook her head. "No. It's something that rightfully should be mine."

"Then why not..."

Yvette didn't care how rude it was to interrupt someone. Not now. "On Saturday." She snapped the box closed and held it out to him. "It should rightfully be mine if I become your wife."

Nicklaus didn't take the box. When she dared look at him, he looked like he was trying to process what she'd said. Rather than wait for him to sort it out, she slid the Van Rensselaer Accord Jewels back into the gift bag and left. She didn't stop until she reached her room, where she threw herself on the bed for that cry.

He'd blown it.

But Nicklaus still wasn't entirely certain how.

It hadn't gone *poorly*, at least not until the very end. Not the best date he'd ever been on, but not the worst he'd heard of either. Not even close. Conversation was a bit stilted. Not unexpected for people who barely knew each other, but were in their position. The dance had been nice.

The *kiss* had been nice. *Really* nice.

"Would you like us to clean up, sir?"

Nicklaus turned to see one of the staff members who'd help him set everything up. "Sure." He started for the table, intending to help, but the uncertain and awkward look on the other man's face told him it wasn't really the way things were done.

Instead, he went back inside and stood for a minute, trying to remember where his rooms were. Christiana and Alexander were also staying overnight in Mevendia. They'd been put in a suite. Somewhere.

"Can I help you, sir?"

A young woman in a maid's uniform stood there, looking at him expectantly. "I'm afraid I'm not sure where to go. I know I'm staying in a suite with Queen Christiana and Duke Alexander, but I have no clue where that is."

"Did security download the map to your phone, sir?"

Security had done something with his phone, and he told her so.

She held out a hand. "May I, sir?"

38

Why not? Nicklaus entered his security code and handed it over. A minute later, she'd showed him the basics of how to use the app they'd installed. She set his suite as his home base and directions popped up.

"You're all set, sir. Just follow the instructions. It's not far."

He thanked her then looked at the instruction list. Not far? Maybe not, but there were about a dozen turns to take. His position was indicated by a dot with an arrow pointing the direction he should go. In just a few minutes, he was in the sitting area portion of their suite.

"How'd it go?" Alexander looked up from his tablet.

Nicklaus sat in one of the chairs and leaned forward with his elbows on his knees. "It could have gone better."

"Could it have gone worse?"

He snorted. "I could have shot her. Accidentally knocked her over the railing. Given her food poisoning. Those would have been worse."

Alexander chuckled, and Nicklaus glared at him. "Sorry." Alexander tried to get it under control. "Did she like her birthday present? What'd you get her anyway?"

Nicklaus held the bag up by one finger. "She gave it back."

"What is it?"

He pulled the velvet case out and tossed it on the couch near his brother-in-law. "Michaela told me it was for Eve. I always thought it was fake, but I realize it's probably not."

Alexander opened it as Christiana walked in from their room. "I don't think it's fake, Nick."

Christiana rested her hands on her husband's shoulders. "You gave that to Yvette?"

"Yeah. Michaela said it was Eve's. Eve is really Yvette. So I gave it to her. I take it that's some kind of major *faux pas*?" He ran a hand through his hair. "She said it was supposed to be hers after the wedding then gave it back and took off."

Christiana came to sit next to Alexander and took the case.

"After Henry's first arrest, we looked into what had happened to the crown jewels. Fortunately, they were untouched. Tony saw to that. This one was never found. We presumed it was lost somewhere along the way. We even contacted Antonio to see if he had it, but had not logged it properly."

It was slowly starting to sink in. "So this thing is a big deal? Besides the fact it must cost a fortune?"

His sister nodded. "It's the Van Rensselaer Accord Jewels. The two countries got into a bit of a tiff a century and a half or so ago. A Mevendian prince, though not the crown prince, was supposed to marry a Ravenzarian princess. There was never a formal arrangement, just an understanding. They married, but the country was at war. He left shortly after the wedding and died in battle. She was then to marry the Crown Prince, but he fell in love with a local girl and married her instead. The Ravenzarians were understandably annoyed, and another of the Mevendian princes was essentially forced into marrying the princess. This was a wedding present from the Mevendian king for the second wedding." She opened the box and showed it to him. "The sapphires and diamonds form part of our family crest. The emeralds and purple sapphires form part of the Mevendian crest. After the wedding ceremony, they signed an accord reinforcing the friendship pact already in place. We both use variations on the same dynasty name so it was called the Van Rensselaer Accord. In the marriage contract Papa signed for you and Yvette, he stipulated that this would be given back to the Mevendian family - or at least to Yvette as your bride."

"And if I don't marry her?"

Christiana exchanged a look with Alexander. One Nicklaus couldn't read. "I do not really know. I presume it would stay in our family as it was a wedding gift for a marriage that won't ever happen."

"Are you considering going through with the wedding?" Alexander had set his tablet to the side.

"I don't know." Nicklaus slouched back in the chair. "Marrying a girl I don't know, one who *just* turned eighteen, doesn't seem fair to anyone involved. But if we don't get married, Michaela, and I are exiled within a week of our families finding out we're still alive, and Yvette loses everything she's ever known. None of this is fair."

"I know." Alexander reached over and took Christiana's hand. "But sometimes God takes 'not fair' and turns it in to something amazing."

Nicklaus just watched as Christiana extracted her hand and touched Alexander's face. "Believe me when I say nothing about my life has been fair, brother. But finding out about the duplicity of my former fiancé, and Alexander offering to marry me instead? I couldn't ask for a better happy ending."

When Alexander turned his head to kiss Christiana's hand, Nicklaus rolled his eyes.

Alexander chuckled at him again. "Just wait. When you fall in love, you'll do the same thing."

And therein lay the crux of one of Nicklaus's biggest fears. "But what if I marry Yvette and don't fall in love with her? What if I fall in love with someone else?"

6

Twenty-four hours after Yvette left Nicklaus standing on the balcony with priceless jewels in his hand, she still hadn't heard from him. The Ravenzarians hadn't left. She did know that. Her father had met with Christiana for several hours on other business. A closed door meeting - though Alexander had been in and out a few times. Yvette suspected it was as much a mentor session as an actual business meeting. Alexander had plenty of business acumen, but Christiana never really had anyone teach her how to be queen.

Yvette had begged off going to church, saying she didn't feel well. It was the absolute truth. After crying for what seemed like forever, she woke with a massive morning-after headache and swollen eyes to match. The family normally didn't attend church Sunday evening, so Yvette had stayed holed up in her room, relying on commentary from Melinda and Belinda to keep her up to date on the goings on in the palace.

Jessabelle knocked then entered without waiting for a reply. "Still nothing?"

"No." Yvette glanced at her sister-in-law but didn't get out of her chair.

"He'll come." Jessabelle sounded far more certain than Yvette did. "Kai talked with Nicklaus for quite some time today. I know he told him about our courtship."

"What courtship?" The two had met at the altar.

"Exactly. We had more than our fair share of challenges to overcome, but we have."

Yvette watched a cloud float along high above the mountains in the distance. "I don't think Nicklaus will marry me because he wants to marry *me*. If anything, he'll marry me because of the effects on Michaela if he doesn't."

"There are far worse things. A man who would marry a stranger to protect his mother is a man who will go to the ends of the earth for his wife."

"She's not his mother, though. He's always known that."

"Who kissed his skinned knee? Who helped him with his homework? Who sat up at night worrying when he was a few minutes late getting home?"

Yvette gave a half-shrug, acquiescing to Jessabelle's point. "Wouldn't that make him a mama's boy who can't cut the apron strings?"

"No. I heard a saying one time. 'Watch how a man treats his mother. Find a man who treats his mother with kindness, because that's how he'll treat his wife.' Michaela may not be Nicklaus's biological mother, but she's filled that role in his life for nearly two decades. Does he take care of her? Is he rude? You've never seen him with Michaela, but that he would sacrifice his future happiness..."

Yvette started to protest but Jessabelle stopped her with a raised hand.

"Or he believes he might be sacrificing his future happiness so his mother can be with her family and the new-found love of her life...That speaks volumes about the kind of man he is. Think about it." With that Jessabelle stood and said good-bye, admonishing Yvette to let her know if anything changed.

"Miss?"

Yvette turned to see her mother's assistant standing in the doorway. "Yes?"

"Prince Nicklaus is here to see you."

Of course he was. "Thank you. I'll be out in a moment."

The woman nodded and dipped into a small curtsy. Yvette stood and glanced down at her clothes. Her favorite pair of jeans and a soft t-shirt. Both would horrify her mother, but she'd wanted comfort, and sitting around all day in her pajamas was even more unacceptable. Deciding not to change, or even check the mirror, Yvette used the band around her wrist to pull her hair into a low ponytail.

In the sitting room, Nicklaus stared out the window with his hands shoved in his pockets. Yvette didn't say anything for several minutes, choosing to watch him while wondering what could be going through his head. Finally, she cleared her throat.

Nicklaus turned and bowed slightly at the waist. "I didn't hear you come in."

"I didn't make any noise," she retorted. "What can I do for you?"

He gestured to the room. "Have a seat so we can talk?"

Yvette crossed her arms in front of her. "I'd rather stand." She was being obstinate, but she didn't care.

"Fine." He shrugged. "Have it your way. I've done a lot of thinking since last night. I've done even more praying. I talked to your brother and my brother-in-law, both of whom have fairly unique perspectives on marrying someone on short notice. Now, I'd like to talk to you about it, about what you think and what you'd expect if we did get married. I thought you'd be more comfortable if we sat down, but we can stand."

Yvette went to stand at the same window he'd been looking

out. "'I lift up mine eyes unto the hills, from whence cometh my help.'"

Nicklaus came to stand behind her and just to the side. "Psalm 121:1."

She turned, feeling his nearness, but brushing past. "It's a verse that's always meant quite a lot to my country and to Montevaro."

"I can see why."

Yvette sank to the edge of a chair, suddenly weary. "What do you want, Nicklaus? I have things to do." Not that she'd been doing any of them.

"I wanted to talk to you about this marriage thing. What do you expect from a marriage to me?"

"I have no idea. I'm still trying to get used to the fact that you're not dead."

"Fair enough."

She drew in a deep breath and blew it out slowly. "I guess I expect my husband, whether it ends up being you this week or someone else later, to be kind. To treat me as an equal but be willing to protect me when the time comes."

"When? You expect to need protecting?" Nicklaus sounded skeptical. "I have a hard time believing you're not capable of protecting yourself."

"I can." Yvette knew how to fight off an attacker if she needed to, and she knew how to handle both a handgun and a shotgun should the need arise. She also knew sometimes escape - or cooperation - was the best way to stay safe. "But you, of all people, should know that being a member of the royal family, no matter how popular, can make me a target for those who are unscrupulous at best."

"Touché," he replied, his manner suddenly more subdued. "But what do you expect from this marriage, if we were to get married Saturday?"

She didn't understand the question, not really. She expected a marriage. What else was there?

When she didn't answer, he went on. "Do you expect a marriage in name only? Where do you expect to live? Things like that."

This time she thought about it more carefully, though she didn't particularly like the answers she came up with. "I suppose I shall have to live with what you decide you want out of a marriage. I have little choice in the matter. All I would ask is that you be far more discreet than my father was."

Far more what? Nicklaus blinked as he tried to remember Mevendian history and what she might be talking about. Then her father's words came back to him.

I was unfaithful to my wife, with a poorly-hidden mistress...

Did she really think...? "I won't be unfaithful, if that's what you're implying."

"I'm not implying anything. I'm flat out saying it." She finally looked up at him, fire flashing from her eyes. "If we get married, and it is a marriage in name only, the one thing I expect is for you to keep your dalliances private."

He wasn't sure if he should be offended or angry at the insinuation. Instead, he refused to give in to either emotion. "Do you think so little of me that you would think I would do such a thing in the first place?"

She just stared at him. "My parents had two children while my father spent much of his time with another woman. Why would I expect any less from a husband in a name-only marriage?"

Red began to tinge his vision. How could she believe such things of him?

But then she stood and turned to leave. He couldn't let her do that. Nicklaus grabbed her arm as she passed by, twirling her until she faced him, stumbling into his chest. Without letting himself think about it, he framed her face in his hands. His fingers tangled in her hair.

And he kissed her.

Like the night before, it took a second for her to respond to him, but when she did...

It caught him off-guard in its intensity. Her hands slid up his chest and around his neck holding him to her. It also served to move his hands off her face. Instead, he wrapped his arms tightly around her.

Time seemed to stand still until finally he moved away. Resting his forehead on hers, breathing heavily, he whispered, "No one else has ever made me feel like that. After we get married, I can guarantee you no one else ever will. Only you."

"After?" she whispered back. "Are you going to marry me?"

His eyes were still closed as he relished the feeling of her in his arms. "I can't let anyone be exiled."

Yvette stiffened and pulled away, not just physically, but he could feel her emotional disconnect as well. She didn't speak until she was once again perched on the edge of a chair. "Thank you. I will see that your assistant gets all of the information you'll need for this week."

"I don't have an assistant." He didn't understand what happened to make her pull away, but he sensed she wouldn't answer his questions about it.

"You will. Or Christiana will assign you one for the time being."

He sat across from her, but she stood again.

"I would imagine we can conduct most of our business via email and text this week. The rehearsal is Friday evening. Your assistant will make sure you have my number and that you're there on time." She turned away and walked out one of the many doors.

Nicklaus sighed and walked back to stare out the same window as he had when she arrived. He turned over the whole conversation in his head, not sure where he'd gone wrong with Alexander's words ringing through his mind at the same time.

"If you make the effort to fall in love with your wife, you will. If you don't make the effort, if you allow yourself to be in situations where you could be tempted into an inappropriate relationship with a woman who is not your wife, you will eventually find yourself in a situation you don't want to be in."

"How do I do that? How do I make myself fall in love with her?"

"Get to know her," his sister said gently. *"Get to know all about her. Guard your time and your heart. Don't let outside pursuits rob her of your attentions, and don't spend time with another woman when you should be spending time with your wife. Never let another woman see more of your heart than your wife does."*

Alexander shifted to look him straight in the eye. *"And never, ever be alone with another woman."*

Nicklaus had thought that might be a bit extreme until his brother-in-law shared a bit about what happened with an old college acquaintance just a couple months earlier.

"My daughter didn't look happy."

He turned to see the king standing there, looking formidable as only a king could. Nicklaus bowed, just a bit, at the waist. Wasn't that what you were supposed to do when you saw the king?

"What happened?"

Nicklaus sighed and sat down in one of the many chairs. "I have no idea. I honestly don't."

"Tell me what happened."

"We were talking. She said the only thing she would expect from me if we had a marriage in name only is that I keep my dalliances out of the public eye." The king's jaw set at that. "I told her I wouldn't cheat on her. I'm not sure she believed me, though. And I kissed her."

"You kissed my daughter?"

Nicklaus managed to keep his internal wince from showing on

his face. "Yes. I kissed her. And it was a good kiss. A very good one. I told her she was the only one to ever make me feel like that, and after we got married, no one else ever would either. She said something like 'so we're getting married?' and I told her I didn't want her or Michaela exiled. Then I could feel her pull away, put up a shutter around herself again."

The king snorted. "I was pretty clueless about women when I was younger, but I think you've got me beat."

"What?" Nicklaus didn't follow.

"You told her you were marrying her so Michaela wouldn't get exiled."

Did he? "No. I said I didn't want either one of them to get exiled. We talked about it last night. She even asked me to take her with her if I went back to the States."

"Maybe. But what my daughter heard was that you were marrying her to protect another woman - who is irrelevant. You want to marry her, not to protect her, to keep *Yvette* from being exiled, but to keep the woman who raised you from being exiled. What she likely needed to hear was that you were marrying *her*, because you *want* to marry *her*. Regardless of the other factors. I am not saying you should have lied if that is not how you felt. I *am* saying that is what she likely needed to hear." He pulled his phone out of the inside pocked of his suit coat and looked at it. "My daughter tells me the wedding is going ahead as planned, with or without the groom, though she believes the groom will be there."

Nicklaus looked up at the king. Cold eyes stared right through him, as though the other man could see into his very soul.

He closed his eyes and sighed. "The groom will be there."

7

"**I**s there anything else, miss?"

Yvette shook her head, dismissing the maid she didn't really know. "Thank you." As the maid left, Yvette's mother walked in.

"The plane leaves in an hour, darling. Are you ready?"

Yvette looked around her room, knowing it would be the last time it would be *her* room. By the time she returned, she would be married, and this room would have been transformed into a guest room for her and her new husband to use when they visited. Or they'd be put somewhere else altogether.

She wanted to throw herself back onto the bed and pull the covers over her head. Hide until this ridiculous nightmare was over. "I suppose I'm as ready as I'll ever be."

Yvette looked at her phone, as though something would have changed in the last minute since she'd looked before. Nothing. No text messages. No voice mails. No direct contact from the man she was marrying in less than thirty-six hours. For reasons she didn't understand, their departure from Mevendia had been delayed from Wednesday to Friday morning. Lizbeth was already there, taking care of the last minute details. She'd been instructed to plan as though the wedding would go off as a *wedding* and not Yvette getting stood up.

But no one knew Nicklaus was alive.

Or very few people did. There had been no public announcement. Everything about tomorrow was being kept very quiet. The guests were coming solely for the train wreck factor. She knew that. Very few were people she would have invited anyway. Given her choice in the matter, if she still *had* to marry Nicklaus, she would have opted for a small ceremony with just a few family members there. Maybe not even that many. Eloping sounded like a good idea.

For the most part, everyone had left her to herself all week. It left her with plenty of time to be alone with her thoughts. Too much time, really.

Even aboard the plane, she was left alone. Fortunately, they went straight to the Baicampo property, with its own landing strip. Unfortunately, it also meant she'd be spending the night alone because with the change in travel plans had come a change in the sleeping arrangements. In the honeymoon cottage where she'd be expected to spend the next night with Nicklaus.

In fact, Christopher, Alexander's twin brother, took them there first so she could freshen up. "Can't I stay in the house with you, Mama?" Yvette whispered, looking around the cabin. It was gorgeous. Perfect for a wedding night.

After a real wedding.

"I'm sorry, love. I can't break the traditions any more than you can."

"And you can't stay with me?"

Her mother reached out to brush the hair off of her face. "No. But I will ask your father if we can find a way."

"Thank you, Mama."

"Now, we have twenty minutes until the rehearsal."

Which was her mother's diplomatic way of telling her she didn't look her best, and she needed to fix that.

It took the full twenty minutes for her to feel even a little prepared for what lay ahead. By the time they reached the chapel, they were ten minutes late. Her father gave her a glare, but there wasn't any real anger behind it. If anything, there was sympathy.

Yvette had been in the building more than once during the planning phase. It never failed to leave her in awe. Stained glass windows. Ancient stone workmanship. A reverent place if there ever was one.

Inside the sanctuary, everyone waited. Lizbeth, who had really done most of the planning for her, held a clipboard and looked a little odd. She must have just found out this wedding really was happening.

Christopher walked in before anyone else could say anything.

"We have a problem," he said without preamble. "Not an insurmountable one, but definitely something we need to deal with quickly."

When he didn't go on, her father encouraged him to.

"As Alexander knows, we've hired some new staff recently. As part of the preparations for tomorrow night, the ballroom floor was being polished and touch-ups made to the woodwork, inside and out." He closed his eyes and sighed. "One of the new, and no longer employed, young men, decided to cut through the ballroom to get to the outside, slipped, and spilled two gallons of green paint all over the floor."

"So we need a new place to hold the ball?" Christiana clarified. "Why not the barn? That's where ours was. It's lovely."

Yvette remembered it well. It was when she realized she was going to have to plan this thing after all.

Alexander jumped in. "The interior is undergoing renovations. When we were planning our wedding, I noticed that things had started to look a little worn. Not too bad, but enough that I wanted to get it fixed back up."

"Right." Christiana shared a look with Antonio. "We need a place for the ball. Canceling it is not an option. Diana can begin making arrangements to have it at the palace."

Diana, Christiana's assistant, scurried out of the room to begin making the arrangements, while others approved of the plan.

Lizbeth jumped in. "Now, can we get this rehearsal started? The dinner will be ready in less than an hour." She took charge, sending members of the wedding party scrambling to get to their assigned spots.

Yvette and her father went to the back of the church to await their signal. She wished Nana Yvette were already here, but she'd been feeling under the weather for the last few days. She was on the upswing, but decided not to arrive until the next morning, preferring to spend the night in her own bed.

Yvette understood her desire.

With her hand tucked securely in her father's elbow, they started down the aisle to the wedding march. They didn't go through the whole ceremony, just explained what would happen. She didn't even have to touch Nicklaus, which was fine with her. He didn't speak to her, and she gladly returned the favor.

By the time they finished the rehearsal, Yvette was ready to just go back to the honeymoon cabin or wherever she planned to spend the night and collapse. Instead, it was time to get her happy on and attend a dinner.

She knew this was a glimpse into what her life would be like after the wedding. Awkward situations, smiling despite everything else, and pervasive loneliness.

How did one get used to that?

"Is everything ready to go?"

Lizbeth looked up from her tablet as Robert Padovano walked into the room, tugging off his tie. "I think so."

"And when the groom doesn't show up?" He toed off his shoes as he tossed the tie over a chair.

Well, that answered that question. Parliament didn't even know the young prince had survived. But could she tell him? "There are contingencies in place for just about everything, even moving the ball to the palace." She'd planned for that, too. Just in case.

Her husband, now in pajama pants, flopped down on the bed next to her. "Care to tell me which contingency is most likely?"

She ran her fingers through his hair. "Sorry, love. It's all on a need-to-know basis. I'm surprised I know as much as I do." She'd only learned of Prince Nicklaus's existence a few minutes before the rehearsal was scheduled to start. "Just remember that I *can't* tell you anything, if you hear shocking news tomorrow."

His eyes narrowed at her. "So something unexpected is going to happen?"

Lizbeth shrugged. "I can't really say."

Robert nodded. "I understand." He rolled over and reached for the remote. "Speaking of news, I was hoping to catch a few minutes of it." It took him a minute to find the right station in the hotel's channel lineup, but he did. "Commercial. Of course." He pushed himself up until his arm brushed against hers. "And I haven't even kissed you yet."

She set her tablet down and lifted her face so he could. What was turning into a very nice kiss was interrupted by the news anchor.

"And in royal news, we've all been wondering what's going to happen at the Baicampo property this weekend. We'll turn it over to Matt Markinson, who's been following the developments."

"Turn it up," Lizbeth whispered. She needed to know what was being said, and picked up her tablet in case she needed to make notes.

The picture switched to a man standing on Bianasola Island, near the entrance to the property. "Thank you. We've not been allowed access to the property yet, though we have been assured we will have a live stream of the events as they unfold tomorrow." It cut to an obviously premade package with a voice over. *"Here's what we know. Nearly eighteen years ago, King Richard of Ravenzario and King Antonio of Mevendia signed a marriage contract for their children. Prince Nicklaus was three-years-old, while Princess Yvette was only a few months old. They both took criticism for it, but in the last year, the rationale has come to light. King Richard likely knew there was a force acting against him and his family, and he needed assurances there would be safeguards in place if something happened. After the plots against Queen Christiana came to light earlier this year, it became known that, in the event of the death of all members of the family, the throne would go to Princess Yvette as the betrothed of Prince Nicklaus, with King Antonio as her regent."*

The pictures, both stills and video, of the relevant people were replaced by the marker on the side of the mountain road. "Not long after the arrangements were made, King Richard, along with Queen Marissa, Prince Nicklaus, and their nanny were killed in a car accident. The betrothal, however, remains in place until *next* Saturday, a week after the presumed wedding date." The camera went back to the live shot. "For the last eight months, Princess Yvette and her planning assistant, Lizbeth Bence, have been preparing for a wedding that will not happen. A joint statement from King Antonio and Queen Christiana stated that there will be events taking place tomorrow, including the reception, which has been moved to the palace with no explanation. Unsubstantiated rumors point to the service being more of a memorial, and the ball a fundraiser for the late king and queen's favorite charities. I'm Matt Markinson, now back to you in the studio."

Robert clicked the remote. "Is that true?"

How did Matt find out? "More or less." It had been the back-up plan, the one they all thought they'd use.

"Can you be done, or is there more you need to do this evening?"

Lizbeth smiled at him. "Oh, I can be done." She set her tablet on the side table before he kissed her.

"There's only thing that bugged me about that story." he asked after one quick kiss.

The same thing that bothered her. "My last name." She kissed him softly. "Soon. After my birthday, he can't keep the inheritance from my mother and grandfather away from me anymore. Once I have control of that, we'll tell the world." And she kissed him.

Nicklaus stood in the ante room to the side of the sanctuary. He could hear the murmur of voices growing louder as more people arrived. He thought about texting Yvette, but decided not to. He'd started many over the course of the week, but none seemed to convey what he was really thinking and feeling.

He turned to Alfred, his new assistant. "Is Michaela up front?"

"Not yet, sir. She will be one of the last ones seated."

Before he could nod, the side door opened. Tony, Christiana's head of security, stepped in with a smile on his face. "Someone's here to see you."

Michaela was right behind Tony. Her hands flew to her mouth as she gasped. "Oh, Nicky," she whispered, coming toward him. "You look so handsome. So much like the prince you were born to be."

He wasn't sure how he felt about that, but he did feel differently. Michaela hugged him, and he held on tight to the only parent he'd ever known. "I love you, Mama," he whispered, hoping no one else would hear.

She clung to him for a moment longer. "Thank you, Nicky. I'm so proud of you for doing what your heart tells you is right."

Nicklaus wasn't sure what his heart thought was right, but this seemed the *most* right out of the options. She straightened his bow tie and then the royal blue sash that represented the family crest. He glanced over at the ornate desk against one wall. They would come in here to sign the paperwork. An armed guard stood next to it.

And he'd give Yvette the Van Rensselaer Accord Jewels again.

This time, he'd put them on her before they returned to the stage for the pronouncement.

Tony put his finger to his ear. "It's almost time, Michaela. They need you in the entryway."

Nicklaus gave her another kiss on the cheek. "We'll spend some time together soon," he promised. He'd met her family briefly, but had spent much of his week in "princely classes."

"Almost time, sir." Alfred stood next to the door leading to the sanctuary.

Nicklaus tugged first on one sleeve and then the other, then the front of his tuxedo jacket. Alexander was walking Yvette's great-grandmother down the aisle as the matron of honor. Nicklaus would enter as Yvette did.

The music changed and the processional started. Nicklaus could hear the murmurs increase even as the music did. Likely everyone wondered why it actually seemed like a wedding.

The music changed again, this time to a wedding march.

Alfred bowed and started to pull the door open. "It's time, sir. You'll be fine."

How did he know Nicklaus's stomach was tied in knots?

When the door was fully open, Nicklaus walked through, marching in time to the music. In theory, he should reach the aisle at the same time as Yvette and her father reached the end of the aisle.

The whispers increased as he walked across the front of the chapel. In less than a minute, he stood next to King Antonio with Yvette on the other side.

The crowd seemed to quiet a bit as the bishop cleared his throat and the music died down. "Who gives this woman to this man?"

King Antonio's voice boomed, no need for a microphone. "On behalf of her family and our people, I, King Antonio of Mevendia, give Princess Yvette in marriage to Prince Nicklaus of Ravenzario."

The whispers picked up again with the confirmation of his identity.

He also knew phones had been confiscated as part of the security procedures and cell phone signals/wi-fi had been blocked for the time being, just in case. The only way any of this was getting out was via the video feed controlled by Tony's men.

After a brief hug and whispered exchange Nicklaus couldn't hear, King Antonio held Yvette's hand toward Nicklaus. When it was tucked snuggly in his elbow, they started for the stairs.

Alexander's words echoed in his head as he tried to listen to the words the bishop spoke.

"Love her, Nick. Love is a verb in many ways. Love her like Christ loves the church. Show her she's beautiful, she's important."

"She is important. She's a princess, for crying out loud. And she's gorgeous."

"And you're a prince. It doesn't matter what her title is or what family she was born into. What matters is how her husband sees her. We hear all the time about how when you belittle your children repeatedly, it sinks in and they start to believe it. The same is true with your wife. Build her up, and she'll start to believe that. To believe that you find her important. That you find her beautiful. And it has far more to do with emotion than physical attraction."

Yvette spoke, and Nicklaus shoved the conversation out of his head. When the appropriate times came, he repeated words and gave the correct answers. It didn't take long for them to return to the ante room to sign the certificate.

Nicklaus found he had to focus when signing his name. He'd

written it over and over during the course of the week, trying to ingrain it in his head. Once both of them had signed it, they had a moment with just the two of them alone.

"You look beautiful." He meant it.

"Thank you."

He took the jewelry box out of the drawer. "I guess it really is time for me to give this to you."

"I guess." They hadn't faced each other during the vows, and he still hadn't gotten a good look at her face, but now they both looked into the mirror. So she could see what he was doing he supposed. Before he could put the jewels on, she removed the pendant she already wore, the one she'd worn to dinner on her birthday.

Very carefully, he extracted the jewels from the box and lifted them up and over her head, settling them into place. She moved the veil aside so he could see the clasp. When he was done, he rested his hands on her bare shoulders. "Beautiful," he whispered as he stared into her eyes via the reflection.

Yvette lifted one hand to touch them. "Yes. They are."

He countered. "I meant you." Nicklaus dug another box out of his pocket. "I know it's a bit late, and I meant to give it to you during the ceremony and was all flustered and forgot."

She turned as he backed away and dropped to one knee. "Yvette, will you do me the honor of being my wife for the rest of my days?"

8

Years of practice helped Yvette keep the emotions from her face. What was she supposed to say to the man she'd just promised to love, honor, and cherish for the rest of her life when he proposed after the fact? Sure? No problem? So glad you got around to asking?

Finally, she just nodded and held out her left hand where the wedding band already rested.

The ring was gorgeous. She would have expected nothing less, though she had no idea which ring it was. Christiana wore the ring their mother had worn. Yvette's mother still wore the one her father had used. Nana Yvette was saving her engagement ring for William, whenever he settled down. But it wasn't a new ring, like Jessabelle's. She did know that.

There was a discreet knock on the door to the hallway two seconds before it opened. Did everyone think they'd be making out in here?

She didn't know Nicklaus's new assistant except by sight. "Straight to the center," he whispered. "Face the audience."

Good thing he told them what to do because she would have

forgotten. Her father and Christiana, both looking very regal, stood on the stage.

When they reached the center, they faced the crowd. The whispers seemed to have stopped. Finally.

"I give you the Duke and Duchess of Berkleyshire." Christiana spoke first.

"I give you the Duke and Duchess of Simonetti." Then her father. A title from each country.

Then it was the bishop's turn. "Your majesties, your royal highnesses, distinguished guests, ladies and gentlemen. It is my honor to present to you Prince Nicklaus and Princess Yvette, husband and wife."

As they descended the steps, the crowd stood, applauding as they left. She could see the questions in so many eyes. In fact, her father had made a special note of telling her there would be an interview tomorrow.

They reached the horse-drawn carriage a moment later, and Nicklaus helped her in. There was no crowd gathered, not like there would be on the mainland. He held her hand but didn't try to talk to her.

Thank goodness.

A fairly large ferry was anchored off shore. It would be used to get everyone from the wedding back to the mainland and to the reception. She and Nicklaus boarded a speedboat, but they would be coming back for pictures.

When they reached the other dock, another carriage waited. The streets were lined with spectators. She put on her happy face and waved, first to one side then the other. Nicklaus looked lost.

"Wave," she whispered. "Pretend you're in a parade."

Homemade signs were held high. Some were obviously made in the last hour. They said things like *Prince Nicklaus is alive!* and *Long Live Prince Nicklaus!* She caught a glimpse of the back of one sign that said something very different. *We miss Prince Nicklaus, too! RIP!* So they'd thought the parade would be for those who would feel his loss the most after a non-wedding.

Questions were being shouted from the crowd.

"Where have you been?"

"Are you really Nicky?"

"You should be king!"

That one stung. Christiana had never been anything but kind to Yvette.

"Are you going to throw Christiana out?"

His hand still held hers and tightened until she thought her circulation had been cut off.

"Ignore them," she whispered.

"How?"

"Just smile and wave. As soon as you hear their comment, they're behind us. Close your ears if you need to." She'd learned how to do that at a young age. "Tune them out."

"How?"

"Focus on something else. Think about something distracting."

"Like what?"

She only knew what had been distracting her all day. "What's supposed to happen later tonight."

"The ball."

Yvette knew her face was turning red as she felt it heat. "After that. When we're alone."

A pause. "Right."

Maybe she didn't want him thinking about that as his wave faltered. "Or find another, steady sound to latch onto. Like the horses clopping or the jangle of the bridles."

He nodded and went back to waving. "I can do that."

The route took them nearly five miles through the city. Even Yvette was getting tired of waving and smiling by the time the carriage went through the palace gates. Inside, they didn't get much of a reprieve. There would be camera angles the news crews would have access to, plus many members of the staff who weren't actively involved in preparations for the ball were lined up in the courtyard.

They reached a portico near an entrance. Nicklaus climbed out then turned to help her. She waved again to the crowds, and he followed her lead. Once inside, with the doors closed, her shoulders slumped. The weight of the world rested on them, and it was too much to bear. It took only a second for them to straighten again. She knew they were being watched.

Melinda and Alfred were already there waiting for them, but it was Nicklaus who took charge. "Where can we have a few moments alone?"

Alfred seemed to understand immediately. "This way, sir."

A minute later, they were alone in a room she'd never seen before. Nicklaus didn't let go of her hand until they reached a chair. "Why don't you sit down for a few minutes, Yvette?"

She did as he suggested, struggling against the tears that had been threatening all day.

He knelt in front of her. "What is it?"

Yvette didn't want to burden him with everything in her heart and mind, so she just shook her head. "It's been a long day, a long week."

"It's more than that, isn't it?"

She hesitated then nodded. "It's eight months of stress getting to this day. I'm ready for it all to be over. To get past tomorrow's interviews, go on a wedding trip somewhere nobody knows us and hide out in my room for a month." He had to have noticed her use of pronouns. She had no expectations of sharing a room, a bed, with him.

Nicklaus clasped both of her hands lightly. "We'll get through this together. I have no clue what I'm doing. You have to know that. I've seen enough weddings to fake my way through, but this royalty stuff? I got nothin'."

Obviously. Her brothers and the Montevarian princes wouldn't dare say "nothin'".

"Can you help me?"

She squared her shoulders. She was Princess Yvette of Mevendia and now Ravenzario, Duchess of Berkleyshire and Simonetti.

Putting on a happy face when she didn't want to was something she'd had years of practice doing.

"Let's go," she told him, standing up. "They're waiting for us for the first kiss."

Nicklaus closed his eyes as Yvette moved around him, getting her dress situated, he supposed. The first kiss. The interviews his sister had mentioned. The crowds outside, both supportive and not. A month long wedding trip where they saw no one else.

All of it was overwhelming. He'd been using his sister as something of a touchstone, looking to her to see what he should be doing and when. Yvette now seemed the most likely one to take on that role.

When he opened his eyes, she was standing next to the door looking back at him. How did she do it? The weight of everything seemed to be crushing her minutes earlier. That's why he'd sought a moment of solitude for her. But now, she seemed to be the bright, sunshiny Yvette he'd seen often in the footage he'd watched of her over the last few days. In his time with her, he'd noticed that veneer slip.

What would it take for her to let it slide off completely with him? To see her be the real Yvette? Not the one overwhelmed with the change in plans the weekend before or the one the public saw, but the real Yvette?

Maybe on that wedding trip she mentioned. But where were they going? Had one been planned? If so, no one had mentioned it to him. He hadn't thought to ask.

When he reached for the door, Yvette slipped her hand into his elbow. By the time they emerged, she had a smile on her face.

Ms. Bence stood in the hallway along with a number of other family members. "Are we ready for the kiss on the balcony?" She addressed her question to Christiana, not himself or Yvette.

Christiana nodded, then shot him a sympathetic glace. She'd been through it herself less than a year earlier. He and Yvette followed Christiana up one of the massive staircases and into an ornate sitting room. Two doormen stood with one hand each on the handles of the massive door leading to the balcony.

His sister nodded at them, and they pulled the doors open. Nicklaus could hear the roar of the crowd even from this far away. With Yvette's hand still tucked into his arm, they walked out onto the balcony, both of them waving.

The yelling soon gelled into a coherent call for a kiss.

"Let's do this and get it over with," Yvette whispered.

Then pucker up, buttercup. The words ran through his head, but even Nicklaus knew better than to actually say them. Instead, he slid his arm around her waist, pulling her a bit closer, then dipped his head for a kiss.

The bolt of lightning from the weekend before paled in comparison to the jolt that shot through him this time.

Physical attraction wasn't going to be a problem.

But this wasn't the time or place to be thinking about physical attraction, was it?

The kiss ended almost as quickly as it began. They both waved to the crowd for a couple more minutes then turned to go inside.

For nearly an hour, they took pictures inside the palace. They returned to the Baicampo property for more pictures, this time taking a much more direct route. The more he had the chance to be near Yvette, the more he found himself wanting to be near her.

To touch her. Hold her. Kiss her.

And either she was a much better actress than he'd thought, or she was feeling much more comfortable as well with or without instructions from the photographer.

They finally returned to the palace and the photographer decided he wanted to get a few more shots. Up to the rooftop they went, with the city spread below them.

Nicklaus was only following the photographer's directions, but he found himself standing behind Yvette with his arms wrapped around her. Her fingers laced with his, hugging herself with him.

"Kiss her cheek," the photographer called.

Yvette, who had long since traded the Van Rensselaer Accord Jewels for the simpler pendant she'd worn during the ceremony, turned her cheek. At some point, she'd also dispensed with the tiara. Nicklaus had done away with his sash and sword. He kissed the side of her cheek and wanted to pull her closer, but the photographer was suddenly pulling them apart.

He took a few pictures of each of them by themselves. Nicklaus stood behind the camera while the man took a few shots of Yvette. With her veil blowing behind her in the wind, her white dress stood out against the gray sky behind her. He'd have to get copies of them to put in his screen saver.

Before he realized what was happening, Yvette was standing on something he hadn't seen. A stool maybe? The photographer pulled him by the arm until he stood directly in front of her.

"Now, princess, put your hands on either side of his face and lean down like you're going to kiss him."

She listened. Maybe too well. With her hands framing his face, he had no choice but to look at her. But Yvette wasn't looking at him. This close he could see the gold flecks in her hazel eyes, but they stared a few inches lower, at his lips.

Was she going to kiss him?

The look on her face said yes.

The call of the photographer meant no.

Pictures. More pictures. Always more pictures.

"Just a couple more," the photographer finally said. He directed Nicklaus to stand behind Yvette once more.

Not a difficult chore, though this time only one arm wrapped more around her shoulders, pulling her closer to him. His other hand rested on her upper arm, her hands clung to him.

Then the next instruction came. "Act like you're going to kiss her shoulder."

There was no acting about it. Nicklaus lowered his face and pressed his lips against her soft skin. Despite the clouds, it was a warm day and her skin attested to that. Warm, soft, silky smooth.

Yvette's head tilted to rest against the side of his.

Two thoughts occurred to him at nearly the same time.

If this was how he felt now, how would he feel about keeping his hands off his wife when they were alone later that night?

And what if she didn't want him to?

9

Yvette didn't know what to think. Nicklaus was being solicitous and kind. The more pictures they took, the more they were forced to be close by a photographer who didn't know the whole story and assumed they were both completely in love, the more she found herself wanting to be close to him. She could tell her smile became more genuine. Her desire to kiss him more real.

In the ballroom, he held her chair, asked her questions about the meal. There were a couple of dishes he wasn't familiar with, but were her favorites. She'd decided on the menu herself, so she'd picked what she'd like to eat.

Speeches would begin before long. She turned to say something to her Nana Yvette, but suddenly, a tinkling of glasses sounded throughout the room.

Nana Yvette's eyes twinkled. "I do believe they want you to kiss your husband, dear one."

Yvette felt her face color as Nicklaus wrapped an arm around her shoulders. She turned his direction and leaned in. He brushed his lips against hers in a soft kiss to the cheering of those assembled.

Nana excused herself a moment later. Lizbeth slipped into Nana's seat. Yvette turned to Lizbeth and could feel Nicklaus behind her leaning in to hear whatever the other woman had to say.

"We've changed things a little bit," she whispered. "Your father..." She nodded to Yvette. "...and your sister..." A nod to Nicklaus. "...don't want to drag this out for both of you. Instead of speeches then hours of dancing, each of them will give a short toast. Then cake. Then there will be a few dances with the two of you and assorted others." She looked at Nicklaus. "Michaela said you know how to waltz?"

"Yes." His breath played with the tendrils of hair near her cheek.

"Okay. First dance is a waltz. After that will be a dance with your father, Yvette, and your sister, Nicklaus."

"Why my sister?" he asked.

Lizbeth hesitated. "I know you consider Michaela your mother, but the queen is your closest female relative. Therefore, you dance with her."

Yvette could see the strain around his eyes, but he nodded.

"After that, a dance with Nana Yvette and Alexander as the best man and matron of honor, then another slow dance." Yvette could hear the sympathy in Lizbeth's voice. "After that, the dance floor will be opened to everyone for the fifth dance. You two keep dancing together. Be into each other. If anyone tries to cut in, just politely tell them no. Nicklaus, work your way to the far corner and then out the balcony door. It'll be open. Someone will be there to show you the other door that will lead to your quarters for the night."

"We're not going back to the island?" Yvette hadn't been informed of a change in plans.

Lizbeth shook her head. "No. With the change in venue for the reception, it was decided that you should stay here. You'll be in Nicklaus's quarters."

Nicklaus had quarters? Yvette supposed it made sense that he had his own rooms. He was a prince of Ravenzario. Of course he had his own designated suite in the Ravenzarian palace.

"Can we skip the speeches?" Nicklaus asked suddenly. "I'd really prefer not to sit through a bunch of words from people I don't know."

Yvette wasn't sure if she wanted to sit through toasts either and said so.

Lizbeth looked a bit shocked but then nodded. "It's not like we handed out programs and order of events and stuff. I would imagine that could be arranged. I'll see what I can do." She slipped back out of the seat.

Yvette turned back to her plate. She'd have to see if someone could make sure to bring a giant piece of cake and some ice cream to drown her sorrows in later.

But as Nicklaus took her hand and led her toward the cake, the warmth of his palm against hers reminded her how wonderful it had felt to be close to him during the last of the pictures. Lizbeth whispered the toasts had been done away with. A moment later, at the direction of the photographer, they held hands to cut a piece of cake off the bottom layer.

Nicklaus held one piece. "I'd kind of like to smush this in your face."

His eyes held a twinkle she didn't yet recognize. "I dare you." She held a piece in her own hand. "Just remember...paybacks."

He chuckled and held it out for her to take a bite. Yvette kept her eyes on his as he fed it to her. No smushing.

But maybe she should. With a demure smile, Yvette held the piece out for him, letting him have just a little bit. Her father would kill her.

But it would be worth it.

She held it up like she wanted to give him another bite, but as he closed in, she saw her opportunity and took it. Shock showed in his eyes as Yvette found herself giggling at the frosting all over his face.

"You asked for it," Nicklaus growled, grabbing her by the waist and pulling her close.

And then he was kissing her, getting the frosting all over her face as well.

The normally semi-stoic crowd in the ballroom became uncharacteristically noisy, with cheers all around. Yvette's arms wound around Nicklaus's neck as he tipped her backward, still kissing her. By the time she returned upright, Yvette knew her face had to be beet red, and she rested her forehead against his chest. She could feel as much as hear his laughter as he wrapped his arms around her to hold her close.

"I think they're ready for the first dance." Nicklaus kissed the side of her head. "But I think we should clean up the frosting first."

Yvette lifted her head, wondering at the tone in his voice. He kissed her again.

"You had some right there," he whispered.

"Thanks for getting it for me," she whispered back.

A throat cleared behind them, and Nicklaus stepped back. They both used napkins to clean their fingers and faces. A moment later, they stood in the middle of the dance floor. Nicklaus bowed to her. She curtsied back.

He'd told them he knew how to waltz, but she hadn't really believed him. In less than a minute, she was impressed and told him so.

"I hated Michaela for making me take lessons. She was right to."

As soon as the first song ended, the second began. Nicklaus stepped closer to her, tucking her hand against his chest. His chin rested against the side of her temple.

"This is nice," he whispered. "If I can pretend everyone else isn't watching us, then it's really nice."

Yvette had never danced with anyone quite like this. She'd never been escorted by anyone who wasn't a family member or a few select friends. None of them ever held her close.

The dances with her father and Alexander passed uneventfully. She noticed Nicklaus seemed to use special care while dancing with her great-grandmother. That earned him some brownie points. Nana Yvette simply wasn't the same as she used to be.

Then she was dancing with her husband again, and she noticed Nicklaus skillfully moving them closer to the open balcony door. No announcement was made but as the next song began, others joined them on the floor. No one tried to cut in. Before the song ended, Nicklaus had taken her by the hand and led her quickly onto the balcony.

"This way," someone called quietly.

In seconds, they'd disappeared through a door hidden by ivy.

Nicklaus wasn't sure what or how he was supposed to be feeling. He didn't know his way around the palace, but he did know how to get to his quarters from the bottom of the stairs. Yvette's hand was still in his as they worked their way through the hallways. They didn't hurry, but they didn't dawdle either. Michaela had often accused him of dawdling as he grew up, but not today.

Yvette, his *wife*, stayed a step behind him. It brought him some comfort to realize he knew his way around better than she did. It wasn't much, but it was something.

He stopped in front of an ornate wood door. "We're here." Nicklaus turned in time to see Yvette blush. "I don't know if you do this here, but in the States, the groom carries the bride over the threshold."

Did he really want to do this?

Yes.

He had to be all in with this marriage thing, and that meant carrying his bride over the threshold. Once he had the door open, Nicklaus turned back and picked her up. Yvette, still a becoming shade of pink, put her arms around his neck.

Then, as he kicked the door shut behind them, she kissed his cheek.

Nicklaus didn't know what to make of that.

"You can put me down now."

He shook himself out of it. "Right." After a few more steps, he set her next to a couch. "Sorry."

She sat down but didn't look at him. "No need to be sorry. You just didn't need to carry me any longer than necessary."

He surprised himself with his next words. "What if I wanted to?"

"I don't know." She took a deep breath and let it out. "Do you have your phone? I don't, but I don't know if I have anything here. Could you maybe ask your guy where my stuff is?"

His guy? Right. Alfred. Nicklaus tapped out a quick message, then started for the bedroom. "I'll look around and see if it's here."

He'd barely walked through the door to the other room when a knock sounded on the main door.

"I'll get it," Yvette called after him.

He went into the closet and found half of it taken up by clothes that certainly weren't his. Back in the bedroom, he found a phone laying on one of the side tables. Purple with sparkles had to be Yvette's.

"Your things are here," he called as he walked toward the door.

She seemed to say something, but he couldn't understand what it was. When he made it to the sitting room, he knew why. Someone had brought a big plate of cake and a tub of ice cream. He'd been told there was a kitchen in the suite, but he hadn't explored it fully yet. He could find the sitting room, the bedroom, the bathroom, and the closet with its own mini-fridge. The ice cream tub wouldn't fit in the mini-fridge, so they'd have to find the kitchen soon.

He could see her swallow.

"That's good," she said. "I'm glad."

He walked toward the sitting area while tugging on the knot in his tie. "It looks like they brought *everything*, though. Not just whatever you might have packed for this trip."

"Not surprising." She looked back at the cake and gave a half-hearted shrug. "I don't live with my family anymore. I'm married. That means I live with my husband. Here. With you."

Right. Made sense. Even though they hadn't talked about where they might want to live.

"If my stuff's here, do you mind if I change?" She took another big bite of cake, likely to avoid looking at him.

"Go ahead. I haven't fully explored the apartment yet, but I'll see if I can find the kitchen and get us something to drink. If you don't mind sharing your dessert that is."

Yvette stood and held her skirts so she could get around the small table. He watched as she walked into the room where he apparently now lived. Once she disappeared, he shed everything he could. No more tie or cuff links or jacket. He rolled up the sleeves of his dress shirt and went to check the other doors off the sitting room. Two led to other bedrooms. One led to a kitchen and dining room. A huge window overlooked the gardens below.

Digging around in the refrigerator, he found bottled water for both of them. Back in the sitting room, he sat in the middle of the couch, using a second fork to take a couple bites of cake himself.

"Ah! That's better."

He looked up to see Yvette wearing dark purple pajama pants with a tank top a few shades lighter. As he watched, she pulled pins out of her hair and let it tumble around her shoulders. The pins went on the table before she sat next to him.

She cut a bite and picked it up with her fork. "You can change if you want to."

Right. He hurried to change into his own pajamas, the most comfortable ones. By the time he returned, Yvette was gone, but he could see her through the now-open door into the kitchen. She came back in with bowls, spoons, and an ice cream scoop.

"We'll want to put the ice cream in the freezer so it doesn't get all gooey."

She had a good point, so they did just that.

Nicklaus didn't know what he expected out of the evening. He really didn't know what she expected, if anything. Once they were both set with dessert, he broached the subject.

"I don't know what you want to happen here tonight, if anything, but I'd really like to get to know you better. Would you tell me what it was like growing up in a palace? I mean you told me some last weekend, but what's it like being a princess as a kid?"

Yvette shrugged. "It was normal for me. I've never known a life without security guards and public events and always having to be 'on' when I'm not home. Never letting anyone see the emotions you might have." She scooped up some ice cream and took a bite. "What about you? What was life like in the States?"

He shared a few stories about growing up. She shared a couple more. The princess, it turned out, had a wicked sense of humor when she wanted to, and she had him laughing.

By the time they finished their dessert, they were sitting shoulder to shoulder on the couch. Both kind of slouched down with their feet stretched onto the table. Yvette leaned her head until it rested on his shoulder, and she slid her hand inside his arm and down to link her fingers with his.

"What do you want out of this relationship, Nicky?"

She'd never called him that before. He rested his cheek on her head. "What everyone wants out of marriage, I guess. A relationship with one person you can count on above all others, a friend, a confidant, a co-parent, a lover." Yeah. He went there. "I know I told you last week, but I would never cheat on you. Ever."

"I know." Yvette sat up and twisted, putting one leg up on the couch between them. "I want all of that, too." She reached out and laid a hand on the side of his cheek. "Regardless of everything else, the fact that we barely know each other, we are married. And I think you're very attractive." She seemed as surprised by her boldness as Nick himself was.

He sat up until he could face her, reaching out to run his fingers through her silky hair. "I find you extremely attractive, Evie." He'd never called her that either. "I want to kiss you. I want more than that. I think there's an incredible chemistry between us I've never come close to with anyone else. But I'll let you take the lead. I won't push you for anything, but just so you know..."

Before he could finish the sentence, she leaned toward him, covering his lips with hers.

Nicklaus wrapped his arms around her and pulled her closer. He trailed kisses down the line of her jaw. "Are you sure, Evie?"

Before answering, she turned her head to kiss him again. She stopped just long enough to say, "Yes, Nicky. I am."

"How long have you known he was alive?"

Lizbeth looked up from her post-wedding checklist to see Robert leaning against a pillar in the ball room. He'd taken off his suit coat and his tie hung loose around his neck. Completely at ease.

"At least, I presume that's the real Nicklaus and not an impostor."

"It is. The DNA testing was done a few weeks ago before the prince even knew he was the prince." She checked off the last thing on her list and set the clipboard down on a table. "And the answer to your question is, yesterday. Queen Christiana and Prince Alexander have known since last Friday. The Mevendians have known since last Saturday. Which explains why Yvette was acting weird when I met with her this week."

"So why did they go through with it if they've only known each other a week? And the prince was raised without knowing who he is. Why not wait a year?"

Lizbeth shrugged and walked toward him, resting her hands

on his hips when she got close enough. "All I know is that it was written into the contract their fathers signed years ago, and both Parliaments at the time approved the language so it's still binding. There must have been some kind of consequences if they didn't go through with it." She moved a half-step closer. "I'd rather not talk about them, though. I'd rather talk about how you have this diplomatic trip to go on and how the king asked me to go, too." She leaned up and kissed him. "I got the impression he might know more than he let on."

Robert wrapped his arms around her waist. "It wouldn't surprise me. He's said a couple of things I wrote off as me misunderstanding him, but could mean he knows about us."

Leaning up, Lizbeth gave him a soft kiss. "And my birthday is while we're in Australia, so when we get back, we can get your lawyer on the paperwork with my father."

He kissed her. "And you can move in with me." Another kiss. "And I can wake up to this beautiful face every day."

"I like the sound of that." One more kiss, and she moved back. "But that night is not tonight." Lizbeth wanted it to be. More than she wanted just about anything. "You have to go back to Mevendia. I'm staying here. After tomorrow, we'll have a couple of weeks together. Then a lifetime." Robert hadn't given her any reason not to believe they'd mesh their lives well together, but they'd never spent more than thirty-six hours in each other's company. Would things change when they saw each other all the time?

Lizbeth wanted to believe they wouldn't, but the part of her that had never been in a real relationship before, wondered if, once they lived together, it would change things. That he wouldn't find her attractive when he'd seen her at her worst. That the traits he now found endearing, he'd find annoying.

That he'd realize he didn't really love her after all.

Warm hands rested on her shoulders. "Don't go there, Lizbeth." His whisper reassured her. That he knew her so well already amazed her. "There will be adjustments that we'll both have to make, but we'll figure it out together."

"I know." She started to hug him, but her phone buzzed. Closing her eyes, she took a step away and pulled her phone out of her pocket. "It's my father. I've been ignoring him all day."

"He knew you were here and were the princess's right hand gal. Did he really think you would answer your phone?"

This time she chose to send an automated text back - I CAN'T TALK RIGHT NOW.

A minute later a text came back.

YOU WILL BE HERE TOMORROW MORNING AT TEN.

The *or else* was implied.

Robert read it over her shoulder. "Your plane doesn't arrive until eleven, and our flight takes off at five." He kissed the side of her head. "And I know you're not packed yet. You'll be home maybe a few hours tops. We don't have to pass through security, but we still have to leave your apartment by 4:15 at the latest."

She closed her eyes and prayed before typing back. MY FLIGHT DOESN'T ARRIVE IN TIME. I'M LEAVING ON A DIPLOMATIC MISSION SHORTLY AFTER.

"Good for you."

She leaned her head against Robert's chest until her phone buzzed again.

MY PLANE IS ALREADY ON THE WAY.

"How do I say no?" she whispered. "If I do, he takes everything away from me. I have no job. I live on the allowance he gives me. If I make him too mad before my birthday, I lose my inheritance."

"I've never understood that, sweetheart. How can he take what your mother left you away?"

She shrugged. "I have no idea, but he's always made it perfectly clear. He wanted me to seduce Malachi so I'd end up pregnant, and he'd be forced to leave Jessabelle for me. When I refused, he threatened me again."

Robert pulled her close and hugged her. "I make enough for us to live on. Don't worry about him. If he can disinherit you, it's not the end of the world."

Lizbeth felt his mouth move and knew he was praying over her.

"And I'll call my lawyer Monday morning. If you don't want to go, don't. I know you have a few loose ends to take care of here before your flight leaves tomorrow."

"I couldn't stand up to him if I didn't know you had my back," she told him.

"I do, love. Always."

"Then I won't go, and we'll see what happens, I guess." Lizbeth stood on tiptoe and kissed his cheek. "I love you, Robert Padovano."

"And I love you." After a quick kiss, he pulled back. "I do have to get going, if I'm going to catch my plane."

She grinned wickedly. "You could always take my place on my father's plane."

Robert winced. "Thanks, but no thanks."

"I know." Someone across the ballroom called her name. "Duty calls." Another quick kiss, and they went their separate ways.

Just a few hours, and they'd get to spend two glorious weeks together.

Lizbeth couldn't wait.

Yvette slipped from the warmth of the covers and into the bathroom. After taking care of her morning ablutions, she wrapped a robe around her and went quietly to the kitchen. Her parents hadn't been thrilled when she'd started drinking coffee at sixteen, but she loved certain kinds. Today, she'd go with whatever she found in the cabinet. Someone must have stocked it with her favorite individual serving cups, because she knew Nicklaus hadn't even known where the kitchen was the night before.

The night before.

Her cheeks heated at the thought of what transpired between the two of them after they finished their cake and ice cream. When her coffee finished brewing, she took her mug and went back into the bedroom, settling into one of the big chairs near the window. Yvette sipped the coffee and wished she could watch as Sunday boaters took to the water.

"What time is it?" Nicklaus's groggy voice cut through the quiet.

"I'm not sure. I think I made coffee around 6:45. It's almost gone so maybe 7:15?"

"Aren't we supposed to have breakfast with our families?"

She heard the rustling of sheets. By the time Nicklaus sat in the chair next to her, he wore his pajama pants. "We have an invitation to breakfast at eight if we want to go. We're not expected to, per se. Then church is at ten. We're expected to be there. After that, we have an interview at three. Supposedly, we have a plane at our disposal any time after the interview, but to the best of my knowledge, no wedding trip plans have officially been made."

"Do you want to go on a honeymoon?"

Yvette thought about it. "I figured I would go somewhere for a few days to get over the whole 'stood up at the altar by a dead guy' thing. Since I found out you weren't dead, I have no idea."

"Where would you have gone?"

Yvette took the last big sip of her coffee. "I don't know. My family has a mountain home in Mevendia, a home on the southern coast of Ravenzario, and a home on the Montevarian coast. I thought about going to one of those. Probably Ravenzario because it's the southernmost one, and it's June in the Med. I thought about our yacht or even getting away from the Commonwealth entirely and going somewhere else not *too* far way, like

Athmetis. I even thought about heading to one of the independent countries in the Caribbean. Nana loves San Majoria's capital city. She told me she thought I would love Cabo Juan-Eduardo, too."

"I'm told Athmetis was our first stop after we left Ravenzario."

Yvette didn't know what to say to that. Finally, she went with, "Where would you like to go? Or would you like to go anywhere?"

Nicklaus shifted, stretching his legs out in front of him as he stared out the window. "I don't think I want to hang around here. I know I'll have to and get the whole 'I was supposed to be king' thing sorted out sometime soon. It's not really high on my priority list right now."

Yvette stared into her cup and wondered what he meant.

"Ah..." He suddenly seemed a bit uncomfortable. "I mean, I don't think I want to deal with the realities of being *Prince Nicklaus* just yet."

She tucked a loose piece of hair behind her ear. "First question to address, I suppose, is do you want to have breakfast with our families?"

Nicklaus looked over at her with a smirk on his face. "I don't supposed hiding for the next week or month or year is an option?"

A small smile crept to her face. "No. I don't think it is."

"In that case, I think I would like to have breakfast with them. I know the queen would like that."

Yvette hadn't really thought about the effect all this would have had on Christiana. She had been too focused on what it would mean for herself. The wedding. The potential banishment. "I'm sure Christiana would love to have you there. Why don't we make that the first part of the plan then?"

"What about church?"

She glanced over at him. He looked...glum was the word that came to mind. "Do you want to go to church this morning?"

"I'm not sure I want to make my debut where everyone knows

who I am at a church I'm unfamiliar with. I'd really love to get out of the interview this afternoon, too."

Yvette stood and stretched. "I guess we should get ready for breakfast and go from there."

In forty-five minutes, they'd somehow managed to get ready without getting in each other's way. It helped that Nicklaus took his things to another room. Yvette put her tablet and phone into her purse and slung it over her shoulder. If they did go to church, she could access her Bible on either one of them. "Are you ready?" she asked as she walked into the living area.

"Not yet."

She looked up to find him walking toward her. He certainly looked ready.

"I haven't kissed you yet." He stopped in front of her. "If that's okay with you."

Yvette blinked rapidly. She hadn't really thought about whether or not he had kissed her yet. It should have occurred to her, but it didn't.

Nicklaus stopped in front of her and rested his hands on her hips. "Is that okay?" he asked again.

She swallowed hard before nodding. Her eyes flickered closed as he leaned toward her. A first soft brush set her nerves on edge, but in a good way. The second, firmer, contact sent her senses reeling. Yvette found herself leaning forward as he moved away. She felt herself falling forward just a bit, until she rested her head against his chest.

Nicklaus chuckled, and she found herself loving the feeling of his arms around her. "That was nice."

She felt his voice rumbling under her cheek. "Very nice."

"But I think we should figure out where we're having breakfast with everyone before we do that again."

A minute later, they walked out the apartment door into a wide hallway. Nicklaus led the way, her hand tucked into his. But she kept turning his last words over and over in her mind.

Yes, they'd truly become man and wife the night before. Two became one flesh.

But was she really ready - were *they* ready - to have that kind of relationship regularly when they barely knew each other?

Nicklaus wasn't sure what kind of reception they'd get when they arrived at breakfast hand in hand. He didn't think their families would be able to tell what transpired the night before, but the knowing looks from several family members made him think they at least suspected. Two seats next to each other were left open, in case they showed up. They were a few minutes late so everyone else had started eating.

"Where's Nana Yvette?" his wife asked as he held her chair.

"She flew home last night to sleep in her own bed," King Antonio answered as someone poured him coffee.

As they started eating, the conversation flowed around him. He didn't know these people, not well enough to converse without feeling awkward. But the only way to get to know them was to talk to them. He'd save that for next time.

About the time they finished, King Antonio spoke to Nicklaus and Yvette. "I cannot imagine either of you would like to attend church this morning or do the interview this afternoon."

Yvette answered for both of them. "We talked about it earlier. I know Nicklaus would prefer not to just yet. I think church would be more of a sideshow if we go today. The interview even more so. All of this is so brand new to Nicklaus. I've lived with the media my entire life. He hasn't. I think it would be good for him, for all of us, if he had a little more time to get used to all of it before going on television." She stood up for him and got his message across more diplomatically than he would have. He needed to pay attention to how she did that.

Christiana jumped in. "I think that is for the best. Antonio, perhaps you and I can sit down with Matt Markinson this afternoon. Answer a few questions and give him enough to hold them over. Offer a longer interview and more access in a few weeks."

"I think that would be the best plan," Yvette said.

Nicklaus wasn't sure what he thought about them talking as though he wasn't here. Since the conversation was going the way he wanted it to, he decided it didn't matter if he was the one doing the talking or not.

"Nicklaus needs time to get used to all of this," Yvette continued. "We need to figure out what, if anything, he needs to do about his claim to the throne. Is he now first in line until the baby is born?"

"We will need to talk to Majority Leader Caruso about that, right?" Christiana looked at Alexander and King Antonio.

"That would be the best place to start," Antonio answered. "You should talk to the official royal historian. He may know if there's any precedent or legal statutes no one remembers because it's been so long since any of them have been used."

Nicklaus watched Christiana nod slowly as she sipped her tea. "He would be a good one to talk to. Nicklaus may still have a claim to the throne right now, despite the statutes passed after the accident."

He couldn't sit still any longer. "Hold on. Why don't you ask Nicklaus if he *wants* a claim to the throne? I have no interest in taking the throne away from you, Christiana, and no desire to be the heir to the throne should, God forbid, something happen to you and the baby."

Christiana exchanged a look with her husband. "If that is truly the way you feel, then you may need to formally renounce any claim to the throne."

The king jumped in. "If he does, and something were to happen to Christiana and the baby, either Yvette would become queen or Ravenzario would be absorbed into the other two countries."

Another guilt trip? Wasn't threatening to exile Yvette and Michaela enough? He'd have to consider carefully whether he really wanted to renounce any claim he might have in case of a catastrophe. Would Yvette even want the throne? Would he want to be prince consort? If it was just about him, he would, but it wasn't. The fate of the entire country would rest on his shoulders. Yvette, at eighteen, would do a much better job than he would.

"So that's settled." Yvette's voice shook him out of his thoughts. "No church. No interview. Nicklaus has some time to think and pray about what he thinks is best as far as any claim he may have in the event of a catastrophe." Odd she would choose the same word he had. "In a month or so, after he's had a chance to settle in, then we'll talk about rescheduling the interview."

Had she gotten all of that from their brief conversation earlier? Or did she understand him in a way he didn't quite understand himself? How?

"So where are you planning to go for your wedding trip then?" King Antonio asked the question, and it seemed to be directed at Nicklaus.

He swallowed his bite of food, and glanced at Yvette. She wasn't looking at him. "I don't know that I have a real preference. We talked earlier about where Yvette had thought she'd go to get away from the press after a non-wedding since she thought I was dead. I'd be good with any of those places."

Yvette detailed the options she'd mentioned, still without looking his direction.

The king seemed to be turning the options over in his head. "I think, if I were you two, I'd take the yacht and spend much of your time at sea. Visit some ports of call, but if you're out on the water, the media can't get to you. Don't plan too much ahead of time and be spontaneous. Worry more about getting to know each other better and not as much about where you're going."

Nicklaus looked over at Yvette. "What do you think?"

She gave a small shrug. "Sounds fine to me. When do we leave?"

"As soon as you're ready." King Antonio pushed back from the table and stepped to the side, stretching his arms toward Yvette. "We must head back home."

Yvette stood and gave her father a hug. He whispered something to her, but Nicklaus couldn't hear what it was. Christiana was coming over to give him a hug herself.

"Just promise you'll come back," she whispered.

"Of course. We'll be back before you know it."

They said their good-byes so the others could make it to church. Suddenly it was just himself and Yvette left in the breakfast room. Something occurred to him. He realized he hadn't seen Michaela but once in the last three days. Had he ever gone so long without seeing her? "What do we need to do to get ready?"

Yvette shrugged. "I'd imagine Melinda and Belinda have my things packed already. Alfred probably has yours mostly done, but since he's only known you a few days, he may have questions."

"So back to my...our apartment?" Would he ever get used to having an apartment in a building this size?

"Yes. Back to our apartment. Then to the yacht and our wedding trip."

Nicklaus stopped in the middle of the hallway. "Actually, there's something I'd like to do first."

Yvette turned to look at Nicklaus. He had something he wanted to do before going to the yacht? What?

"I'd like to see if we can see Michaela before we go." There was something of a lost little boy in Nicklaus's eyes. "I'd love for you to officially meet her. And..." He hesitated.

"And what?" she prompted when he didn't go on.

"I've never gone several days without talking to her before all this started." He shifted his weight from one foot to the other. "So much has changed in the last week, and I'd like to talk to her before we go."

Yvette nodded slowly. "If we can work it out, I'd love to meet her. I'll talk to Melinda and have her check into it."

They arrived at their apartment a few minutes later. As she expected, Melinda and Belinda were putting the last things in her suitcases. Alfred looked to have completed most of that task for Nicklaus. Alfred began asking him questions while Yvette motioned to Melinda.

Once out in the sitting area, she turned to her assistant. "Do you know anything about where Michaela is?"

"No ma'am. I can find out, though."

"Nicklaus would like to see her before we leave."

"About that..." Melinda looked like she had information she wasn't sure she wanted to share. "There are a couple of options. Your father didn't quite think it through. The Mevendian yacht is still in Montevaro. They're preparing to get underway, but you wouldn't be able to leave here until early tomorrow. You could fly there and drive to the marina, but there's no airport near the marina, so you'd end up driving a couple of hours."

Yvette crinkled her nose. "I'm not crazy about either of those options."

"The only other one we came up with was for you to take the

Ravenzarian yacht and leave as soon as it's ready and meet up with the Mevendian yacht. You can take a small suitcase with you that could be easily moved from one to the other and the rest of your things meet you at your first port of call." Melinda seemed to reconsider. "You *could* take everything with you now, but it would be more difficult to move between the ships. The queen and Duke Alexander are taking the yacht tomorrow morning to visit some of the islands for the next few days, or you would be able to just take it to Mevendia."

"I'll check with Nicklaus, but I'd imagine we'll want to leave as soon as possible on the Ravenzarian yacht." She started for the bedroom. "Let me know as soon as you find out if we can meet with Michaela."

Melinda nodded and headed for the door. Yvette went back into the other room to find Nicklaus in the closet with Alfred.

He walked out shaking his head. "A week ago I had less than half as many clothes as I do now. I've never even tried most of these on. How do I know what I like to wear?"

"Trust Alfred and whoever else helped you obtain the clothes. Did he or she ask a bunch of questions?"

"Yeah. I know the suits came from the shop in Pagosa Plaza where Christiana hid during the whole assassination thing a couple months ago. I have no clue about the others. No one else asked me anything." He ran a hand through his light brown hair.

"Trust me, then. Whoever it was didn't get his or her job by buying uncomfortable clothes." She shuddered. "Except some of the formal dresses or high heels, but that's not something they can do anything about. I'd imagine almost all of the clothes are ones you'll find comfortable."

"We don't even know where we're going. How do I know what to tell Alfred to pack?"

Yvette walked toward him, stopping a few inches away and took his hands into her own. "For now, you need clothes for a few days on the yacht. That's it. Let Alfred handle the rest. He knows what he's doing."

"She's right, sir." Alfred's voice came from the closet.

He sighed. "Okay. I'll trust you both. When do we leave?"

Yvette glanced over at the door to see Melinda nodding her way. "As soon as we're ready. We'll go see Michaela then go to the marina and get underway."

Nicklaus's shoulders slumped in relief. "That sounds great."

"Then why don't we head for the car? We'll stop and get some flowers for me to give her so she'll like me." Yvette grinned to take any sting out of her words.

But Nicklaus still pulled his brows together in confusion. "Why wouldn't she like you?"

Yvette hoped she wasn't about to offend him. "Because I'm the girl who represents everything taking you away from the life the two of you had for the last decade and a half."

"You may have a point. But I still think she'll like you, even without the flowers."

Yvette leaned up and kissed his cheek. "You're sweet to think so. But we'd better get going. I think we probably want to be out on the water by the time the interview was scheduled to begin."

He agreed, but bent down and kissed her, for real. Yvette found that she liked it, very much, and could get used to it, quite easily.

But the kiss didn't last long. Yvette doubted Alfred meant to interrupt, but some noises came from the closet and reminded her they weren't alone.

"I think that's our cue," Nicklaus whispered. He stepped back and held his elbow out her direction. "Shall we?"

Yvette slid her hand into the crook, loving the feel of his strong arm under her fingertips. "We shall."

After conversing with Melinda for a moment, they left the apartment. When the door closed behind them, Nicklaus looked first to the left, then the right. "Um, you don't happen to know how to get out of here, do you?"

She laughed and leaned her head against his shoulder. "Not really, but we're two pretty smart people. I bet we can figure it out."

Nicklaus stopped at another junction between hallways.
"Um...I'm not sure where to go from here." He looked
one way then the other. "If we keep going this way, we
should eventually get to the other end of the palace, right?"

"You would think so." Yvette looked straight ahead. "Of course,
back home, most of the hallways are laid out pretty straight. It's a
giant courtyard with palace on all sides. Most of the floors have
one long hallway right down the middle. Some have smaller hallways going across in places." She went straight ahead to the next
hall. "But here, some of them go at odd angles."

"I need to see if there's a simplified map I can use to get
around. A blueprint would be too much. Something simple."

"You should talk to your sister and Tony about an app." She
pulled out her phone.

Nicklaus watched as she tapped a couple of times. An app
opened up with what looked like a floor plan.

"Jessabelle, my sister-in-law, calls it her 'you are here' app. I
don't know how they did it, but you can preprogram certain

places in it so I can pick 'go to my room,' and it'll give me several options of how to get there."

"Someone put that on my phone when I got to Mevendia." What a weight it took off his shoulders. "That would be great. I wonder if they could do something like that while I'm gone." He noticed what he said immediately and amended his statement. "While *we're* gone."

"It would sure help both of us until we get this place figured out."

"Until you get what figured out?"

Nicklaus turned to see Tony walking down the hall.

"Lost much?" The smirk on the head of security's face didn't annoy Nicklaus as much as he expected.

Yvette crossed her arms. "You know very well neither of us knows our way around this place."

The head of security chuckled. "I know. I also know you were planning to go see Michaela. It just so happens she was already on her way here." He tilted his head to the right. "Let's go this way."

The three of them walked in silence for a couple of minutes. As they reached a large set of double doors, Tony turned to them. "I have a bit of work to do. Let Michaela know I'll be back in a few minutes?"

Nicklaus nodded.

Tony winked at Yvette. "And I'll see what we can do about that app while you're gone."

She grinned. "Thanks, Tony."

"My pleasure, ma'am."

Yvette wrinkled her nose. "I'm only eighteen. I'm too young to be 'ma'am.'"

"But you're married. You're no longer a miss."

"I know." She heaved a dramatic sigh. "But that doesn't mean I have to like it."

Tony chuckled again as he pulled open the door. Nicklaus

walked in to find Michaela standing across the room staring out a window.

She turned and smiled, giving a small curtsy. "Good morning, Your Royal Highnesses."

Nicklaus rolled his eyes and held out his arms for a hug. "You've been my mother for so many years. Please don't start calling me that." Michaela hugged him close, as though she hadn't seen him in days. And, truth be told, she kind of hadn't. He'd talked with her for a moment the night before, but that was the most time he'd actually spent *with her* since the week before. After a minute, she squeezed him a bit tighter then let go. He put his arm around her shoulders and turned. "Have you met Yvette?"

Yvette held out a hand. "It's a pleasure to meet you, Michaela. Thank you for taking such good care of Nicklaus for so long."

Michaela shook her hand. "It was my pleasure, ma'am."

Yvette rolled her eyes. "Please call me Yvette."

She looked uncomfortable at that idea.

"Why don't we see what happens after you've gotten to know each other a bit?" He motioned toward the couches. "We can't stay long." He really, *really* wanted to be gone by the time that interview was supposed to start. "But I'm glad I got to see you before we leave. I don't even know how long we'll be gone."

"Probably a month," Yvette interjected. "At least that's pretty typical. My brother and sister-in-law only went to Ravenzario for a few days because of her father's illness. Adeline and Charlie only took a couple of days because her coronation was the same week. Anastasia and Jonah also only took a few days. Richard and Ellie did take a whole month, but they're the adventurous ones. They spent part of it dog-sledding across Greenland." Another roll of her eyes told him what she thought about that idea.

"We're kind of playing it by ear, I think. Yachting around the Med." Nicklaus grinned at Michaela. "Didn't we talk about that a few times?"

"We did," she confirmed. "When you were about ten, one

summer we did a dream trip around the Mediterranean. Ravenzario was the first place you wanted to go."

Had he known, somehow, even then, that he belonged here?

"You told me you were going to take Eve, remember?" Were those tears in Michaela's eyes?

"You planned to take Eve? Me?" She looked back and forth between them.

"We talked about taking 'my father's best friend's daughter Eve' on our cruise around the Mediterranean."

Michaela looked between both of them then spoke to Yvette. "I did my best to prepare him for yesterday without being able to tell him everything. I always wanted him to know you were out there waiting for him to come home."

"He told me that." Yvette wiped away a tear. "I can't thank you enough for that. If you hadn't, when the time came for him to decide to marry me or..." She looked at him and hesitated.

"Or we'd all be exiled," Michaela confirmed.

"I still don't understand why," Michaela went on.

Nicklaus leaned toward her. "King Antonio explained it. It was to prevent Henry from bringing a fake Nicklaus in who refused to marry Yvette. Fake Nicklaus would have been exiled, too."

"And if you were alive but not here?" she asked.

Yvette answered that one. "My guess is the exile would still have been enforced if the wedding didn't happen, unless his reappearance was so late I'd already married someone else."

Yvette saw how Nicklaus looked at Michaela, like her brothers looked at their mother. He'd said it, but part of her hadn't wanted to believe it. He'd married her only to make certain the woman who raised him wouldn't be exiled.

Yvette didn't know how she felt about that.

But it was too late now. They were married. The marriage had been consummated. She was about to spend a month on board a yacht with this man. All she could do was hope and pray that one day he'd be glad he married her because of who *she* was, not because of the consequences to his mother.

"I have something for both of you." Michaela must have decided a subject change was in order. She stood and walked toward a table on the far side of the room. When she turned, she held a beautifully wrapped box. Yvette expected her to hand it to Nicklaus, but she didn't. "It's for both of you, but I want you to know that I've done my best to watch you grow up from afar. I know you've grown into a beautiful young woman, but I also know that you're kind and gentle and all of those other fruits of the Spirit. I know King Richard and Queen Marissa would be incredibly proud to have you for a daughter-in-law."

Yvette took the box from her and tugged at the ribbon. The gold box wasn't wrapped in paper so she shook the top until the bottom fell out. Unfolding the tissue paper, she got her first glimpse of white and emerald green. Cloth of some kind. She didn't know quite how to describe the feeling of it. Standing, Yvette set the box next to her and pulled the whole thing out.

A quilt.

"It's gorgeous." Her voice held the awe her mind couldn't describe. There was also shiny royal blue, the same color Christiana had used for an accent color on her wedding dress.

"The quilt shop in Mallard Lake made it. The blue comes from the Rensselaer family crest, and the purple from the Van Rensselaer crest. I know you have access to the best bedding money can buy, but I kind of hoped you'd keep it somewhere. Maybe in your room at one of the other houses."

Yvette didn't know what to say. "It's beautiful. I'm not quite sure what we'll do with it." Or what Nicklaus would want to do with it. "I'm certain it will have a place of honor for many years to come."

"Definitely, Mickey."

Yvette looked over to see Nicklaus hugging the other woman again.

"Thank you."

A throat cleared on the other side of the room. Tony stood there and held up the arm with his watch on it.

Nicklaus gave Michaela one more hug, but then Michaela turned to her. "Do you mind?" she asked, holding out her arms.

Yvette walked into them and held on for dear life.

"I've prayed for yesterday for so many years," Michaela whispered to her. "He needs time and help adjusting to all of this. I believe this marriage has had God's hand in it, even from the very beginning. It will take you both a while to get to the point where you know each other well enough to honestly say you would *choose* each other, if given the chance to make a choice. I know the reasons why he decided to marry you. Give him time. Let him get to know you. Before you know it, he'll be very glad none of us were exiled." Michaela let go and took a step back. "Have a wonderful trip. I look forward to hearing about it when you get back."

Yvette hugged the quilt close as Nicklaus hugged Michaela once more. They followed Tony until they reached the front entrance to the palace. The portico covered a limousine waiting for them. Once seated in the back, Nicklaus kept his distance, staring at his clasped hands. Yvette continued to hold the quilt to her chest until they reached the marina. Even then, she didn't let go, but kept it with her as they boarded a small boat that would take them to the larger one anchored in deeper water.

Once on board, they were shown to the room she would expect to share with him, if things hadn't become so awkward. Rather than doing something else, Yvette went out onto the balcony, still holding the quilt. She didn't know why, but she didn't want to let go of it.

Nicklaus followed her out. "Any idea how long until the rendezvous with the other yacht?"

Yvette shrugged. "Probably five or six hours depending on exactly when both get going."

"So we don't even really need a stateroom?"

That was one way to look at it. "I suppose not. Unless you want to change into something more comfortable, like shorts and a t-shirt."

"That might be good. Swim trunks?"

She arched a brow as she looked at him. "Do you expect to spend much time swimming alongside?"

"Good point." He rested his forearms on the railing. "I think we need to talk."

13

"**W**hat do you want to talk about?" Yvette could think of any number of things they probably needed to discuss.

She wanted to talk about precisely none of them.

Before he could say anything else, there was a knock on the stateroom door.

Nicklaus sighed and went back in to open the door.

"Are you ready for lunch?" he called a minute later.

It was about that time. "Sure. You go on. I'll be there in a minute."

He hesitated then left. Yvette went back into the stateroom and refolded the quilt. She'd enjoyed the evening in the apartment with Nicklaus. He called her Evie. She called him Nicky. They'd kissed. Before that, they'd talked and spent time getting to know each other better.

She wanted to spend her days with that Nicklaus. To be that Yvette. Not the two who were awkward around each other.

It would take time. She knew that, but did it have to be *so* uncomfortable. Maybe it was the quilt. Because Michaela had handed it to her? Or because seeing Michaela reminding Nicklaus of the life he'd had no choice but to leave behind?

Yvette laid the folded quilt on the bed and ran a hand over the blue and purple material where they intersected.

In just a few minutes, she'd made her way to the deck where lunch was waiting. She could still see Ravenzario in the distance, but it was getting smaller all the time.

Nicklaus stood against the rail, the wind making his loose shirt flap. He turned and smiled. "There you are. Ready to eat?"

"Sure."

He held her chair for her then sat across the table. "What do you want to do today? I mean, I know we're on this boat for the next few hours and then we transfer over to the other one, but until then, any ideas?"

Yvette took a bite of her sandwich and thought about it. "We could take naps." One of her favorite Sunday afternoon activities, one she rarely had the opportunity to indulge in. "Or watch a movie or go for a swim in the on-board pool."

His eyes sort of bugged out. "There's a pool on the yacht?"

"Sure." She shrugged. "So you can swim when we're under-way." Yvette pointed toward the railing. "You couldn't exactly go for a swim right now."

"Good point." He took another bite. "Why don't we do that then?"

Yvette nodded then finished her meal. She wished the silence wasn't quite so awkward, but she didn't know what to do about that. Once finished, they made their way to the stateroom. Nicholas found his new swim trunks easily and went into the bathroom to put them on. He made some excuse and then left, so she could change on her own, she supposed.

Once in the tankini, Yvette pulled a cover-up on. Hopefully, there would be towels available on the deck. The pool wasn't really a pool per se, but more like a hot tub, without the hot. Just enough room for several people to sit in and enjoy the cool water with the hot sun overhead or watch a movie on the screen nearby.

Yvette sat on one of the deck chairs and pulled the ponytail out of her hair. It had taken her weeks to convince Belinda to teach her how to braid her own hair, but once she learned, the skill came in handy. The French braid wasn't the best one she'd ever done, but it didn't matter. No one else was around.

Just Nicklaus.

Her husband.

Speaking of, where was he?

"I got lost."

The voice behind her made Yvette jump.

"Sorry." She could hear the apology in Nicklaus's voice as he sat in the chair next to her. "I don't know how, but I managed to end up in the lowest level and in the crew quarters." He gave her a look of utter disbelief. "You would have thought I cut a hole in the side. I had no idea being in the wrong area would be such a big deal."

"It depends on who you work with. Who you are. Who's running the boat." She pulled her cover up off and headed for the pool. "I would imagine most of these people worked for Henry Eit, and he would have had a very different opinion about..." She made air quotes. "...'the help' than you or even your sister. My family has a pretty close relationship with some of the staff members we work with regularly, like Melinda and Belinda, or my parents' assistants. My father loves the water, so he and the captain get along famously. He loves spending time in the wheelhouse."

"All right, so these folks are going to have to learn that I'm not Henry?"

"Probably. And it's not like they know either one of us." She stepped down into the water. "They have no idea what they might do or not do that could get them fired."

"That's kind of ridiculous." Nicklaus stepped in next to her. "Short of trying to kill one of us, I can't imagine myself trying to get any of them fired."

"But they don't know that. We're both unknown quantities to them."

They both settled onto the seat. Yvette let her legs float up in front of her a bit. Easier to stare at her toes than deal with whatever Nicklaus might be about to say. Would he still want to have that talk? Whatever it was?

Nicklaus took her hand in his, linking their fingers together. "I think I'm glad we decided to get out of Dodge for a while."

She didn't understand. "Get out of where?"

"Never mind. It's an American reference to the Old West. It means to get out of somewhere before it's too late for some reason." He leaned his head back and looked at the sky above them. "I just mean that I'm glad we have some time to get to know each other without worrying about being around so many other people at the same time. I find I like this plan better by the minute."

"You know my mother gave me some very strict instructions for this trip." She didn't look at him, didn't know what he'd think about what her mother said.

"I don't think I want to know."

"Probably not. But you get to have more prince lessons."

"Prince lessons?" Nicklaus stared at her. "I already got prince lessons."

Yvette shrugged. "Apparently you need more." She gave him a sympathetic look. "We can wait a week though."

"Am I going to be walking around with a book on my head? Practicing my wave?" Over his dead body.

"Well, the book thing isn't a bad idea. Helps give you good posture, but..." Yvette suddenly ran her hand over his head. Water dripped down the side of his face. "I'm not sure your head is flat enough. I know it's this big thing princesses are supposed to be able to do. I've seen *Princess Diaries*. But sometimes a head just isn't flat enough to balance a book on."

Nicklaus suddenly felt self-conscious. "My head's not flat?" He ran his own hand over it. "Since when isn't my head flat?"

Yvette just looked at him.

"Right. Since birth most likely."

"Or when Christiana tried to carry you and dropped you on it."

He looked over at her and could tell she was trying to hide a grin. "For all I know she may have." Nicklaus flicked a little bit of water at her, getting her face wet.

"Hey!" Her eyes widened in surprise, but then narrowed, taking on a wicked gleam he wasn't sure he liked.

And he took a wave full of water to his face. Sputtering and coughing, he splashed back. She returned his splash, quickly turning it into a full-fledged war.

Laughing, they circled the small pool, alternately splashing each other and ducking to avoid the next spray of water.

Yvette slipped, just a bit, not enough to fall, but enough for her to be just a bit off balance. Nicklaus took the chance and moved across the pool instead of around, his arm wrapping around her waist and pulling her to him.

"Truce?" He was more out of breath than he thought he should be. But then, he'd never had a splash war with his wife before. Could it be the nearness of this beautiful woman more so than the physical exertion?

"Truce." She didn't try to get out of his embrace. Instead, she rested her arm on top of his.

Nicklaus only let himself press a quick kiss to the side of her head before letting her go. They both sat back down, close but not actually touching. The water came nearly to his chin when he relaxed down far enough. He could handle water like this, but he didn't like moving water. Or water in the dark. "So, prince lessons."

"They do *not* include water fights." Yvette held her nose and took a deep breath before submerging completely. She came back out of the water with her hair slicked straight back.

"So they probably don't include balancing books on my head because my head is egg shaped. And no water fights. They sound completely boring."

Yvette gave him a small smile. "They probably are, but you likely already know more than you realize. I'm sure Michaela raised you to be a gentleman. That goes a long way."

"I never understood why she was so adamant that I learn certain stuff or why I had to spend my summers learning about European geography and politics."

"It's good you did."

"I even studied the history of the Commonwealth." He stared up at the sky. "I learned all about the daughter of the English guy who had the relationship with Charlemagne. He was in love with her, but they couldn't get married. So Charlemagne *allegedly* gets her pregnant and gives her father the land that includes Montevaro and Mevendia. The daughter marries one of her father's knights. They have three sons and rule Belles Montagnes. The daughter was shipped off to Athmetis to marry a prince. They conquered what is now Ravenzario. The three sons split the kingdom upon the death of their father. All three royal families are still descended from those three brothers."

Yvette looked impressed. "I doubt I could have recited that quite so well. Do you know their names?"

Nicklaus winced. "Nope. Except for Charlemagne."

"You know Prince Charlie who married now-Queen Adeline of Montevaro?"

"Sure. I know who he is, and I think I met him at the wedding."

"I'm sure you did, briefly anyway." Yvette let her arms float in the water. "Anyway, the land came from Charlemagne, which is who Charlie was named after."

"Wait. So Prince Charlie is really Prince Charlemagne?"

"Yep. But he's gone by Charlie his whole life, for obvious reasons. Then he marries a princess a couple of days before she becomes queen, and all of the sudden everyone knows his real name."

That made Nicklaus chuckle. Neither one of them said anything for several minutes. He wasn't sure what to say. Before he could try to make another joke about prince lessons, a uniformed member of the crew walked out onto the deck.

He bowed at the waist, though there was no accompanying heel click. "Sir, ma'am, I've been informed that we have about four hours until we rendezvous with the Mevendian yacht. Would you like to have your dinner on board here or after the transfer?"

Nicklaus looked at Yvette only to find her looking at him, waiting for him to answer. What was he supposed to say? "What do you want to do, dear?" It was the best he could come up with.

Yvette responded with a smile that warmed Nicklaus's heart. A real, genuine smile. "The food here is excellent, but if you could ask the chef on board the Van Rensselaer yacht to prepare my favorite, that would be wonderful."

The man bowed again and left.

"Your favorite? What exactly is your favorite?" And would he like it? He'd discovered over the years that he was fairly particular about which foods he really enjoyed. Michaela had made certain he knew how to behave when dishes he did not like were placed in front of him. He had no known food allergies which made getting out of the shellfish he detested a bit more difficult.

"You'll have to wait and see." Yvette moved across the pool and climbed out, finding a remote control next to the television on one wall. "How about a movie to pass the time? We can't really swim in this pool, but it's a nice place to sit and watch."

Nicklaus simply nodded. When she sat back down, Yvette was far closer than she had been a moment earlier. And after she rested her head on his shoulder, he wondered what on earth was keeping him from kissing her like he wanted to.

14

"Sir, ma'am, we have about ten minutes before we'll be ready for your departure."

Yvette blinked her eyes open. Had she fallen asleep? She looked around and realized the sun was lower in the sky than it had been, though it wasn't yet sunset. As she sat up, Yvette also noticed she'd been snuggled next to Nicklaus on one of the couches.

"Thanks for letting us know." Nicklaus answered for both of them. The steward turned and left.

Yvette sat up, moving away from Nicklaus in the process. "We should probably change and get whatever we've got here together to make the transfer easier." She started for the door.

"How close will the two boats be?"

Yvette shrugged. "Not too far, I guess."

"Then I've got a challenge for you."

He had a gleam in his eye that Yvette didn't know how to interpret. "What kind of challenge?"

"You know how to swim, right?"

"Of course. All of us do." What was he getting at?

"Then I challenge you to a race." He tilted his head toward the railing. "The water's calm right now. When it's time, we'll see who can get to the other one first."

Yvette tried to decide if he was confident or foolhardy. She was a good swimmer, though she seldom swam any distance in open water. "What's the winner get?" Would the prize be worth it?

Nicklaus stood up and crossed his arms over his chest. "What are you willing to give up?"

"Give up?"

"Yeah. What item are you willing to give up? Control over the remote? The thermostat? Ports of call? What we do there?"

"Okay. You're on. Winner..." She tried to come up with something creative. "Winner gets to pick what we do at any one port of call. Winner's choice of port and activity."

Nicklaus grinned and walked toward her, resting his hands on her hips when he got close enough. "Sounds like a plan to me." He bent his head a bit lower. "But I don't intend to lose."

She looked up at him, searching his eyes for something, though she wasn't sure exactly what.

He leaned down a bit further capturing her lips with his. Her hands rested on his chest, the warmth of his skin from the late afternoon sun counteracting the delicious chill his kiss sent spiraling down her spine. When he backed away, Nicklaus rested his forehead on hers.

Yvette whispered back. "I don't intend to lose, either."

"Then I guess one of us will be disappointed."

She closed her eyes again relishing the feel of him close to her. "Why does either one of us have to be disappointed?"

"Only one of us can win," he pointed out.

"But just because I win doesn't mean you won't enjoy it, too."

"Are you that sure you're going to win?" She could hear the teasing challenge and imagined the look on his face.

"Maybe." This close to him, for this long, caused her stomach to do weird flip-floppy things. "Or maybe we'll tie."

She thought he was moving to kiss her again, but a cleared throat stopped whatever motion there was.

"Sir, ma'am, is there anything you'd like to get from your stateroom or shall we pack it up?" The same steward was back.

Nicklaus didn't move or say anything, so Yvette answered for both of them. "If you could make sure everything is packed up, that would be wonderful. Thank you. I think the prince and I are going to swim to the other ship if the captains can get close enough without any danger."

"I'm sure that can be arranged, ma'am." The combination of amusement and embarrassment in the steward's voice told Yvette he'd thought he'd interrupted something far more intimate than he actually had.

Or would it have become something more if he hadn't come along? He'd only been gone a couple of minutes. They needed to be more aware of their surroundings.

Thinking like that made Yvette wonder just how much there would be to interrupt in the future. They'd gotten carried away the night before. Would they again?

Nicklaus moved back and cleared his own throat. "So where is this race going to start?"

"The water."

That brought the chuckle she'd been hoping for. He walked over to the railing and whistled. "I thought this ship was nice, but wow! The Mevendian family's is pretty okay, too."

Yvette shrugged. "It's a difference in preferences, I guess. My father likes new toys. The last yacht was great, don't misunderstand, but it was older than me. He decided he wanted a new one a couple years ago. The old one was auctioned off with the proceeds going to charity. I heard Henry was planning to get a new one to one up my father even though this one isn't all that old. He was arrested before he could." She headed for the staircase. "Come on. As soon as the ship stops, we go."

His voice caught up to her. "You're on."

Yvette leaned against the railing at the back of the ship. They would lower a small boat out of the side and take the suitcases over. She hoped they remembered the quilt. Frowning, she wondered if she should double check, then decided not to. Not yet. She would once they made it across.

"I hear there's to be a race."

Yvette and Nicklaus both turned to see the captain standing there, a smile hidden by his bushy beard.

Nicklaus started to shift his weight from one leg to the other. "Uh, yeah. If that's okay, sir?"

Was he afraid they were getting caught doing something wrong? They weren't as long as they waited until it was safe.

"It's fine with me." The captain winked at her. "I happen to know the Mevendian royal family are all fabulous swimmers, though. I certainly wouldn't have taken her on."

Yvette grinned. "Thanks, Captain. He has no idea what he's getting into." Neither did she. Maybe he'd blow them all away with his own ability.

"Well, if you'd like to take your spots, I'll give you the signal."

The ships were situated facing away from each other. It was a straight line for a couple hundred meters. No flip turns required.

"Are you both ready?" the captain asked.

"Yes!" she and Nicklaus replied at the same time.

"On your mark. Get set. Go!"

Yvette took a deep breath and pushed off the boat, arms in front of her in a perfect dive. Time to win.

Nicklaus caught Yvette's dive out of the corner of his eye as he dove in himself. She had nice form. The water swallowed him and when he surfaced, he realized she was already several yards beyond him. Daytime and gently moving water like this he could handle. Taking a deep breath, he followed, kicking and pulling himself through the Mediterranean.

Just as he finally caught up with Yvette, as she was only half a body length ahead of him, she grasped the rung on the ladder of the other yacht.

Nicklaus tagged it a second later, looking up to see a big grin on Yvette's face.

"I won!" she exclaimed gleefully.

He gave her a quick kiss. "You did, but I would have had you in a couple more yards."

"But you didn't."

"And I probably won't ever live it down, will I?"

"Nope." She motioned for him to go first. While he climbed the ladder, she went back under the water, smoothing her hair back off her face as she reemerged. He held out his hand pulling her on board after she'd climbed to the top rung.

"So where are we going, and what are we doing?" Someone had left towels lying nearby, and he handed her one. She wrapped it around herself, tucking the other end in near her other arm. Nicklaus used another one to dry himself off, then wrapped it around his waist.

"I don't know yet." She started for the stairs leading up to the next deck. "I'll have to think about it."

Chuckling to himself, Nicklaus followed her.

The next hour was spent separately, each of them taking a quick shower in separate bathrooms and getting dressed for dinner.

Nicklaus met Yvette on the top deck. "I'm told dinner is about ready."

"Probably."

"Where are we eating?" He knew there were several possible locations.

"Wherever we want."

"Are you okay?" She seemed off.

Yvette shrugged. "I'm not sure what I am. Yesterday was over-whelming but adrenaline helped with that. Today's been...I don't know what it's been. Long. I was up early. We've been on the go a fair bit. It's been emotional. Seeing Michaela and leaving on our wedding trip." She turned and leaned her back against the railing. "Trying to figure out what the new normal is. We're married. The marriage has been..." She glanced down, her skin turning a becoming shade of pink.

"Consummated?" he offered.

She didn't look at him, but nodded.

"And what does that mean for our new normal? Are we sleeping in the same bed? Smooching or consummating more?"

She nodded.

"Hey." Nicklaus walked toward her, resting his hands on her mostly bare shoulders. "It doesn't have to mean anything. I'd like to sleep in the same bed with you, but that doesn't mean we have to or that anything more than sleeping will actually happen."

"You mean that?"

"I do." He pulled on her shoulders until she leaned against him with her arms around his waist. "Why don't we see if we can eat in our suite - change into our most comfortable clothes, and go from there?"

She nodded against him. "I like that idea. In fact, I think that's where dinner is supposed to be served unless we say something."

When they reached the suite, Nicklaus did a double take. Sliding doors had been opened and a table and two chairs had somehow been extended outside, almost like a pop-out section of a motor home.

"You never told me what your favorite is. What are we having for dinner?"

"They would have had to stop at a port somewhere because they didn't have the ingredients. We'll have it another time."

"Sounds like a plan." He went to a stereo system and hit play. "Mrs. Rennselaer, may I have this dance?"

15

Yvette tilted her head to one side. "You have never thought of yourself as 'Mr. Rensselaer,' have you?"

Nicklaus chuckled. "Nope. Never have. I've always been Nicholas Metcalf. I'm working on it though."

"You never thought your wife would be Mrs. Rensselaer, either."

"No," he answered slowly. "I never did."

"And you never really thought you'd marry Eve."

Why was she doing this to herself? Nicklaus *had* married her. He'd promised before God and man to love, honor, and cherish her. None of the fake half-promises Malachi had made during his wedding to Jessabelle the year before. Thankfully, the wedding had used the Ravenzarian traditional vows rather than the Mevendian ones. It wouldn't have made a difference, though. Malachi told everyone he'd taken his own vows after the ridiculous ones at the wedding.

Would Nicklaus have done the same thing?

Would it even have occurred to him given that he'd really only married her to keep Michaela from being exiled?

"You never answered my question." His gentle voice brought her back to the present.

"What?"

He still held out his hand. "May I have this dance?"

Yvette nodded and moved into his arms. Despite whatever rationale he had for marrying her, he held her far closer than he had the night before. She loved the feeling.

She felt safe.

Yvette knew she'd never truly known danger, never known anything but safety. She always had the best drivers, pilots, and security her country could provide.

But here, in the arms of her husband, she felt safe in a way she never had before.

Before she quite knew what happened, he was kissing her. Soft, gentle kisses. Kisses for the sake of the kiss.

After a couple of songs, they moved to the table where dinner waited. Nothing hot or too heavy after such a big day. They happened to have a perfect view of the sunset as they ate. Neither one of them said much, just took it in. After dinner, they moved to a couch where they could still see the view to the west.

Yvette snuggled into Nicklaus's side as they sat there, neither one saying anything for what seemed like an eternity. Staff worked quietly to clear the table and bring the balcony section back inside before closing the doors.

Only a soft light coming from around the ceiling lit the room as the sun finally said it's good night, disappearing completely beyond the horizon.

"I know it's fairly early." Nicklaus's soft voice broke the stillness. "But I'm still not quite acclimated to the time change, and it's been a few very busy days. I think I'm ready to turn in."

"Go ahead." Yvette lifted her head from its spot on his shoulder. "I think I'm going to sit here for a bit longer."

He kissed the side of her head and stood.

Yvette continued to sip her tea, trying not to listen to the shuffling of sheets and Nicklaus settling into the bed.

Her mind wandered here, there, and everywhere, not settling on anything specific. After taking her final sip, Yvette decided Nicklaus had the right idea. Being careful not to bother him, she slid into the other side of the bed and settled in to sleep.

The next several days were spent lazing around the ship. They ate together, talked, swam when the ship slowed down so they could, though Yvette noticed Nicklaus spent more time on the back of the boat than he did in the water with her.

It was a week after the wedding when something changed.

Yvette woke out of a deep sleep, sitting straight up in bed, wondering what woke her.

The engines hummed quietly in the background, but that wasn't it.

And then she heard it again, only this time it was accompanied by jerky movements from her husband still sound asleep on his side of the bed.

What was he mumbling?

"No!" That wasn't a mumble.

He thrashed about and Yvette scooted as far as she could to the other side.

Were you supposed to wake someone up when they had dreams like this?

It continued for another minute before he seemed to settle down.

Cautiously, Yvette worked her way toward him. Except for that first night, they hadn't touched much, except incidentally, while sleeping. But now, she slid over until she was behind him and molded her body to his, wrapping her arm around his chest.

She could feel the tension radiating off him and the sweat clung to his skin. Prayers from her heart winged their way to the heavens. Prayers for peace and comfort - and for her to know what to do.

116

"Eve?" Nicklaus's startled voice didn't surprise her.

"I'm right here," she whispered back. He hadn't called her Eve in days, but it didn't matter.

"Don't let go." His hand found hers as she tightened her hold on him.

"I won't."

He seemed to drift off again, and Yvette closed her eyes, the prayers continuing.

They slept until the sunlight streaming through the windows woke them hours later.

Yvette still held him.

"Are you awake?" Nicklaus asked quietly.

"I am now," she answered back, not wanting to move or break the spell woven over them.

"Did something happen in the middle of the night? I can't remember..."

"You had a nightmare."

"I don't remember what it was. I remember being scared. Did I say anything?"

"You asked me not to let you go."

"Thank you."

"It's what I'm here for." She tightened her hold again. "Do you remember anything?"

He stayed still for a moment then shook his head. "No. I don't think so. I think I might remember dark. Maybe cold. But that's it." She could feel the tension in his shoulders begin to release.

After several more minutes, Nicklaus moved, her arm sliding off as he sat up. Yvette pushed up on her elbow as he stood and went to the bathroom. Before she could decide what her own plan was, a knock sounded at the door.

Yvette slid a robe on, tying it around her waist as she went to the door. On the other side stood the captain.

"Good morning, ma'am." His serious tone caught Yvette off-guard. Though excellent at his job, the captain was a generally happy man, often laughing and joking with the family when he talked with them off-duty.

"What is it?" A million thoughts ran through her head. Had something gone horribly wrong? Her parents? Christiana and the baby? Had former King Jedidiah taken a turn for the worse?

"I don't know, ma'am. I just know that you and the prince have been summoned back to Ravenzario post haste." He bowed slightly at the waist. "We've already started for the closest port. Depending on the timing, a helicopter may be sent to take you both to the nearest airport straight from the ship."

"Is everyone okay?"

"As far as I know, ma'am. I was only told there is a pressing matter that requires you both to be present."

"Thank you." The captain bowed again, and Yvette shut the door.

Nicklaus came out of the bathroom, pulling a shirt on over his bare torso. "Who was that?"

Yvette explained the little she knew, then looked around. "I guess we should get dressed and get our things together so we're ready to go when the time comes."

For the next hour, they did just that. With another knock at the door came a steward informing them the helicopter would be arriving shortly.

Yvette looked around the room as Nicklaus left.

So much for their wedding trip.

No one had told Nicklaus anything except it was imperative that they return as quickly as possible and that everyone was fine. As they walked through the palace hallways, he couldn't help but wonder what could be so big as to bring them home.

They were led to a conference room in his sister's office. She,

Alexander, King Antonio, two members of the Ravenzarian Parliament, Tony, and several others waited for them. After a few hugs, handshakes, and introductions to members of Mevendia's Parliament, they all sat down.

Tony spoke first. "When we were in Mallard Lake Township, I got a sample of your DNA from a water glass when you joined me while I ate lunch in the diner. I sent it back here and had it compared to Christiana's. The DNA came back as a sibling match, just as we expected. But the original sample from right after the accident was locked up where no one could get to it."

Nicklaus leaned back in his chair. "So what's the problem?"

"We compared your DNA to the official DNA on file from after the accident. It was taken from your toothbrush, just in case anyone came around, trying to claim you were alive."

"An Anastasia Romanov type thing," Alexander added.

"Okay. So what's the problem?"

Everyone else at the table seemed to look at each other, but not at him or Yvette.

"What?" Yvette finally demanded.

"It didn't match." Tony gave the answer.

Stunned, Nicklaus couldn't find any words.

"So? We all know Michaela is who she says she is." Yvette didn't have the same problem. "His DNA matches Christiana's. Why or how could Michaela have substituted someone who matched his sister, but not his own DNA? And who's to say the DNA from eighteen years ago is still good? Or still the right DNA sample and not mishandled somehow or switched by Henry?"

"It probably was switched," Tony admitted. "But now we're in a bind."

"How? He's Christiana's brother. That DNA matches." Yvette leaned forward. "Why would anything else matter?"

King Antonio answered. "Because it brings into question Christiana's parentage as well. Is there any proof that she's biologically the child of King Richard and Queen Marissa?"

Nicklaus looked at his sister, but she wouldn't look at him.

Yvette jumped up. "That's ridiculous. Isn't that like looking for a zebra when you hear hoof beats? You have a known criminal. A man who has tried repeatedly to kill Christiana, who *did* kill the last king and queen even if you can't prove it, who did *all* this other evil stuff. Doesn't it make far more sense that he screwed it up somewhere? That's the horse. Christiana not being who she says she is, who everyone *knows* she is, that's the zebra."

"We all agree on that." Nicklaus's new father-in-law gave Yvette a look, one that told her to sit down.

She ignored it. "Then why is any of this an issue?"

"It's a legality thing," Tony tried to explain. "In order for Nicklaus to reclaim his titles and portion of the inheritance and so on, even without the throne to go with it, the DNA has to match."

"And there's no untainted DNA? No DNA of their parents to compare theirs to?"

"Not without exhuming their bodies." The answer came from Christiana.

"We have mutual ancestors!" Yvette still didn't sit down.

Then Nicklaus took in what she said. "We do?" His stomach began to churn. "How far back?"

"All three countries are descended from the same couple." Alexander answered when no one else would.

Right. He'd known that. "So we're related from a thousand years ago?" That made them cousins of the millionth order or so. He could handle that.

"A hundred and fifty years ago." Yvette finally sank into the chair. "A Ravenzarian princess who was the oldest in her family, but not the heir because of male primogeniture, married a Mevendian prince. That's where the Van Rensselaer Accord Jewels came from. We're all descended from the parents of that prince. Us through the Mevendian Crown Prince. You and Christiana through the oldest son of the Ravenzarian princess and Mevendian prince."

Closer cousins but still plenty far enough away.

"Isn't there some way we could test our DNA to prove we're related?" So that's where she was going with it.

"Not really. The relationship is far too distant." Tony seemed as thrilled to give the answer as the rest of them were to hear it.

"So what happens now? Why does it matter? Except for the inheritance thing." Yvette glanced at her father. "And, let's be real, I may be the spare's spare, and I may have been demoted a slot after the baby was born, but I'll get enough of an inheritance someday that it won't matter much. And if Ravenzario is going to be all dumb about it, why couldn't we go back to Mevendia to live? Or somewhere else? Nicklaus is my husband, and I'm a Mevendian princess regardless of whatever his legal status is here."

"I'm afraid it's more than that." Prime Minister Caruso spoke for the first time. "You're aware that there was a small movement to get rid of the monarchy all together last year? It picked up steam again this year after the news about the queen's ex-fiancé came to light. It has died off somewhat again. If news gets out, and it eventually will, that Nicklaus doesn't match the DNA, it could easily strike up again, bigger this time. Because if Nicklaus doesn't match that DNA, but does match as a sibling to the queen, then the queen doesn't match the DNA officially belonging to the royal family."

"Not all DNA results come out." Yvette gave her father a look. He glared back. What was that about? "Is there *no* other way to prove they're who they say they are? Some other DNA sample somewhere? Is there really only one sample?"

"There could also be accusations that Ms. Engel is really the mother of both children, which is why they match as siblings."

"That's ridiculous." Nicklaus was too shocked to say much of anything. Fortunately, Yvette was doing a good job of speaking for him. "Do they think she slept with King Richard? Seriously?"

"No way!" He couldn't keep quiet about that. "There is no way she had an affair with the king." He didn't believe it for one second.

"Of course she didn't," Tony interjected. Nicklaus should have known Tony would help protect her. "But the allegations could come out. Sometimes, often, allegations are all it takes."

Nicklaus pinched the bridge of his nose with his thumb and forefinger. "Okay. So all of this is a mess. How do we fix it?"

16

Yvette had never wanted to hit anyone so badly in all her life. It was a good thing Henry Eit was behind bars for life. Otherwise, she'd get someone to hold him down while she punched him a few times.

And no one seemed to be really listening to her. Or not understanding.

She tried again. "Wouldn't it be easier to prove the sample that we all know Henry swapped out is false? Without exhuming the king and queen's bodies, which none of us want to do, there's no way to prove Christiana and Nicklaus are who they say they are. Unless there's other DNA laying around somewhere?" She looked around. No one answered. "So why can't we find a way to prove the DNA sample has been tampered with? After everything else that's come out about Henry, after he tried to assassinate Christiana a couple months ago and *shot* Alexander, why on earth would *anyone* believe he didn't have the samples switched? Or even put his own DNA in there?"

"Very few people would," Christiana pointed out. "But it only matters how vocal they are and how good they are at drumming up support. Just because something isn't true doesn't mean it won't get out of hand."

"So we'll do the interview from last week. Get Michaela to do one. Get the story of what really happened out there so that when the..." She turned on the sarcasm and air quotes. "...'truth' comes out, the real version is already out there."

Tony tapped out a message on his phone. "I'll get Charlyn on setting up the interview with Markinson. He's always been truthful and fair. He did the queen and duke's first joint interview last fall." He set his phone back on the table. "We need to decide what we're going to say."

"Don't say anything," Yvette challenged. "If anyone asks, say Nicklaus's DNA is a sibling match to Christiana. Leave it at that. I don't know why anyone would ask about an official sample most people don't know is supposed to exist. If they do, say it was tampered with or hadn't been stored properly and therefore was unsuitable for use. Both are true statements."

No one would listen to her. No one ever listened to her. She was only eighteen. Why would she have anything of value to add to the "grown-up" conversations? Yvette hated that's the way it was.

"She might have a point." Her father? She looked over to see him smiling. "It's been nearly twenty years. It's completely plausible that something happened to the DNA sample in the meantime, even without Henry doing something to it. Are there any other mementos lying around somewhere that might have some DNA on it?"

"Not that anyone's aware of." Tony answered the question. He picked his phone up. "Markinson has some time this afternoon. Guess he didn't want to put it off."

Yvette glanced at her husband. He'd been strangely silent through all of it. "Then Nicklaus and I should probably sit down with Charlyn or whoever and go over what questions might be asked and the best ways to answer them without lying, but also without telling the whole truth when we need to."

Everyone began to push back from the table. "We'll be going over the legal ramifications with our Mevendian counterparts," Prime Minister Caruso told them. "I don't think we'll have much trouble since we all know what Eit was capable of."

"Will we need to pass new legislation?" Christiana asked.

Caruso shrugged. "It's too early to tell. We'll keep working to see if we can prove Henry switched the samples. If we can do that, we won't need to."

"Will he talk?" Yvette demanded. "He's in prison for life. He has nothing to gain by staying silent."

"And he has nothing to gain by talking, either," Alexander pointed out. "His life sentence will get shortened? More dessert? Not going to happen, and he knows it."

"Then can we find out who it belonged to?" Everyone turned to look at Nicklaus. "I mean, if whoever the DNA belongs to is in a database of some kind, couldn't that prove that he is *not* me and that the sample must have been switched."

Tony blinked twice. "We could run the DNA against the databases and see if there's a hit. Identifying who it is could work."

"Then do it." Yvette couldn't believe no one else had thought of it earlier. "Meantime, we'll get ready for this interview." She looked up at Nicklaus. "What topics, besides this DNA mess, are off-limits?"

"Huh?"

Yvette could picture her mother wincing. Princes did *not* say "huh" anywhere, but most especially not to the press.

Christiana answered. "General questions about your upbringing are acceptable. Specifics about Michaela or where you lived or how you got there, those kinds of things, are not."

Yvette would do her best to keep the interview on track. She just prayed things wouldn't get too out of hand.

Nicklaus had never been so nervous in his life.

And he'd found out he was a prince and married a stranger in the last couple of weeks.

This eclipsed them all.

Everyone told him Matt Markinson would be a great first reporter to meet with. He was well known for being fair to the royal family. Christiana even almost *liked* him. She didn't like *any* reporters. Ever. Or so he'd been told.

Given his choice, Nicklaus would have put this interview off indefinitely, but he knew that wasn't a feasible option.

"Are you ready?"

He looked to his left to see Yvette standing there in a simple blue dress that probably cost far more than he could guess. "I'm as ready as I can be." He fiddled with the cuff of his dress shirt where it came from under his suit coat.

"Here. Let me." Yvette took his hand and in seconds had fixed the cuff link he'd managed to mess up.

She looked up at him with those big hazel eyes of hers. "You'll do just fine." Leaning up, she brushed a kiss against his lips. "I believe in you. You can do this."

"That makes one of us."

When Yvette slid her arms around his waist and rested her head on his chest, Nicklaus took a deep breath and let it out slowly. He liked this. Standing here with his wife in his arms, he felt like he might actually be able to do the things she believed he could. He felt strong, almost invincible. He felt his phone vibrate in his inside coat pocket. "I'm guessing that means it's time for us to go."

"Probably."

Neither one of them moved until a soft knock at the door told them their momentary reprieve was over.

"Time to go." Yvette squeezed him lightly then moved away. He missed having her close.

What did that mean? Did it mean anything?

They walked to the door to find Alfred waiting for them. "Mr. Markinson is waiting for you in the reception room."

"I think I even know how to get there on my own," Nicklaus whispered to Yvette who grinned back at him.

"The Information Technology team is working with the Mevendian IT team to create the app Princess Yvette mentioned previously. I believe your phone will be the first device it is uploaded to."

Before he could answer, Alfred's phone buzzed. "I need to take this, sir. I'll see you after the interview."

The assistant answered his phone in Italian while Nicklaus and Yvette continued on their way. Charlyn, the head of PR for the palace, waited for them outside the reception room. "Mr. Markinson has been given the parameters of the interview, including what questions are off limits. However, we would expect him to try to push a little bit because that's his job. If any questions make you feel uncomfortable, don't answer them. Try to redirect." She turned to Yvette. "You likely have much more experience with this, Your Highness. Do your best to help the prince if he needs it?"

"Of course."

And with that, Charlyn opened the door in front of them. When they walked in, Nicklaus immediately noticed the camera equipment, and that it was already focused on them. The reporter introduced himself and shook hands with both of them, directing them to the love seat afterward. Nicklaus noticed Charlyn in the background, to make sure things stayed on track maybe.

Matt got started. "Good afternoon, Your Royal Highnesses. Thank you for taking the time to sit down with me."

"It's our pleasure," Yvette answered for the both of them. "We want to thank you for your understanding when we postponed last week. Our travel arrangements had to be changed."

The reporter answered with a comment Nicklaus didn't really hear. His gut had started to churn as the pressure on him increased.

Yvette squeezing his hand brought him back to the present. The reporter was addressing him. "The question foremost on everyone's mind, I'm sure, is how are you even alive, Prince Nicklaus?"

Nicklaus glanced at Yvette, her eyes conveying to him how much she believed he could do this.

He cleared his throat. "To be honest, Mr. Markinson, I have no idea. I don't have any recollection of my life in Ravenzario as a child or the journey we took to escape Henry Eit."

"You said 'we'. How many people escaped with you?"

"Just the two of us. Myself and Michaela Engel, our nanny."

"And you don't remember anything about how you survived the auto accident?"

"No, sir. Ms. Engel..." He needed to remember to refer to her that way as much as possible. "...has told me bits and pieces over the years, but not everything, and I don't remember any of it."

"Did you always know who you were?"

Nicklaus shook his head. "I always knew Michaela wasn't my mother. We told everyone she was my aunt who took me in after the death of my parents. I think I always knew that wasn't entirely accurate either, but I don't recall when I learned she'd been my nanny. I did know my parents were powerful, influential people who were killed by a business rival. Not quite the truth, I suppose, but close enough to keep me from looking further and unwittingly jeopardizing our safety."

"Did you know about your sister? Remember her?"

"No, sir. I didn't know I had a sister until about a month ago. Michaela, Ms. Engel," he corrected, "believed we were being chased again about six weeks ago, so we moved on. Once we realized the person doing the chasing was, in fact, the head of security for my sister, Michaela told me more. I didn't know the whole story until a few days before my arrival in Ravenzario."

"Did you know you were engaged?" the reporter pressed.

"I knew my parents had hoped I would marry their best friends' daughter, Eve. There were pictures of her in our home the entire time I was growing up. Now I know it wasn't Eve, but Princess Yvette the whole time. Telling me the true circumstances may well have led me to researching and discovering things that would put myself and Ms. Engel in danger. She did her best to prepare me for as much as she could, including my marriage to the princess, without actually telling me everything, for my own safety."

"So when did you discover you were engaged to the princess?"

Nicklaus did the calculations in his head. "About two weeks ago."

17

Yvette rubbed her thumb along the side of Nicklaus's hand. He was doing well, better than everyone had hoped. So far, Markinson had stuck to the agreed upon areas of discussion and not tried to press further. That Nicklaus genuinely didn't remember many of the details likely helped.

"So you only knew you were getting married for a week?"

"Correct."

"Princess Yvette, when did you discover the prince was still alive?"

Markinson startled her with the question, but she knew better than to let that show. "The queen, duke, and Prince Nicklaus came to see us a week before the wedding, less than twenty-four hours after Queen Christiana learned the truth of what happened that night."

"So the queen didn't know there was a possibility the prince and Ms. Engel had survived?"

Yvette hesitated, something she rarely did in the few interviews she'd given. "I'm afraid you'd have to ask the queen that. I do know she was not aware Mr. Browning, her head of security, had gone on a quest to see if he could find Nicklaus and Ms. Engel. I believe the duke was the only one with that knowledge, but I've not been fully briefed on the situation." She should have told Nicklaus earlier that was a phrase he could use to get out of questions he wasn't quite sure of the answers to.

Fortunately, Markinson dropped the line of questioning. "So you had no idea until a week before that the wedding might actually be a wedding?" he asked instead.

Yvette shook her head. "No, sir. I believed we were planning a wedding that would be turned into a celebration of the four lives taken far too soon."

"Did either of you consider not going through with the wedding?"

Yvette glanced up at Nicklaus who didn't seem inclined to answer. She jumped in. "We talked several times and decided, for a variety of reasons we won't go into today, that going ahead with the wedding was the best course of action."

"But why?" he pressed. "Why go through with a wedding to a man you didn't know was alive just a few days earlier?"

Yvette gave him her best fake smile. "Mr. Markinson, I believe I just told you there were a variety of reasons that we have chosen not to discuss publicly. You are a smart man, sir. I'm sure you can appreciate and even understand our desire not to have our most private discussions about such a momentous occasion on full view for everyone to see."

He appeared to acquiesce but Yvette noticed a bit of a gleam in his eyes. "Speaking of private discussions, and given the circumstances surrounding the wedding, has the marriage been consummated?"

She squeezed Nicklaus's hand lightly as she sensed his anger at the question. Instead of letting him answer, she turned that best smile up another notch. "Now, Mr. Markinson, do you really expect an answer to such an intrusive question?"

"It's something that's on everyone's mind, I'm sure," he countered.

"Then it's a curiosity they will have to continue to live with. What happens behind our closed doors is not for public consumption. I am quite certain you would not ask anyone else such a question, even if you believed it to be politically expedient to do so."

"Touché, Your Highness." He shifted slightly in his seat. "What about children? Have you discussed when, or even if, you'd like to start a family?"

Nicklaus answered before she could. "I do believe we started a family last week." They did? "We both come from a family. Getting married creates a new family, with or without children. As for the discussion of children, I'm fairly certain those conversations take place in private, behind those closed doors, and are also off-limits."

Markinson stared at them both for a moment then nodded. "Very well. Let's change the topic then. Prince Nicklaus, where did you grow up, once your flight from Ravenzario was complete?"

"In several places in the United States. For the time being, I can't be more specific than that."

"If you grew up in the United States, how do you expect to lead Ravenzario?"

"I don't." Nicklaus answered before Yvette could even process the question. "My sister is queen of Ravenzario. Despite any claim I might have had to the throne as a young child, and any possibility that I *could* claim the throne, I have no intention of trying to unseat Queen Christiana. My understanding is that I *might* be able to, if gone about the proper way, assert my claim to the throne, but I see no point in adding turmoil to an already tumultuous situation. I believe God made sure my sister was sick so she, and I, would survive that car accident. She is the one chosen for such a time as this, not me."

"Then what do you intend to do with your life?"

Yvette squeezed his hand again. They hadn't really talked about that.

"I'm evaluating a number of options at the moment. I completed several years of college in the States and may continue to earn my degree there."

She managed to keep her surprise under control. Was he really thinking about returning to the States?

"Or, more likely, see if those credits can transfer here, so I can finish my degree locally. As for my long term plans, I would imagine I will be involved in any number of charities. What my vocation will be, beyond Prince of Ravenzario, I am not certain."

It didn't look like the reporter was happy with that answer, but he let it slide. "Princess Yvette, what are your plans for schooling? You recently graduated secondary school, correct?"

Did he have to make her seem so young? "Correct. I am also planning to attend university, but those decisions have not been made or are not ready to be made public." It did explain why her father insisted she apply to universities in Ravenzario. She hadn't thought about that before.

Movement behind Mr. Markinson caught Yvette's attention. Charlyn was making a move to wrap it up. "I do believe we are about out of time for the moment, Mr. Markinson. Thank you for rearranging your schedule to meet with us today." The three of them stood and shook hands.

Once the cameras were off and being put away, Charlyn joined them.

Mr. Markinson turned to her. "Where are we on the documentary?"

"We're finalizing the details on our end. I expect to contact you by the end of the week."

Yvette glanced up at Nicklaus and saw her own questions reflected in his eyes. Documentary? Was he going to have to relive the whole thing? Could that have been what his nightmare was about? Would a documentary make it worse? Or help clear up his confusion?

And more importantly, should she tell someone about the nightmares before a final decision was made?

NICKLAUS LAY IN THE DARK AND STARED AT THE CEILING. OR AT least in the general direction he believed the ceiling to be. The complete and utter dark of his bedroom in the palace took some getting used to. There were lights outside, but heavy curtains prevented any of it from illuminating the room at all.

Yvette's even breathing should have helped relax him, but it didn't. She was curled next to him, with his arm wrapped around her, holding her close after one kiss earlier had turned into more.

Much more.

He went over the interview in his head. Everyone told him he'd done well, even his sister, Alexander, and Tony who'd all been watching from another room. Yvette had reassured him of that as well. They had far more experience with the press than he did. He had no reason not to believe any of them when they said it.

But the almost off-handed comment about a documentary was eating away at him.

He couldn't explain it, hadn't even mentioned it to Yvette. Thoughts and fears tumbled around is mind until he finally fell into a fitful sleep.

"Come on, Nicky." Michaela's frantic voice drifted to him. "We've got to get out of here."

Nicklaus tried to move but was restrained in place. Screaming reached his ears. He realized they were his own screams and tried to stop, but couldn't.

"*Come on, Nicky.*" *The desperation caused him to struggle harder. Where was Michaela? He couldn't see her in the darkness.*

And why was it so cold?

Moans. He heard moaning coming from somewhere in front of him.

"*Run, Michaela!*" *Nicklaus didn't recognize the voice, but the man was somewhere ahead.* "*Get Nicklaus and run!*"

The restraints he struggled against suddenly released him, and he fell forward. Someone picked him up, but he couldn't see who.

Dark

So dark.

He tried to move, but couldn't as this person held onto him.

They fell.

He couldn't breathe.

So cold.

Wet.

Gasping for air.

"*Nicky? Sweetheart?*"

Another voice sounded panicked but much closer. And warm.

Nicklaus sat straight up, gasping and nearly hitting Yvette as he did.

"Hey." She laid her hand on his bare back. "You're okay. I'm right here. You're safe."

Safe?

Was he really?

Slowly, his heart rate and breathing slowed. At Yvette's gentle urging, he lay back down, his head on the pillow.

"You had another nightmare." Yvette lay close to him again, reassuring him with her mere presence.

"I did?" Physiologically, he seemed to be more stable, but his mind still raced a thousand miles a minute. Kilometers. He needed to think in kilometers.

"You were yelling."

Nicklaus reached up with his free hand and pushed his hair back off his face. He felt cold and clammy even to his own touch.

"Do you want to talk about it?" she asked softly.

He shook his head. "No. I don't remember much." More than the last time, but he knew there was more to it than he could remember.

"I'm always here to listen when you're ready."

"I know." The thought reassured him. "Let's try to get some more sleep." He didn't want to talk about it any further. Not yet. Maybe not ever.

Once again, he stared into the dark. This time when he dozed off, the dreams were less specific, and yet, somehow, more scary.

Yvette woke him again, and he kissed her. Desperate. Frantic. Afraid.

The touch of her hands on his face began to calm him, but the kiss turned no less intense. He clung to her in a way borne of the desperation he couldn't shake. This time he found himself in her arms, on her pillow. His eyes closed, and he slept peacefully for the first time that night.

When he awoke, Nicklaus discovered Yvette already gone for the day. A note on his side table explained more. She had an early, unexpected meeting but didn't want to wake him. She'd be back soon.

He took a shower, letting the hot water sluice over him, washing away the remnants of the dreams that still clung to him. By the time he dressed and headed into the living area, Yvette was walking in the door.

"Hi!" A smile lit up her face. "You look like you're feeling better."

"How did I look before?"

"Like you hadn't slept well. You finally looked like you were sleeping peacefully when I had to get up. I even showered in the other room so I wouldn't bother you."

Her upturned face begged him to kiss her, but he held back. "Thanks. I appreciate that." Instead, he headed for the kitchen. "Did you already eat?"

"Yes. I had breakfast with your sister and brother-in-law to talk about what comes next for me specifically."

For her? Not him? "What did you decide?"

He couldn't see her but could imagine her shrug. "That it really depends on what you decide to do. I've been accepted into several schools here in Ravenzario. I've also been accepted in Mevendia. You could easily get into any of those schools as well. Until then, I'll settle into life here in Ravenzario and take over some things from Christiana as her pregnancy progresses and then as she settles in as a new mom. Not all of it is something you or Alexander could do."

"Like what?"

"Like spearhead a committee for women and children." He could hear the amusement in her voice. She had a point. "You'll get your share of things to do. Don't worry."

He wasn't. Not even a little bit.

"They've also decided to air the special tonight."

"Already?" Weren't they going to wait until Friday?

"I guess they decided not to wait. I'm not sure why."

Nicklaus suddenly felt very claustrophobic. "Are we going back on our honeymoon?" *Please, God.*

"Not right now, at least not that I'm aware of. I guess we might in a few weeks, but right now the plan is for us to stay here. Alexander told me more about the documentary Matt Markinson was talking about yesterday. It looks like they'll start filming next week, if everything works out as planned."

"What is it going to entail?" He filled a glass of water.

"Interviews with all of us. Returning to different places, like the scene of the accident with Michaela, I guess. Maybe going to the places you hid out. I'm not really sure." She walked into the kitchen as he guzzled the glass of water. "Are you okay?"

Nicklaus nodded as he kept drinking. "Just thirsty," he said when he set the glass back down. After another deep breath or two, the world seemed to expand, to stop closing in on him.

He reached for his wife and pulled her close. "Now, how about a good morning kiss?"

"Do you think the king knows about us?" Lizbeth leaned against the door frame separating the two hotel rooms.

"I think it's very likely." Robert set his suitcase on the rack. "Why else would he set you up as my assistant and insist on adjoining rooms everywhere we go?"

"I think you're probably right." It had been the best week Lizbeth could remember, despite the ever present jet lag.

"Your birthday is tomorrow, but we won't have any time to celebrate together with everything else planned. Do you want to do anything special tonight?"

"Just spend it with you. Maybe room service for dinner."

Robert grinned and moved closer to her. "Dinner in bed?" he whispered.

Blood rushed to her cheeks. "Maybe."

He chuckled. "I think I'd rather take my girl out for a night on the town. A fancy dinner." Robert rested his hands on her hips. "Champagne. Dessert. Dancing."

"I do like the sound of that." She kissed his cheek. "Thank you."

"Did you bring a dress with you?"

Lizbeth did a quick mental inventory of her wardrobe. She had brought a little black dress that would be perfect. Before she could say anything else, Robert's phone buzzed at him. He pulled it out of his pocket and glanced at it.

"Sorry, love." He gave her a quick kiss. "Duty calls for both of us."

Lizbeth went back into her room, closing the adjoining door. The day passed far too slowly, though she kept busy. When she finally made it back to her hotel room, she made sure the door to Robert's room was unlocked before collapsing on the bed.

She startled awake when the bed tilted next to her.

"Sorry," Robert whispered.

Lizbeth pushed up into a seated position, noticing the darkness.

"I didn't mean to wake you," he went on. "I was just going to give you a forehead kiss. I know you're exhausted."

She reached for her phone to see what time it was and groaned when she saw the display. "We missed dinner."

"You needed your rest. You've been extra tired lately."

Lizbeth nodded as she scrolled through the other notifications. Multiple calls, voice mails, and texts from her father, none of which were very interesting. "I have been. I'm not sure why. I must not be adjusting to the time zone changes." That's what she told him, but she wasn't a hundred percent sure that was the only reason.

"I ordered some room service," he told her, standing and heading for his room. "I got that salad you liked so much if you want it. I figured it would keep a lot better than a hot dish." He walked back in holding it. "That way you don't have to wait half an hour for them to get here with something either."

Her stomach growled as he set it in front of her. "Thank you, Robert. That was very thoughtful."

He sat in the desk chair while she ate on the bed. They talked about their day a little bit and about their plans after everything was settled. She'd move in with him as soon as possible. He insinuated that he was ready whenever she was, something she'd known for quite some time.

Lizbeth put her dish on the side table when she finished and turned back to see Robert had disappeared into his room again. Before she saw him, she heard him singing.

He reappeared in the doorway, one hand sheltering a candle on top of a chocolate cake as he finished his song. She closed her eyes and made a wish, blowing the candle out quickly. Robert pulled the office chair close to the bed, and fed her the cake bite by bite, taking bites for himself in between. Once finished, he set the plate on the side table and leaned in to kiss her.

Lizbeth wrapped her arms around his neck and pulled him closer. Finally, she was able to spend her birthday with the one man who knew her better than she knew herself. The one man she was going to spend the rest of her life with.

Her phone buzzed, the triple buzz of her father's ring tone. She reached over, still kissing Robert, and turned her phone off all together. Her father wouldn't be happy, but she didn't care.

Everything she needed sat just inches away from her.

And she wouldn't have it any other way.

The late night meal and two bottles of water necessitated a middle of the night bathroom trip for Lizbeth. As long as she was up, she decided to turn her phone back on and make sure she hadn't missed anything of import. She did listen to her father's last voice mail, just in case there was something, some emergency, where he really needed her.

He didn't.

It was about what she expected. Threats to cut her off, to refuse to allocate her portions of her inheritance, and anything else he could threaten to do, if she didn't cooperate. She wasn't sure what she was supposed to cooperate with, but she'd bet anything, even her life with Robert, that it wasn't any good.

18

Yvette wasn't about to say no to a good morning kiss, despite how odd he was acting. She had to remind herself the dreams were likely still affecting him, whether he realized it or not. The part of her that was rapidly falling in love with this prince kissed him back with a fervor at least equal to his. The rational side reminded her they had another function to attend in less than an hour.

"As nice as this is," she murmured between small kisses, "we have to leave soon."

"We do?"

She held up her phone as she moved away from him. "Our calendars are being synced with the palace scheduling system. We have our first official public appearance today."

"Where?"

"An orphanage not too far from here. Ravenz-by-the-Sea is a small town on the other island. It was hit hard by a medicane almost two years ago. Princess Anastasia of Montevaro and her husband, Dr. Jonah Fontaine, were there working with the orphanage and nearly lost their own lives in an effort to save one of the little girls. A lot of the damage was a direct result of Henry lining his own pockets rather than taking care of the infrastructure like he was supposed to."

"The more I hear about that guy, the less I like him."

"No one likes him. Not anymore. Almost everyone thought he was this benevolent uncle who took care of his niece the best he could after the death of her family. The reality was so very different. It's taken time for the people to come to terms with that. Christiana was scheduled to attend, but she's not feeling great. Instead of Alexander going by himself, they asked us to go. The orphanage was back up and running fairly quickly, but they've built a new facility on the other side of the river. Today's the ceremonial ribbon cutting."

So stand around and look pretty for the cameras. Not something she thought Nicklaus would enjoy, but something he could handle. As far as she knew, there would be a tour of the facility following the ribbon cutting, but that was about it. No speeches or too much mingling with curiosity seekers.

She rested her hand on his back. "You've got this, Nicky. You are more than capable of doing this."

"I know." He leaned his side against the counter. "You grew up in the public eye. I didn't. It's going to take some getting used to."

Her phone buzzed in her pocket. She pulled it out to see Charlyn had sent her a message saying the deal had been reached on the documentary, and they needed to leave for the orphanage in ten minutes.

"It's time to go." Because leaving in ten minutes meant they had about nine to get to the vehicles, not ten until they needed to leave the apartment.

"I wish someone had woken me up then," Nicklaus grumbled. "I haven't eaten yet." He grabbed a couple of sticks of something white out of the fridge. "String cheese," he told her, answering her unasked question. "Probably a bit too plebeian to be found in most palaces, but I asked for some."

His defensive answer wounded her, though she couldn't really explain why. He walked out of the kitchen without saying anything else. She followed and wondered what had brought this mood on and whether it was to be a common one.

Yvette hadn't thought the travel arrangements through. Rather than taking a boat, they boarded a helicopter outside one of the palace doors. They could have taken an airplane, but the drives to and from the airports would have been nearly as lengthy as taking a helicopter the whole way. They made it to the motor pool with a couple minutes to spare, but they'd been redirected to another entrance where the royal helicopter waited. No media waited to watch them walk out. At the helicopter, a couple of uniformed men saluted and helped them both inside. Once seated and buckled in, the helicopter rose from the lawn and took off for the other island.

She stared out the window on her side, watching the water below. A few boats, yachts, cruise ships, and other water craft passed below. She glanced over at Nicklaus occasionally, and found him doing the same thing on his side.

Before she knew it, they were landing near the new orphanage. A car waited to take them the rest of the way. A few minutes later, the door was held for her by a man she immediately recognized.

"Dr. Jonah!" She gave the other man a big hug. "What are you doing here?"

He hugged her back then let go. "I wouldn't miss this day for the world, but I'm here in my capacity as a doctor and long-time supporter of the orphanage, not as a representative of the royal family."

Yvette turned to Nicklaus. "I'm sure you met at the wedding, but I know I wouldn't be able to remember everyone. Nicklaus, this is Dr. Jonah Fontaine, Duke of Pantiori, and married to Princess Anastasia of Montevaro."

The two men shook hands. "A pleasure to meet you, sir," Nicklaus said.

"The pleasure's all mine," Jonah replied. He started to say something else, but turned when he heard someone calling.

"Papa!"

Dr. Jonah picked up the little girl who ran into his arms. "And this munchkin is my daughter, Stacy."

Yvette could see the wheels turning in Nicklaus's head. How could she give the answers without reminding the little girl of all she'd lost?

"My first mummy and papa live with Jesus now." Stacy took care of it for her. "Dr. Jonah and Princess Ana are my new mummy and papa."

Nicklaus smiled at her. "That's fabulous. I'm so glad you found a new set of parents who are so wonderful."

Stacy looked at him and tilted her head. "Do you have a nice mummy and papa?"

Nicklaus looked at her and shifted his weight from one foot to the other. "My parents both died when I was littler than you are. I was raised by a wonderful lady named Michaela instead."

"Oh." She seemed to shrug it off. "Are you a prince like my uncle Rick and Charlie?"

Nicklaus chuckled. "Yes, sweet girl. I am, but I didn't always know I was. When I was a kid I didn't know."

That puzzled her and her little brows pulled together. "How didn't you know?"

"I was being chased by a bad man, and it wasn't safe for me to know."

"Is the bad man gone now?"

"Yep. He's in jail forever."

"I'm glad." Stacy leaned over and gave Nicklaus a kiss on the cheek. "Bad men belong in jail."

"You're right they do."

"Pardon me, Your Royal Highnesses, but it's time to get started." Another voice joined the conversation.

Nicklaus smiled, nodded, and answered simple questions when they were asked. He enjoyed getting to know Dr. Jonah a bit better. Stacy was a sweetheart who had latched onto him as a fellow orphan.

Before long, they were on their way back to the palace. When they arrived, they were taken into a conference room, where Matt Markinson and several other people waited.

After polite greetings, they got down to business.

"Your Royal Highnesses, thank you for agreeing to meet with us," the woman introduced as a producer started the conversation.

Like we had much choice, Nicklaus thought, wondering *why* they didn't have a choice in this.

The producer droned on about how this was going to happen. They would have to decide how much, if any, of their private quarters would be on camera. The producers wanted to record the two of them together in their apartment.

Nicklaus didn't know what to think about that.

Yvette answered for both of them. "I think, for now, we're going to decline any time in our residence. The palace doesn't belong to just us. It belongs to the queen and duke as well. I don't think either of us is comfortable granting access that isn't really ours to give."

Nice and diplomatic. Nicklaus didn't think he'd ever master being polite while still telling someone to stick it.

"So when can we get started?" The producer looked between them. "Today?"

Yvette shook her head. "Not today. Perhaps later this week."

The producer and Yvette negotiated a start date a few days

later, far earlier than Nicklaus would have liked - both date and time of day. The camera crews would arrive at seven in the morning.

They would also have a shooting schedule with them that day. Letting them know what days they'd be filming what.

When they'd be returning to the scene of the accident and the escape route.

Nicklaus already dreaded that day.

The meeting ended an hour after it began. He headed back to his apartment. Yvette went somewhere else. Nicklaus didn't know where.

The windows in this apartment didn't face anything very interesting. Some of the windows overlooked the courtyard. A couple others were above the gardens. Nice views, sure, but not want Nicklaus wanted. Christiana's looked out over the Mediterranean. He didn't really know what he wanted to look at, but a courtyard and the city beyond or the gardens wasn't it.

Before he could figure out what it might be, the door opened, and Alfred walked in.

"Good afternoon, sir. Are you ready for lunch?"

Nicklaus shook his head. "I'm not hungry, but thanks."

"You need to eat, sir. You didn't have breakfast."

The man had a point. "Fine."

"Good. Your sister requested you join her. Shall I let her know you're on your way?"

"Yeah." It would take ten minutes to get to her office. On the way, he was told to go to the apartment, which meant turning around and doubling back, taking even longer.

"Oh, Nicky! There you are!" His sister welcomed him with open arms. "I am so glad you could join me."

"Happy to." He wasn't sure he meant it. Christiana was a wonderful person, but his reappearance in her life meant far more to her than him. She'd thought he was dead for years. He'd known she existed for less than a month before returning to Ravenzario.

"How was the orphanage?"

"Good. I got to meet Dr. Fontaine and his daughter." The thought reminded him of why he and Yvette had gone in the first place. "How are you feeling?"

"Better. I was extremely tired this morning, so I slept a bit longer." She rested her hand on her belly. "This little one is taking a toll on me sometimes."

"I'm not even sure I know when you're due."

She led the way to the nook overlooking the Mediterranean. "September 14," she told him. "The exact date is not public knowledge."

"I won't tell anyone." Nicklaus stood next to the window and looked out over the ocean. "I don't want to sound ungrateful, because I'm not and the rooms you've given me are great." He hesitated then went on. "But I don't suppose there's another suite available? One that has this view?"

"You like the ocean?" She came to stand next to him. "You always did. Even when you were little, you loved being out on the yacht or playing in the waves near the beach."

He had? Nicklaus shook his head. "No, it's not that. In fact, I can swim pretty well, but I've never really *enjoyed* being in the water, especially moving water. I like looking though." When he and Yvette had been racing between yachts, he'd been more focused on her than the water. He glanced over to see his sister watching him with a puzzled look on her face. "What?"

Christiana shook her head as though to clear her mind. "Nothing. You were so crazy about the ocean when you were little."

"Maybe being carried through a river trying to escape with my life had something to do with my change of heart." Bitterness he didn't know he carried seeped through.

"It's very possible." His sister rested a hand on his back. "I am so incredibly grateful you are alive."

"I am, too." But if he'd died in that river, he never would have known any differently.

"And I do believe there is another suite of apartments on the top floor of the palace that have a view similar to this one. In fact, I believe it is even a bit better. I will have Diana make sure it happens after lunch."

"Thanks."

"My pleasure."

They spent lunch talking more about him. About his life in the seventeen and a half years since the car accident. Nicklaus would have thought they'd exhausted all possible topics in the week before the wedding but apparently not.

"Your tutor arrives tomorrow," his sister added, almost as an aside, as they finished dessert.

Nicklaus nearly choked on his sip of water. "Pardon?"

"You need to learn Italian, French, Spanish, and passable Modern Greek. We use English for most dealings with other countries, but it is a very useful skill."

Right. He should have expected it. "Michaela made sure I took French in high school. I managed to pass two years' worth, but that's about it. I'm not sure I could find a bathroom if I needed to."

"Yvette will help. She speaks all of them fluently. Working one-on-one with a tutor is far different than working with one teacher in a large class."

Before he could respond, Christiana's phone rang. While she spoke with her assistant about something, he checked his own phone. A text message from Michaela caught his eye. He needed to talk to her and soon. To tell her about the documentary. He replied asking when they could meet.

Her response told Nicklaus all he needed to know. He could read between the lines of her text.

She already knew, and she wasn't happy about it.

19

Lizbeth cut right to the heart of the matter. "I need your help."

"What is it?" She could hear concern in her friend's voice. "Is everything all right?"

"Mostly. I need a favor, though, and since you're now a duchess and married to a prince in Ravenzario, I was hoping maybe you could help me."

"Of course. I'll help if I can. What do you need?"

"My father owns a home in southern Ravenzario, right on the beach. I need to know who actually owns the property. My father? A trust? One of his companies? With me being so far away at the moment and with the time difference, I'm having a hard time connecting with anyone to find out." Those things were absolutely true. They also weren't the only reasons. She'd managed to squeeze in a couple of phone calls only to find herself stonewalled.

"I'll see what I can do." Yvette still sounded puzzled. "Can you email me the address and any other particulars that might help me figure it out?"

Lizbeth detailed the little she knew, including that her grandfather's will dictated that Marie and Giuseppe, long time servants of her grandfather's, would have a place to live on the property until their deaths, even if they retired. "Thank you, Yvette. Your help means a lot to me."

Yvette laughed. "You've helped me more in the last six or eight months than anyone. It's the least I can do."

Lizbeth looked up to see Robert standing in the doorway. "I've got to go. I'll email you in a few minutes and talk to you soon." She hung up without waiting to hear Yvette's reply.

"Who was that?"

She turned back to her suitcase. Their flight was scheduled to leave in about two hours. It was a private plane so there was no possibility they'd miss it, but she didn't want them to be running late because of her. "Yvette."

"What did she want?"

Lizbeth wouldn't lie to him, even though she knew he wouldn't like the answer. "I asked her to see if she could find out who owns that property in Ravenzario. With her connections, she can get answers a lot easier than either of us."

"Why didn't you wait?" She could hear the frown in his voice. "I thought we were going to get my solicitor to look at all of it when we returned."

She laid one shirt in the suitcase then picked up another. "I know that's what you said, but I've got this funny feeling in my gut. Something's not quite right, and I don't want to wait any longer."

Even without looking, she could tell he took a deep breath in and blew it out slowly. "All right. I defer to your gut instinct, but I wish you would have talked to me about it first."

She had tried. He hadn't listened. Just insisted it could wait until they got back. The last piece of clothing went into the suitcase, and she zipped it closed. "I'm going to email Yvette some information. Then I'm ready to leave."

Robert moved behind her and wrapped his arms around her waist. "I love you, Lizbeth. This is all going to work out somehow."

"Thank you for everything." She leaned her head back against his shoulder. "I love you, too."

"You know what's coming up, right?" He kissed her neck.

"Our anniversary."

"We'll be back in Mevendia by then."

Lizbeth could hear the unspoken question. Would she be ready to tell the world they'd been married a year already?

She didn't answer, because she didn't have one to give.

It all hinged on what Yvette discovered and what the lawyer said when they returned.

Yvette was worried about her husband. He hadn't said much to her since he had lunch with his sister a few days earlier. She still found him tossing and turning in his sleep, but no more nightmares had woken him.

With her eyes closed so Belinda could finish applying her make-up, she walked herself through the day. The producers and crew were already setting up in the Reception Room. They would begin with some fairly innocuous questions. She prayed the news team would hold true to their word and work into everything gradually.

She didn't know where Nicklaus was. He'd been gone when she woke up. Surely, he wouldn't run off and not show up.

"All done, ma'am."

Something occurred to Yvette as she opened her eyes to see Belinda putting her things away. "I don't think I ever asked either of you if you're okay with moving to Ravenzario. If you'd rather go back home, I'd understand."

Belinda shook her head. "We're both very happy to be here with you, ma'am. But I promise, if anything changes, we'll let you know."

"Thanks."

She was going to say something else, but before she could the door opened into their suite and Nicklaus entered. His hair clung to his head, and the stains on his t-shirt let her know he'd been working out somewhere. Going for a run perhaps?

He didn't say anything, but headed into the bathroom. The shower turned on a few seconds later, confirming her thoughts.

Yvette headed for the reception room. Nicklaus didn't want or need her there. He was making that clear by his deeds and his lack of words. He hadn't kissed her since before they went to Ravenz-by-the-Sea. He didn't turn to her in the night when the dreams worsened. The touch of her hand on his back did seem to calm him some, though.

Alexander had already arrived, doing what he seemed to do so well. Taking charge of the situation and looking out for the best interests of his family.

She, Alexander, and several others made some inane chit chat while waiting for Nicklaus to arrive. He appeared a few minutes later, dressed nicely, but she could see the strain around his eyes. Ten minutes after they were supposed to have started, she and Nicklaus were seated on a love seat with Mr. Markinson in a chair across from them.

The reporter spoke first. "Okay, let's get started. You both have microphones on, but just ignore them and all the other paraphernalia around. We're just going to talk. We're going to cover some of the same ground we did last time. That was a short interview, and we didn't use most of what we had. We'd rather not use the footage from that interview, combined with this one. Different clothes and all that. We'd rather have it with just one."

Yvette gave him her best fake smile. She refused to be real. Not yet. He hadn't earned her trust.

"Let's start with something simple," Markinson went on. "How did you two meet?"

She didn't wait for Nicklaus to respond. "We met when I was an infant. I have seen photos of Nicklaus holding me when I was just a couple months old." The picture would probably be on the screen when this aired.

"Was that before or after this contract was signed?"

"About the same time, I believe. Our fathers signed the pact when I was just a few months old."

"So you would have been about three, Prince Nicklaus?"

He shrugged. "I guess. I don't remember any of it."

Great. Semi-surly Nicklaus had shown up. She turned her smile up a notch. "Neither do I, of course. My point was simply that we met not long after my birth."

"Prince Nicklaus was declared dead the same year, though. So you must have re-met at some point. How about that story?"

Yvette made a point of smiling at Nicklaus and patting his leg. "Well, as everyone knows by now, the bodies of Nicklaus and Ms. Engel, nanny to both Nicklaus and the queen, were never found. There had been a plan in place to escape from Mr. Eit should the need arise. Most people heard the rumors off and on about the bodies, but yes, everyone believed they'd been declared dead. Very few people in the world knew about the plan. My father, king of Mevendia and dear friend of King Richard, was one of those."

"Did you know the whole time?"

She snorted. Quite unladylike, but the question was ridiculous. "Of course not. I was an infant. I was told when the time was right."

"Which was when?"

"None of your business, sir." She didn't like the thought of the entire world knowing she'd been kept in the dark. "Some time after I was old enough to understand the potential ramifications if word leaked out. As for when we were reintroduced, the day after the prince's return to Ravenzario, he visited Mevendia with

Queen Christiana and Duke Alexander. That was our first face-to-face meeting since the auto accident."

Markinson turned slightly to face Nicklaus a bit more. "When did you know you were supposed to marry the princess?"

She rested her hand on his knee, hoping to reassure him. "For as long as I remember, Michaela, the nanny who escaped with and raised me, told me my father wanted me to marry his best friend's daughter. She kept fairly recent pictures around most of the time. I didn't know about the arranged marriage and contract until much later."

"So you essentially met for the first time a week before the wedding?"

"Yes," they replied in unison.

"So why go through with it? Why not postpone it until you'd had a chance to get to know each other better and then decide?"

So much for starting with easy questions. Yvette squeezed Nicklaus's knee. The exile portions of the contract were not public information and needed to remain that way. "The wedding was already planned, for one thing." She gazed adoringly at Nicklaus. At least she hoped that's what it was. "And after we met, we just knew it was right. Sometimes God answers prayers in very specific ways. I had prayed for many years that when the time came, I would know the right thing to do. Our first meeting answered those prayers in spades."

"Did he kiss you?"

Nicklaus wanted to reach out and deck the guy. He didn't and was quite proud of his restraint. "No," he answered for Yvette. "I didn't kiss her at the first meeting."

"So the kiss on the balcony was your first?"

154

"Our first kiss is no one's business but ours." He kept his gaze steady.

"Is it safe to say the marriage has been consummated?"

"Also no one's business." Yvette's tone was much gentler than his had been, but the underlying steel couldn't be denied.

"Very well." Markinson's attention turned completely back to Nicklaus. "You said you didn't know about the contract to marry the princess until much later. Have you always known who you were?"

"No. For my own safety, I wasn't told until fairly recently." Did this guy want to know everything?

"So who did you think you were? Who did you think Ms. Engel was? Your mother?"

There was an insinuation there Nicklaus didn't like. "Ms. Engel, Michaela, is the only mother I've ever known. I always knew she wasn't, though. I *know* I had a mother and father who loved me very much. I knew they were killed in a car accident caused by a man who wanted my entire family dead, and Michaela would do anything to protect me. That said, we always said she was my aunt. It invited far fewer questions than if we told everyone she was my nanny."

Had he really thought through everything Michaela had done for him?

Matt Markinson looked at someone behind Nicklaus. "Okay. I think that about wraps it up for now."

Nicklaus glanced at his watch. Several hours had passed, though it didn't seem like it. The stops and starts between questions. The touch ups to their hair and faces. The technical issues at the beginning. All of it conspired to take half of forever to get maybe twenty minutes of potentially usable footage.

The producer handed a piece of paper to Nicklaus. "We're done here for today. We'll be taping with Ms. Engel and her parents later and be back here tomorrow with all three of you.

We're scheduled to leave for the mountains about ten and will be there most of the day."

Great. Reliving a night he couldn't remember and didn't want to. Even worse, making Michaela remember.

Despite his run earlier in the day, something that normally put him in a good mood and made his day go better, the following hours were interminably long. Christiana told him about the suite that would be ready for him to occupy soon. He stood up there, staring out the window for an eternity. The cleaning and maintenance crews would arrive tomorrow to get it ready. It wasn't in bad shape by any stretch of the imagination, but it could use a good cleaning and some touch ups in places.

The next morning came far too early. He hadn't slept much and not well when he had. Another run through the gardens and rarely used corridors of the palace didn't help any more than it had a day earlier. Yvette was already gone by the time he returned to take a shower. She didn't join them in the reception room.

Michaela and the television crews were already there. He gave her a big hug and whispered his love, which she returned. Rather than interview either of them, they spent a couple of hours in the gardens, taping a bunch of random footage that would be spliced in later. Supposedly natural or candid shots, they were completely staged.

Nicklaus was constantly aware of the microphones they wore, though they weren't saying anything meant for the cameras to pick up. For that reason, he didn't ask about Tony or how she was doing or any number of other things he might have wanted to. Instead, they talked about the flowers and other aspects of the garden or the architecture of the palace itself.

Midmorning, everyone there loaded into a variety of vehicles. Nicklaus found himself in the back of a dark SUV with heavily tinted windows. Michaela sat in the middle row of seats, but Yvette slid in the other side of his.

"Why are you going with us?" He winced under Michaela's

disapproving glare. "I mean, I'm glad you are, I just didn't know you were." Not entirely accurate, but close enough.

Matt Markinson sat in the passenger seat and several cameras were mounted inside. Everything they said was fair game.

Yvette reached over to cover his hand with one of her own. "I didn't want you to do this by yourself."

"I have Michaela." He was more concerned about his nanny.

"I know. And she has you to lean on, if she needs to. You have me."

Okay then.

The reporter did ask a few questions on the drive, but most of it was spent in silence.

When they reached the pull-out, just big enough for a few cars, Nicklaus felt a chill sweep over him. He already didn't like it here.

Camera crews waited for him to step out of the vehicle. Because of the way it was situated and the order they'd gotten into the car, he was the last one out. As soon as he was clear of the vehicle, he looked around, knowing they would be recording. Before he could decide what he really thought, his eyes landed on the marker. Without anyone telling him to, he walked toward it reading the words to himself, his breath catching as he read his name and then Michaela's.

"Tell us your thoughts, sir?"

Nicklaus barely heard Markinson asking the question. "It's surreal. I've known it was here, but I can barely grasp it."

"Are there any plans for a new marker, now that it's known you and Ms. Engel survived?"

"I have no idea." He should ask Christiana.

"What are your thoughts, Ms. Engel?"

Nicklaus turned to see Michaela wiping tears from her cheeks. Yvette stood next to her with an arm wrapped around Michaela's waist to support her.

"I'm not sure what I think," Michaela answered. "I'm not sure I like it here. So much sorrow is attached to this spot."

Silence permeated the area.

"You're right, Michaela." Yvette startled him when she spoke. "There is sorrow here. The death of the king and queen was tragic. But there is hope here, too. With his dying breath, the king passed on information how to find you. His last concern, his last thoughts, were prayers for your safety. What one man meant for evil, God has turned to good. I spoke with Mr. Browning about it yesterday. If the car had gone over the side pretty much anywhere but right here, all the planning in the world wouldn't have saved both of you."

Michaela nodded, though Nicklaus had a hard time believing her words.

"Would you walk us through what happened?" Mr. Markinson's voice came from somewhere behind them.

"The brakes went out half a mile or so up the mountain. King Richard managed to keep the car on the road and was even able to slow it down some by putting it in a lower gear, but it wasn't enough. This turn was too sharp, and he couldn't keep it on the road."

Nicklaus wanted to go to her, to hug her and thank her for everything, but instead he stood in front of the marker with his hands shoved deep in his pockets, staring out over the valley. Yvette had said she'd be there for him today, but as push came to shove, she stood next to someone else instead. Bitterness began to take root deep in his heart.

And he didn't care enough to try to stop it.

Yvette followed Michaela down the steep trail toward the river. What had possessed anyone to think it was a good idea to actually go down the side of the mountain and look more closely?

Someone needed their head examined.

About the time the producer told them the plan, Nicklaus seemed to snap out of whatever funk he'd been in and was most solicitous of Michaela as they worked their way down. One of the trees on the bank still bore the scars of that day. Gouges in the trunk and a noticeable tilt one direction were testament to the strength and resilience, not only of the tree but of her husband and Michaela as well.

Michaela had a wind breaker on. It wasn't nearly as cold as that night must have been, but the other woman had wrapped her arms around herself. It was as though the memory chilled her to her core.

Finally, the crews were set up, and Matt Markinson asked her the question again. "Walk us through what happened."

She pointed near the tree. "The car came to a stop right there. The queen was already unconscious. My understanding is that she died around the time emergency crews arrived on the scene. The king was badly injured." Her voice shook. This time Nicklaus was there to support her. "He'd hit his head, there was blood everywhere. All over his face. I think I'd hit my head, too, because I feel like maybe I blacked out for a short period, but I'm not really sure. I remember going off the road and praying for God to send angels to help us. The next thing I remember is the king yelling at me to take Nicky and go."

"Was this something you'd worked out with him ahead of time?"

Michaela nodded. "He knew there were threats to the family, serious ones. I believe he knew Mr. Eit was behind them, but if he did, he never said anything about it to me. Just that it wasn't safe. He'd given me a couple of names and phone numbers of people who would help me should I ever need to take the children and run. When he told me to go that day, I unbuckled Nicky from his car seat and opened the door. I could hear sounds up near the road and knew people were coming. I didn't know if those people were trustworthy. So I carried Nicklaus down the river. It's not terribly deep through here, waist high at its worst. It hadn't stormed recently so it wasn't running wild. The cold was the worst part of it."

She pointed downstream. "That bend isn't very far when you have adrenaline pumping. Around it, the bank has a couple of good places to get out. Every morning when we would go anywhere in the car, the king would point out places that were likely safe. So that morning, before we left, he took out an aerial map of this area. He pointed to this barely visible roof and said 'if anything happens while we're on this road today, go to this cabin. The woman who lives there can be trusted implicitly to get you somewhere safe.'"

"How far away was the cabin?"

Michaela swiped at her cheeks. "Maybe a two-mile hike. It seemed like forever, but he'd pointed to a creek that would take me to the cabin. Once I found it, I didn't have to worry about getting lost."

Yvette could hear more in her voice. Had she been worried she'd found the wrong creek? Had Nicklaus cried the whole time? How had she dealt with the fear that had to hound her every footstep? Had she worried this woman wouldn't be home?

Clouds rolled in while they talked, bringing a cold front with them. About the time they finished several takes of different things there, a fine mist appeared. Not a true rain, or even a drizzle, it was just enough to make things a bit miserable.

Apparently, the news crew already knew about the cabin, because a boat appeared from down river to take them to the next stop. Rather than following the same path, it took them to a town a bit farther downstream. A comment from the producer led Yvette to believe they wanted footage of the three of them working their way down the mountain from the marker, but didn't need it of them going back up. Instead, they would get out at the town and drive to the cabin.

Yvette had to bite her tongue to keep from saying some rather un-princess-like things. Another SUV met them near the small dock, and they took a dirt road back into the woods. Her heart constricted when the small building came into sight.

The small log cabin had been left to the elements for some time. Dilapidated and neglected, it had likely been rickety even in its best days.

"Oh, my," Michaela whispered. "It's changed quite a lot."

"We wondered about that," Markinson replied from the front seat. "No one has lived here for about fifteen years."

"I can see that." The mist continued to fall as Michaela walked slowly toward the cabin.

Nicklaus followed behind her, leaving Yvette to stand at the SUV and wonder what her place was in all of this. She couldn't hear what was being said, but Michaela pointed out several things, including what looked to be a cellar. Could that be where they hid until it was safe to move?

Her phone buzzed in her pocket. She pulled it out to see it was Lizbeth. Yvette hit the end button then opened a text message. With a microphone clipped on, she couldn't have a private conversation. She leaned against the SUV and sent a few more texts back and forth with her friend. By the time all of this wrapped up, Lizbeth would be asleep in Australia. Lizbeth promised to call when she woke up in the morning.

Shooting at the cabin took several hours despite the camera crew that had been at the palace in the morning beating them to the location. When they headed back to the palace, Yvette found herself sitting alone in the back seat while Nicklaus rode with Michaela in the middle. Fortunately, their microphones had been removed, the cameras had been turned off, and Matt Markinson rode separately. They wouldn't see him again until the next day.

When they arrived at the palace, Michaela disappeared in the direction of the security office. She had no idea where Nicklaus went, but he may have another meeting with his language tutor. He was making progress on his Spanish and Italian. When she got to the bedroom she shared with her husband something was quite obviously wrong. A few empty boxes were strewn about the room, and all of his things were gone.

Nicklaus had gone to the new quarters after a text from Alfred told him his things had been moved and Yvette's would be shortly. Changing quickly back into running clothes he went for another run. A few members of the staff looked at him oddly when he jogged past them in the far reaches of the unused portions of the palace. Maybe he should just stick to his new floor from now on. There were plenty of hallways there to get a good run in.

He rounded another corner as music pulsated through his ear buds. The whole day had been too much to take. Though he had no memory of the accident or the trek to safety, a sense of loss pervaded the entire scene. The effect on Michaela was almost unbearable. He could see her remembering every detail, and he was quite certain she hadn't told him or anyone else the whole truth about that day.

In fact, he suspected it had been a far more harrowing experience than anyone else realized.

He'd figured out a circuit of hallways that came to about a quarter mile total. As he began his fifth round, he came face-to-face with his very angry wife.

"Hey." He stopped and pulled his ear buds out. "What's up?"

"You moved out."

"What?"

"Everything you own is gone. I get to *our* room in *our* apartment, and all of my things are still there. But *everything* the not-dead prince owns is gone. From the graduation picture of you with Michaela to all those brand new suits you said you didn't know what to do with. Care to tell me why you didn't let me know you're leaving me?"

His mind had been in such a different place that it took him a few beats to catch up with what she was saying. "Leaving you?" Was that what she thought? "I'm not..."

"I *thought* we were working. That we were going to give this thing our best shot because divorce is *not* an option for either of us, whether we wanted to or not."

"Yvette, stop."

"Don't tell me to stop." Her voice was getting louder, the anger less apparent as the hurt pushed its way to the forefront.

"You've got it all wrong. I'm not leaving you." He reached out and put a hand on each of her shoulders. "I wouldn't leave you."

Her eyes searched his face. "Then what's going on?"

"I asked Christiana the other day if there were rooms available with a view of the Mediterranean. She said there were but it would be a couple weeks before we could move. I just found out half an hour ago that they'd already moved all of my stuff, but hadn't gotten to yours yet. That's all."

He could feel her shoulders, her whole body start to relax. "We have a new apartment? That's it? You're not leaving?"

"No. I'm not leaving."

The hurt in her eyes fled, but some of the anger returned. "And you didn't think asking me if I wanted to move, or at least *telling* me we were going to, was appropriate?"

Nicklaus let go when she shrugged his hands off her shoulders. "No. I didn't. I should have, but I didn't. I'm sorry." He felt so much beginning to slip through his fingers. "I can have them move my things back. It's fine."

"No." Her gentle tone caught him off-guard. "It's not fine. I don't care if we live in a different apartment. I like the view from Christiana and Alexander's quarters better than ours, too. But it's not about the living arrangements. It's about talking to me. Making decisions *together*." She reached out and clasped his hand. "Now, care to show me our new rooms?"

They had to go up four more stories to get to the new apartment on the fifth floor of the building. She held his hand the whole way.

As they finally reached the top floor, she remarked, "I guess I won't need to use the stair climber in the gym anymore."

Nicklaus turned to see the delightful twinkle had returned to her eyes. "No, I suppose not. And there's not a whole lot going on up here, I guess. These will be the only rooms occupied for the time being, anyway."

"So you can run up here on days when it's too yucky to go outside?"

"Probably smarter than running downstairs where everyone looks at me weird."

"Just don't slip and break something priceless."

Nicklaus winced and looked around the wide hallway. "Good point. Maybe I should ask Alfred to have someone remove all the important stuff for now."

She let go of his hand as he reached to open the door to the new apartment. He bowed and gestured with his other hand. "After you, Your Royal Highness."

Yvette walked into the sitting room and headed straight for the windows on the other side. "This is a beautiful view," she admitted.

"Then you'll love the one in here." He led the way into their new room where more expansive windows looked over the sea.

She went to the one on the other wall. "This is definitely the winner." She leaned in a bit further toward the window and looked to the side. "Wait. Is this next to the turret?"

Nicklaus shrugged. "I guess."

Yvette left the window and went to the corner of the room. It was a corner. Just like any other corner, in any other room, except it boasted a fireplace. "Christiana was telling me..." She didn't finish her sentence but pressed on a rock before tilting a sconce next to the mantle. With a groan the wall opened.

"What was my sister telling you exactly?" And why hadn't he known there was a secret passage of some kind?

"She said the turrets are all open in the rooms below the top floor, so right below us, the turret is part of that room or is a separate room or whatever, but not blocked off. All of the turrets on the top floor, though, are blocked. She told me how she got into the passage in the garden cottage, and I wondered if it might work here." Yvette turned around, a genuine smile covering her face. "Let's check it out."

"Won't it close on us?" Hadn't he heard that?

"Good point." Yvette chewed on her bottom lip and looked

around. She found her phone and tapped out a text message. "There. Belinda will talk to Christiana if she doesn't hear from me in half an hour."

Half an hour? What did she think she was going to find up there?

With a feeling of apprehension surrounding him, he followed her into the darkness.

21

N ervous anticipation filled Yvette as she shone the flashlight from her phone into the turret. The floor was made of stone and a bit dusty, but otherwise in good shape. Very few cobwebs could be seen. The seal between the fireplace and room must be a good one. A stone staircase was built into one wall. She started up it despite a sound of annoyance from Nicklaus.

Since he hadn't told her they were moving, he could deal with her exploring their new quarters.

The top of the staircase opened into a room. Sheets covered furniture, but didn't seem to be organized in any particular fashion.

"What do you suppose it all is?" she whispered.

"I have no idea." Nicklaus's voice echoed in the chamber.

"Can't you just imagine? A little girl, a princess in real life, sneaking up here to dream of fighting her own battles?" She looked around, shining her light upward.

"Sure."

The light coming through the windows meant she didn't need

her flashlight any longer. "You are such a party pooper. Don't you have any imagination?"

"My imagination works just fine. It just doesn't lend itself to wondering what some girl from a century and a half ago did in some abandoned room."

"Then what does it lend itself to?" She lifted one corner of one sheet.

"Villains and super heroes, I guess. Running through the woods chasing bad guys."

His words struck her though she tried not to show it. He'd run through the woods being chased more than once. That could easily explain their different outlooks on life.

"Do you think we can uncover all of this stuff? Or should we wait and let someone who knows about preserving historical stuff do it?"

"I don't know."

The *I don't care* was implied.

No matter. She'd come back later. She'd get Melinda to see if she could find out the best way to handle it. Yvette didn't want any of it touched though. Not unless it needed to be for preservation purposes. She wanted to discover it herself.

She looked out a window then turned and headed for the staircase. "I'll look more later."

Halfway down, she felt a hand on her arm, stopping her in her tracks. "Don't come in here alone."

The intensity in Nicklaus's voice both surprised and concerned her. "Okay. I won't come in without telling someone where I am."

"I mean it, Yvette." His grip on her arm tightened just enough to pinch. "Don't come in here alone."

She pulled her arm out of his grasp. "Fine. I promise that if I can't find someone to come with me, I'll tell someone where I am and when to expect me to return."

He glared at her. She glared right back.

"Is that the best I'm going to get?"

"Yes. Unless you can explain to me why you'd make such an outrageous request when I've outlined other precautions, that's the best you're going to get."

"Did you feel any air moving around in there?"

"No, but it didn't smell old and musty either. That air is not nearly as stale as you'd like to think."

"Maybe not, but it's obvious there's not much of anything living in here. After being closed up for who knows how long, wouldn't you expect to see signs of spiders or mice or something? If there isn't any, why not?"

Yvette rolled her eyes. "I think you're worrying for nothing, but I promise I'll be careful. Surely there's a way to prop the door open, then it's not an issue. But," she hurried on. "I'll still tell someone just in case it shuts anyway."

They reached the bottom of the staircase to find the fireplace had remained open. Whether that was because it was designed to or because of some flaw, she didn't know. Tilting the sconce back closed the door. It did seem to stick a bit, so maybe it was supposed to close on its own.

As it closed, she texted Belinda to let her know they were fine. Yvette turned to Nicklaus to see him staring out the window. "So have you looked around the rest of this place, or just at the view?"

He didn't turn around. "Just the view."

Well, okay then. She left him standing there and went to explore a bit on her own. The master suite not only had a fireplace and a secret passage, but an enormous walk-in closet half filled with Nicklaus's things, and a lavishly appointed bathroom. No surprises there. Off the sitting room, two more bedroom suites sat on the same wall as the master suite. There were several large windows while the opposite wall had several more doors. One led to a water closet for guest use, she supposed. Another led to a third bedroom suite. The next one led to the kitchen. Before going in, she checked the last door on that side. A smaller office with two desks for them to "work from home." It would be a good place for Nicklaus to work on his language lessons. She went into the kitchen. Through it was a dining area that extended to the outer wall, with windows of its own.

She had just reemerged into the sitting area when Nicklaus walked out of the master suite, putting his ear buds back in. "I'm going to finish my run."

Without giving her any time to respond, he was out the door. Yvette let a sigh escape then sat in one of the chairs near a window. She wanted to go back up to the hidden room where windows looked out all sides of the room, but she'd promised Nicklaus. She also knew if she went, she would have a hard time stopping herself from looking at the treasures and the last thing she wanted to do was accidentally ruin something.

Before she could make any more decisions about what to do next, her phone buzzed.

She found herself smiling as she answered. "Hello, Lizbeth. Happy belated birthday. I can't believe I didn't say that when we talked the other day."

Lizbeth didn't take the time to reply to Yvette's well wishes. "Did you find anything yet?"

Yvette sighed on the other end. "No. Things have been sort of crazy around here, and I haven't had a chance. I will put Melinda and Alfred on it as soon as we hang up. They probably know who to talk to far better than I do, anyway."

"Is everything all right?" Something was off in her friend's tone of voice.

"More or less."

Which Lizbeth knew meant less.

"It's just been a very long week."

"Well, I'll be back in Mevendia tomorrow. Maybe we can get together soon? I can visit Ravenzario, unless you're going to be home."

All she got back was a noncommittal, "maybe."

"Thanks, Yvette."

"No problem. I'm sorry I don't have answers for you yet. I'll let you know when I do." There were voices in the background. "I've got to go. I'll talk to you soon."

There was no need to disconnect the call as Yvette had already done so.

"Did she find anything?" Robert came out of the conference room where they were finishing up for the day.

"Not yet." Lizbeth shook her head. "There's something else going on, but she wouldn't tell me what."

"We'll be back tomorrow."

"I know. But my father has something up his sleeve. I wish I knew what."

"We've been over this."

She glared at him. "I'm aware we've been over it. But the thought of it is nagging at me day and night. I've prayed about it. I've asked God to take my worry away, and He has. I'm not *worried*. At the same time, there's an urgency I can't describe or define or explain."

"His eye is on the sparrow, Lizbeth," Robert gently reminded her.

"I know. And He knows the number of hairs on my head. He also gives people jobs to do. Joseph had a dream to take Jesus and flee to Egypt so He wouldn't be killed by Herod. The magi had dreams telling them to go home and not report back. Moses had a burning bush. Noah knew to build the ark. It took half of forever to build. If he hadn't started really early, it never would have been done in time. How many times do you hear stories about people who listened to their gut? Who wouldn't have checked on a grandparent that day but did anyway and found them in some danger? Or to take a different route to work or took a different flight or any number of other things and found out later it would have been bad if they had done the usual?"

"True." Robert looked around to make sure no one else could see them before resting his hands on her waist. "If you're so driven by this, then we'll keep looking. I can call now and get my solicitor started."

"He can't do much without my paperwork, can he?"

"It's in the safe in my office. I have an aide who can get to it. But even if he didn't have access to it, he could get started. Most of it will be filed with the courts so your grandfather and mother would have their wishes on record. It's far easier to have your own copy, of course."

"Go ahead then." It didn't completely put her at ease, but at least Robert seemed to be taking her seriously. She glanced around before leaning up to give him a soft kiss. Though everyone traveling with them knew they were an item, they had worked hard to keep their personal and professional lives separate in public. "Thank you."

"My pleasure." He kissed her forehead. "Now, we need to get back to the hotel for dinner."

Rather than spend another night away from home, the flight would take off not long after the meal ended. By morning, they would be back in Mevendia. Lizbeth had no idea what time that would be locally, but at least they'd be home.

Yvette smoothed the white crushed velvet of her dress as she twisted from side to side to get a good look at herself in the mirror. The dress was a replica of a replica of a replica of the one worn by the very first queen of Ravenzario on Independence Day. They hadn't fought for their freedom like many other countries that celebrated such a day, but Mevendia and Ravenzario had split off from Montevaro many centuries earlier. The exact date was lost in the annals of time, but it had been celebrated the second Saturday in July since the 1500s.

Normally, the queen wore this dress, but since Christiana wasn't feeling well, she was going to wear a different one and only make a brief appearance at the Independence Ball, if she was able to come at all.

"Remind me why I have to wear this get-up again?" Nicklaus walked out of his closet also in period wear.

"The land that is now Mevendia and Montevaro was given to a man from the British Isles after Charlemagne fell in love with, and possibly impregnated, his daughter." Yvette knew he knew this. Why did she need to recite it all again? "The daughter married one of her father's knights. After her father died, they became king and queen of Belles Montagnes. Under their rule, these islands became part of the kingdom. They had three sons. Each son inherited a section of the country, splitting it into thirds. The couple had ruled from what is now Montevaro, so Mevendia and Ravenzario claimed independence. Every year, both countries have big celebrations. Since the Van Rensselaer Accords, the ruling families alternate which country they celebrate in. This year, the celebration is in Ravenzario." And the reason why her mother wasn't wearing this dress. As the most senior female of the Ravenzarian family after the queen, Yvette got to.

At least someone had been thinking ahead and had one made especially for her, and she didn't have to try to fit Christiana's. They were built too differently for that to work well.

Melinda let them know it was time for them to leave the apartment. Yvette led the way, though Nicklaus was only a half-step behind. They reached the ante room near the ballroom and found Alexander waiting.

He kissed Yvette's cheek. "You look lovely."

"I look goofy," Nicklaus complained.

Alexander chuckled. "Sorry. It's the way it goes. Girls get the gorgeous dresses. We guys get the funny lookin' outfits."

Yvette wasn't sure the medieval gown was much better than the Robin Hood looking outfit Nicklaus wore.

In a few minutes, they were ushered into the ballroom, announced by someone unseen. Normally, Alexander and Christiana would have the first dance - a traditional dance going back centuries. With Christiana absent, it *should* fall to Yvette and Nicklaus, but he didn't know it. Her parents were forbidden by tradition since the celebration was in Ravenzario. That left Yvette and Alexander.

It wasn't the first time they'd danced. In fact, he'd escorted her to an event or two before he married Christiana. But this dance was a very specific routine, led by Alexander and covering the entire dance floor. By the time they finished, near the small stage at one end, Yvette was quite out of breath. Alexander went to the podium to greet the crowd while Nicklaus came to stand by Yvette.

"That's a lot faster than I remembered," she whispered. "I remember it being a much slower dance."

"You did great," he whispered back.

She shook her head. "I missed a bunch of steps. I just hope no one noticed or it'll be all over the society section of the papers tomorrow."

Alexander apologized for Christiana's absence and noted he would be going to be by her side, leaving Yvette and Nicklaus as Ravenzario's representatives. Yvette sipped her water, though every eye was on her.

"Dinner will be served before the dancing begins," she told Nicklaus, clapping politely as Alexander left the podium. He shook a few hands on his way to the door. Nicklaus took her hand and led her onto the stage, holding her chair for her at the head table. As soon as they were seated, the staff began serving the head table first, then the rest of the room.

Yvette's father sat on the other side of her. "You did well, Yvette."

"I missed some steps."

"I doubt anyone else noticed."

She wished she could believe him, but as she glanced around the room, Yvette caught the society editor for the local paper eyeballing her. There was an almost predatory gleam in the other woman's eye.

Great.

"Promise you'll save me a dance?" her father asked.

"Of course."

Small talk dominated the next hour as they ate. Dancing followed, beginning with Nicklaus and her father. Yvette then danced the rounds with assorted other men of import - like Majority Leader Caruso and Minority Leader Michaels. Lizbeth and Robert were both there, so Yvette made sure to share a dance with him.

As her dance with Robert came to an end, a man in his mid-to-late twenties tapped Robert on the shoulder. "May I?"

Yvette managed to keep a long-suffering sigh in as she curtsied slightly to begin the dance. "I don't believe we've had the pleasure of being introduced."

"Lord Peter of Gregorson, Your Royal Highness."

"Gregorson? Isn't that title Montevarian?" What was he doing at a Ravenzarian Independence Ball?

"It is," he acknowledged. "My mother is Ravenzarian by birth."

"I see," Yvette murmured, as though that explained how the second son of a minor duke came to be at the ball. And really he was holding her a bit more closely than she was comfortable with. As they turned around the dance floor, she tried to add a bit more space, but he was having none of it.

Until he stepped on the hem of her gown.

She pushed him away as forcefully as she could without landing him on his rear end. "Excuse me. I believe I'm going to sit out the next round." She turned and walked off, smiling as though nothing was wrong.

"Our dance isn't over," he called after her.

Yvette ignored him and kept walking until she reached her seat. An attendant held it for her, and she nodded her thanks. Sipping on her water, she let her eyes wander over the dance floor. If she was being honest, she wanted nothing more than to escape to her quarters and put this night behind her.

Though she didn't stop to look directly at him, Yvette did notice *Lord Peter* still standing on the edge of the dance floor, staring straight at her.

A chill ran up her spine. If she never ran into him again, it would be too soon.

22

Nicklaus tried to keep his mind on dancing with the young lady in front of him, but found it wandering to his wife instead.

And the way that guy had looked at her when she danced with him. Who was he? Nicklaus couldn't see Yvette's face as they'd danced, but they were dancing far closer than she had with anyone else. Could it be an old boyfriend? Someone she'd hoped would be more than a friend before Nicklaus had come back from the dead?

Had he ever flat out asked her if there was someone else?

The woman he was dancing with asked him a question about his upbringing. He focused his attention on her and gave the same vague, innocuous answer he gave everyone else. After that dance, there was another. Then another. And another. A seemingly endless line of women he didn't know and would never remember.

Finally, the last dance came around, and Nicklaus found his wife in his arms again.

"Have you enjoyed yourself?" she asked.

He shrugged. "It's been fine. I'm ready to get out of here, though."

"Me, too."

Nicklaus glanced over at one of the staff members, the one who seemed to be in charge of this thing. She nodded at him so he let go of Yvette and took her hand, leading her out the side door and on the long walk to their room. As they reached the top of the first set of stairs, Yvette stopped and kicked her shoes off.

"Much better." They kept walking, hand in hand, as she went on. "You know what Malachi and I used to do?"

"What's that?"

"We used to slide around on the ballroom floor in our socks." She didn't look at him. "Did you ever see *Frozen*? The Disney movie with the ice queen Elsa?"

"Um, maybe?" He had. He should just tell her that. "Yeah. I watched it with Michaela because it was her kind of thing."

"Remember when Anna and Elsa go play in the ballroom as little girls?"

"I think so." Kind of.

"Like that, but without snow. We'd pretend we were ice skating or just play tag. He always let me win."

As soon as they reached their room inside their apartment, Yvette flopped into the overstuffed chaise lounge.

"You okay?" he asked, sitting down to pull off the blasted boots.

"Yeah. My feet just hurt."

Nicklaus went into the closet and quickly changed into his favorite pajama pants and a t-shirt. He pulled the chair from the writing desk they never used over next to the chaise and sat down, picking up one of Yvette's feet. She'd pulled off her stockings at some point. With his thumbs he kneaded the bottom of her foot until he heard a relaxed sigh escape.

"That feels good." He could barely make out the words.

Instead, Nicklaus set that foot down and picked up the other foot, massaging it until he realized she'd fallen asleep. Now, the questions came to him. Did he try to change her clothes? Leave her where she lay in her dress? Move her to the bed and cover her up?

Finally, that's what he decided to do. After flipping the covers down, he lifted her carefully and laid Yvette on her side of the bed. A small sigh escaped her lips as she snuggled down into the covers. Nicklaus pulled the sheet over her and finished getting himself ready for bed.

He didn't know how long he'd been asleep when something woke him. Nicklaus blinked, until he recognized the shape of Yvette sitting on the bed next to him.

"Sorry," she whispered. "I need your help."

Nicklaus pushed himself into a seated position. "What's up?"

Yvette swept her hair to one side. "I can't get the back undone."

He resisted the urge to kiss the base of her neck, and unhooked the dress before untying the ribbon that held the two sides together. He loosened it until she would be able to remove it herself. He couldn't stop himself, though. Nicklaus pressed a kiss to her shoulder. "There you go." The husky tone to his voice surprised even him.

Yvette turned, her dark eyes bigger than normal in the dim nighttime lighting. "Thank you." She leaned back just enough for him to understand the meaning of her slightly parted lips.

So he kissed her. And she kissed him back.

And she pulled away and whispered, "We should go to the ballroom in our socks."

Not exactly what he'd thought she had in mind.

Yvette bounced up, holding the dress in place with one hand. "Come on. It'll be fun."

Nicklaus chuckled, because what else could he do?

In a few minutes, Yvette was in her pajamas and they both wore thick socks. Yvette held his hand but practically tiptoed through the halls.

"You know we won't get in trouble, right?" he whispered.

"Sh!" She peeked around a corner. "Just because we won't get in trouble doesn't mean we want everyone knowing we're acting like little kids."

Yvette had a point. And really, she was still just a month or so past her eighteenth birthday. His wife wasn't far from a child herself.

They made it to the ballroom without being seen, though Nicklaus would bet some security guard could see them on a camera display somewhere.

Yvette turned, a twinkle in her eye, as they entered the dimly lit room. "Race ya to the other side."

Before he could agree or not, she took off, slipping and sliding her way to the other side of the floor. Nicklaus took off after her, his arms wind-milling as he managed not to fall on the slick surface.

Yvette beat him to the column that must have been the finish line. "I won!" she declared with a triumphant grin. "You owe me a dance."

"I danced with you twice earlier," he reminded her.

"You owe me an Independence Dance. I had to dance it with Alexander." She slid her way to the center of the floor. "Come on."

Nicklaus sighed. Not exactly what he'd had in mind, but he'd go along with it.

"Here." Yvette reached for his hands and positioned them just so. Then she stepped far closer to him than she had been to Alexander. "It's really a dance for lovers," she whispered. "Designed to be danced very close together. Obviously, that's not what happened earlier."

He swallowed hard as she helped him through the steps. They didn't make it very far before she nearly fell when he stepped on her foot.

"Sorry."

Yvette winced but then smiled. "I'm fine. Let's keep going."

They managed to make it to the end of the dance and when Yvette spun back into him, she rested her hands on his chest and looked up at him, that same breathless look he'd seen on her face before. He didn't think about it.

He kissed her.

Then he picked her up and carried her to their quarters. The walk took forever, it seemed, but they stopped and he kissed her again several times.

And this time when they reached the privacy of their room...they shared the dance as old as time itself.

Nicklaus stared at the wall after Yvette went to sleep. Thoughts, feelings, impressions all roiled around in his mind, leaving him unable to even contemplate sleeping. It wasn't until his eyes refused to stay open any longer that he went into one of the other bedrooms and collapsed. It wasn't that he didn't want to sleep in the same bed as his wife. On the contrary, he didn't want to disturb her.

Blackness enveloped him.

"Come on, Nicky." Michaela's frantic voice drifted to him. "We've got to get out of here."

Nicklaus couldn't see and tried to move, but was restrained in place. His own screams echoed in his ears.

"Come on, Nicky." The desperation caused him to struggle harder. Where was Michaela? Where was his mother? They were the same person, weren't they?

And why was it so cold?

Moans. He heard moaning coming from somewhere in front of him.

"Run, Michaela!" This time he knew the voice. His father was yelling. A voice he never remembered hearing before, but he knew. "Get Nicklaus and run!"

The restraints he struggled against suddenly released him, and he fell forward. Someone picked him up, but he couldn't see who.

Dark

So dark.

He tried to move, but couldn't as this person held onto him.

They fell.

He couldn't breathe.

So cold.

Wet.

Gasping for air.

Getting water instead.

Coughing. Crying.

Someone holding him tight as the water finally receded behind them.

"Nicky? Sweetheart?"

Another voice sounded panicked but much closer. And warm.

"Nicky. Are you all right?"

This voice calmed him. It wasn't Michaela, but the person behind the voice meant something to him. He knew that much.

"It's okay, Nicky. You're safe. God protected you. He sent His angels to protect you and Michaela. You're safe."

Her voice was the voice of an angel. His breathing slowed. The darkness ceased being scary and stars seemed to appear.

"Just rest, Nicky. You're safe."

Nicklaus sat straight up in his bed, alarm blaring from his phone.

"What time is it?" The sleepy voice didn't surprise him, though maybe it should have.

He turned to see Yvette propped up on her elbow. "It's early. You don't need to be up yet. I must not have turned it off from yesterday." He didn't really need to be up yet either. After double checking the alarms, he laid back down.

"Are you okay?" Yvette wrapped an arm around him.

"Yeah. Why?"

"You had a nightmare."

That's when he remembered. He'd slept in another room so he wouldn't bother her. "Did I wake you up?"

"No. I wanted a drink and on my way to the kitchen I heard you. Why'd you sleep in here?" Traces of fear tinged her voice.

"I didn't want to bother you if I had another dream."

"It's part of why I'm here."

"I don't want to hurt you. I almost did one night."

"You won't hurt me."

He remained unconvinced but decided arguing wasn't the best plan. "What's our schedule for today?"

"We have a meeting about ramping up your charity work. Christiana, Charlyn, and a couple others have some suggestions for you. I'll be joining because, although I work with a number of charities back home, I need to start working with more here."

Back home. This wasn't her home. It really wasn't his. Not yet. Maybe not ever. He never thought he'd miss Edwardsville, Illinois or Boaz, Louisiana or any of the other places he'd lived with Michaela, but maybe he did.

She was still talking, but he didn't really hear what she said. Would he ever fit in here? Be the prince everyone said he was?

"I had an idea about how to prove you and Christiana are who you say you are."

That caught his attention. "What's that?"

"The real question isn't who your mother is. I mean, we all know Queen Marissa was your mother, but as far as the legalities go, it only matters who your father is, right?"

He tried to think that through. "I guess. Though if Queen Marissa isn't our mother, we'd be illegitimate children. Is that a big deal?"

Yvette shrugged. "In some countries it could be. I don't know about here. But mitochondrial DNA passes from mother to child. Men don't pass it on, but women do. We could find out if your mother has any cousins, or even your second or third cousins as long as it goes through the maternal line, and compare mitochondrial DNA. It would prove your mother is Queen Marissa."

"How does that help? Someone could always say she'd been cheating. It happens."

"Tell me about it." There was an exasperated tone to her voice he didn't think was directed at him.

He rolled until he could see her. "What? Is there something I should know?"

She waved a hand. "It's not important now. It has nothing to do with us or this. What I was wondering, though, is if there's something similar, maybe on the Y-chromosome that is passed from father to son that could prove a relationship through the paternal line. If so, we're good. Because we're descended from the same king in Mevendia like a hundred and fifty years ago. I know my family line is through the paternal line. My father's father was king. So was my father's father's father. And so on."

"How does that help us? Yeah that son married into this family, but she wouldn't have been queen. Christiana is the first queen of Ravenzario, right?."

"You're right. And I'm not as up on my Ravenzarian history as I should be, but I'm *pretty sure* that the princess who married the Mevendian prince didn't become queen. *But*," she hurried on. "I *think* her son became king."

"How would that work?"

"Her brother was king, but died without any heirs. She was already deceased which made her son next in line for the throne. So he was king. His son was king. And so on, down to your father."

He was starting to see where she was going with this. "So if there's some sort of male version of mitochondrial DNA, maybe your father or one of your brothers and I could get tested to see if we came from the same paternal line."

"Exactly!"

"Aren't Malachi and..." What was Malachi's wife's name?

"Jessabelle," Yvette prompted.

"Aren't they coming here in a couple of days? We could do some research and have it done then."

She wrinkled her nose. He kind of loved it when she did that. "That won't work. It's a long story I'll tell you another time. I don't think anyone outside of my immediate family knows, but Malachi is my half-brother. We don't have the same father." Before he could assimilate that information, she went on. "Of course, Jessabelle is also my half-sister, but she and Malachi aren't related."

Nicklaus shook his head to clear it. "I don't think I followed that at all."

Yvette looked at her phone. "I'll explain it all some other time. For now, it's enough that Malachi wouldn't work for that test." She stood up and stretched. "I do need to get moving though. I'll do some research before we talk to your sister about the testing."

"Good idea." Even as he said it, he wondered. Did he really want to know if he belonged to a family he already knew he didn't fit in with?

23

Yvette held the phone against her ear. "I did some Google searching, and it turns out you *can* compare Y chromosomes to determine if there's a common male ancestor as long as it goes straight through the paternal line."

Her father sighed. "I fail to see how that helps Nicklaus and Christiana prove they are who everyone already knows they are."

"Remember the Van Rensselaer Accords?"

"Yes," he answered slowly. "The son borne of that union became king after his mother and uncle both died."

"That's what I thought."

"So comparing my Y chromosome and Nicklaus's should prove relation."

"We'd want to talk to someone who knows what they're talking about, but Internet research says that it should work that way." She hesitated for a second. "Malachi will be here in a couple of days, but..."

Her father sighed. "Right. I will make arrangements to have my DNA sampled here today or tomorrow and have the results sent wherever we need to. Then Malachi will not be asked to."

"That would be a good plan."

"I am proud of you, Yvette. You are thinking outside the box to find a solution to a problem." She could hear something she hadn't heard nearly enough until a year earlier. Approval and affection from her father. "I love you, Yvette."

"I love you, too, Papa. I'll talk to you soon."

Good. That would be taken care of before Malachi got there, and they wouldn't need to have any uncomfortable discussions about why his DNA couldn't be used. Her conversation with Nicklaus replayed in her mind. Technically, he was her immediate family now, but she hadn't talked to her father about whether or not the rest of the family would be all right with her telling him the whole story. He'd want to know the whole story later. Maybe she should call her father back and tell him she'd let it slip. The buzz of her phone meant it would have to wait. She had people waiting for her arrival, and it wouldn't do to be late. With a sigh, she headed out.

Before she got far, Melinda caught up with her, reminding Yvette that her schedule had been changed. The palace decorator was waiting for their meeting in her new office.

After a long day of decorating decisions and meetings, she collapsed back into bed. She prayed for peace for Nicklaus as he slept, but she didn't know where he spent the night. All she knew for sure was that it wasn't in their room with her. The next day was more of the same. He wasn't in their room again when she turned in. Pounding footsteps in the hall meant he was likely trying to run off his discontent.

Sometime in the middle of the night, she woke, though she couldn't quite define why. Deciding a drink was in order, she headed toward the kitchen. Nicklaus didn't share her bed again. As she padded through the sitting room, she heard it.

Nicklaus's agonized groans came from the other bedroom. Sneaking through the door, she found him much as he'd been the other times. The bedsheets were twisted around his legs, and a sheen of sweat covered his back. When she reached the side of the bed, Yvette sat down and rested her hand on his back.

"It's okay, Nicky," she whispered, just as she had the other times. "You're safe. I'm here." Over and over she repeated it until he started to calm down. His muscles finally began to relax under her hand. Trying not to disturb him, she walked around to the other side of the bed and slid in until she was close enough to wrap an arm around him.

When she touched him again, Nicklaus rolled and sat straight, his elbow swinging around.

Yvette tried to move, but it connected with her cheek, knocking her over.

She cried out as her hand came up to her face.

Nicklaus turned, his breath coming rapid and shallow. "Evie?"

"I'm okay." She wasn't but she didn't want to tell him that.

"Did I hurt you?" He sounded like a scared kid.

"I'm fine. Are you okay?"

His breathing started to slow as she rested her hand on his back again. "I think so."

"Do you remember what the dream was?"

"The same thing it has been. It's dark and cold. There's water everywhere. Sometimes I feel like I'm drowning."

That was more than he'd told her before. He laid back down, his head on the pillow. "Thanks for being here."

"Of course. What's a wife for?"

"Thanks."

The tears wouldn't stay put any longer and leaked down her cheeks. "Are you all right?"

"Fine."

"I'll be back in a minute." She tried to keep the crack out of her voice, but failed. He didn't say anything as she headed out of the bedroom and back to their suite. In the light of the bathroom, she saw the swelling had already begun. Belinda was a wiz with make-up. Surely she'd be able to cover it. Nicklaus hadn't hurt her on purpose. She had a feeling he'd withdraw even further if he realized what he'd done.

Going back out to the kitchen, she looked for an ice pack in the freezer but didn't find one. There *was* a package of corn and a couple steaks. Nicklaus's favorites. She was *going* to learn how to make them someday. Wasn't meat supposed to be good to put on a black eye? But she didn't have one of those. He'd caught her cheekbone.

After taking some pain killers, she held the bag of corn to her cheek. Wincing, she wondered if she'd be able to sleep at all.

Deciding it would be better to tough it out and make sure Nicklaus wasn't alone, she put the corn away about ten minutes later. Nicklaus was asleep again when she slid back under the covers next to him, though she kept her distance this time. Yvette didn't know how long it took, but she did eventually fall asleep. When she awoke, Nicklaus was already gone. Belinda waited in the sitting room.

She gasped when she saw Yvette. "Oh no! What happened?"

So much for hoping it wasn't noticeable. "The prince had a nightmare, and I'm afraid I got in the way of his elbow when he awoke."

"Does it hurt?"

"Some, but not as bad as before." That wasn't entirely accurate. It did feel better in that it wasn't throbbing anymore, but it ached worse. She needed more pain killers. "Do you think we can cover it? I'd prefer no one else know about it. I'm not certain the prince even realizes it happened."

"I'll do my best, ma'am." She sounded dubious. Maybe it was best Yvette hadn't looked at it again.

Once Belinda had worked her magic, it was time to head to the reception room. Her brother and sister-in-law would arrive any minute. She prayed they wouldn't notice.

But mostly she prayed Nicklaus wouldn't.

Nicklaus couldn't keep his eyes off his wife's face.

And that wasn't a good thing.

Belinda had done a fabulous job covering what had to be quite a bruise on Yvette's cheek. When he woke up for the morning, he prayed it was just part of the bad dream. As soon as he'd turned to look at her, he'd seen the green and purple on the side of her face.

He'd done that to her.

That it had been an accident didn't matter.

Had anyone else noticed? No one said anything.

Her brother and sister-in-law joined them for breakfast after half an hour or so in the reception room. Her words about the DNA testing came back to him. Malachi couldn't be tested to see if they were related through their paternal lines. That meant he wasn't King Antonio's biological child. A quick Internet search hadn't turned up any gossip about Queen Alicia having an affair. The king had made no secret of his past. It seemed likely that must be where Jessabelle came from - if she was related to Yvette but not Malachi.

No Internet gossip had turned up about the mistress having the king's child either, though.

Whatever the secrets were, they were very well kept.

Nicklaus picked at his breakfast. Michaela would have scolded him, but she wasn't here. Except for the time taping for the documentary, he hadn't seen her since right before they left for their honeymoon. He hadn't even heard from her. They hadn't exactly had time to catch up or talk during the filming.

He missed his mother.

She wasn't, of course, and she would insist she didn't deserve the title, but no one else had ever filled that role for him. He wanted her insight. Her wisdom. To spend some time with her.

Maybe he could sneak out and find her. She was likely

spending her time with her family and wouldn't want to be interrupted. He'd give it another week.

"Nicklaus." His sister's voice held a reprimand much like Michaela's might have. Clearly he hadn't been paying attention to the conversation.

"My apologies. I believe I was wool gathering." For crying out loud. He was even starting to sound stiff and formal.

Malachi spoke next. "I just wondered if you'd completed your university degree."

"No. I haven't. I'm about half done. Honestly, I'm not sure what my plan is from here. If I'm going to finish a degree here or just stop or what."

What he wanted didn't matter. He'd have to do whatever what was expected of him. If he could figure out what that was. Besides not accidentally hitting his wife. He already knew that was on the to-be-avoided-at-all-costs list.

Nicklaus managed to keep his attention on the conversation at the table and join in when appropriate. He hated the slight wince he noticed on Yvette's face when she opened her mouth too widely. Did anyone else notice? No one seemed to.

As soon as breakfast ended, almost everyone went separate ways. Nicklaus found himself with Alexander at the men's clothing shop near the palace. New suits and ties were picked out, and Nicklaus lost track of everything he chose or was chosen for him. Hadn't they already done this once?

He prayed they were nearly done when he looked around and noticed Alexander was gone.

"The duke was called away, sir." The proprietor of the shop hung up the last jacket Nicklaus had tried on.

"Thanks." Where were the ubiquitous guards? He looked around the front of the shop and saw them standing outside. The phone rang, pulling the proprietor's attention away from Nicklaus.

This was his chance.

Double checking to be certain no one watched him, he snuck out the back door of the shop and hurried away. His wallet contained his Nicholas Metcalf identification and credit card, even his passport thanks to the large wallet Michaela had gotten him for their European trip. With those, maybe he could get out of here and clear his head. Figure out what needed to happen in his life before he hurt Yvette again.

With cash he bought a baseball cap and sunglasses from a nearby vendor, then caught a cab to the airport. Where would he go?

He didn't know. Hadn't decided.

He paid the cab driver and went to look at the departure board. He didn't have a clue which one would be best.

"Can I help you, sir?" A woman at the kiosk near the screens caught his attention. "You look a bit lost."

"Yeah. What's the first flight I can catch out of here?"

"Where to?"

"Doesn't matter." Yvette's bruised cheek wouldn't leave him alone. He needed to get away.

"There is a flight leaving in just over half an hour for Paris. From there, you can go just about anywhere."

"What's the quickest I can leave there? Headed to the States maybe."

She tapped on her computer. "There's a connecting flight to Atlanta that you shouldn't have any trouble making."

"I'll take it."

She asked him for his identification and hurried him through the process. The security line didn't look too long. In fact, he made it to the gate with plenty of time to spare. She'd even upgraded him to first class. He'd offered to pay for it, but she wouldn't let him.

By the time the plane actually took off, he'd made a decision. Once he landed in Atlanta, he'd fly on to St. Louis and rent a car to get to Edwardsville. He knew where the key was hidden, and they hadn't yet packed up the house or anything so there would be plenty of clothes and non-perishable food, at least for a while.

Part of him knew it wouldn't take them long to figure out he'd used his other identification to get out of the country and where he'd gone. Maybe he should take a note from Michaela's playbook and drive from Atlanta. He could do that in a day, easily. With that settled in his mind, Nicklaus decided sleep would be a good thing. He finally dozed off sometime in the second leg of his flight back to the States.

"Where is who?" Yvette sat in the new chair in her new office and looked up at Alexander.

"Nicklaus."

She shrugged, though a feeling of dread began to build in the pit of her stomach. "I have no idea. Last I heard, he was with you."

Alexander ran a hand through his hair. "I got called away. Security went in to check on him, but he was gone. The only thing we can figure is that he snuck out the back. I hoped he'd contacted you."

"No, he hasn't."

"Any idea where he might have gone or why?"

She opened her mouth to say something but the ache in her cheek stopped her. "I might know why."

He glared at her when she didn't say anything else.

"You can't judge him. He didn't mean to. But he hit me last night."

The look on Alexander's face changed to one of fury. "He did what?"

"Calm down. He was having a nightmare. I startled him when I touched him, and his elbow caught my cheek. That's it. He didn't mean to."

Alexander seemed to calm a bit. "Did he realize it?"

"Not at the time. I didn't want him to. It was an accident. You haven't seen his nightmares. He won't tell me much about them. I don't know that he knows much about them. My guess is he saw the bruise this morning before Belinda covered it with make-up."

"That would make sense, but where did he go?"

"That I can't help you with. Maybe to see Michaela?"

Alexander pulled his phone out of his pocket. "Time to get Tony on this."

He left while speaking to the head of security on his phone.

Yvette turned in her chair to look out the window behind her desk. Maybe she should rearrange things so she could actually look at the view while she worked. Where could Nicklaus be? Why didn't he just talk to her?

She decided work could wait - there wasn't that much of it at the moment anyway - and went to look for Christiana. If Nicklaus really had disappeared, his sister would be devastated.

By the time she reached Christiana's office, Alexander was already there. Tony and Michaela, who happened to be in the palace already, were on their way.

When they arrived, Michaela looked nearly as distraught as Christiana.

"Before we get too worked up, let's talk this through." Tony nodded at Yvette. "You said he caught you with his elbow when he woke up after a nightmare?"

She gingerly touched her cheek. "It's bruised but it was an accident. I don't blame him."

"He probably blames himself anyway," Michaela noted.

"So where would he have gone?" Christiana rubbed her stomach. "The yacht hasn't moved. He doesn't have a car. There's no surveillance cameras in the back alley or on either end."

"My men are looking for footage from nearby to see if we can figure out what he did."

"He couldn't have gone anywhere," Alexander noted. "He doesn't have any credit cards or anything in his name yet. Just an ID."

Michaela leaned forward. "He may still have his Nicholas Metcalf cards and ID though. Princess Yvette, has he been carrying a normal sized wallet or a larger one?"

Yvette shrugged, not understanding the importance. "A bigger one in his coat pocket I think. Maybe this big." She held her fingers about six inches apart.

The former nanny sighed. "That's what I thought. I bought it for him for our trip to Europe. It has a pocket for your passport and for identification, money, credit cards, you name it."

Tony picked up on the thread. "So he could have used his alternate identification to travel under. Can you access his credit or debit accounts?"

"Unless he's changed the passwords, I should be able to."

Tony slid a laptop toward Michaela. Yvette wasn't sure how she felt about it. She, Nicklaus's wife, had no idea what his passwords could be. She knew it wasn't logical. Nicklaus had no idea what her passwords were either, but it still rubbed her the wrong way.

"Here." Michaela pointed at the screen. "Airline tickets at the airport. Pretty expensive. Then a meal of some kind in Paris."

Tony tapped on the keyboard. "A flight left for Paris less than an hour after he was last seen. Given the cost of the ticket, I'd imagine he was headed somewhere else afterward." A few more clicks on the keyboard. "There were a couple of flights leaving from the same terminal not long after he reached the gate. Where was the food purchased?"

Michaela named a restaurant.

"Let's see..." Tony studied a map of the airport. "There it is. Given the time he landed and the time and location the food was purchased...I'd guess he took the flight to Atlanta. Let's see if that would be about the right price." His fingers practically flew over the keyboard. "That looks right. The prices of the flights to New York or Chicago were a bit cheaper. Doesn't mean he couldn't have taken them because prices fluctuate, but I think Atlanta is the best choice."

Alexander stood. "I'll have Martin pack a bag for me and I'll go."

Yvette jumped out of her chair. "I'll go with you."

Everyone else glanced at each other, and she sensed they wanted to tell her no.

"Why not?" she demanded before anyone spoke. "He's my husband. Why shouldn't I go with Alexander to find him? Would any of you stop Michaela from going? No. Of course not. Because she's his mother." A brief flash of pain crossed Christiana's face. "Not biologically, but she's the one who raised him. We all know that." She looked at the other woman. "And I have no problem with you coming, too. You know him better than any of us. But why can't I go?"

Another round of looks was exchanged.

"I'm going," she reiterated.

Finally, Alexander nodded. "Get your things together, and we'll leave as soon as we can."

Michaela brushed her hair back off her face. "I will, too."

Yvette didn't listen to the rest of the conversation. Instead, she hurried from the room and up several flights of stairs to their new quarters. She had no idea where Belinda and Melinda were, so she'd have to pack herself.

No way was she getting left behind.

Atlanta lived up to its nickname - Hot-lanta. Stepping out of the airport and looking around, the sweltering heat rolled over Nicklaus. First, a car rental place. One where you didn't have to be at least 25 to rent a car. He took the first car rental shuttle that came along and found out that, for a minimal "under 25" surcharge, he could get a vehicle.

Part of him wanted to go with a sports car, but the practical side won out, and he went with a more reasonable sedan. Before long he cruised northward. He'd slept some on the plane and thought he could make it all the way to Edwardsville without needing to stop overnight.

The miles rolled by under the tires, first in Georgia, then Tennessee. He stopped only to grab a bite to eat and use the facilities. By the time he hit Kentucky, he was rethinking his plan to drive straight through. His airplane sleep had been anything but truly restful. Between occasional pockets of turbulence, other passengers, and recurring dreams where he hurt Yvette over and over, he finally admitted it couldn't have been much better than no sleep at all.

When he reached Paducah, Kentucky, Nicklaus decided it was time for a longer break. Finding a park, he retied his new tennis shoes, grateful he'd thought to get a change of clothes in the Atlanta airport.

As he ran around the asphalt trail, Nicklaus found himself missing the palace and its wide hallways. A bit unconventional, sure, but there was something to be said for climate controlled. He set a slow pace to account for the heat and only went a bit over a mile. After guzzling some water, he got back on the road.

He finally made it to Edwardsville over eleven hours after he started, instead of the eight and a half his phone had quoted him. The accidental detour through Carbondale hadn't helped.

A car he vaguely recognized sat in the driveway when he pulled up. A girl walked down the stairs from the front porch as he put the car in park.

Tessa.

A girl he'd gone out with three times and thought he might like before everything went haywire.

"Nicky!" The endearment sounded off to his ears. "There you are! Where have you been?"

He shut the door behind him, trying not to roll his eyes as she extended a cheek for a kiss. Who did that in the States? No one he knew. Everyone in Ravenzario seemed to, though. "Hey, Tessa."

"Where have you been? And what happened to your phone?" she practically demanded.

"Sorry. Mom and I had something come up. My phone broke." Or, he now suspected, Michaela had broken it. "It wasn't backed up, and I had to get a new number when I got a new one." A phone vetted by security in Ravenzario.

"It's okay." She linked her arm through his. "You're home now."

He extracted his arm. "Not really. I'm not here long. In fact, we'll be packing everything up and selling the place soon." An assumption, but a reasonable one.

"Is that why you're here? To tell me you didn't miss me at all?"

Yeah. That was why he'd spent nearly twelve hours in a plane and nearly a dozen more driving. To tell a girl he'd dated a couple of times he didn't miss her. "Sorry, Tess. A lot's happened in the last couple months."

"I haven't talked to you since you left on the cruise."

And she hadn't found another guy yet? "Sorry." Not sorry.

He flipped through his keys looking for the one for the front door. "I don't mean to be rude, but I have a few things to take care of."

"You're not even going to invite me in?"

He held up a hand. "No. Sorry, Tess. Not today." Not ever.

Tessa grabbed his hand. "What's this?" She tugged on his finger.

"Hey!" He pulled his hand away. "Leave it alone."

"What is it?" she demanded.

"What's it look like?"

"It looks like a wedding ring."

"You got it in one. I'm married."

Her insipid blue eyes blazed at him. "You went on dates with me while you were *engaged?*"

"No. It happened very quickly. We met and got married in about a week. That's all you need to know. There's no future for us." He turned to the door with the right key in his hand. "Now, if you'll excuse me, I have some things to do."

He left her fuming on the doorstep. Too bad. Michaela had tried to warn him about Tessa. He had a feeling Tessa wouldn't much care that he was married.

With the door locked behind him, he went up to the room that had been his just a couple months earlier.

So much had changed in such a short time period. This house had seemed quite nice at the time - and it was. But it didn't hold a candle to the grandeur of the Ravenzarian palace. The halls were nearly claustrophobic, his room maybe half the size of the room he'd slept in the last several nights. Smaller still compared to the room he was supposed to share with Yvette.

He flopped onto the twin bed he'd spent most of his nights in. Before he could even change into a pair of pajamas he'd left behind, he dozed.

Nightmares didn't wake him, but yelling did.

"Nicklaus David Richard Antonio Rensselaer, where are you?"

He sat up in the twilight. "Mom?" he called.

Michaela stormed into the room, her eyes flashing. "What do you think you're doing?"

"How did you find me?"

"Your phone." Michaela used her best mom look on him. One he still hated.

"It's been turned off," he pointed out.

"Not the whole time. It was on for a few minutes when you landed in Atlanta and again in Carbondale."

Right. When he'd gotten directions and then tried to figure out where he'd gone wrong. There had been missed calls and text messages, but he'd purposely avoided looking at them. Nicklaus ran a hand through his hair. "I needed to get away."

"And you think running off is the best plan? Really? Didn't I teach you to stay and work out your problems?"

He shot a glare at her. "No. You taught me to run."

"When you were in danger! Not because of bumps in a relationship!"

She had a point. "Fine. I should have stayed. How could I, though? I've tried sleeping in a separate room because I didn't want to hurt my wife when I wake up from a nightmare. But even if she's asleep when I go to bed, somehow she knows and finds me. And last night, the night before, whatever it was, I hit her. I didn't mean to, but I did. And I hurt her. I saw the bruise on her cheek before Belinda covered it up. How could I stay knowing I could hurt her again? And it could be far worse next time." He looked behind Michaela to see a stern Alexander. "Where is she? Is she here?"

"No." Alexander crossed his arms over his chest, looking even more intimidating. "She's at home. We didn't want her to get hurt again either."

Lizbeth pressed her forefingers to her temples. "I'm not following whatever it is you're saying. Could you repeat it?"

Robert's lawyer nodded. "Between the papers you've provided me, the information on the trust and the property in Ravenzario, and what I could find available in the public record, it appears that you, Mrs. Padovano, are a wealthy woman."

For a second she wondered at the name, but of course he knew they were married. Legally, he couldn't say anything about it. Plus Robert trusted him implicitly, or they wouldn't be here. "How exactly does that work? My mother and grandfather left me some of their individual estates in their wills, but I always thought it was a small portion."

"Not according to these documents. It appears everything can be distributed to you any time after your birthday last month, provided a couple conditions are met."

"What conditions?"

He flipped a piece of paper up to look underneath it. "You have to be married and not be involved in any illicit amorous activities. The marriage clauses would probably be overturned if we challenged them."

She glanced at Robert. "What exactly counts as illicit amorous activities?"

The solicitor let the paper come back to rest on top. "The generally accepted legal definition in Mevendia is that you are not involved romantically with a married man."

Lizbeth looked at Robert. "Only my husband, and I'm pretty sure that doesn't count."

"It can also be a premarital relationship that results in a child, though that definition is not enforced today like it would have been a few decades ago or before."

Lizbeth felt the blood drain from her cheeks. Robert reached over and took her hand, silently telling her they'd face whatever it was together.

"Is there something I need to know?"

Hot tears leaked down her face. "Last spring, a little over a year ago, I got drunk one night. I don't know anything about the guy except he was staying at the house in Ravenzario, and he seemed nice enough. I got pregnant. When I told Robert, he proposed, wanting to be a family with me and the baby, but I miscarried not long afterward."

The solicitor leaned back in his chair. "That's a legal gray area then. Some judges might enforce it. Most wouldn't, but very few enforce that regardless, unless it was specifically spelled out."

Another thought crossed her mind. "What kind of proof does there have to be of a relationship with a married man?"

He frowned. "I'm not certain. I can look into it, though."

She looked over at Robert. "There were rumors in the tabloids last year that I had something going with Prince Malachi. They weren't true, but they did exist."

"I remember. The palace vehemently denied it, didn't they?"

Lizbeth shrugged. "To be honest, I don't remember. If Prince Malachi had left Jessabelle for me, I wouldn't have shed any tears over their broken marriage. Not then. Things changed a lot over the next few months. I do know my father desperately wanted me to be caught in compromising positions with Malachi, and did everything short of come right out and tell me I should try to get pregnant with his baby."

Robert squeezed her hand as the other man leaned forward. "Do you have any proof of those conversations?"

"I don't think so. There was never anyone else around when he'd say stuff."

"Okay. I have some paperwork I need to get in order to submit to the trust. The way it looks, once the paperwork is done, there will be a short period where someone could object based on the criteria. After that, it's all yours."

"And if my father objects?"

"The trustee would decide, though we could force it in front of a judge if we felt the need." He went on before she could say anything. "And I would. I know this law firm, and it's known for its integrity, but we don't want to risk it."

"Could my father pay off the judge?"

"It's possible," he conceded, "but unlikely. Your father has had unlimited use of the assorted properties owned by the trust, including the house in Ravenzario, the home here, and several others. He's had an allowance of sorts until now. There's a way built in for him to force a decision if you're not married by your *next* birthday. Then, or if he proves illicit amorous activities, he would get everything. A judge would see the conflict of interest and likely look for proof outside what your father would bring. They wouldn't just take his word. Your father probably hasn't had access to the kind of money needed to pay off a judge."

Lizbeth relaxed, just a bit. "Okay. So what do we need to do?"

He turned some papers around. "The first thing is that I need you to read and sign some forms."

She took the stack, prayed for wisdom, and thanked God for the man at her side. Without Robert, she wouldn't have had the first clue about how to do any of this.

25

Yvette fumed and yelled and stormed about. No one heard her, but it made her feel better anyway. By the time she'd finished packing, Michaela and Alexander were already gone, leaving her behind. Nicklaus had been gone more than a full day. They'd been gone over eighteen hours, and she hadn't heard anything from any of them.

Once Nicklaus should have landed in Atlanta, she'd called him. Repeatedly. But it always went straight to voice mail. He must have kept it turned off. Alexander and Michaela were both ignoring her calls, too.

She made another circuit around her room, this time punctuating her arguments with pointed fingers, though she spoke only to the air.

"Are you quite finished?"

Yvette turned to see Christiana standing in the doorway of her bedroom. "Sorry. I didn't know you were here."

"I understand your annoyance, Yvette." Christiana had a gentle way about her that immediately began to calm Yvette down. "I was also a part of the decision to leave you here. Nicklaus needs some space. He needs not to see the reminder of what he did. Not yet."

"Fine." She plopped unceremoniously down onto the settee at the end of the bed. "So what do I do here?"

"Whatever you wish. Continue working with your charities. Find new ones. Look at our universities and possibly apply to a few so that when Nicklaus decides what he wants to do, you'll be ready as well."

"I already applied to and was accepted by pretty much every university in the Commonwealth." She'd done that when she had no idea Nicklaus was alive. She wanted options for after the wedding didn't happen.

Except then it happened, and she had done nothing else about university.

"Now, I heard you found a secret passage in here." Christiana walked toward the fireplace. "I am told the historian and preservationists have looked at everything in there and said that, as long as you are careful, they will leave it all for you to discover."

Yvette felt her face light up. "Really? I would love that, but I definitely don't want to accidentally ruin anything."

"They did not look through everything, but if you come across something you think may be too old or fragile for you to handle yourself, please call them."

"Of course."

"Would you show me?"

How could she not? But still Yvette hesitated. Nicklaus had gone in there with her, but only reluctantly. Part of her wanted to claim sole ownership of the area, though that was ridiculous of course.

Christiana turned and smiled at her. "I do not think I would want to share such a treasure either. Not right away."

"But it's your palace," Yvette protested weakly. "Whatever is in there likely belonged to one of your ancestors."

"Perhaps, but I still understand." She started for the door. "If you would let me know of anything you discover of historical significance, I would appreciate it."

"Of course."

Before she walked out the door, Christiana looked back. "They also tested to see how the door stayed open. As long as you leave the sconce tilted, it should not close on its own. If it does, there is a lever inside that will open it."

"Thank you."

Christiana looked like she wanted to say something else, but left. Yvette texted Melinda to let her know where she was and how long she expected to be in there. With Christiana's reassurance the door wouldn't close, Yvette wasn't sure it was necessary, but did it anyway, because she had promised Nicklaus.

Yvette found a flashlight and opened the hidden door. She looked around the first floor much more carefully than she had before, but discovered nothing new. Once up the stairs, she stood still, trying to take it all in. Sheets still covered the furniture. What should she uncover first? Maybe she should come back in the morning or see if some lights could be set up in here. The rest of the palace was electrified, surely they could add some in here.

Finally, she decided to look at one piece. Holding the flashlight under her arm, she carefully removed the cloth, gasping as it came into view. Rich wood surprised her. Not in its ornate design, but in its elegant simplicity. It seemed that, often, royal families of the past thought the more ornate the better. Whoever had commissioned or purchased this desk clearly didn't subscribe to that theory. After folding the cloth, she tugged gently on the top drawer. It slid open easily, revealing a dark brown journal.

Yvette gasped, reaching out to touch the cover. The soft leather had held up surprisingly well. She picked it up and set it on the top of the desk. Opening to the first page, she found an inscription.

To Princess Victoria Abigail Amelia Grace
on your sixteenth birthday

All my love, Papa

Princess Victoria? The name sounded familiar. If only "Papa" had written his name or the actual date. That would be a clue. She carefully turned a page. There was a date, but no year. The fancy script would be easier to read in a well-lit area. Yvette closed it and took it down the stairs with her. After texting Melinda, she got ready to turn in. Once in her pajamas, she sat cross-legged on the bed.

Prince David is scheduled to arrive tomorrow, the diary read. *I have not seen him in several years, though Papa travels to Mevendia occasionally. I remember that he was quite handsome. Perhaps now he is even more so. Will he find me beautiful? I am the plain one in the family. Gisele is the beautiful one. Though she is only twelve, everyone knows this. I am afraid it will turn her head. Now that I am sixteen, we will begin to plan our wedding. We have known since we were children that we were to marry, but what if he changes his mind? What if Prince David decides he wants a wife who is not as homely as I am?*

Yvette realized who this must be. The princess who was first widowed then jilted for another woman. She then married another Mevendian prince. The Van Rensselaer Accord Jewels were originally Princess Victoria's. How ironic that Yvette should be the one to find the journal.

Or how preordained, a voice inside whispered. *Perhaps the God who was, is, and always will be knew you would benefit from her words?*

The still, small voice had a point. She set the journal on the side table. In the morning, she would ask the preservationists what needed to be done to maintain the integrity of her find, but ask that she be allowed to read it first.

Though she knew he would ignore it, she texted Nicklaus a good night message anyway then tried to find the rest she knew she needed.

"Wait a minute." Nicklaus glared at Alexander who seemed completely unintimidated by his yelling. "You'll let me stay in the States." That he needed permission ground against Nicklaus's independent streak. "But I can't stay here?"

"Watch your tone, young man." Michaela's steady gaze nearly caused him to wilt.

He wanted to lash out, to remind her that she wasn't really his mother, but he couldn't.

"And yes," Alexander answered. "You can stay here. It's your choice."

"I can stay here with a security contingent bigger than the Pope's."

Michaela's look told him he hadn't contained his exasperation.

Alexander shrugged. "That's the deal. You can stay here with security, you can return to Ravenzario, or you can go to Serenity Landing and stay with a friend of mine who has a secure home."

"I'd still need a security team," he muttered. If he went back to Ravenzario, he would too, but that was irrelevant.

"But, because his home is already secure, you will only have two security team members with you, and they won't follow your every move unless you leave the property."

"I can't stay somewhere else?" He chafed under the restrictions, but he'd likely take them.

"Anywhere else and you get the full complement of security members."

"I have to stay with some random guy I don't know?"

Alexander chuckled. "I'd let you stay with my folks, but I doubt you'd want to. Christopher has his own drama going on right now. Our house also isn't secure. Jonathan's is. Plus it's huge, and you'll likely only see him when you want to."

"Fine." Did he really have any other choice? He didn't want to go back to the Commonwealth. Not yet. Not until he could figure out how to keep the dreams from coming.

Alexander gave directions. "So if you're going to Jonathan's, you and two of the security guys with us will take Michaela's car and head to Serenity Landing. You'll get there by dinner. My friend will be home this evening. He'll show you around, and we'll head back to Ravenzario from here."

"Fine." He felt like the rebellious teenager he'd rarely been. "Sorry." Not really. And she knew that. He could tell by the look she gave him.

Alexander's phone buzzed, and he went into the kitchen to take the call.

"I love you, Nicky. I'm pretty sure Yvette does, too, even though neither of you may realize it yet. You love her, too, don't you?"

He didn't answer the question. He didn't know how to. Did he have feelings for Yvette? Of course. Far more than he'd expected to have such a short time after the wedding. But did he love her?

That question was one he wasn't ready to answer.

"While we're here, I'm going to arrange for movers to come and pack everything up. It'll be shipped to Ravenzario. So, if you want to take anything with you, you should grab it now. I have no idea how long it'll take to get this stuff shipped or if our things will get mixed in with each other. We could have a hard time finding stuff."

Emotions rolled over Nicklaus like a freight train, and he stood, wrapping his arms around Michaela. "I love you, Mom," he whispered. More and more he was beginning to understand all she'd done for him. He may not like the decisions or things he was asked to do, but the only reason he hadn't died that night in the river or several other times since was because of this woman.

"I love you, too, Nicky." She didn't chastise him for his use of "mom."

Alexander walked back in. "We've got to get going, Michaela. There's an event I need to be at tomorrow. I wasn't supposed to go, but Charlyn asked me."

Nicklaus could hear the unspoken, though mild, rebuke. It was something Nicklaus was supposed to have done. Michaela gave him another squeeze then let go. "I'll see you when you get back."

He just nodded. In an hour, he was in the back seat of a sedan. Not enough leg room, but the security goons sat in the front and hadn't given him much of an option. They crossed the Mississippi River into Missouri, headed southwest on I-44. Nicklaus wanted to ask them to stop, to go back to Edwardsville, or anywhere else, but they didn't seem inclined to conversation of any kind, so he kept his opinion to himself. Mostly, he played inane games on his tablet, brought to him by Michaela, until the battery was nearly dead. He didn't dare ask for a charger. The glare he'd gotten over his radio request was enough to keep him quiet.

Somewhere past Ft. Leonard Wood, he dozed off.

He didn't sleep deeply, but he did dream. Maybe more of a memory than a dream, but vivid.

"Mickey, my tummy hurt."

"I know, sweet boy." They rocked back and forth as metal clanged around them. "We'll be there soon."

Nicklaus couldn't see much. He sat snuggled against Mickey on a bunk somewhere. A boat maybe? That would make sense. It explained the yelling and metal and rocking.

"We in a boat, Mickey?"

"Yes, Nicky. We're on a boat."

"I wanna see."

"Not right now. We have to stay here where it's safe." She sounded scared.

"Mickey..."

Nicklaus startled awake as the car slammed to a stop.

The driving goon glanced back at him. "Sorry, sir. A deer decided to cross the road in front of us."

"No problem." He turned the dream over in his mind. It was new. Not the same one he'd had over the last couple weeks. Had Michaela told him how they got from Ravenzario to Athmetis? The only reason he knew they'd been in Athmetis was an off-hand comment from Tony when he and Michaela told him the whole truth. Maybe they'd been in a boat. Not a yacht or cruise ship, but something else. He'd have to ask her about it later.

They were nearly at their destination. The security goon in the driver's seat punched a button on an intercom by a wrought iron gate. After he spoke to someone for a minute, the gate opened, and they drove in.

Nicklaus contained his whistle as they pulled up to a house less impressive than the palace, but not by much, especially for this part of the world.

"Nice place," non-driving goon commented. Nicklaus should probably learn their names.

Nicklaus opened his own door and walked up the steps to ring the bell. Before he could, the door opened. A smiling, dark haired man a few years older than himself opened the door.

The other man held out a hand. "I'm Jonathan Langley-Cranston. Come on in."

26

Yvette read the text message again.

SORRY I LEFT WITHOUT SAYING ANYTHING. STAYING WITH A FRIEND OF ALEXANDER'S IN THE STATES. I'LL BE BACK SOMETIME SOON, I GUESS. I DON'T KNOW WHEN.

Fabulous. At least she'd heard from him now. Better than the nothing she'd had before. Did she want to text back? Not particularly. She was hurt and annoyed at him for ignoring her for so long already. Two wrongs didn't make a right, but at the moment, Yvette couldn't make herself care.

She sat on the bed she was supposed to be sharing with him and opened Princess Victoria's diary again.

Prince David arrived today. He is far more handsome than I remember. His smile is among the most genuine I have ever seen, but there is sadness in his eyes. I feel he has something to tell me, but does not want to. There is to be a ball tomorrow night. Papa told me to save all of my dances for the prince, except for one with him, of course. What if the prince does not want to dance with me? What if someone else turns his head? Papa has already spoken to him again of the plan for us to marry in the next year, but I do not know Prince David's thoughts on the matter. Or do his thoughts matter as little as mine do?

Victoria's words struck a chord with Yvette. She wanted to be loved by Prince David just as Yvette longed to be loved by Nicklaus. Yvette had looked the history up on the Internet. The difference, of course, was that Victoria would be married to his brother first, widowed, stood up by his other brother, then finally marry David. Maybe the sad thought, the thing David needed to talk to her about, was that his father had decided Victoria would be married to Richard instead of him. Yvette almost didn't want to read any further and find out the inevitable truth. Victoria, though she didn't love David, would still have her heart shattered into a thousand pieces. Her father would be furious. It would lead to nearly breaking up the Commonwealth. Surely that wouldn't have been the other king's intention.

Her phone rang tearing her away from Victoria's world. She closed her eyes and prayed for wisdom when she saw the name on the screen. "Hello, Lizbeth. I have some news for you."

"You do?" Her friend's voice sounded so hopeful. Yvette had no idea if her news would be welcome or not.

"The property is owned by a shell company that is in turn owned by a trust." Yvette wasn't sure she understood what all of that meant.

"Who runs the trust?"

"A lawyer in Mevendia." She looked over her notes again. "Or maybe it's a law firm and this particular lawyer happens to be the one handling it at the moment. I'm not quite clear on what the notes say."

"Thanks. I appreciate your help."

"My pleasure." Yvette leaned back against the headboard. "How was your trip abroad?"

"It went well. It was nice to use some of my skills for something besides shopping and wedding planning."

She could hear the frustration in her friend's voice. "Your father still doesn't want you to work?"

"No, but he let me go on this trip because King Antonio specifically requested my assistance."

Something about her wording bothered Yvette. Why would Lizbeth, who was now in her mid-twenties, need permission from her father to have a job? Or to take a trip?

"I am going to be heading on holiday for a couple nights this weekend, but that's not a business trip."

"Good for you." Yvette glanced at the clock. No wonder she was feeling tired. "I've got to go. Say hello to Robert for me."

"I will." They exchanged a few more words then hung up. She carefully set the diary back on the side table and settled in to get some rest.

With no Nicklaus to keep her company, and already tired of making excuses for where he was, Yvette decided to spend her weekend back in Mevendia. With her family. Who loved her.

First thing the next morning, she took a flight to Mevendia and arrived in time to have breakfast with her brother and sister-in-law. She hadn't seen much of them while they were in town not long before. Malachi apparently had some meetings he'd needed to attend. They also hadn't brought baby Catherine with them, which irked Yvette. How was she supposed to spoil her niece if she never got to see the little girl? She would have to fix that on this trip.

"Have you heard from Nicklaus?" Malachi asked.

Yvette shook her head. "A short text. That's all."

"But Alexander and Michaela found him, right?" Jessabelle asked.

She turned to half-sister/sister-in-law. "He was in Edwardsville, Illinois. I guess that's where they lived until a few weeks before they came back here. They found out someone - Tony - was looking for them and moved somewhere else briefly, but that was the last place he called home. He's in Serenity Landing now. I think he's at the same house you two stayed at."

Jessabelle sipped her water. "We went to Edwardsville, didn't we, Kai?"

"I think so. We stayed somewhere in Illinois for a couple of days." He chuckled. "Wouldn't it be odd if we'd run into them? We didn't meet a Michaela or Nicklaus though."

"She went by Michelle," Yvette reminded him.

Malachi's eyes grew wide. "She did?"

"Yes."

"For weeks, I've been trying to figure out why they both looked familiar. It's not even familiar enough to begin to place where I might know them from, but I couldn't have known them, right?"

"Of course." Yvette didn't know what she was supposed to say.

He turned to his wife. "Remember that barbecue restaurant we went to? The one that claimed to be the best for miles."

Jessabelle nodded. "It was good." Her eyes grew to match his. "The two people sitting next to us? You think that was them?"

"It was a kid about twenty or so and his mom. His name was Nick. Hers was Michelle, wasn't it? And you said something after they left, about something you couldn't quite put your finger on. You weren't sure what it could be."

"Assuming that was them, Nicklaus looks quite a bit like his father, though occasionally there are flashes of Christiana. I'd met Michaela a few times, but I was young. Five or six, I guess, so I wouldn't remember her well."

"Well, there you go." Jessabelle's smile grew. "We met your husband before you did." She glanced at her watch. "I do have a meeting to go to in town. I'll see you both later." She kissed Malachi and left.

Yvette waited for her brother's attention to turn back to her. "That would also explain why Michelle left in a hurry. She probably knew who I was at least. Did you say she kept track of us?"

She shrugged. "Some I guess. I know she kept pictures of me around so Nicklaus would know his father and mine wanted us to get married someday. It's plausible, I think, that she'd know who you were."

Yvetted turned back to her breakfast. "Small world," she muttered. Why couldn't the world get a bit smaller and bring her husband home?

Lizbeth walked into her apartment and tossed most of the mail on the table with her keys. One envelope, though, stood out. She opened it and stared at the note from her father's attorney.

She sank onto the couch. The words came as a blow and a huge surprise, but it probably shouldn't have.

Closing her eyes, she thought through her situation. The note said her father had cut off all of the allowance from the estates of her mother and grandfather. She'd been getting the money since she turned eighteen, and had no idea he could stop it on a whim. Could he do that? Legally, could he stop what was rightfully hers?

And what was rightfully hers? What else didn't she know about the inheritances?

She needed to double check, but first she should have enough money in her personal account, the one her father wasn't supposed to have access to. She wouldn't put it past him to try though.

There was enough money in that account to keep her going for several months. The first thing she needed to do was check.

No.

The first thing she *should* do was call Robert and tell him. He wouldn't let her go hungry or get evicted from her apartment, even though he'd rather she finally moved in with him. She'd rather do that, too, to be quite honest, but not until they got this whole inheritance thing sorted out.

Lizbeth pulled her tablet toward her and checked the account. Her income - the first real earned income of her life - from the diplomatic trip had been deposited the day before. Her heart pounded as she waited for the website to log her in. She closed her eyes and prayed, but when she opened them, her worst fears were realized.

The account had less than half of one percent of what had been in there the day before. Just enough to keep it open because it couldn't be closed without her signature.

Tears streamed down her cheeks as she tried to assimilate everything. A knock on the door cut through her frustration. She ignored it, but the person wouldn't be deterred.

"Ms. Bence, I know you're home," the unfamiliar voice called.

With a groan, she stood and headed for the door. "What?" she demanded as she yanked it open.

The man held out an envelope and waited for her to take it. When she did, he gave a maniacal grin. "You've been served."

"What?"

He didn't answer her question, just headed down the hall, pushing past a surprised looking Princess Jessabelle as he did. Her security team looked annoyed.

Jessabelle turned to look behind her as she approached the door. "Who was..." She stopped and gasped. "What is it, Lizbeth? What happened? Was he bothering you?"

Lizbeth shook her head and went back inside, wiping her tears as she did. "It's nothing."

"Don't lie to me," her friend warned.

"Fine." Lizbeth sank to the couch and opened the envelope. The contents didn't come as much of a surprise. "My father has asked for a hearing to have my inheritances stripped away from me."

Jessabelle sat down next to her, a hand resting on Lizbeth's back. "He can do that?"

"He can try. Robert's attorney doesn't think he has the grounds." Lizbeth flopped back on the couch. "I hate to even ask, but I might need Malachi and even you to vouch for me."

Jessabelle leaned back into the couch and propped her feet up on the coffee table, looking very un-princess-like. "We'll help however we can, but why us?"

"Because one of the ways he can try to get it taken away from me is if I was having an affair with a married man." She didn't look at her friend. There was a time, not long after Prince Malachi married his princess that Lizbeth wouldn't really have thought twice about sleeping with him.

Jessabelle looked puzzled. "No one actually believed those accusations, did they?"

Lizbeth shrugged. "Sometimes it only matters if they think it *could* be true, not if it is. That's why I might need you two to help. I just hope he gets it over with quickly."

"Why quickly? Besides wanting to put it behind you?"

Lizbeth sighed and handed Jessabelle the note from the attorney. "Because I'm quite broke at the moment. I have, literally, no money."

Jessabelle scanned the note. "We'll help. You know that."

"So will Robert. But that's not the point." Fresh tears streaked down Lizbeth's cheeks. "I *finally* made some money of my own, from the trip we went on, and all of that money is gone. That money alone would have lasted me quite a while, but he managed to get to it, too." She sank into the side hug Jessabelle gave her. "I just wanted to prove myself, you know? Just for a few minutes, even."

"I know."

They sat there until Lizbeth took a deep breath and blew it out slowly. She sat up and reached for a tissue to wipe her cheeks with. "We didn't have plans I forgot, did we?"

"No, nothing like that. I was in the neighborhood and wanted to stop by for a few minutes. I haven't seen you since you got back." She reached down and picked up a gift bag. "Happy late birthday."

Lizbeth managed to force a smile to her face and took the bag. At least there was a bit of happiness in this otherwise miserable day. A weekend away with her husband was just what the doctor ordered.

Nicklaus found himself quite unexpectedly enjoying Jonathan's company.

They sat on the back porch of Jonathan's house, each with a beverage. No alcohol. Nicklaus had only just turned twenty-one when he returned to Ravenzario, and Jonathan was a long-recovering alcoholic. His new friend wouldn't say more than that. "So you dated Queen Adeline?"

"I did. In fact, we talked about getting married. We'd already decided not to when they found out she could marry Charlie after all, but if they hadn't been able to, I think we might have given it another shot. No matter, though. She and Charlie are perfect together."

Nicklaus nodded his agreement. He'd met the queen and her husband briefly, but had no clue if they were a good match.

"My grandmothers never knew," Jonathan added with a chuckle. "They would have been over the moon, and it would have been the only acceptable reason for my children to not have my name."

"Valid point I guess. Who do you dare bring home after you dated a queen?"

"She wasn't queen yet, not until a couple days after their

wedding, but she already knew she would be soon." He sighed. "Have you met King Jedidiah?"

Had he? "I'm not sure."

"He's a good man and a good king, but he has Parkinson's. Combine that with a skiing accident that left him pretty banged up, and he had already told her he was going to step down by the end of the summer. After her, I dated Ellie a couple of times. My grandmothers would have grudgingly accepted her because her cousin married the queen. It never really went anywhere though. She was in love with Prince Richard, and we both knew it."

"So you never brought her home?"

"No. The only girl I've even sort of brought home in ages was actually Princess Anastasia." Jonathan didn't say anything else, but sipped on his drink.

After a couple minutes waiting, Nicklaus prodded him. "What happened with her? She's married to a doctor, right?"

Jonathan nodded. "Yep. Dr. Jonah Fontaine, award winning pediatrician, philanthropist, and all around good guy."

"I sense a story." He'd met Dr. Jonah and liked the man.

"I guess. I fell for her. She fell for the doctor. The doctor fell for her, but they had some fundamental disagreements on what her role as a celebrity should be. She liked me well enough. My brother went missing almost two years ago. She came and helped us deal with the press surrounding it. My parents had some issues with her, but they weren't thinking clearly."

"Wow. You've had an eventful dating life." Nicklaus had gone out with exactly five girls, none more than twice, except Tessa. He'd gone out with her three times.

"You don't know the half of it." Jonathan took another gulp of his drink. "I've sworn off dating for a while. I'm focusing on other parts of my life. When the time is right, it'll happen. And if it doesn't, then I guess I'll find a way to be okay with that, too."

"I'm not sure if this arranged marriage is better or worse then."

"From what I know of your father and King Antonio, it wasn't a decision they entered into lightly. They would have sought counsel and direction through prayer, I'd imagine. If that's the case, your marriage to Yvette has God's hand in it, even if the two of you didn't have much choice."

"I suppose." Nicklaus turned those thoughts over in his mind for a while as the sun set in the distance. He could see a few slivers of the lake. They turned the color of fire, marred only by the occasional boat as the sun finally disappeared behind the horizon.

Saturday dawned bright and clear. As much as he hated to, Nicklaus knew he needed a quick trip to the mall. He needed clothes. Nothing outlandish, but a couple pairs of jeans or pants and some shirts. He'd been so annoyed when he left Edwardsville that he hadn't grabbed any of the clothes he'd left there. He did have the suit he'd been wearing when he took off, so he didn't need to worry about that. He didn't expect to need a suit, but if he did, he didn't need to buy one. Nicklaus didn't want to think about the things he was supposed to do back in Ravenzario. Or the language tutoring sessions he was missing. Or the time with his wife and sister he should be enjoying.

Goon One and Goon Two drove him to the local mall then followed him around like puppies.

He held a shirt up and tried to decide if he liked it enough to buy. As he hung it back up, the person next to him spoke.

"You should get it. It would look great with your eyes."

Nicklaus turned to her. "Pardon?"

"I said the shirt would look great with your eyes. That's all." She gave an exasperated roll of her own eyes and went back to looking at the rack in front of her.

"Um, thanks." He'd never enjoyed picking out his own clothes. Though he wasn't sure he needed as many as they'd bought him at the palace, he was glad he didn't have to shop for most of them.

Goon One started to walk over but Nicklaus waved him off. This girl had no idea who he was. Most of the time, Nicklaus didn't either.

"You should try..." She dug through a stack on a nearby display table. "This one." She held out a nice collarless shirt. "It'll look great on you."

He took the shirt and held it up. "Thanks again."

She stuck out her hand. "I'm Eliza."

"Nick." He shook it, but made sure his wedding ring was visible in the hand that held the clothes.

"Why don't you go try those on and see if they fit? I can help you find something else if you need it, too."

He spun in a slow circle. "Jeans and slacks."

"What size do you wear?"

Nicklaus's eyes narrowed. "Why?"

Eliza sighed. "Because. You can go try those on, and I'll pick some out for you. Trust me. I'm good at this."

Reluctant, but glad he didn't have to do the choosing, Nicklaus headed for the dressing room. When he came back out to look at the shirt in the three-way mirror, he had to admit it looked nice, though he couldn't define exactly what it was about this particular shirt.

"Here you go." Eliza walked into the men's dressing area, completely unconcerned about any other men who may have been around.

"Are you supposed to be back here?"

Eliza shrugged and held a pair of pants his way. "Try these on, and let me see."

He kept his sigh inside, but tried them on. She dragged him back out to the floor to look at something else. He had no idea why she didn't bring it to him instead. Then back into the dressing room where he spent probably twenty minutes trying on different clothes.

Eventually, Eliza decided he should only get the one shirt and pants they'd picked up when she'd dragged him back out. Why did he care what this woman thought?

Because it was easier than fighting with her. She was persuasive. Did she work for the store, and he just didn't realize it? Maybe she'd forgotten her name tag?

He finally emerged from his dressing room with his original clothes back on.

"Sorry we didn't find anything else for you, Nick." Eliza leaned up against the wall across from the fitting room. She reached up and rumpled his hair. "Want to try somewhere else?"

"You don't work here?" There went that theory.

"No." She seemed puzzled. "You just looked like a nice guy who needed some help."

They walked toward the entrance to the rest of the store. "Well, thanks anyway, Eliza. I've got to get going, though. No time for another store."

"Oh." Eliza seemed disappointed and turned right in the doorway to the floor. Her voice got louder. "I had fun though." She rested a hand on his chest.

Nicklaus felt his insides twisting. He needed to get out of here, but didn't want to be rude.

And even louder. "Thanks for showing me a good time, Prince Nicklaus."

Before her words could register or he realized what she was doing, Eliza leaned up and kissed him.

27

Yvette sat in her father's office, in the chair she'd loved since she was a little girl and sipped hot cocoa. It was too warm outside, but her father always kept his office cool, and the drink was one of her comfort foods.

"Malachi told me what happened." The kindness in her father's eyes warmed her heart. He had changed so much in the last year.

"He didn't mean to, Papa. I startled him while he was having a nightmare."

He gave her his "I'm the king" look. "Promise me that's what happened?"

She sighed. "Yes. He didn't hit me or abuse me in any way. Nicklaus was in the middle of a bad dream. I touched him. He twisted and sat up all at once, and my face got in the way of his elbow. *That's all,*" she stressed.

"I believe you. If I had believed for one moment he was the kind of man who would do such a thing on purpose I would have found a way around the exile."

"Then why didn't you do that anyway? Why did you insist on the wedding?" She took another sip of the drink.

"Because it likely would have involved fabricating evidence against a man I believed to be a danger to my daughter. It would have been extremely unlikely the evidence would exist."

She gave a half-shrug conceding his point. "I did say something to him I probably shouldn't have without talking to you first, though I made sure he knew the information was a secret."

Her father bowed his head as though praying for strength. "What?"

"When I had the idea about the DNA, he mentioned Malachi was coming, and I told him that wouldn't work. I didn't tell him the whole story. It was enough that he could definitely put together that you're not Malachi's biological father, but that you are Jessabelle's. As for the circumstances surrounding it, we never got into all of that. Yet. I told him I'd tell him the whole thing later."

Her father chuckled. "I expected he'd find out sooner or later. I'd imagine Christiana and Alexander will, too, as you are part of their family now. I also know they all understand the need for discretion, as do you. Granted, I had not thought he would find out so soon. I don't know why it never occurred to any of us that there could be some Y-chromosomal testing we could do since we are descended from the same paternal line."

She changed the subject a bit. "Do you remember the name of the prince who was supposed to marry the Ravenzarian princess?"

He leaned back in his chair and closed his eyes, thinking. "The brothers were Luke, Richard, and David, I do know that much. I'm afraid I'd have to look up any further details. I believe the princess was Victoria. Why?"

She wasn't ready to tell him about her find, the one she'd left hidden back in the turret. She didn't want to share it with anyone just yet. "I'm curious about the other woman who wore the Accord Jewels, that's all."

"How did they come to be in Michaela's possession? Do you know?"

Yvette shook her head. "I haven't asked her. I'd guess it was part of the escape plan for her and Nicklaus."

"I would imagine so."

She sipped on her drink some more while her father turned his attention to his computer, tapping out a quick email. Though she wished he'd pay attention solely to her during this time, he was far better than he used to be. Two years earlier, this conversation would have lasted maybe thirty seconds at most, and he would have had his eyes on a screen of some sort the whole time. As king, he rarely had any time truly to himself. Almost always, his attentions were divided. He'd gotten much better, but she wondered if he'd ever truly be able to break away. Even the times he wasn't on his phone or tablet or computer, there was the chance he'd get called away.

It wouldn't be the same with her children. She'd decided that long ago. Nicklaus had not expressed his thoughts on the matter, but if she had to guess, he felt the same way. Neither of them would be king or queen, barring something happening to both Christiana and the baby - or her older brothers and niece. The odds were long at best.

"Other than the nightmares, how are things with you and Nicklaus?"

She stared into the foam on the top of her drink. "Fine, I guess. I still don't know him well, not really. The nightmares started before we returned to Ravenzario. Since then, he's seemed preoccupied a lot. The documentary days have been hard."

"What excuse have you given them?"

"The same as everyone else. He's not feeling well. As long as no pictures of him in the States show up online, they should buy it. Hopefully, he'll be back soon. It was raining and cool the other day when we were shooting the special. It's plausible he caught something, I guess."

"Does he remember?"

She shook her head and took another sip as a chill ran through her thinking about that night. "Not really. I think it's what the nightmares are about. He's trapped in the car, then in the freezing water." Yvette wrapped her hands more tightly around the mug. "I can't tell you why I think this, but I think it was a much closer thing than Michaela has let on."

"You think they almost didn't survive that first day?"

"If I had to guess, from his nightmares and what I've gathered, I think they almost didn't survive the first half hour."

"I need to talk with Ms. Engel, I think." He tapped his pen. "I know Christiana is planning some sort of thank you for her. Likely she'll be given an order of the highest honor of service to the crown. I forget what they call it. It wouldn't surprise me to find she and Tony are both given titles upon their wedding." His voice turned contemplative. "I think maybe I need to talk with her and come up with a way for Mevendia to thank her as well. If not for her, things could have turned out much differently all those years ago."

Yvette wasn't sure what her father meant, and he didn't seem inclined to explain further. As she took the last swallow of her drink, he stood.

"Let's go find that granddaughter of mine. I think she needs some time with her papa."

It felt more like an excuse to get out of his office all together. With his arm around her shoulders, Yvette leaned into his strength and thanked God he was the father she needed him to be. He may not have always been, but he was now. She had a feeling she would need his strength even more in the days to come.

Nicklaus balked at the idea of going to church with Jonathan, but finally decided it was probably the best idea. He needed to be in church. Had he gone since they'd left Edwardsville? Only once or twice in Mallard Lake?

He sat next to his new friend on the right side of the sanctuary at Grace Community Chapel. It had been converted from an old grocery store according to Jonathan. The service was a good one, similar to the churches he'd gone to growing up. He left feeling a bit convicted about putting everything in the hands of his loving Father.

In the foyer, Jonathan was stopped by a couple with two small girls. The older one was maybe five and the younger probably not yet two. At least that was his guess.

Jonathan introduced them. "Nicklaus, this is Josh and Stephanie. They live not too far from me."

He shook hands with Josh, but Stephanie was pulled the other direction by the older girl.

"That's Alyssa," Josh explained, picking the toddler up and flipping her over his shoulder. "She doesn't know how to sit still."

"Josh and Stephanie own the local comedy club," Jonathan explained.

"That's great." Nicklaus didn't know what he was supposed to do with that information.

"You should come next weekend. We'd love to have you."

Nicklaus rubbed the back of his neck. "I'm not sure I'll still be here next weekend."

"Then let me know next time you're in town. My treat."

Jonathan jumped back in. "Remember the girl your nanny taught to swim last year?"

Josh looked to be thinking it over. "Yeah. Some friends of yours from Europe, right?"

"Nicklaus married Malachi's little sister not too long ago."

Recognition appeared in Josh's eyes. "Oh! Right. Well, still, if you're ever in town, you and your entourage are welcome."

So Josh knew Malachi and Jessabelle? That meant he knew Malachi was a prince and his younger sister would be a princess.

If nothing else, that meant he knew Nicklaus was royal by marriage. Didn't Jonathan know how to keep his mouth shut?

"You don't have to worry about them," Jonathan told him quietly. "They have more security at their house than I do. I'm pretty sure his late, former father-in-law was the richest man in the state. Josh's first wife and father-in-law died in the same car accident, and Josh inherited almost everything."

Okay. Nicklaus wasn't sure what he was supposed to do with that information either.

"There's someone else I think you should meet." Jonathan did a full three hundred and sixty degree turn looking around the foyer. "There's her son. Travis!"

Nicklaus had little choice but to follow in Jonathan's wake. By the time he caught up, Jonathan was asking the other guy where his mother was.

"She's home sick today. Not feeling great." He held out a hand Nicklaus's way. "Travis Harders."

He shook the other man's hand. "Nick." He didn't know what last name to give.

"How're things going for you?" There was concern in Jonathan's voice.

Travis shrugged. "They are what they are. God's got it under control." He gave Nicklaus a wry grin. "Sometimes I wish He'd clue the rest of us in a bit sooner."

Nicklaus surprised himself by voicing his agreement, then going on. "My mom always told me God's weaving this tapestry, and we're all a part of it. If you look at the back all you see is the mess, but when He's done, the front is beautiful. I wish He'd show us the front a little more often."

Travis chuckled. "You and me both, my friend. I'll tell you this, though. I've gotten a glimpse at the front of that tapestry a few times. I see bits of it every time I look at my daughter. God's got a plan for all of this, even if He's not letting us in on it. Your mom was right. It's a beautiful tapestry. Sometimes it's rough when you're going through it. No one knows that more than I do, but in the end, it's worth it." He clapped Nicklaus on the shoulder. "And speaking of my daughter, she's glaring at me to hurry up. See ya later." He waved as he walked off.

"His mom is a retired counselor," Jonathan explained as they walked out to his car. "I thought she might be a good one for you to talk through some of this stuff with. But you know, Travis might be a great one, too. I don't know his whole story, and he's a high school drama teacher not a therapist, but there's something about him that screams wisdom, you know?"

Nicklaus nodded, though he had no intention of talking to either Travis or his mother. Back at the house, he went to his room and shut the door behind him. Suddenly, he found he didn't particularly want to talk to anyone. He needed to go home, to his new home, talk to Michaela and get the whole story about their trek to safety. Then hug his wife and apologize to her again. And again. And again.

And set out to try to be the man he knew God wanted him to be. The husband. Eventually the father. Until then, the brother, the friend, the son God designed him to be. Travis and Michaela were right about one thing. The tapestry had to be beautiful on the front. If the messiness was any inverse correlation to the beauty, it would be stunning.

He flopped on the bed and stared at the ceiling. "Okay, God. You've got my attention. Now what?"

There was no audible voice. No whirlwind. No fire or storm. No still, small voice. Just a pervasive sense of peace when he thought about returning to Ravenzario. Finally, he pulled out his phone and sent a text to Goon One.

Time to go home.

28

Y vette woke from a sound sleep when someone slipped
into bed next to her.

"It's me."

Nicklaus. She closed her eyes again and breathed prayer of
relief for several reasons. "When did you get back?" she whispered
back.

"A few minutes ago. I asked them not to tell you I was on
my way."

She pushed up until she was sitting straight. "Why did you
come here and not Ravenzario?"

"Because you're here." He rested the palm of his hand on her
cheek, his fingers tangling in her hair. "I wanted to be where
you are."

"I'm glad you're here."

"How's your cheek?"

He'd remembered, and his thumb brushed against her other
cheekbone. "Better. Not healed yet, but better than it was."

He rested his forehead on hers. "I'm so sorry, Evie. I didn't
mean to."

"I know." Yvette tilted her chin until she could kiss him. "If you'd done it on purpose or in a fit of rage, you wouldn't be here now. I'm a member of two royal families with connections around the world. You wouldn't get anywhere near me again."

He snorted. "Royal families, nothing. You would take me out. Or Michaela if she heard about it. Or both of you."

She giggled. "Most likely."

Nicklaus sobered. "I would *never* hurt you on purpose, Evie."

"I know."

"Do you really?"

"Yes." But now he was scaring her. What could he have to tell her?

"Then there's something else I need to tell you. I don't quite understand what happened or how it happened, but you should know because I have a feeling it's going to come back to haunt me."

She searched his eyes in the dim lighting. "What?" It couldn't be that awful, could it?

He shifted until he sat next to her. "I didn't take much with me, and there wasn't much at the house in Edwardsville that I wanted, so I went to the mall yesterday."

"Okay." Nothing earth shattering there, though she typically didn't shop at Aeropostale or Old Navy.

"I was looking at shirts and some girl offered to help me pick out clothes. I thought she might work there or something. I didn't really think much about it. She kept coming into the outer part of the dressing room and giving me more clothes. Sounds like an employee, right?"

Yvette nodded slowly, unsure of where this was going.

"After trying on a bunch of clothes and deciding I didn't want most of them, we're walking back out of the dressing room area, and she stops me." He rubbed the back of his neck. "She leaned against me pretty hard, so I grabbed her waist to keep us both from falling, and she kissed me. That's it," he hurried on. "One kiss where I was so surprised I didn't push her away. I certainly didn't kiss her back."

She blew out a slow breath. "I'm not crazy about it, but I have no reason to believe you'd be lying to me about what happened. So I believe you, and just promise you won't kiss some other random girl any time between now and forever, and we're good."

"Thank you, and I have no intention of it, but that's not the part that worries me."

Yvette waited for him to go on.

"She knew who I was. Right before she kissed me, she called me Prince Nicklaus." Even without a lamp on, Yvette could see the worry in his eyes. "The whole time she was grabbing clothes and back in the dressing area alone with me, she knew who I was. She was never in the..." He made a square gesture with his hands. "...actual dressing room thing, just in the outer part. The vestibule or whatever, but the goons who were with me weren't back there."

"Goons?"

"Yeah." He winced. "I wasn't happy about the security guys going with me. I didn't remember their names so I called them Goon One and Goon Two in my head. Not very kind or princely of me, I know, and I promise I'll do better in the future. My point is that they were out on the floor. I'm sure if I'd started yelling or something, they would have been in there fast." He ran a hand through his hair. "But she had an agenda of some kind. I don't know what it could be, but why else would she have done all that?"

Yvette slid her hand between his bicep and his chest, sliding it along his arm until she could link her fingers with his. "I don't know." She rested her head on his shoulder. "But whatever it is, we'll face it together. We may never hear from her again," she added optimistically, knowing it was unlikely.

Nicklaus let go of her hand and wrapped his arm around her, pulling her close to him. "I don't deserve you, Evie. All of you have warned me about this stuff, now that I'm alive again and all. I didn't listen."

She snuggled into his side. "I don't think any of us deserve each other. Deep down, the reality is that all of us have faults. We're petty or jealous and vindictive, needlessly cruel to others, something that makes us unworthy, not only of the love from our family and friends, but from our Heavenly Father. If some of the thoughts I'd thought when I was planning the wedding ever came out, you'd know I don't deserve you either. I thought some pretty unpleasant things about a dead guy."

He kissed the side of her head. "You might have a point."

"Of course I do. Ask my father sometime about how much he deserves my mother."

"He told me a little bit. Warned me about ever cheating on you."

She picked at the sheet. "I insinuated some stuff when we were talking a while ago that I never explained. My father knows I'm telling you, but otherwise no one outside of my immediate family and Nana Yvette know."

"No one will hear it from me."

"My father had the least secret affair in the history of affairs. An employee who was in love with his mistress drugged and assaulted my mother. No one knew about it until several years later when he returned to work at the palace and Mother freaked out. He was arrested and is in prison forever. At the time, they realized there was a chance this man was Malachi's father. For all his other faults, my father never even considered that Malachi wasn't his son. He knew it was a possibility, but it never mattered to him. He ended the affair, and the mistress disappeared into the night."

"Okay, but what does that have to do with Jessabelle?"

"Only Nana Yvette knew that his mistress was pregnant. She also knew about the drugging and rape. Sometime in the intervening years, she had the testing done and knew Malachi wasn't my father's biological child. A little over a year ago, it all came out. They had the DNA testing done again, just to make sure Malachi and Jessabelle weren't half-siblings. They're not, though they're both half-siblings to William and me. If anyone knows what it's like to watch your family fall apart because of stupid things you've done, it's my father. He blamed himself for what happened to my mother. It turned him into a hard man for many years. It's only in the last year or so that he's becoming the man he should be. He's admitted that."

Nicklaus's hand rubbed up and down her arm. "I can see why he'd make his position on infidelity extremely clear, then."

"Whatever comes from this girl, Nicky, we'll deal with it together. I believe you. I trust you." She tilted her head up so she could see him. "It's you and me."

He kissed her. "You and me," he repeated, then kissed her again.

Lizbeth sat outside the king's office on the first floor of the palace and waited. She'd been summoned by him, but had no idea why. Could she have done something wrong on the trip? Violated some protocol she was unaware of?

Jessabelle walked out of the office door and smiled at her. After exchanging a hug, Lizbeth's friend whispered, "Go on in. He's waiting for you, but there's nothing to be scared about."

All right then. Jessabelle knew what all this was about. Time for Lizbeth to find out. She curtsied as the king rose from his desk chair. "Good morning, Your Majesty."

King Antonio walked around the desk and held out his hand for her to shake. "None of that nonsense today, Ms. Bence." He gestured toward a chair. "Or should I say Mrs. Padovano?"

Lizbeth felt her face heat. "We wondered if you knew, and that's why you asked me to go on that trip."

The king chuckled. "Oh, I knew, but that is not why I asked you to go. Or not only why I asked you to go, rather. After watching you plan Yvette's wedding, I knew you were the perfect person to assist Robert, wife or not."

"Thank you, sir."

He sat back down in his chair and leaned on his forearms. "Now, it has come to my attention that the funds you were sent the other day have been absconded with?"

She nodded, embarrassed he knew about it. "That's correct. No one is supposed to have access to that account but me."

"Do you know who did it?"

Lizbeth hesitated then shook her head. "I have suspicions but no proof."

"Duly noted. Who do you suspect?"

She didn't look him in the eye. "My father."

"I see." The king pulled a manila envelope out of the drawer and pushed it across the desk. "In there is a checkbook and card associated with a palace account. In that account is the amount of money you were paid. You will not be able to overdraw, but the funds are yours to do with as you see fit. They are not accessible by anyone else."

Lizbeth took the envelope, her eyes blinking rapidly in surprise. "Wow. Thank you, sir. You didn't have to do this. It wasn't your fault."

"I know, but I believe in taking care of those who are in my employ, even temporarily, when a catastrophe strikes. I will also see to it that this is not counted twice as income for your taxes."

She hadn't even thought about that yet. "Thank you, sir."

He gave her a kind smile, one she'd never seen from him before. "Promise me something, Mrs. Padovano?"

"Of course."

"If you have any further troubles with your father, please come to me. I may not be able to help personally, but I can certainly pull some strings if I need to."

She couldn't believe her ears. Sure, she was friendly with several members of the royal family and had spent holidays with the family at one of their other homes, but she'd never had an informal relationship with the king. "Thank you, sir." She didn't know what else to say.

"My pleasure, Mrs. Padovano. The only thing I ask is that you keep this between us for now. I have my reasons for wanting your father especially not to know about this for the time being."

Lizbeth nodded and stood as he did. "Of course. Thank you again, sir."

She left his office clutching the envelope and giving thanks for how her fortunes had suddenly changed. If only they could get through the hearing in one piece, it would be okay.

29

Nicklaus opened the door to their apartment to let Michaela in. He gave her the biggest hug he'd given anyone in a while. The early morning flight had returned him and Yvette to Ravenzario. The first thing he'd done was ask Michaela for a meeting. Yvette would join them in a few minutes. She wanted to hear it, too.

"I'm so glad you're back." Michaela gave him another hug as they reached the sitting area.

"Me, too."

"What is it you want to talk about?"

He glanced toward the bedroom where Yvette had gone to freshen up. "Yvette will be out in a minute, but I think it's time you told me everything about the accident and what happened afterward."

She stared at her hands. "I'm not sure I want to do that. What's the point in reliving it all?"

"The point is that I'm having nightmares about it. Things I can't quite see or understand. And when Yvette touched me at the end of one of them, I hit her in the cheek with my elbow. I *need* to know, to understand. Then maybe the memories won't have a hold on me anymore.

Michaela nodded slowly. "All right." Before she could say anything else, Yvette walked in and sat next to him. "I'll tell you everything."

Nicklaus leaned back and let Yvette take his hand, linking their fingers and covering them with her other hand. She was there to support him.

"The river was higher and faster than I've led all of you to believe." She pinched the bridge of her nose.

Nicklaus glanced up to see Tony walk in, but Michaela didn't notice.

"We were almost swept away a couple of times. We both went under more than once."

That explained that part of the dreams.

"I prayed desperately. I think your father was still alive and praying, too. Every time, getting us to the next spot where we weren't under water wasn't something I could have done in my own strength, not even with all the adrenaline running through me. We finally made it around the bend and got out. That part was pretty much the way I said it, except we were more thoroughly soaked. I was so scared I'd fall and not be able to get back up, that we'd freeze to death. When we finally made it to the cabin, the woman there got us dry blankets to wrap around us while she dried our clothes in front of the fireplace. We hid out in a root cellar for two days. In the middle of the night, she put us in the back of a delivery truck, hidden by boxes. I don't know how long we drove. We may have taken a ferry between the two islands even. I'm not really sure."

She swiped at the tears streaking down her cheeks. Tony stood behind her, his face the picture of compassion. "Eventually, a man I've never seen before or since moved the boxes and took my hand. He never spoke to me. Over the years, I've wondered if he wasn't an angel, not human at all. He took us to another spot to hide, but when I looked around to see where he went, he was gone. All I really remember is a bushy beard and green eyes."

Michaela took a deep breath as though to strengthen herself and sat a bit straighter. "A while later, another man showed up and asked if we were the special cargo bound for Athmetis. I knew that was supposed to be our first real stop so I said yes. We hadn't eaten since we left the cellar. You were crying but doing such a good job being quiet. It was like you understood."

"Did he put us on a boat? A ship of some kind?"

Yvette's hand tightened around his.

"Yes. It was a fishing vessel. We hid in one of the bunks they weren't using. Someone brought us food a few times, but it took several days to get to Athmetica. They even stopped at another port in Athmetis first."

Nicklaus looked over at his wife. "I'm pretty sure that's what I was dreaming about the other night when I hit Yvette with my elbow. I know Christiana called you Mickey, but did I?"

She nodded. "Until I told you it was important you call me mom or Michelle. You both called me Mickey when we lived here. Before long you didn't remember it."

"I asked if I could go out and see the ocean, didn't I?"

"You did," she confirmed. "After a while, we made it to Athmetica. Yaya came to the docks that morning to get some fish. The man who'd asked if we were the special cargo pointed at her and told me to follow that lady. I did. She never looked at us until we reached the courtyard of her home. By then were exhausted and asleep on my shoulder. She opened the secret door and pointed to the room without ever looking at us and said, 'You wait here. I bring you food and clothes.' We spent most of the next month in there. She brought us food several times a day, and when no one was home or everyone was asleep, we'd go inside."

"I don't remember any of that," Nicklaus admitted. "All I remember is what's come in those dreams."

"Maybe it'll come back to you, but I hope not. It wasn't a fun time. We had a little bit of light in there. Enough to see, but that's it. We needed to make sure our trail had gone cold. Police came to Yaya's a couple of times while we were there, saying people had heard strange noises at night. Yaya never believed it was the neighbors calling the police. She thought they were part of the group coming after us. It wouldn't surprise me if she was right."

Nicklaus didn't think his admiration for Michaela could grow any further, but it had.

"After no one had come for two weeks, she took us to another man, an old man this time, who had fake papers for us. He put us on a cruise ship to France. This time we were regular passengers, but we'd changed our appearance. Your hair had gotten long and scraggly. I cut mine super short and dyed it. We kept mostly to ourselves except for meals. I didn't want to have them delivered because I didn't know if room service would cost extra. The story was still all over the news, though no one knew our bodies hadn't been found. I often wondered if that wasn't divine providence."

"It was." Tony finally spoke.

Michaela didn't look surprised but looked over her shoulder to see him.

"You know how there are stories that came out of the Holocaust where those in danger prayed, and the eyes of the searchers were closed?"

They all nodded.

"I was the first one to the car. I knew you were gone, but didn't know what happened. It had to be about the time you got out of the river. The king grabbed my hand. I've told a few people, like Alexander, that he gave me the name of an obscure file, but it was more than that. He said, 'They're alive, Tony. Don't let anyone find them. Pray harder than you've ever prayed.' Then he gave me the name of the file. It was like he'd been waiting for me to get there, to pass on the information. His hand went slack and, when I checked for a pulse, it was gone. I checked the queen, and she was gone, too."

He rested his hands on Michaela's shoulders. "I took his words to heart. I prayed harder than I'd ever prayed before. I prayed that your survival would remain a secret, though I had no idea how to orchestrate that. Later, I overheard some of the emergency personnel talking. All of them knew *they* hadn't seen your bodies, but knew someone else who had. They didn't think about it too deeply. I've long believed it was the opposite of what happened in the Holocaust. God caused those men to believe they saw something they didn't, because He had a bigger plan all along."

Yvette rested her head on Nicklaus's shoulder, watching the tender moment between Tony and Michaela.

"I prayed for you constantly in those first few weeks. I prayed for your safety. I prayed Nicklaus wouldn't be afraid, that he wouldn't inadvertently give you away. I prayed for the right doors to be opened and the wrong ones to be closed. Over time, the frequency decreased, but I still prayed. Daily. Usually more often. Every time either of you came to mind, I prayed. Every time I suspected Henry of something dirty, I prayed. Every time, I asked God to tell me when you needed my prayers most."

He leaned over and kissed Michaela's head. "I haven't told you this yet, but having talked through some of the history with you, I'm pretty sure those times that I knew one or both of you were in danger were real. When Nicklaus had surgery that didn't go as planned. When he had a bee sting that nearly killed him. When you were in the car accident that should have been much worse, and if it had been, they might have dug further into your background and discovered not everything was as it seemed."

"Thank you," Michaela whispered. She reached up and squeezed his hands where they still rested on her shoulders. "Thank you."

"At the same time, I prayed that once Henry was taken care of, I'd find the right woman to settle down with. Someone who would understand my devotion to the royal family will have to come first sometimes. I never could have imagined that I was praying for the same person."

"It's part of the beautiful tapestry God is weaving out of our lives." Yvette wiped the tears off her own cheeks.

"I told Nicklaus that all the time." Michaela smiled at both of them. "You two are definitely something beautiful."

Tony's phone buzzed, and his head dropped. "And duty calls. Thank you for telling us the whole story, love." He kissed the top of Michaela's head again. "I love you."

"I love you, too." She squeezed his hands one more time before he removed them and left. She turned back to them. "Are there any other questions I can answer for you, Nicky?"

He shook his head. "I don't think so. Not now. I might have some more later."

Michaela stood, and Nicklaus rose to meet her. Yvette watched as he hugged her, bringing healing to both of them.

"Maybe now the nightmares will stop." Nicklaus left his arm around her shoulder. "You shouldn't have to sleep in fear, Evie."

She rolled her eyes at him. "I don't. It was an accident. Move on."

Michaela jumped in. "I don't plan to tell anyone else all of the details, you know. Not unless I need to for some reason. That's why I didn't tell you for so long. I didn't see the point."

"We won't repeat the stories unless we have to," Yvette reassured her. "There's no need for anyone else to know. Christiana, especially, has no need to know the whole truth. She's torn up enough about it as it is."

Michaela rested her head on Nicklaus's shoulder. "I thanked God she wasn't in the car. If she had been, you'd both be dead. Even if I'd gone with you, and squeezed in the middle, I never could have carried both of you through that river. I probably couldn't have made it with Christiana if it had been her in the car instead of you."

"God does things for a reason." Yvette stood and stretched. "Not to rush you guys, but I haven't eaten yet."

"There's string cheese in the fridge." Nicklaus grinned at her.

She wrinkled her nose. "No, thank you."

"Suit yourself."

Michaela shook her head. "I tried to refine his palate. I really did."

"I know." She checked her phone as it gave a single buzz. "I have a meeting in ten minutes, all the way down on the first floor. I guess I'm going to have to grab one of those cheese things." She also grabbed an individual serving of juice Nicklaus liked to keep in the fridge. Not her favorite breakfast, but it would have to do.

Once on the first floor, Yvette found the conference room where the leaders of a local charity waited for her. They were trying to convince her to become a patron of their organization. She probably would, but she wanted to hear the presentation first. It wasn't overly impressive but it wasn't completely forgettable either. She promised to think it over as they went on their way. The charity was a worthy one, but she had only so much time to go around. She wasn't nearly at her capacity yet, but if she wasn't careful, she'd find her schedule overly full and have no time for causes she found herself more interested in - or for schooling or starting a family when the time came.

She needed to talk to Nicklaus about their schooling plans. If they were going to attend university this fall, they needed to get that arranged soon. When she reached the apartment again, Nicklaus was there reading over some paperwork. He invited her to join him and asked about her meeting. They talked about it and just a few random things, nothing deep or serious.

A knock on the door caused them both to turn.

"Come," Nicklaus called.

Tony walked in, looking much more serious than he had when

he left an hour and a half earlier.

"What is it?" she asked.

"Do you two know Lizbeth Bence?"

Yvette nodded. "Of course. She helped me plan the wedding. She's been friends with Malachi for years and is friends with Jessabelle, too."

He looked at Nicklaus waiting for an answer.

Nicklaus shrugged. "I guess. I think I met her the day before the wedding. I don't know that I talked to her at all, though."

Tony held up a picture. "Do you recognize this woman?"

Yvette squinted. The photo had been taken from a distance and wasn't terribly clear. "Is that Lizbeth?"

"That's what we need to know."

"Why?"

Nicklaus took the picture from him and looked at it more closely. "I think I know this girl."

She and Tony both looked at him.

He turned to look at her. "Remember what I told you last night? About the girl at the store?"

Her heart stopped in her chest. "Yes," she whispered, afraid of where this was going.

"I think this is her. I'm not completely sure, but I think so." He handed it back to Tony. "I think she said her name was Liza or Eliza, something like that."

"Not Lizbeth?"

He shook his head. "No. I would have remembered that. I knew her name even if I don't really remember her. Why?"

"Lizbeth is in the middle of some court stuff about her inheritance. Her father produced this photo." He picked up another one but didn't show it to them yet. "There's a video to go with it."

Tony turned the photo around.

There was Nicklaus. His arms locked around this woman's waist, and her lips on his.

"Her father is accusing the two of you of having an affair."

30

Nicklaus paced around the room. "How is that even possible? I've met her once. Maybe. Twice, tops."

Tony sighed. "Unfortunately, unless she gets a sympathetic judge, the burden of proof rests on her, not on her father."

"Well, I guess I have proof of where I was, but without proof of where she was, I don't know that it matters."

"Is Lizbeth claiming to have had an affair?" Yvette asked.

Nicklaus looked over at his wife. "Good question."

"No, she's vehemently denying it, though last I heard she hadn't told anyone where she was this weekend either, just that she was away."

"Will I need to testify?" Nicklaus stopped his pacing. "I mean, I will if I need to, but then I'd have to explain why I was in the States. I'd rather not have to tell the entire Commonwealth that I'm having nightmares and accidentally hit my wife."

"Hopefully it won't come to that, but it might," Tony warned.

"In the meantime," Yvette interrupted. "We need to finish filming the documentary and get Nicklaus out among the people.

The more they know him and see him advocating on their behalf, the more likely they are to give him the benefit of the doubt. That's not the only reason to do it, but it won't hurt." She pulled out her phone and started to make arrangements.

A few hours later, Nicklaus tried to keep his knee from bouncing up and down, but failed miserably. It was annoying Yvette, but she didn't say anything.

"Why are you nervous?"

Her quiet voice helped soothe his nerves.

"I never liked public speaking."

"Unfortunately, it's something you're going to have to get used to."

"I know. Doesn't mean I like it."

The car pulled to a stop in front of the museum. "What kind of place is this again?" He should remember but all he could think about was the speech coming up.

"The reopening of the Ancient portion of the Ravenzario Historical Museum." She hesitated. "We will be expected to tour the entire facility with a guide, since neither of us has been here before. I would imagine there is a section on the death of your parents." She stopped, though he sensed she had more to say. "And you and Michaela. There's probably still a whole display about your death."

The mere thought made Nicklaus feel sick to his stomach.

A security guard opened his door, preventing him from asking any more questions. Nicklaus turned to offer Yvette a hand. After she emerged, she linked her fingers with his. Using gentle pressure, she urged him toward the crowds nearby.

"Princess Yvette! Prince Nicklaus!" Many of the onlookers were girls, not too much younger than Yvette. Most of the rest were women, though, with only a few men scattered about.

One woman held tight to his hand as he shook it. "I am so glad you're alive, Prince Nicklaus. We mourned your death for weeks."

"Thank you." Was that the appropriate response?

She turned to Yvette. "And you, Your Highness. Welcome to Ravenzario! We've watched you grow up, and my family was always so sad you wouldn't end up as a Ravenzarian princess as well. We are glad you're here!"

Yvette inclined her head slightly. "Thank you. I have always loved my time in Ravenzario. I am glad it is now my home."

Was she really? Or did she wish they'd remained in Mevendia?

They worked their way down the line, mostly just saying hello. They took a few pictures, both selfies with a few who asked for them and more posed photos of the two of them.

Once they walked inside, Nicklaus hoped he would get a few minutes to let down his guard, but no such luck. A number of people already there waited to meet them. After about ten minutes, they walked into a full auditorium. The director of the museum made a few opening statements then introduced Nicklaus. He walked to the podium, shaking hands with the man when he was near enough.

He took his spot and looked at the speech prepared for him. With less than two hours' notice, they'd put it together, but he'd only skimmed it.

"Good afternoon, members of the conservation society, honored guests, ladies and gentlemen, and..." He turned toward Yvette. "...my wife, one of Ravenzario's newest residents. Though, to be honest, I've really only lived here about a week longer than she has. I know. I was born the Crown Prince and would have been the monarch someday, if not for the accident that killed my parents and sent myself and my nanny on the run, in fear for our lives. I remember very little of my first few years. My mother made sure I studied Ravenzarian history." He glanced down realizing what he'd said and hearing the murmurs. "That is, Michaela, my nanny." He hadn't wanted to get into all of this, but felt he had no choice. "I always knew Michaela wasn't my biological mother, though I never knew the true circumstances surrounding my family of origin. As a young child, I began calling her mom most of the time. It was easier than explaining a story I didn't understand, but inherently knew was a very painful one." Hopefully that was enough.

"Every summer, she taught me about two countries. One in Europe and one of the Belles Montagnes countries or some other country around the world. I studied Ravenzarian history through World War II two or three times. I hated all that summer studying." The crowd chuckled. "But knowing what I know now, I understand and appreciate her rationale. I am grateful I know as much about the countries of the Commonwealth as I do. I look forward to spending quite a bit of time here and at the sister museums in Mevendia and Montevaro, learning more about my heritage."

After he finished speaking, Nicklaus returned to his front row seat next to Yvette. She squeezed his hand, letting him know she thought he'd done well. There were a few closing remarks, followed by a reception in the rotunda. Yvette stayed close to his side, her hand often sliding into his elbow or holding his own, reminding him he wasn't alone.

As the reception wound down, the curator of the museum walked with them through the ancient wing. Just a quick tour. Nicklaus would come back later and look much more closely. In the 1800s area, he found a display that made him especially curious. A replica of the Van Rensselaer Accord Jewels hung around the neck of a wax figure identified as Princess Victoria. He read the plaque as the curator explained the story.

"Princess Victoria married Prince Richard of Mevendia. A few days later, he went off to war and died. She was to have married Crown Prince Luke, but Prince Luke decided to marry someone else and ran off with her, despite the wedding being just two days away. At the last minute, she married Prince David instead. They went on to have several children. Their oldest son eventually became King of Ravenzario."

"Why?" Nicklaus asked the man. Yvette had told him about this, hadn't she?

"Her brother became king, but only reigned for about ten years. He died without an heir. Their son was the next in line."

"Why didn't Princess Victoria become queen?" He should know this.

"She had already passed. And technically, she was a princess of Mevendia by then. According to the laws of the time, she was no longer eligible. Her son, though, was in line for both thrones, though much further down the line for the Mevendian throne."

The rest of the story came back to him. This was why the Y-chromosome testing was possible - and being done. Prince David's son became king of Ravenzario and was Nicklaus's eighth great grandfather or something to that effect. Prince Luke, brother of Prince David and uncle to the eventual Ravenzarian king, became King Luke of Mevendia. Both royal families could be traced, through the patrilineal lines, to that set of male siblings.

He turned, managing not to show his surprise at the television camera there. Of course. The documentary. How could he have forgotten they were still being followed? They followed the curator around a corner and into the modern history portion of the museum. The next hundred years went by quickly. The curator hesitated before approaching the next display. Nicklaus knew why even before he saw it.

It was the display proclaiming his death.

Yvette hated the display they were about to see. It represented so much wrong in the last twenty years. The official family photo, all four of them, was the centerpiece. The king sat in a chair in the reception room, with the Christmas tree behind and to his left. Behind and to his right stood the queen, with Christiana in front of her. Young Prince Nicklaus stood in front of his sister. All were wearing their royal best.

"This photo was taken just a week before..." The curator didn't finish. He likely didn't know how.

Yvette felt the corners of her mouth twitch. "You were cute." Complete with sash proclaiming his Crown Prince status.

He winked at her, though she knew it was only because there were others present, making himself seem much more confident than he really was. "I'm still cute."

Yvette rolled her eyes, but rested her temple against his shoulder. "Of course you're still cute."

His grip tightened on her hand. The next parts of the display would be difficult at best. Another picture showed the whole family the day before the accident, taken by the official photographer as they spent some time at an orphanage. The next photo was from that morning with the king and queen, Nicklaus and Michaela leaving the hotel to climb into the auto driven by the king. Then came emergency vehicles blocking the mountain road as the rescue mission must have been underway.

Those had all been medium sized pictures. The next two were larger. Four coffins at the front of the largest cathedral in Ravenzario. Then a little girl, blond hair, big blue eyes, and a crown far too large for her small head, surrounded by those coffins.

Was that a teddy bear peeking out from the folds of the coronation robes?

She'd only been five. Her world turned upside down.

"I've never seen her coronation photos." Nicklaus's somber tone fit the mood.

"All of us were shocked the coronation was held at the funeral." The curator sounded the same way. "Most coronations are held several months later because you don't want to celebrate when you're in mourning. Queen Elizabeth II became Queen of the United Kingdom upon her father's death in February 1952, but her coronation wasn't until June. Her grandmother, Queen Mary, died in May of that year, but the coronation went ahead, as her grandmother wanted. Queen Adeline's was different because King Jedidiah stepped down, but generally it's some time later."

"So why was it done then?" Nicklaus asked the question, but Yvette knew the answer.

The curator answered first. "All we can ascertain is that it had something to do with Henry Eit consolidating his power."

Yvette wondered how much was public knowledge, and if it even mattered anymore. "My father tried to become her regent. Perhaps the coronation had something to do with keeping him out of power, keeping my father from taking control on Christiana's behalf. He might not be a Ravenzarian, but he'd have been a far, far better regent than Henry was."

"I don't know that your father's efforts were ever public knowledge." The curator turned thoughtful. "But I doubt it would surprise anyone."

They took a couple more steps, and something else caught Yvette's eye. On a fancy easel, a large placard contained an update.

"Prince Nicklaus and his nanny, Michaela Engel, were long believed deceased in the December 23, 1999 car accident," she read. "In June 2017, Prince Nicklaus and Ms. Engel reappeared, just in time for his wedding to Princess Yvette of Mevendia. The details of their escape and sojourn have not yet been made public. More details will be added as they are available." Below the text was one of the official photos from their wedding. Not her favorite of the photos, but a nice one. Her favorite ones, the most intimate of them, where their fledgling feelings began to seep through, hadn't been released to the public.

"I think I'm ready to go."

Yvette glanced up at Nicklaus to see him staring at the pictures of the funeral and coronation. "Let's go." She squeezed his hand.

He took one last look at the photos then turned away, and they left.

A few days later, their plane landed in Mevendia. The interviews for the documentary were complete, and it was time to help Lizbeth deal with her father. Rather than going to the room she'd grown up in like she had while Nicklaus was in the States, Yvette found herself in a guest suite reserved for visiting dignitaries.

"Is this weird for you?" Her husband's voice startled her.

She turned to see Nicklaus closing the door behind a departing Alfred. "How so?" If anything, this had to be weird for him.

"This is the room I stayed in when we came before the wedding. This is your home, but not your room."

He'd been walking toward her, but stopped a few feet away. She closed the distance between them, wrapping her arms around his waist and resting the side of her head on his chest. "More and more I'm learning that home isn't a particular location, a building or a room, but where my family is."

"Your family *is* here."

She breathed a contented sigh. "You're my family, Nicky. That's part of the whole leaving your family and becoming one flesh thing. I think the most important thing isn't where we are, but that we're together."

He ran a hand up and down her back. "My whole life Michaela did her best to give me a stable home, to make sure I fit in, and I did for the most part, but there was always something a bit off. A part of me that knew I wasn't where I was supposed to be. Once I was old enough to understand that, I figured it was because of my parents' death and that I always knew we weren't ever completely safe. To an extent I think that was part of it, but..." His voice trailed off.

"But..." she prompted.

"I don't want it to sound like I'm slighting Michaela, because I don't mean to, but the more I think about it, the more I think it was God's way of making sure I wasn't too comfortable. If I'd been too comfortable with my life in the States, with a girlfriend or a big group of friends I would have missed, would I have said no when I found out about our wedding or the exiles?"

Yvette turned that over in her mind. "I wish we hadn't been forced into the wedding, but I can't say I'd prefer to be exiled, either. Thank you."

A knock at the door interrupted whatever else they would have said. Nicklaus kissed her hairline then called, "Come."

Alfred walked into the room. "Your family is waiting, ma'am. Breakfast will be served upon your arrival in the dining room of your parents' apartment."

She didn't move her head from Nicklaus's chest. Not yet. "Thanks, Alfred. We'll be there in a couple minutes."

The door closed behind him, and Nicklaus kissed her hairline again. "I'm glad I stayed, Evie. I'm glad you're in my life. I'm glad you're my wife."

"Me, too." Deep down, despite the comfort of his arms, she wondered at his statement. Was he glad *she* was his wife? Glad he'd gotten married? Glad for the...benefits of marriage? Even once she realized they'd be getting married, she hadn't anticipated those kinds of intimacies so soon. Not even after their incredible first night together.

Was he being kind, placating her, or was he glad to be with *her*? And if so, was he falling in love with her?

Because she was pretty sure she'd fallen in love with him weeks ago.

Nicklaus smoothed his hand over his tie. Being called to testify about someone he'd met once or twice and barely remembered wasn't high on the list of things he was comfortable with.

"Your name?"

He tried to shake himself out of his stupor, but Lizbeth's lawyer objected before he could say anything.

"If it pleases the court, please remind the barrister that Prince Nicklaus is a member of the Ravenzarian royal family by birth and the Mevendian royal family by marriage. As such, he is to be treated with the same respect as the rest of those families. He has a title, multiple titles in fact, and should be addressed either using one of them or sir at all times."

The judge nodded. "He's correct. Please remember this in your dealings with the prince."

The other attorney stood in front of judge. "I understand that, Your Honor, however, based on the most recent information I have available to me, there is some question about whether or not this man is, in fact, the real Prince Nicklaus."

Lizbeth's lawyer jumped in again. "Even if he isn't, which is a ridiculous assertion, he is the husband of Princess Yvette, son-in-law of the king, and holder of several titles based on that fact alone."

The judge nodded at both of them. "I understand the questions that have been raised in Ravenzario. However, I recommend you tread very, very carefully, sir."

The other attorney turned, but Nicklaus saw him roll his eyes. The judge couldn't. "Fine. Can you please tell me your name, *sir?*"

Could he remember the whole thing? "Prince Nicklaus David Richard Antonio of Ravenzario. Would you like my assorted titles as well?" *Please, no!* He'd never remember all of them.

"No, that will suffice. Is that the name you've used your entire life?"

"I have used the name Nicholas Metcalf."

"Why?"

"Because Henry Eit tried to kill me and the rest of my family. My nanny managed to escape with me and raise me in the States until it was safe to return home."

"And how are we supposed to know, *for certain*, you are the same Prince Nicklaus who disappeared from the car that day when your DNA doesn't match the sample left?"

Nicklaus wanted to give the man a piece of his mind, but kept his answer civil. "Michaela Engel says I am. She spent her life protecting me. The DNA in question was under the control of a madman who tried repeatedly to kill my sister and me, and did succeed in killing my parents. He tried again to kill Queen Christiana in the last couple of months. Who is more believable? A maniac with an affection for assassinations or a beloved nanny, daughter of close friends of the queen, who left everything behind to protect her charge?"

"There is validity to your comment, but not proof."

"New DNA tests are being done. Until they are complete, I

cannot comment further on what kind or how they are expected to prove who I am."

Lizbeth's attorney jumped in again. "What is the point of this line of questioning?"

"Just trying to ascertain the true identity of the witness." He flipped the page in his notepad. "Now, sir, where were you last weekend?"

"I was in Serenity Landing, Missouri in the United States."

"Why?"

Nicklaus forced himself not to shift uncomfortably in his seat. "I needed a few days away to think about some things."

"Rumor says you attacked your wife and that's why you left."

"Those rumors are untrue."

"And her black eye?"

How did he know about *that*? "Pardon?" Nicklaus tried to stall for time.

"Princess Yvette has been seen with a black eye in the last week. Is that from you?"

He had to tell the truth, no matter how damning. "She did not have a black eye. I unintentionally bruised her cheek."

"Isn't that what all abusers say?"

Nicklaus's hands clenched into fists. "I have no idea."

"Did she make you mad? Is that why you hit her?"

"Your Honor!" Lizbeth's lawyer finally jumped in. "This is argumentative and irrelevant."

"I'm trying to establish what kind of man he is," the other lawyer countered.

The judge addressed him directly. "Your Royal Highness, if you would be so kind as to tell us what happened, I would appreciate it."

"Yes, sir." He didn't want to, but he would. "I'd been sleeping in a separate room from my wife the last few nights. Ms. Engel, Michaela, told me I had nightmares for weeks after the car accident. They started again after the wedding. Yvette woke me up in the middle of one more than once because she was scared for me, not for herself. I nearly hit her once when I sat upright. After that, I slept in another bed in our apartment. That night, she was going to get a drink of water and heard me. She came in. I sat straight up and managed to hit her with one of my elbows. I would never intentionally hurt my wife. Ever. I went back to the States to get a bit of space, and hopefully, figure out how to stop the nightmares."

"Have you?"

"Not yet."

"Do you still sleep separate from your wife?"

Nicklaus shifted and raised an eyebrow. "I fail to see what that has to do with anything."

"Just answer the question."

"She has insisted on sleeping with me, and to be honest, the nightmares aren't as bad when she's there. Selfishly, I like that part."

"And while you were away, in Missouri, what was the name of the girl you had sex with in the stores?"

Talk about argumentative. "Excuse me?"

"You heard the question."

"I have never had sex with anyone but my wife. I never will."

"And this photo?" He held up the same picture Tony had shown him.

"I was shopping. This girl offered to help me find some clothes. I thought she was an employee."

"You were in the dressing area alone with her for over half an hour."

"No. I was in the dressing area. She went in and out getting clothes. When I left, she threw herself at me and called me by my name and title."

"And you didn't recognize her as Lizbeth Bence?"

"I didn't recognize her at all. She was not Lizbeth Bence."

"She looks like Lizbeth."

"Ms. Bence looks similar," Nicklaus shot back. "But it

wasn't her."

"How many times have you met LB?"

LB? Really? "I met her once or twice in the planning of the wedding and at the wedding itself. I am not well-acquainted with her, but this girl is not Ms. Bence."

"How do you know?"

"Because it wasn't her." Nicklaus couldn't keep his exasperation under control. "And, let's say, for the sake of discussion, it was her. I didn't sleep with her. Therefore, it doesn't matter if it was her or not."

"But it could have been and you wouldn't have been able to say for certain, not 100% because you've only met her once or twice in the middle of the craziest few days of your life, correct?"

"It wasn't her."

"There is absolutely no doubt in your mind, not even the teeniest, tiniest bit that it could have been?"

Nicklaus hesitated, just for a second, but it was long enough.

The lawyer gave a smug grin. "No further questions."

Lizbeth's attorney bolted from his table. "Was the woman in question Lizbeth Bence?"

"No, sir."

"Have you ever slept with anyone but your wife?"

"No, sir."

"Have you ever had non-intercourse, sexual relationship with anyone but your wife?"

"No, sir."

The lawyer turned to the judge. "In that case, I fail to see what relevance this witness brings to the case. I ask that the witness be excused and his testimony stricken from the record as completely irrelevant."

"I will dismiss the witness, but will not strike his testimony." He turned to Nicklaus. "Thank you for your time, Your Royal Highness. You are dismissed."

Nicklaus left the witness stand, unsure as to what the purpose had been. Even Mr. Bence's attorney had to know what he would have said, more or less. At least the relevant parts about Lizbeth. The nightmare stuff didn't matter at all. He just hoped he'd helped Lizbeth with whatever it was she needed help with.

Lizbeth paced outside the courtroom. She wasn't allowed inside so it wouldn't taint her testimony when the time came. She hadn't even spoken to Prince Nicklaus in ages and had no idea what he would say, though there was no truth to any rumor of an illicit relationship.

The door opened, and Prince Nicklaus emerged, but as instructed by her attorneys, they didn't say anything to each other, simply gave a polite nod.

"Ms. Bence, they're ready for you." The bailiff held the door open for her. She walked down the aisle with her head held high. Her father sat at the table with his attorneys. Why had he been allowed inside when she hadn't?

She took her seat and swore to tell the truth.

"Can you please identify yourself for the court?" Her attorney gave her a reassuring smile.

"Lizbeth Diane Bence Padovano." She couldn't help but glance at her father, but did manage to resist a smug smile at his shock.

"Padovano?" Her attorney wasn't as shocked as he seemed.

"Yes, sir."

"When did this name change happen?"

"I suppose it hasn't happened legally, however, unofficially it happened upon my marriage to Mr. Robert Padovano."

"And when was that?"

"Last summer." She gave the date.

"Over a year?"

"A little bit over, yes." She twisted the engagement ring and wedding band she'd worn in public for the first time.

"And why did you marry Mr. Padovano?"

"Because I love him." It wasn't what the lawyer was after, not really, but what they'd discussed.

"Did you have a big wedding?"

"No. We eloped."

"Why?"

"Neither of us wanted a big wedding, and to be completely honest, I didn't want my father involved."

"Why not?"

"Any number of reasons which are likely irrelevant, including the feeling I've had for most of my life that he's been controlling and manipulating me. I was done with that."

"So why did you marry Mr. Padovano, eloping with him?"

She stared at her hands for a moment. "I was pregnant."

"With Mr. Padovano's child?"

"No, sir."

"With Prince Malachi's child?"

"No, sir."

"There were many rumors last year about your relationship with the prince. Was there any truth to them?"

"No, sir." Could she sound any more like a broken record?

"Then who was the father of the child?"

"A man I met while on vacation in Ravenzario. We spent a couple of days together. I don't know enough about him to find him again, though I would imagine my father does."

"And what happened to the child?"

Tears filled her eyes. "I miscarried a few weeks after the wedding." One snuck down her cheek, and she wiped it away with her freshly-manicured nail.

"Who else knows about that?"

"Robert and my doctor."

"No one else?"

"No, sir."

"Have you ever had an affair with a married man?"

"No, sir. The only married man I've ever slept with is my husband, after we were married."

"And this other man wasn't married?"

"Not to my knowledge. He mentioned being single several times, but I didn't run a background check."

"What about Prince Nicklaus?"

"What about him?"

"Have you ever had an affair with him?"

"No, sir. I met him a couple of times in the days leading up to his wedding to Princess Yvette, but I don't believe I've ever spent any time alone with him. I have never kissed him or had any relationship with him beyond a short conversation or two." What was the point of all of this? Hadn't Nicklaus covered all of it?

"At any time were you aware that the bulk of your mother and grandfather's estate went to you?"

"No, sir."

"What was your understanding?"

"That my father inherited everything, and he would be kind enough to give me some of it on my last birthday." When she heard it out loud like that, it sounded ludicrous.

"And when did you find out the truth?"

"In the last couple of weeks."

"Do you have any idea why that might be?"

"I would imagine he wanted to keep it all, and his lifestyle, for himself, and didn't want me to know the details."

"Objection!" Her father's attorney stood. "She has no direct knowledge of what Mr. Bence may or may not have known or intended."

"She may not have had direct knowledge, but she can speak to what he told her or what he intended her to believe," her attorney shot back. "As his daughter, she can speak to his lifestyle and make educated inferences as to his intent."

The judge nodded. "I'll allow it."

The other attorney took his seat.

"You found out about recently that infidelities could lead to your father being able to claim all of the inheritances. Has he ever done anything that would lead you to believe he was encouraging those infidelities, even if you didn't understand why?"

"Yes." She took a deep breath and plunged forward. "He tried to convince me to put myself in compromising positions with Prince Malachi. His stated rationale was to force a divorce between the prince and Princess Jessabelle, but knowing what I know now, there may have been more to it."

"Is anyone else aware of this?"

"Not to my knowledge. I have reason to believe the king may have suspected, but I don't know for certain."

"King Antonio of Mevendia."

What other king would be relevant? "Correct."

The attorney turned to the judge. "Your honor, I would like to reserve the right to call on the king for a deposition if necessary."

"Not in open court?" the judge asked.

"Only if we deem it unavoidable. I would not presume on the king's busy schedule any more than necessary."

"Very well. I have it noted."

The lawyer turned back to her. "Now, we have heard accusations of a clandestine meeting with Prince Nicklaus last weekend. You said earlier there had been no relationship with him, but to clarify further, did you meet with him last weekend?"

"No."

"You have not told anyone where you were. Will you do so now?"

"Robert and I went away for the weekend."

"Where to?"

"Some friends of my husband run a boutique hotel in Ravenzario. They understand our desire for discretion until we decide it is time to go public with our relationship."

"Is there proof of your location?"

He hadn't prepared her for that question. "We took a couple of selfies. I know it can be possible to determine location from the information encoded in the photos, but I'm not sure what the settings on my phone are. I also don't know if there's anything identifiable in those photos."

"Can you give us names of people who can corroborate your story? Besides Mr. Padovano?"

"The owners of the hotel and perhaps a member of the staff or two, but we tend to keep to ourselves while we're there. It's been one of the few times we've had time alone together since we've been married. I will provide the names. My husband may have a few more."

The attorney turned to the judge. "Your honor, unless Mr. Bence and his attorneys have significantly more substantial proof that my client engaged in the kind of affairs that would lead to Mrs. Padovano being stripped of her inheritances, I ask that this entire proceeding be dismissed."

The judge nodded and addressed her father's table. "Do you have anything more substantial?"

"We believe the evidence we have presented so far is substantial enough to prove the claim that Ms. Bence..." A glare from the judge forced him to change his wording. "Pardon, Mrs. Padovano has been involved in relationships that are inappropriate and would preclude her from receiving the inheritance."

"Do you have any evidence, besides that which we've already heard, or simply more of the same?"

She could see the defeat in the lawyer's face. "We have no evidence of any other relationships at this time."

The judge banged his gavel. "Then I will adjourn to consider the evidence, and return with my decision tomorrow."

After the judge left, Lizbeth followed her attorney to an office down the hall. Robert met them there, pulling her into his arms. They both looked at the other man.

"I have a really good feeling about this," he told them. "We can't know for sure until he announces the decision, but I get the feeling he wasn't all that impressed with your father and his attorney or their evidence of your alleged misconduct."

"Would you really call the king as a witness?" She rested her head against Robert's chest.

"If I need to. It wouldn't surprise me to find out the judge reaches out to the king, kind of unofficially, to find out if he has anything of interest in this matter. The king saying yes could be enough to sway the opinion of the judge, without him even needing to testify."

"Is that legal?" Robert asked.

"Maybe. Maybe not. If they were to challenge it, it might get overturned, but I doubt they'd challenge it. They'd lose. The king wouldn't imply he has relevant information if he doesn't. For them to challenge it would make it all much more public. The king would come out against them, and they wouldn't want all of that."

"So it's probably over?" Stress began to bleed off of her.

The attorney nodded. "I think so."

Lizbeth lifted her face to Robert's. He kissed her firmly. Once and then again.

"It's over, sweetheart," he whispered. "It's over. And now we can be together like we've dreamed."

Tears began to stream down her face.

It was over.

Yvette walked into the suite to find Nicklaus staring out the window. "How'd it go?"

"Fine, I suppose. Some of the questions caught me a little off-guard, but nothing too out there. Questions about whether or not I am who I say I am."

She walked behind him and wrapped her arms around his waist. "Any idea when those tests are supposed to be done?"

"Soon, but that's all I know."

"Do you want to stay here tonight or go home?"

Nicklaus turned in her arms and held her close. "Like you said earlier, wherever we're together is home."

Did he really feel that way? Yvette pushed the thoughts aside. She needed to learn to trust him and his statements and not question him all the time. "Okay, so if we're together we're home, where do you want home to be tonight?"

"You know what I really want?" She could hear heaviness, weariness in his voice.

"What's that?"

"I want to get away. To go somewhere, just the two of us. Away from the cameras, away from prying eyes, away from the questions about my identity, away from the public, away from everyone and everything. Finish our aborted honeymoon."

She smiled, though she knew he couldn't see it. "I can get on board with that plan."

"On board? Like back on the boat?"

"Sure." That sounded fantastic. Another week or so in the middle of nowhere.

"We never did do that excursion. And I can avoid a few more weeks of language lessons."

Yvette gave an exasperated sigh. "You can't get out of them forever. Plus, I can help you."

"Fine," he grumbled. "But only because you're a lot prettier than the other guy."

They stood there for another moment before Nicklaus pulled out his phone. She watched him text Alfred and ask him to make the arrangements. Either yacht would do. A minute later a text came back letting them know the Mevendian yacht was still docked in Ravenzario. A quick flight home, and they'd be on board.

Did they need to say good-bye to her parents and siblings, or could they just go? She'd bet they both wanted the same thing - to just go.

"Can we have someone pack our stuff in Ravenzario and head straight to the marina?" Nicklaus asked her.

Yep. They were thinking alike. "I like that plan."

Another text to Alfred and a minute later a response telling them their flight would leave in under an hour, just long enough for them to get to the nearby airport and for the pilots to get ready for take-off. They left their suite a few minutes later, only to have her parents meet them near the door to the portico where their car waited.

"You're leaving without talking to us?" The amused tone behind her father's words was very different than it would have been a year earlier.

"We just want to get away," she explained, walking into his waiting arms. "We need to get away from all of this."

He gave her a hug then let go. "I understand. When will you be back?"

She shrugged and moved away to hug her mother. "We planned this in the last fifteen minutes. A week? I don't think either one of us have anything on our schedules that can't be rearranged."

"What about the documentary?"

Nicklaus answered that question. "We can either find a way to stream it or watch it later. I'm sure we'll see the comments if we do any kind of looking online."

"If you need anything, let us know."

"We will," Yvette promised. She took Nicklaus's hand, but looked back. "Thanks for everything."

Her father looked at Nicklaus. "Thank you for helping Lizbeth. I've had suspicions about her father for many years. The judge called me a few minutes ago, looking for any unofficial information I might be able to give him. I got the impression he would let them call me as a witness if needed, but just the confirmation that I might know something seems to have been enough."

"Do you know anything?" Nicklaus asked. "Or just implied that you might?"

"There are a lot of things that *could* add up to something, but I do not have specific knowledge. I am certain Mr. Bence does not want me testifying in any form - affidavit, deposition, or especially not in open court."

"If you hear the ruling, would you let us know?" she asked.

Her father nodded as the door opened, their car waiting for them on the outside.

Before they could leave, another car pulled up. Yvette glanced back at her father who looked puzzled.

Mr. Bence was out of the car almost before it came to a stop.

"You and I are going to have a talk, Antonio," he yelled as he barged toward the door.

Nicklaus let go of her hand and stepped in front of the charging man, physically restraining him.

"It is all right, Nicklaus. Mr. Bence knows better than to attack me. He would not survive the encounter, even if my security team was not nearby. Shall we talk in my office?" Yvette wondered why Mr. Bence hadn't been taken off the approved guest list yet.

Nicklaus let go of the other man, but all of them headed for her father's formal office on the main floor. She knew why. His office in the apartment wasn't wired for sound. This one was. It wouldn't surprise her to know there was also video. Her father took a seat behind his desk. Mr. Bence remained standing, his arms folded over his chest.

"I want money." No equivocation. No stalling. Just right out there.

The king chuckled. "Why would I give you money?"

"To keep what I know a secret."

"And what is it you think you know?"

"That you're Lizbeth's father."

32

Nicklaus managed to keep his mouth closed at that revelation. Surely there wasn't any truth to the allegation.

The king's face remained impassive, something Nicklaus took to mean there may be something to the story. "Pardon?"

"I know you slept with my wife. I have proof. And I have proof you're Lizbeth's biological father."

Nicklaus glanced at his mother-in-law. She looked grim, but not surprised.

"My wife has known about that particular, potential, indiscretion for many years. I fail to see what the blackmail is supposed to accomplish."

So he had slept with Lizbeth's mother. But what did he mean by potential?

"In fact," the king went on. "If I had to guess, given what I know now, you put her up to the seduction in an effort to eventually blackmail me into doing something you wanted. You likely had not planned for it to take so long to need, but here we are."

"Don't think I won't go to the press!"

"With what? And do you think they'll believe you? And if they do, what does it matter? All that will happen is more rumors of another affair many years ago. My infidelities were never much of a secret. Neither has my faithfulness to my wife for the last two decades. Besides, I was never convinced I actually slept with her." The king was the picture of nonchalance. "I know she tried to seduce me, but I'd had quite a lot to drink that night."

Mr. Bence pulled something out of his pocket and set it on the desk, pushing a button as he did. "Your Majesty..."

A woman's voice came out of the digital recorder, followed by a man's. It sounded like King Antonio, but the king didn't look too impressed with it. There was conversation about the tryst about to take place, refusal to wear protection, a creaking door as it closed behind them, and the squeak of bedsprings.

And King Antonio laughed.

"That's your proof? Really?"

Mr. Bence turned off the recording. "It goes on. Much more explicit, but out of respect for your wife and daughter, I'll stop it there."

"That recording won't hold up to even the most cursory scrutiny, and you know it."

The other man blustered, but didn't really say anything.

The king leaned forward in his chair. "This liaison supposedly took place here in the palace, correct?"

"Where else?"

"Do you really think we have doors or bed springs that creak around here? Those two things alone prove this recording is fabricated."

"Does it matter if it is?" Mr. Bence countered. "All that is necessary is for the public to believe it is true."

"And what would that accomplish? Even if it were true, it wouldn't be a shock to anyone to learn there had been one more woman, many, many years ago. In fact, I think it might be a good idea to call a press conference and clear the air. I never have, you know. Thank the people for their continued trust and faith in me and my ability to lead the country despite my past indiscretions. I can let them know that, yes, I did help Mrs. Padovano by replacing the money her father stole, but there's no truth to anything else."

Mr. Bence turned white, then started to fume.

The king turned to his wife. "And I thank you, publicly, finally, for standing by me all these years." His smile turned tender. "I don't deserve you. I never have."

The queen returned his smile before shifting to face Mr. Bence. "Sir, I have no idea what it is you hope to gain or what my husband might know that would lead you to threatening him, but trust me on this. You will never gain the upper hand as long as I have breath in my body. You would do well to remember that."

Something seemed to snap in Mr. Bence. With a roar, he propelled himself toward the queen.

Without thinking, Nicklaus sprang to action, launching himself at the other man. Nicklaus felt his shoulder connect with the other man's torso. They crashed into the desk, but didn't break it, sliding a few inches until they landed on the floor.

Before Nicklaus could decide what his next move would be, doors opened, and security streamed into the room. He was helped off Mr. Bence who was pulled roughly to his feet.

The older man glared at Nicklaus. "I'm having you charged with assault."

King Antonio chuckled as he moved to comfort his wife. "I dare you to try."

"We'll be back in a few moments to sort this out, sir," one of the security guards told him as they practically dragged Mr. Bence out of the room.

Nicklaus rotated his right shoulder. It stung a bit. "Sorry about the mess, sir." Papers, pens, and assorted other desktop materials were now scattered across the floor.

"That is the least of my worries, Nicklaus. Thank you for your prompt action. If he had succeeded in touching Alicia, I might be concerned about whether it could be considered justifiable homicide or not." He reached up and brushed the hair off the queen's face. "Are you all right, sweetheart?"

"I was not scared." She gave the king a tremulous smile. "Not a little bit. If Nicklaus had not jumped in, you would have. I knew security was mere seconds away regardless."

Nicklaus felt Yvette's arms wrap around his waist, and he used his good arm to pull her close.

"Thank you," she whispered.

"My pleasure," he whispered back, watching the tender moment between his in-laws.

The door opened behind them and the head of the security team walked in, followed closely by several attorneys.

"He's been arrested and detained in the cell in the security offices, sir," the head of security began. "I'm certain you will want to file charges?"

"Of course. An attempted assault on the queen as well as attempted blackmail using falsified information should be a good start. I am certain more charges will be possible once we finish looking into all of his dealings with Lizbeth Padovano's inheritance."

Yvette lifted her head off his shoulder. "Padovano? She married Robert?"

The king nodded. "Over a year ago. They had their reasons for keeping it quiet, including her father's reaction."

For fifteen minutes, they discussed assorted security related issues. Nicklaus and Yvette weren't involved except as observers. She turned further into him, settling more closely to his chest.

The king turned to them after several moments. "Your car is still waiting outside. You should go on. I do not blame you for wanting to get away for a bit. We do not need you here at the moment, and if something comes up, we know how to find you."

Nicklaus ran his hand up and down Yvette's back. "I think that sounds like a great plan."

Yvette moved away from him to hug both of her parents a little longer than she would have an hour earlier, he thought.

A few minutes later, they were in their car, headed for the airport and a week with just the two of them and the Mediterranean Sea.

Yvette rested her head on the back of the seat and closed her eyes as they drove to the airport.

When Nicklaus leaned forward and knocked on the window, she opened them.

"Where are we going?" He sounded a bit concerned but not panicked.

Yvette sat up a bit and looked out the window. She looked around, hoping to see a landmark she recognized, but all she could see was trees.

Nicklaus turned to her. "This isn't the way to the airport, is it?"

"No." She twisted the other way, looking toward the road behind. "I think we may still be on palace property. The road's not wide enough for anywhere else."

He knocked on the window again, but there was no reply.

Yvette pulled her phone out of her purse only to find there was no signal. Nicklaus checked his as she watched.

"This isn't good, is it?" he asked, his voice grim.

"Probably not."

"So now what?" He looked around, on the edge of the seat.

"We wait." She sighed. "When we don't leave through the front gate or when we don't arrive at the airport in a few minutes, they'll start looking for us."

"Where will we be by then?"

"Good question."

The car turned off the road and bumped through the woods on a small, rutted trail, barely big enough for it to pass. Branches scraped against the sides of the car and caused Yvette to jump as one smacked the window.

"What do we do?" Nicklaus's voice started to sound a bit panicked now.

"We pray." Yvette had to remain calm if he wouldn't. She'd likely spent far more time than him in training to deal with situations like this - despite his history. "That's the first thing we do in a situation like this. And while we pray, we assess." You didn't have to bow your head and close your eyes and get down on your knees in order for God to hear you. She looked around the cabin of the vehicle as she prayed. "God, you know where we are, and You know where we're going. You know who has us and what their purpose is. Help us stay calm. Give us wisdom to know when to fight and when to keep still. Send Your angels to protect us and keep us safe." She didn't add an amen because she wasn't done praying. She wouldn't be done praying for a long time.

"Can we jump out?"

Yvette looked at her door. They'd never be able to get it open far enough to get out. Would they? She turned and checked Nicklaus's side. It didn't seem to be as bad.

"Can you open it, or are we locked in?"

He reached for the handle and pulled, but didn't push the door open. "Yeah. I think it opens."

"Then watch for an opening and jump. I'll be right behind you."

"You go first."

Yvette saw what she was looking for, a slight gap coming in the trees. "Now!"

Nicklaus reached for the handle, and she pushed him out, leaning forward to follow him, only to find herself thrown backwards as the car lurched to the side. She scrambled to her knees and stared out the back window to see Nicklaus kneeling on the ground and looking at her with wide eyes.

"Go!" she whispered. "Go!" He wouldn't hear her if she yelled, and she didn't know if the man up front knew he'd made it out.

Nicklaus pushed himself to his feet then disappeared into the woods.

Good. He needed to stay under cover and get back to the palace. Maybe his phone would work away from the car.

Yvette knew she needed to keep her wits about her. Could she jump out? As she leaned over toward Nicklaus's door, she groaned and closed her eyes as she took a deep breath.

Nicklaus's phone was on the floor. He wouldn't be able to call. She picked it up and tucked it inside her boot. Maybe they wouldn't check her and turning over her phone would be enough when they got where they were going. She stuck it in her other boot, hoping they'd think it was the only thing she was trying to hide.

Before she had a chance to jump out herself, the car slowed and drove through a gate of some kind. Rather than coming out the other side and into daylight, Yvette was surprised to find herself in some sort of cave or tunnel. After just another minute, they came to a stop.

To her surprise, no one opened any doors. No one said anything.

Could she get out here? Find her way back outside somehow?

A careful examination showed her she wouldn't be able to open either door far enough to get out. Would the windows roll down? Which side would be safer? The driver's side - where the driver was - or the passenger side where he might be idly staring?

Breathing another prayer, she pressed the passenger window button. It rolled down, but not very far. Not far enough to wiggle her way out. She pressed again, but nothing.

She had no choices for the moment. Could she *do* anything but wait?

No. Not really. There was no way out of the passenger compartment at the moment, and nothing in there she could fashion into a weapon.

Instead, she decided she would try to relax, rest even, but keep her ears open for the smallest sounds that could mean something was about to change. She wasn't sure how much time had passed when the car started again and began to slowly roll forward. Yvette opened her eyes and watched the walls on either side pass until they opened to a slightly larger room.

The car came to a stop situated next to another car, this one older and more nondescript than the limousine she'd been riding in. It did have dark, tinted windows so even if there were someone inside, she wouldn't have been able to see who it was. Someone unseen opened the passenger door.

"Get out," the voice ordered.

She did as she was told, knowing resistance was futile at this point. When she could see the man who held her door, Yvette had to purposely not show her surprise.

A man known to her by sight. A member of the minor nobility from Montevaro, maybe. Hadn't she danced with him at the Independence Ball?

Without another word, he opened the door to the other vehicle. This time she couldn't hold back the gasp that ripped from her throat as she recognized the man.

Mr. Bence.

Lizbeth's father.

The one who had been arrested in the palace that afternoon.

He was her captor.

This couldn't be good.

Nicklaus pulled himself up as the car disappeared around a

corner. He cursed under his breath. How could he have left Yvette behind?

Truth was, Yvette was probably better equipped to free herself or to not make her captors mad. He'd fight when he should sit down and shut up.

Once he made it several feet into the woods, he stopped to think. Where was he? Did he follow the car or go for help? Finally, he said a quick prayer and decided to follow the road from the woods and head back the way they came.

When he reached a fork in the road, Nicklaus went with his gut and headed to the right. They hadn't been driving *that* long but it took him nearly an hour before he saw his first sign of civilization.

The palace came into view in the distance, and he reached for his cell phone. Realizing it wasn't in his pocket, he frantically patted himself down. Had he dropped it when he fell out of the car?

Stupid!

Instead of being able to call, he picked up his pace, trotting along the paved road. As he got closer to the palace, and the wrought iron gates, he heard a shout and saw a rifle leveled at him from a guard post on top.

"Don't shoot!" he yelled, holding his hands up. "I'm Nicklaus!"

Several other guards poured out of door near the gate, running at him with guns drawn but pointed at the ground.

Nicklaus stayed still. "Don't shoot!" he yelled again.

He could see recognition on several faces. Immediately, he was surrounded by the men, this time, facing out toward any possible threat, he supposed. One of the men took his arm, and they picked up the pace, practically running toward the open door. Nicklaus was rushed through corridors he'd never seen until they finally reached the security office.

King Antonio had a look on his face Nicklaus couldn't quite identify. Fear. Relief. Concern.

Rage.

"What happened?"

Nicklaus was out of breath by this point, but he bent over, his hands on his knees. "I don't know. I know we didn't go out the main gate. I thought maybe we were taking some other way to the airport. Yvette's eyes were closed, but after a few minutes, I asked the driver where we were going. He didn't answer, but she realized something was wrong. Our cell phones had no signal, but the doors were unlocked, so we decided to jump out. My door had more room between it and the trees. I was going to let her go first, but she saw an opening and pretty much pushed me out. I couldn't see her through the back window but the door slammed shut, and they went around a corner." He blew out a breath. "I decided to come back here where I could get help."

"Why didn't you try to call again after you got out of the car?"

"Because I thought the lack of signal was a middle of the woods thing. It wouldn't have worked any better out of the car."

"The entire property has service," one of the guards said. "It must have been a localized jammer or something."

"Most likely," the king agreed.

"I was going to when I saw the palace, but I must have dropped the phone somewhere. Either in the car or when I fell out, I guess." He dropped into a chair, everything from the last hour washing over him. "She's alone. I should have stayed with her. I should have gone after the car."

His father-in-law knelt in front of him. "You did the right thing. You got help. You can give us information that can help find her. If her side of the car had been the better side to jump out of, Evie would have done the same thing. You haven't been through the training she has when it comes to what to do if you've been kidnapped and with different kinds of kidnappers." Antonio rested his hand on Nicklaus's shoulder. "She's in God's hands, Nick. Just like you were."

Nicklaus nodded his head. "I know that."

"But it's not always easy to trust God." Antonio squeezed his shoulder and stood. "We'll work on it together."

"Sir?"

They both turned to look at the new voice.

One of the guards stood there, one Nicklaus recognized as one who'd taken Mr. Bence away earlier.

"What is it?" Antonio asked, clearly agitated that information wasn't more forthcoming.

The guard shifted uncomfortably. "Mr. Bence is gone, sir."

Nicklaus blinked as the king stiffened noticeably. "What? How?"

The other man shook his head. "I don't know. Both of the men stationed to keep an eye on him are gone, too. There's some blood outside the holding cell, but not much."

"So he overpowered his guards?"

"Maybe." The head of security, Tony's counterpart, stepped in. "Or he managed to sneak past them, and they pursued without checking in hoping they could re-apprehend him without anyone else knowing."

."So do we presume he has something to do with Yvette's disappearance?" The king crossed his arms over his chest.

Someone walked in wearing scrubs and pulled a chair up next to Nicklaus, beginning to treat the minor wounds he'd forgotten he had. The medication stung as it hit the scratches and scrapes, but he didn't let himself cry out.

The head of security spoke to the king. "It's possible. I've contacted Tony Browning to see if there are any threats on that end we don't already know about. He's checking a few things and will get back to me, but nothing immediate."

"Given everything else today, and Mr. Bence's disappearance, I would think these things are all connected."

"Most likely," the security man agreed.

Nicklaus looked up from where his hand was getting bandaged. "So what does he want? How do we get her back?"

"If it is Bence who has her, he probably wants money and safe passage to a country without an extradition treaty. The court case will not go his way, and he has to know that. This was his insurance plan." Antonio leaned against the table, bracing himself on his arms. "Maybe not the arrest, but the kidnapping."

An aide walked in, his face grim. "There's someone to see you, sir."

"Who is it?"

Before the aide could answer, another man pushed his way in. Robert Padovano, his face ashen. "Lizbeth is gone."

33

Yvette didn't let her fear show on her face. Whatever he wanted, he surely needed her alive to get it.

"I understand your husband ran like a schoolgirl." Mr. Bence pulled a cigar out of the inside pocket of his suit.

Yvette didn't answer as he prepared to light it.

"No matter. It's you I need, anyway. Your father will do what I ask to make sure you remain safe."

She still said nothing. At least this was a devil she knew. Kind of.

He jerked his head toward the back of the car. One of his goons, a man she vaguely recognized, gripped her arm.

"Into the boot, Princess." Mr. Bence cupped his hand around a gold plated lighter. A few puffs later, smoke curled from the end.

The goon opened the trunk and motioned Yvette over.

"I would recommend you go quietly, Princess," Mr. Bence warned. "I would hate to drug you like I did my daughter." He chuckled. "If she's my daughter. Even if she's not the spawn of Antonio, I doubt she's mine."

Even as a thump came from the trunk, Yvette refused to say

anything. At least she wouldn't be alone in this. Following the goon's grunted instructions, she stood near the back of the vehicle and let him restrain her hands behind her back, holding her arms so that they weren't as tightly bound as he thought they were. Maybe she'd be able to work loose.

"Get in." Mr. Bence gave the instruction from where he was standing.

It wasn't easy, but Yvette did as she was told situating herself so she was facing Lizbeth. She saw that Lizbeth's ankles had also been secured with duct tape. Yvette prayed he wouldn't tape hers also, and not just because her favorite boots would be ruined.

"We've got to get moving," Mr. Bence called as she got as comfortable as she could.

Yvette stared into Lizbeth's closed eyes and wished she could reassure her friend. Lizbeth had been gagged, too, but they bothered with none of that for Yvette. The goon just shut the lid and left them there. She couldn't see anything but she could whisper.

"It's going to be okay, Lizbeth. Nicklaus got away. They know something about where we are and who might have us. I'm sure they know by now that your father escaped from custody at the palace." How had he managed that? Beat someone up? Have someone on the inside?

She had a pretty good idea where they'd gone when they left the palace itself, though she hadn't known there was a gate of any kind at the end of that road through the woods.

Yvette tried to follow the twists and turns they took, but without any reference for where they were or where they were going, she really couldn't. How would she use the information if she could?

A sudden lurch to one side, and she both heard and felt muffled panicked sounds.

"Lizbeth, it's Yvette. It's okay." She repeated the words several times before it seemed to sink in and the attempts at flailing stopped.

"I know you can't talk, and I don't think I can get the gag out of your mouth. My hands are tied behind my back and without seeing what I'm doing, I just don't think I can."

A muffled sound of frustration came from Lizbeth.

"I know. Listen. I'll ask yes or no questions. You answer with one noise for yes and two for no, okay?"

The answer came in the form of a single grunt.

"Do you feel okay? Are you hurt?"

Three grunts.

"Right. One question at a time. Are you hurt?"

Again three.

What could that mean? "You're hurting but mostly okay?" she tried.

A single grunt.

"Good." What information could she get with yes or no questions? "Do you remember what happened?"

Two.

"Okay. You don't remember." There was one grunt, despite it not being a question. "Here's what I know. Your father was arrested at the palace for threatening my father and attempting to blackmail him. He escaped somehow. The guy driving the car Nicklaus and I were in has to be working for him. I've met him before, though. He's the son of a duke or something in Montevaro. Nicklaus managed to get out, but I couldn't." She didn't mention the phone. Just in case someone was listening. "Then your father had his goon put me back here with you. Can you think of what your father might want?"

One grunt.

"Okay." What could it be? "Money?"

Another one.

"He thought he was going to lose his lawsuit, and he thinks kidnapping the three of us would get him a payoff and probably a trip somewhere he could hide?"

Lizbeth answered yes.

"So he needs us alive then. That's good." She'd really been musing to herself, but Lizbeth answered in the affirmative anyway. "I'm sure my father and the best of the best are on this already." She leaned her forehead toward her friend until they touched. "We're going to be okay."

Three grunts in response.

"I've been praying. I know you have. So has Nicklaus and Robert and everyone else. His eye is on the sparrow. He knows where we are and where we're going."

Lizbeth made a noise that sounded vaguely like "I know."

"So we keep praying, and we keep our wits about us. We'll have a chance to escape. Or he'll let us go. God's got us in His hands. He didn't bring both of us this far to abandon us now."

A series of bumps felt almost like a set of railroad tracks. Followed by more of the same bumps, it gave Yvette an idea of where they might be. "The rail station on the north side of Erres?" she whispered. There were few other places where there would be several sets of tracks together.

Lizbeth grunted her agreement.

So what did it mean that they were at the rail station? Lots of trains coming and going. Passenger and freight trains both headed toward the rest of Europe. If he could get them out of Mevendia, it would be much more difficult to rescue them.

"They're going to put us on a train," she told Lizbeth. "From there, we could end up anywhere." In theory, they could even end up on ship headed overseas.

He could take them anywhere.

And for the first time, Yvette wondered if they'd ever be found.

Nicklaus sat in the security office with his face in his hands. His soul prayed, but his mind couldn't focus enough to form words. Yvette was out there, alone or with Lizbeth, not knowing for sure if anyone was coming for her, not knowing how hard everyone here was working to find them. Not knowing for certain if he made it back to the palace or to a police station or somewhere else to find help.

A hand rested on his back, and he turned to see Nana Yvette sitting next to him. The peace on her face made him more than a bit jealous.

"God has her, you know. He knows where she is and who she's with and how this is all going to turn out."

"I know." He did. Kind of. "I want to believe that."

"When you 'died' all those years ago, some of us knew your father had feared for your lives."

Nicklaus looked up at her. "I didn't know you knew."

"I didn't, not officially, but I knew." She took his hand in her own. "I prayed non-stop, just like so many of us are praying now. For days, I fasted and prayed for you and Michaela. It wasn't until I felt a release from God that I stopped the continuous prayer. Even then I prayed often. Right now, all of us, those left in Ravenzario, and I would venture to guess, others you don't even know - who don't understand why, are praying for your wife and Mrs. Padovano right now."

"I hope you're right."

Nana Yvette squeezed his hand. "I know I am."

Nicklaus leaned back in his chair. "Can we talk about something else? Anything else?"

"Of course." She smiled. "What would you like to talk about?"

"We were planning to head back out on the Med to spend some time together. We had a bet on our first trip that she still hasn't collected on. She gets to pick an excursion some place we stop."

"Where would you like to go?"

He shrugged. "I have no idea. Where would you recommend?"

Nana Yvette gave a wistful smile. "Oh, I don't know."

"Where was your favorite place to go with your husband?"

"We didn't travel like you do. We didn't have the freedom of instant communications or rapid travel like there is today. Oh, better than it was before, of course, but my husband became king quite young, and then died quite young, you know. We rarely had the opportunity to travel for pleasure, not outside of the Commonwealth."

"And since then? Your children were grown, weren't they?"

"My oldest three children were." She smiled softly. "My youngest, my only daughter, Beatrice and I went on some trips."

"Where was your favorite vacation spot?"

She chuckled. "Oh, my favorite vacation wasn't taken with Bea. Last summer, I went to San Majoria in the Caribbean." Nana Yvette leaned closer and whispered. "Incognito. No one knew who I was, but after the revelations with Antonio, Malachi, and Jessabelle, I needed the anonymity. For several glorious weeks, I wasn't a former queen, or Queen Grandmother." She shuddered lightly. "I was just Yvie." She gave him an eye. "With a Y, of course."

"Yvie? I had no idea anyone called you that."

With a wry chuckle, she shook her head. "No one ever has, not since my father many, many years ago. It was a lovely time. I spent much of it near the water." She shook herself out of the memories. "I'm not sure it's something you younger people would enjoy as much as I did. I did enjoy the excursions I took, but I spent most of my time resting and reading."

"Honestly, Nana, resting and reading sounds perfect." With no worries, no stressors.

No wife being held captive by a madman.

He looked around the room. Small knots of people poured over computer screens. "Any word?" he asked Antonio when the king glanced over.

"Not yet." Antonio motioned to one of the men who put the map up on a large television screen. "This is the road you took, where you jumped out." He pointed to a thin line, barely visible between the foliage of the trees. "But it ends at the wall surrounding the property. We have no idea where they may have gone from there."

"There's an entrance into the wall there, you know."

Everyone turned to look at Nana Yvette, too stunned to reply.

"Those walls are hollow." She looked at Antonio. "You used to play in them sometimes."

"I did?"

She rolled her eyes. "My goodness. Are all the maps with the secret passages missing?" She stood and pointed to the wall. "There are several of these wooded roads that end at the wall. They all end at an angle, you see. When the door into the wall is opened, the cars are able to angle their way in without needing to make a sharp turn. The tunnels lead all the way back to the palace."

Antonio turned to the head of security. "You didn't know this?"

The man shook his head. "It's not been on any map or drawing I've ever seen. I've never seen any with passages outside of the palace itself."

"So where are the exits, Nana?" Antonio turned back to his grandmother. "Once they get into the wall, how do they get out?"

"See the roads leading into the woods?" She pointed to the screen.

"There are exit doors there?"

Nana Yvette smirked. "If you're leaving the wall, yes, it is an exit. If you're coming from the other direction, it's an entrance."

"I wonder if that's where Bence ended up."

Robert Padovano jumped in. "What are we waiting for? Let's go."

Antonio motioned for him to sit down. "A team of men will go. You and Nicklaus will remain here."

Nicklaus sensed Robert's frustration. He agreed. He wanted to go, too, but they weren't trained for these things. They would just be in the way.

"We stay here and pray," he reminded his new friend. "Let the professionals do what they do best."

Robert sank back down into his seat and bowed his head. Nicklaus did the same.

And prayed like he'd never prayed before.

Yvette had no idea where they were. At the rail station, they'd been put into a shipping container. Their hands had been moved from behind them to in front and Lizbeth's feet left free. There was a bit of food and water, enough for several days. Yvette didn't like that. Too long. He expected them to be in here, unable to be found due to movement, and traveling to heaven only knew where.

At least he didn't gag them again, but did warn that no one would hear them, and he would know if they tried anything. He didn't say what he'd do if they did try to get help, but the implication wasn't good.

The rolling clickety-clack of the train might have been soothing in another context, but not here, not now. Their watches had been taken away. Yvette had looked at the phones just long enough to turn them both off to preserve their power. Though both had been fully charged when they left the palace, there was no telling how long they would last.

And Lizbeth's father had been sure to tell them that no phones would work in the rail car. She'd checked before turning them off. No signal.

"Get some rest," she whispered to Lizbeth. Her friend was still shaken and not quite free of whatever drugs Mr. Bence had used to sedate her.

"How? What if someone comes for us?"

"I'll keep watch," Yvette promised. "You rest." She wouldn't sleep until Lizbeth was more coherent.

The train rattled on for hours, or possibly days, lurching to a halt occasionally, then starting again. Yvette spent her time looking around for a way to escape, then resting. She spent quite some time staring at her engagement ring. She never had asked Nicklaus where it came from.

Eventually, the train stopped, and the container was moved. The rolling, jerking, then swinging motion threatened to make both of them sick, but they managed to keep the little they'd eaten down. Fortunately, the cargo in their container was well tied down.

The container settled with a clang. Yvette could hear what sounded like other containers being placed around - and one even on top of - their container.

"Where are we now?" Lizbeth asked, reaching for a bit of the bread they still had left.

"I don't know." Yvette leaned her head against a box behind her. "We've been moved off the train. We were set on top of something metal and it sounded like another container was put on top of us. They wouldn't put them three high on a train. Perhaps we're on a ship?"

"Where would he be taking us on a ship?" Fear colored Lizbeth's voice, much more so than Yvette would have expected. Could it be the drugs still affecting her?

"Anywhere," Yvette replied with a sigh. "Hopefully not far." The food and water, which they'd rationed, wouldn't last too much longer. They were already getting dehydrated.

He needed them alive. She had to keep believing that.

After an undetermined period of time, they were underway again. The motion and sounds were different.

"I think we are on a ship this time." Lizbeth flexed her hands and tried to rotate her wrists. "There's something I haven't even told Robert yet." She glanced around. "Do you think my father can hear us?"

Yvette shook her head. "I doubt it."

Regardless, Lizbeth leaned close enough to whisper. "We're having a baby."

Yvette gasped. "You are?"

Lizbeth nodded, tears streaking down her cheeks. "I was going to tell Robert the day after the hearing. Instead, I'm here."

That explained Lizbeth being more scared than Yvette would have expected her friend to be.

Yvette reached over with both of her hands and took Lizbeth's. "They're looking for us. They'll find us. I don't know when or how, but God's got *all* of us in His hands. We're going to be fine." She couldn't explain how she knew that, but she did. Deep inside, she knew their captivity would be a difficult few days, but ultimately, they would be all right.

The rocking motion put both of them to sleep. As Yvette dozed off, she prayed again.

Lord, let them find us in time.

Nicklaus should have shaved, but he couldn't bring himself to care enough to.

The crowd of reporters waited in the press room for Nicklaus, Robert, and King Antonio to make their appearance and answer a few questions.

He hadn't slept in two days. Antonio had managed a few winks, as had Robert. Not much, but some. More than Nicklaus. He wouldn't want to see a photo of himself right now.

The press secretary made a short statement before Nicklaus and Robert followed the king into the room. Antonio stood at the lectern, his hands braced on either side and looking older than Nicklaus had ever seen him.

"Thank you for coming on such short notice." He straightened the papers in front of him. "Two days ago, at about seven in the evening, my daughter, Princess Yvette, my son-in-law, Prince Nicklaus of Ravenzario, and Mrs. Lizbeth Bence Padovano, wife of Parliament member Robert Padovano, were kidnapped. Prince Nicklaus and Princess Yvette's vehicle was commandeered by someone in the employ of the man we believe to be behind the kidnappings. As the vehicle drove through the woods near the palace, Prince Nicklaus was able to escape the vehicle, injuring himself in the process. For reasons we still don't understand, my daughter was unable to follow him as planned. Mrs. Padovano disappeared somewhere between her apartment and the home she was moving into with her husband."

He cleared his throat. "Not long before my daughter and son-in-law left the palace, Mr. Bence was arrested and detained within the palace for attempting to blackmail me before attacking me, the queen, Princess Yvette, and Prince Nicklaus. In the informational packet we'll give you after this press conference, there will be more information about what we believe his rationale to be, both with the blackmailing and the kidnapping. About the time Nicklaus returned to the palace, it was discovered Mr. Bence was missing, leading us to believe he is behind the kidnapping. We are investigating how he managed to escape and will share the details of that investigation when the time comes. However, there has not yet been any ransom demands or demands of any other kind."

Antonio took a deep breath before continuing. "At this time we would ask two things. First, prayers for Princess Yvette and Mrs. Padovano, as well as their husbands and families during this difficult time. Second, if you have any information, or see anything suspicious that you believe could be connected to their disappearances, please call the number provided. Your help is needed to find Princess Yvette and Lizbeth Padovano and to bring the assailants to justice. I will answer a few questions."

All of the reporters shouted at once. The king pointed to Matt Markinson. How had the Ravenzarian reporter known to be here?

"Two questions, Your Majesty. First, will Prince Nicklaus be answering any questions about why he was able to escape, but not the princess?"

Antonio leaned closer to the microphone. "Not at this time. There are too many unknowns as to why she was unable to follow him out of the moving vehicle."

"In that case, is there any reason to believe the women have been moved out of the country?" Markinson sat back down.

"Yes. We have reason to believe they were taken to the rail station north of Erres. From there, they could have been taken anywhere. We are reasonably certain they were not taken anywhere by plane from any location within Mevendia, but if they were traveling by car, it is possible they were across the border before we were able to increase security checks."

A woman stood before anyone else could. "When did Mr. Padovano get married?"

Nicklaus knew the king would be annoyed by the question. He'd said as much before they headed to the press conference. "That is a question for another time. Suffice it to say, Mr. Bence's discovery of his daughter's marital status is likely part of the reasoning behind all of this. He had requested a hearing in an attempt to retain all of the inheritances due Mrs. Padovano from her mother and grandfather. By the end of the hearing, two days ago, he had to know he would lose. Her marital status would have played a role in that decision."

A man Nicklaus recognized, but couldn't place, asked the next question. "If they have left the country, where do you believe they would have gone?"

"Our belief is that their most likely stop would be in the Commonwealth, at least at first, before possibly going elsewhere. Mr. Bence owns property in all three Commonwealth countries."

He took several more questions before announcing the press conference over and leaving the room with Nicklaus and Robert in tow, despite questions called out to all three of them.

They headed for the king's official office. "Thank you for not letting them ask questions about my escape."

"There's no reason for them to. We all know you would have let Yvette go first if you'd had a choice or that both of you would be gone if she hadn't pushed you." He used the remote to turn on his television. "I want to see what the general reaction is."

Matt Markinson was standing in front of the palace, but still on palace grounds. He moved quickly to be out there already. He gave a short intro then they cut to several of the king's comments already spliced together. Antonio clicked it off before it went back to Markinson or the studio.

"Never mind. Someone will let me know if there's anything for me to know." He leaned back in his desk chair before standing up instead.

Nicklaus and Robert glanced at each other then followed him down a level to the security headquarters.

"Do we know what train they were on yet?"

The head of security looked even more exhausted than Nicklaus felt. "We think so. It headed to port in Mevendia. Several of the containers were transferred to ships bound for Ravenzario, Athmetis, Italy, or one of several other destinations. Ravenzario is probably the most likely, though."

"Have you coordinated with Mr. Browning."

"Of course. Every container ship will be searched upon arrival."

"They have to be hungry." Everyone turned to Robert, who looked ashen. "Lizbeth hasn't said anything to me yet, but I think she might be pregnant."

"If he wants a ransom, he has to be taking care of them." Nicklaus looked over at Antonio. "Right?"

"You'd think." Antonio sank into a chair. "What else can we do but trust God?"

It was at least another day before the ship lurched to a halt. They had finished the food and water, despite their best rationing. Yvette tried to give Lizbeth more than she took without her friend noticing. Lizbeth needed it more than she did. Yvette knew she couldn't be pregnant.

The container moved again, swinging as it was lifted and then set down. A truck rumbled for a short distance before coming to a stop.

The doors to the container opened and Yvette blinked at the sudden influx of light. It hadn't exactly been dark, but certainly not well-lit.

"Get out." Mr. Bence stood there with goons holding guns.

Yvette and Lizbeth did as they were told. They were told to stand next to the truck and were handed a newspaper. Yvette didn't get a good look, but saw their photos on the front page, plus a picture of her father, Nicklaus, and Robert at what looked like a press conference. One of the goons took a picture.

Proof of life.

Good.

He needed them alive to make a ransom demand.

A few minutes later, they were taken through a series of hallways and hidden in an empty office.

As soon as they were left alone, Yvette stood on her tiptoes to look out the single high window. Could she recognize the town?

She couldn't see much through the grime, but she did see one spire that gave her hope. "We're in Zarifan." The coastal Ravenzarian town was familiar to Yvette. Not greatly so, but enough. Poppo and Nanny had moved here. Could they get to him? Get a hold of him somehow?

Yvette knew she could break the duct tape, but she didn't want to, not yet. Not until she knew they could get away. Otherwise if the goons came back, they wouldn't be kind, or she would have done it days earlier. She reached into her boot and pulled out Nicklaus's phone. She held the button until it came on. It had a fair bit of power, but there was a pass code.

"What could it be?" Lizbeth asked in hushed tone.

"I have no idea." She tried her birthday. His birthday. She only had a few before she was locked out. What other important dates? Their wedding?

Too obvious, but so were the birthdays. She tried it anyway. Then Michaela's birthday. The day he returned to Ravenzario. The date of the car accident? His second chance at life...

She tried it and muttered a curse. Locked out for a minute.

"What else could it be?" Lizbeth asked her. "What about the date of the contract signing?"

"What contract?"

"The marriage contract."

Why would that be it? Yvette didn't know, but waited a minute then tried it anyway.

And breathed a sigh of relief.

Finding Poppo's number was easy. It even had an address, but there was still no service.

"Okay." Yvette looked around. She'd seen out the window that they were on the first floor, so they could jump down, if they could find a way out the window. She looked around. Nothing they could climb on, not really. She came to a conclusion, texting herself the address. It would go through when they got to a better reception area. "Here's what we're going to do. You're going to climb out the window. I'll boost you up, then I can pull myself up. We'll head to Poppo's house." She slipped the phone into Lizbeth's pocket and telling her the pass code. "Go to his address and tell him everything."

"Won't you be with me?"

"In case we get separated." She really didn't hold much hope they'd both get out the window. With her hands still bound together, she managed to get the window open. Time to go for broke.

With a deep breath, she raised her arms and yanked them down and apart at the same time. The duct tape split. She didn't take the time to pull the rest of the tape off, but went right to work ripping Lizbeth's apart.

"Let's go." Yvette stood next to the window and cupped her hands.

Yvette bent her knees as Lizbeth put her foot in Yvette's hands and pushed the window open. "1...2...3." On three, Lizbeth pushed herself off with her other foot, and Yvette straightened, boosting her. Lizbeth's head disappeared, and she swung her other leg out the other side of the long window. Once Lizbeth dropped to the other side, she called back. "Come on."

"Hide!" Yvette grasped the windowsill and hoisted herself up, climbing up the wall until she could swing one leg up and over to the outside. She rolled out, lowering herself carefully. As she landed on the ground, she whispered a prayer of thanks and crouched, making herself as small as possible.

"Over here."

She looked around and saw Lizbeth hiding behind a rubbish bin across the alleyway and down a bit. Together, the two of them ran away from the water and toward what seemed to be the outside of the facility. In ten minutes, they were still on the property of the shipyard, but far away from the building they'd been in.

Hidden behind another rubbish bin, Yvette pulled her phone out of her boot and turned it on. A signal! She didn't make a call, but hoped the security teams would be watching. The text from Nicklaus's phone came through, and she used the map app to find out where to go. Five miles. Not close, but not overwhelmingly far either.

"We don't trust anyone," she told Lizbeth as she pulled the information up on Nicklaus's phone for her friend to use. "Not a kind stranger. Not the police. No one until we get to Poppo. If we get split up, go to Poppo's house. If we get there, and it doesn't seem safe, hide and call Christiana."

"It's a plan, but how do we get out of here, and how do we keep from being recognized? Especially you. You're a princess here in Ravenzario."

"No one expects us to look this awful." They had to. Lizbeth did. Yvette probably looked worse. "If we find some clothes we can snag, maybe a shirt or hat, we do and return it later."

With a better idea where they were going, they stayed as hidden as they could. When they stopped behind a large truck, Yvette tried the door. It opened easily and she found two flannel shirts, ball caps, and two bottles of water. A minute later, as they finished putting the clothes on, Yvette spotted a middle-aged man watching them.

He glanced around and held a finger to his lips.

Yvette knew she shouldn't trust him, but something about him calmed her. When he motioned for them to follow she did, despite Lizbeth's whispered protests. In seconds, they were through a well-hidden gate and out of the shipyard property. She turned to thank the man, but he was gone.

The next four hours were spent trying to stay out of sight, going down back streets and alleys as much as possible, refilling their bottles in a park drinking fountain when they had the chance. Finally, they reach Poppo's back yard.

Yvette knocked on the back door and hid, waiting.

Poppo opened the door and looked around. "Hello?"

"Poppo?" Yvette whispered, tears finally beginning to fall. "Is it safe?"

"Evie?" he whispered back. "Is that you? It's safe."

She came out from behind the bush and rushed into Poppo's waiting arms.

"You're safe, sweet girl." He held her tightly with one arm, ushering her inside, and motioning to Lizbeth with the other. "You're both safe." His other arm came around Yvette, and she collapsed into him as they made it to the living room.

They'd made it.

Nicklaus had tried to sleep in his own bed the night before.

It hadn't worked.

All he could think about was Yvette curled up on her side of the bed or resting her head on his chest as they talked.

But she and Lizbeth were in Ravenzario. They just knew it. Everyone said so. Nicklaus wasn't so sure.

He sat in Tony's office, waiting for more news. The ports and shipyards were being searched with dogs, but there was no way to know if they hadn't somehow missed the container with his wife inside.

"We got something!" The call came from down the hall.

Nicklaus bolted from his seat, beating even Tony who'd been deeply engrossed in something on his screen. They made it to the command center two doors down at the same time.

One of the men looked up from the computer screen and clicked a button, sending the picture to a large television. "Nicklaus's phone is on and moving through the shipyard in Zarifan."

"Do we have men there?"

"Yes, but on the other side. It'll take at least ten minutes to get over there." Tony pointed to another dot on the screen. "The yard is huge. It'll take time."

The dot labeled with his name was moving quickly. Then stopping. Then moving. Then stopping. Then joined by a second dot. "Who's that?" Nicklaus pointed.

"Yvette's phone."

"So she has both?" he asked.

Tony shook his head. "They're far enough apart that Lizbeth probably has one, but yes, they're together. That's the important part."

The dots kept moving and stopping, moving and stopping.

And then left the shipyard.

"Where are they headed?" he crossed his arms. If they weren't on the other island, he would have been in his car already.

"I don't know." The dot representing security teams split into three separate dots. Two stayed in the shipyard, but one left. "They're going to follow from a distance and make sure they stay safe. But with everything that's happened, Yvette likely doesn't trust anyone. If they try to approach, she'll bolt and hide and know enough to turn off the phones or leave them behind."

The dots seemed to stay to back roads and side streets most of the time. The security teams stayed not far behind.

Tony turned to him. "Who does she know who lives in Zarifan?"

Nicklaus wracked his brain until it hit him. "Poppo!"

That was all Tony needed to hear. "Let's go. Get the helicopter ready." It was already waiting on the lawn. Nicklaus didn't think anyone else was supposed to hear him mutter, "Why didn't I think of that?" By the time they reached the lawn, the helicopter was ready to go.

Nicklaus, Robert, Alexander, and Tony boarded. The second the door was secured, they took off.

"Call the king," Tony shouted to Alexander over the sound of the rotor blades. "I'll call Poppo."

Nicklaus didn't know how long it took to get to Zarifan, but it seemed to take half of forever. Finally, they touched down on top of the local police station. Dark SUVs waited to whisk them away. They parked a few streets away from Poppo's house, on the other side from where Yvette and Lizbeth were. They were only a few blocks away.

It was half an hour before the phone call came, and the SUVs sped away. The vehicle hadn't come to a complete stop before Nicklaus managed to get the door open and jumped out, racing to the front door. Nanny opened it in time for him to barrel through.

"Sorry!" he called, knowing he'd bumped her. "Where is she?"

"In here," Poppo called from another room.

Nicklaus slowed his steps as he entered the sitting room. Yvette sprung up from her seat and out of Poppo's embrace. She ran the three steps, and he caught her in his arms as she leapt toward him.

Her arms gripped his neck as his held her as close as he could. He would never let her go.

Never.

He loved her.

He loved her and didn't know how he ever could have considered *not* marrying the beautiful, kind, compassionate, caring woman now weeping in his arms.

It wasn't the right time to tell her, though. Not with the teams of security streaming into the house, and Robert having his own reunion with Lizbeth.

Yvette's body shook with the sobs she probably hadn't let go of since her ordeal began. Tears ran down his own cheeks and into the four day beard growth.

"You're safe," he whispered. "I'll never let go of you again."

She laughed through her tears. "Yes, you will, but I won't let you out of my sight for days."

He smiled. "Okay. I can live with that."

Yvette moved away from him, just enough to look him in the eye. "I knew you would find us."

"You rescued yourselves."

"But you knew where we were going, or you wouldn't be here so quickly."

Tony broke in. "I'm sorry to interrupt the reunions, but we need to talk. We need to find whoever did this. We've got teams at the shipyard, but where were you *exactly*?"

Nicklaus linked his fingers with hers as she walked to Tony and looked at his computer.

"We first saw Nicklaus's phone here." He pointed.

"We'd turned it on before that, but Mr. Bence said he had jammers." Her finger traced along the screen. "I think this is the building we were in."

Tony spoke into a walkie and the dots on the screen began to move again. She told them about a marking she'd noticed on the side of the building, and he passed it along.

"Do we have to wait here?" Lizbeth asked. She looked more nervous and scared.

Yvette looked straight at Tony. "She needs medical attention."

"You both do. You've both lost weight."

Nicklaus hadn't planned to say anything. A few minutes later, Tony was running things from his laptop and cell phone as the SUVs took them back to the police station. In minutes more, they were all back on the helicopter and headed for the palace.

Toward safety.

Toward home.

With his wife now safe from a madman.

Yvette refused medical treatment until she'd taken a shower and brushed out her hair.

Then she allowed a doctor to look at her.

In her own room.

Her own bed.

The doctor wasn't crazy about the idea, but Yvette didn't care. Lizbeth was being taken care of in one of the hospital rooms in the palace, but Yvette wasn't pregnant.

Under doctor's orders, a nurse put in an I.V. with fluids. A couple bags of saline and she'd be good as new. Maybe they'd even take it out before bedtime.

A girl could hope.

Tony came in and took a seat. "I need you to tell me everything you remember."

Yvette closed her eyes and began to tell her story. She could sense the tension in Nicklaus as she rubbed her thumb along the back of his hand.

"Why did you give Lizbeth more of the food and water?" Tony asked.

Yvette glanced at her husband. "Because I knew she was pregnant, and I'm not." He didn't want children yet, did he? She wasn't ready.

"Robert told us he suspected," Nicklaus said.

It took another half an hour, but Tony finally left. Yvette carefully slid closer to her husband and rested her head on his shoulder.

"Are you really all right?" His voice held a tone she couldn't determine.

"I'm *fine*." She'd been trying to reassure him, but to no avail. Was it impolite to wish he'd go take a shower? He likely hadn't had one in just as long, though he hadn't spent any time in a shipping container.

He pulled his hand from hers and stood up so fast she nearly fell over. He walked to the windows and shoved his hands deep in his pockets. "I'm so sorry, Evie."

Yvette knew she couldn't hide her shock. "For what?"

"For leaving you in that car. For not getting you out when I could."

"Nicky, look at me." He didn't budge. "I'm serious. Look at me." He still didn't move. Exasperated, she swung her legs over the side of the bed and held onto the I.V. pole. She rolled it with her until she reached his side and could turn him with pressure from her hand. "Look. At. Me." She glared at him. "Don't make me use your middle name."

"Which one?" he muttered.

"All of them."

With a sigh, he turned.

She looked him straight in the eye. "Nicklaus, none of this is your fault. None of it. I knew when I pushed you out that I might not get out, too. And you know what? It's a good thing I didn't."

"How do you figure?"

"What would Lizbeth have done if she'd been there alone? Or with just you? Which one of us is the better option to be with Lizbeth?"

"You," he admitted, though it seemed to be grudging at best.

"God worked it for good. You left your phone behind. We weren't trying to split that little bit of food three ways. Without your phone, I wouldn't have had Poppo's address. I'm sure we would have found some other way, but I'm glad we had Poppo."

"Michaela will be, too."

She reached up with both hands and cupped his scruffy face. "But it is *not* your fault I was kidnapped. It's *not* your fault you made it out and not me. *None* of this is your fault."

Nicklaus nodded, but still seemed unsure. He took a deep breath. "There's something I need to tell you, though. Something I realized over the last few days."

She tilted her head at him. "What's that?"

He took another breath and blew it out slowly. "I love you."

Yvette blinked twice. "What?"

"I love you, Yvette." His earnest eyes warmed her heart. "It took this awful thing for me to realize that. I haven't known you very long. Only a few weeks, really, but I do. I don't know why I realized it so quickly or that it took so long, because it seems like it's both. I don't know why our path to each other took such a circuitous route, but I'm glad I stayed. I'm glad I married you. I'm glad you're my wife." He kissed her, soft and gentle. Their first kiss since he walked into the room at Poppo's. By unspoken agreement, they'd waited until they were alone. "I love you."

"Oh, Nicky." She kissed him the same way he'd kissed her.

Before she realized what was happening, before she could tell him what else she wanted to, he'd picked her up into his arms. "Good. Now you're going to bed. You need rest."

She sighed. "Fine. But promise me you'll take a shower."

He chuckled. "I can do that. I think I might keep the beard, though."

Yvette wrinkled her nose. "Please don't."

"Fine. I'll shave." He set her down then kissed her forehead. "Rest."

She waited until he closed the bathroom door behind him before she reached for the drawer in the table next to the bed. Time to check in with Princess Victoria.

For some reason, the diary opened to the last entry.

It's been many years since I last wrote in this diary. The time has often gone by as though it has wings, while at other times it has crawled frustratingly slow. Prince David has been a good husband to me. I have loved him as I could have loved no other. I believe he has loved me as well. I believe him when he says he has been faithful to me and me alone. King Luke has not been faithful, and I believe it was God's favor that spared me marriage to my brother-in-law. I grow more tired by the day and believe the time I have left in this world is short.

All of my children will survive me. Many women do not have this blessing. In fact, unless something changes, my son will inherit my father's throne. I could not ask for more of this life. I have been loved and loved well by a good man, a prince among men, no matter what his hereditary titles may have been. I have been loved by my children and done good with my life. I could not ask for more.

Yvette looked at the date and then picked up her phone to do a search. It had been written just days before Princess Victoria's death and mere weeks before her son would take the throne.

Yvette set the book back in the drawer as she looked up to see Nicklaus coming out of the bathroom clad in pajama pants and drying his hair.

"Nicky?" He looked at her. "I love you, too."

He grinned, that electric smile she loved. "I know you do." He put a knee on the bed and leaned on his hands until he could kiss her. "But you're supposed to be asleep."

Yvette hadn't planned to sleep just yet, but suddenly it sounded like the best idea she'd heard in a long time. She pulled the quilt Michaela had given them up over her chest, closed her eyes, and slept.

Nicklaus kissed Yvette's forehead and tucked the quilt around her a bit more tightly. He went out to the living area and closed the door quietly behind him.

"She's asleep," he said still keeping his voice down.

Michaela and Tony sat on one couch, while Poppo sat on the other.

"How's she doing?" Poppo asked.

"Okay, I think." He sank into a chair. "She was very adamant that leaving her behind was the right thing to do."

"It was," Tony confirmed. "I think it's more likely you would have been less inclined to go along until it was time to fight back. That would have gotten all three of you hurt. You would have done it with the best intentions, but it would have backfired."

Nicklaus nodded. "She pointed out the same things and asked what would have happened to Lizbeth if we'd both gotten out. Or if I'd been there instead of her."

"We're having a press conference tomorrow," Tony told him. "We'd like Yvette to be there, but I don't think Lizbeth will up for it."

"How is she? The baby?"

"They should be just fine, but they want her to rest for a couple more days."

"I'll let Yvette know." He ran a hand through his hair. "Did you get everyone?"

"As far as we can tell. We'll keep investigating, but we got Lizbeth's father, the two members of your father's security team who helped Bence escape, Lord Peter from Montevaro, and several others."

"What about the man who helped us find the gate?"

Nicklaus, along with everyone else looked over to see Yvette walking slowly into the room, dragging the I.V. pole with her. Nicklaus hurried to her side, putting his arm around her waist to support her until they reached the chair. She sat in it while he leaned against the arm.

Tony shook his head. "We haven't found anyone matching the description you gave us, and no one seems to know him either."

"Some guy helped you?" Michaela leaned forward. "What did he look like?"

Yvette described him.

"Did he have incredibly green eyes?" Michaela asked.

Yvette's brow furrowed. "Yes. He did."

Michaela pointed at her forehead. "And a scar right here?"

"I think so."

Tears started to streak down Michaela's cheeks. "That sounds just like the man who helped me and Nicky all those years ago. Older, but the same."

"You think?" Nicklaus was skeptical.

"Maybe, maybe not, but maybe God's got an angel or two working down at the docks."

Tony looked at his phone then kissed Michaela's cheek. "I've got to get back downstairs. I'll see you later."

Poppo stood as Tony left. "I need to get home as well."

"There are no more ferries tonight, Dad." Michaela went and

put her arm around him. "I told you and Mom you shouldn't have moved."

Poppo chuckled. "I've got connections, sweetheart. I have a friend who will take me. He'll be going back soon anyway." He moved away from her and gave both Nicklaus and Yvette hugs. "Thank you for coming to me, Evie. Anytime you need anything, I'm here."

She smiled, but Nicklaus thought it seemed a bit weak. "I know, Poppo." She squeezed his hand. "Thank you."

A minute later, they were alone in the apartment. Nicklaus gave Yvette a mock glare. "It's time for you to get back to bed, young lady."

He picked her up again, more carefully than he had in their room earlier. She held onto the pole as it rolled with them. Nicklaus settled her onto the bed and covered her back up with the quilt from Michaela.

"Stay with me?" she whispered.

"Of course." Nicklaus settled onto the bed and took her hand in his. They lay there until Yvette fell asleep again a few minutes later. Nicklaus stayed with her, afraid the nightmares would come for her as they did for him.

But when sunlight streamed in the window, waking him, he realized she still slept soundly. The bag of saline was about half full. He wasn't sure how he felt about a nurse sneaking in while they slept to check on Yvette.

Several people waited in the living room when he made it out there. Great. Maybe they could get to that trip on board the yacht again soon. Just the two of them and staff members who knew to stay out of the way.

When had he gotten so used to having staff members?

The nurse bobbed a curtsy and went past him to check on Yvette. Melinda and Belinda were both there waiting to work their magic to help Yvette look her best for the press conference he still hadn't told her about.

A couple hours later, she'd directed her aides in packing both of their bags and tried to avoid using the wheelchair to get to the press room. Her doctor insisted, though, and Nicklaus backed him up.

And then they were standing in front of the press corp.

"Good morning, ladies and gentlemen." Yvette was far more poised than he ever would be. "I will make a brief statement, but won't take any questions at this time. I would like to thank members of law enforcement, security teams, and countless others who spent the last several days tirelessly searching for myself and Mrs. Padovano. Out of an abundance of caution, her doctors have asked that she be given a couple more days of rest. They have tried to insist on the same with me, but..." There was a twinkle in her eye. "I refused. In fact, they wanted me to address you from a wheelchair, just to be safe, but I'm not about to take that suggestion sitting down when I feel mostly fine. Still a bit weak perhaps, but not *that* weak."

Quiet chuckles sounded.

"The prayers of the people of both Mevendia and Ravenzario kept us going and gave us the strength we needed when it became possible for us to escape. Fortunately, we weren't kidnapped by the brightest bulbs in the box, and we were able to sneak away once we arrived in Ravenzario. More details will likely be available at a later date, but for now, please know that you have my eternal gratitude as well as that of my family. I was able to speak to them by video conference earlier and look forward to spending some time with them before long."

Antonio looked years younger than he had just two days before when his daughter was missing. The whole family had talked with her for a moment, though Nana Yvette had cut her visit short when she was told she had a guest.

Yvette neared the end of her speech. "I would also like to thank all of you for keeping the public informed and giving them the information they needed to help find us. Thank you."

She turned and walked away from the podium, ignoring the questions called from behind her. Nicklaus rested his hand on her back as they walked out. When they were down the hall, she spoke again.

"How soon can we get to that ship?"

In a couple of hours, they were back in their suite on the yacht as it headed for the open sea. Yvette stood on their balcony, leaning her forearms against the railing.

The wind blew her hair back from her face as the islands disappeared behind them. She didn't hear him coming, but Nicklaus didn't surprise her when he slid his arms around her waist.

"Are you all right?" he asked, loud enough to be heard over the breeze.

"I think so. I keep thinking about the day in my father's office. I knew, intellectually, that my father hadn't been the most upstanding man. I was there when the truth about Jessabelle's paternity - and Malachi's - came out last year. But to see and hear, even a faked recording, the proof of his infidelities was a bit of a blow. I wasn't even born yet."

"I won't do that to you," he vowed. "I wouldn't cheat on you."

"I know." She sounded unconvincing even to herself.

They stood there for several minutes before he spoke again. "Why don't you believe me? I know your father didn't set the best example in the early years of their marriage, but not all men are like that. Most aren't. Look at Alexander. Or Malachi. Both have had opportunities to cheat and didn't."

"I know."

"So what is it?"

Everything she'd been storing inside tumbled out, exacerbated by the trauma of the last few days. "My father loved my mother the whole time he cheated on her. It was an arranged match, to an extent, but they didn't marry until they were ready to. I even have it on good authority that he was faithful to her before the wedding, but within six months, he had taken up his philandering. Until I was missing, you didn't love me. How can I be sure that's enough to stop you should you find someone else you're attracted to?"

He let go of her, and Yvette found herself feeling more alone than she had in quite some time. Before she could let herself sink into despair, Nicklaus took her hand and led her back into their suite. He led her to the bed and motioned for her to sit down.

Before her mind could register what he was doing, he was on one knee. "Princess Yvette of Mevendia, we've done all of this a bit backwards. Engaged before either of us were potty trained, before you could talk. Married when we barely knew each other. Intimacy based on attraction but not love."

Was he trying to make her feel better? If so, he was failing. Miserably.

"But things have changed in the last month." He took her hand and kissed the back of it. "I've seen you, gotten to know you, to know the real you. Not the you we see on television, but the tender, compassionate, funny Yvette. The one who believes in me and is on my side no matter what. The Yvette I've fallen head-over-heels for. I can't ask you to marry me, because you already did. I can ask you to spend the rest of your life with me. I love you. I loved you before you went missing, but it took something big to knock some sense into me. I want you to be my best friend, my only lover, the mother of my children, and my help meet in whatever God has planned for us. Will you?"

Tears had begun streaming down her cheeks as he spoke. "Yes," she whispered. "I love you, too, Nicky." She leaned down and kissed him with all the love in her heart. "But I have a question. It doesn't change anything, but I've been meaning to ask."

"What's that, love?"

"Where did this engagement ring come from?"

Nicklaus fiddled with it. "It's Princess Victoria's ring from when she married the second time. I actually didn't know that until the other day."

Yvette looked more closely at the sapphire, emerald, and diamond ring. "It's fitting," she told him. "The Van Rensselaer Accords and all."

Nicklaus sat next to her on the bed. "I never thought to ask if you like it, or if you'd like something else. Someone gave it to me and told me to give it you. With everything else at the time, I just sort of went along with it."

A sheen of tears clouded Yvette's view for a moment as she wondered at the connection between her life and that of a princess nearly two centuries ago. "It's perfect," she whispered, looking up at Nicklaus. She leaned up and kissed him again.

He kissed her back, and she showed him how she felt about him, how much her feelings had grown since the first time they came together as man and wife.

For the next two days, they spent most of their time in the suite. They talked like they hadn't before, sharing much of their innermost thoughts and feelings. Planning their future. Sharing their dreams.

Friday night, Yvette curled up next to her husband in a big chair, her head resting on his bare chest. They hadn't heard from anyone in either family since they left, and she considered that a good thing. But now it was time for the documentary to air, and they'd decided to watch it in real time.

"You ready for this?" she asked softly as he clicked the television on.

"As ready as I can be I suppose."

Matt Markinson appeared on the screen giving an introduction to the evening's program. It began with a brief history of the royal family leading to the accident and including their betrothal. The picture of Nicklaus holding her when she was just an infant made its expected appearance. After a commercial, they came back to the cliff side where the car had come to rest. Michaela-on-the-screen told how she'd gotten Nicklaus out of the car and walked along the shore, pointing out where they'd gone in the water and where they climbed out.

The story was interspersed with the interviews with all three of them, though they focused mostly on Nicklaus and Michaela until they reached the point in the story where they returned to Ravenzario before the wedding. By then the hour was nearly up.

The last few minutes surprised both of them. There was a short interview with Michaela done just the day before.

"And there's something new about you today, Ms. Engel."

Michaela blushed and held up her left hand. The picture changed to show Tony sitting next to her. "Yes. Since we first began taping, Tony asked me to marry him. I said yes."

Nicklaus pumped a fist in the air. "Yes! It's about time!"

"Did you know he was going to?"

"I suspected. He'd talked to me about it, but I didn't know when."

Matt Markinson asked Tony the next question. "So all those years doing your best to keep Henry Eit from finding out Prince Nicklaus was still alive also served to keep the love of your life safe?"

Tony took her hand. "We didn't meet until I went searching for them." He looked at her. "I think we may have met once, in passing, many years ago, but we never had a conversation. But yes. In protecting Nicklaus, I was protecting the woman I want to spend my life with, even though I wouldn't know that until much later."

The shot cut back to the studio. "We'll be doing another special soon, interviewing all of those involved in this week's dramatic events. The kidnapping, the rescue, and everything in between. But before that, we've also received some information just today. For obvious reasons, it's been kept fairly quiet, but there were allegations that Prince Nicklaus wasn't who he said he was. His DNA didn't match the official DNA on file. The presumption was that Eit had tampered with it at some point, but the palace knew they needed to prove the prince is who he says he is. A constitutional crisis could result if they were unable to, as the DNA did prove he was a full sibling to the queen - and she was also not related to the official DNA on file."

The camera angle changed. "Just this afternoon, new DNA results were made available to us. Using mitochondrial DNA, they were able to prove that both the prince and the queen are the descendants of Queen Marissa's mother through the maternal lines. A yDNA test was also done, comparing Prince Nicklaus's DNA to King Antonio of Mevendia's DNA. Prince David of Mevendia married Princess Victoria of Ravenzario in the mid-1800s. It was this marriage that led to the Van Rensselaer Accord, the jewels the princess wore for the second half of the wedding, and the princess's engagement ring. When Princess Victoria's brother died without an heir, their son became king and the ancestor of King Richard. Prince David's brother Luke became king of Mevendia and the ancestor of King Antonio. Both lines trace back to the father of those two princes. The yDNA is passed down from father to son, virtually unchanged."

He held up a piece of paper. "As expected, the yDNA of King Antonio and Prince Nicklaus is a match, indicative of sharing a male ancestor some eight to ten generations ago." Matt smiled. "With those questions laid to rest, the private reign of terror instigated by Henry Eit comes to a final conclusion. The country, and the royal family, can put it behind them and move forward to a future filled with promise, including new little princes and princesses running around the palace. The country is waiting with bated breath for the appearance of Queen Christiana and Duke Alexander's first child." His eyes twinkled. "From those I've talked to, they're also waiting anxiously for news that Princess Yvette is expecting."

He wrapped up the broadcast while Yvette gaped up at Nicklaus then back down at her stomach.

"No!" She shook her head. "Not yet! I want kids, several of them, but not yet!"

Nicklaus chuckled. "When it happens, it happens. The country will be excited. I'll be ecstatic." He kissed her. "In the meantime, it's just the two of us. And I love that." Another kiss. "And I love you."

She felt her cheeks color as he kissed her again, more intensely, this time.

Yvette whispered her love for him as he showed her how he felt about being her future.

A future she finally looked forward to.

With the prince from her past who showed up at the last minute to be the love of her life.

LETTER TO READERS

Dear Reader,

Thank you for joining Princess Yvette and Prince Nicklaus in *Prince from her Past*! I appreciate you and hope you enjoyed it! This is the third book in the Brides of Belles Montagnes series! Next up will be Christopher Bayfield's story, likely picking up where we left him - on a plane back to Serenity Landing with Julia. Then a second Serenity Landing Lifeguards - this one a "short novel" that will lead right into... Jonathan's story! YAY! I know all of you have been waiting for that one! Don't worry, his happily ever after is on the way! In just a few swipes, you'll find chapter 1 of *Finding Mr. Write*, book 1 in the CANDID Romance series which is FREE on all retailers! Many of you have likely already read *Good Enough for a Princess*, but if not, it too is FREE on all retailers!

I see a meme floating around Facebook from time to time that tells readers what they can do to help their favorite authors. Buying their next book or giving a copy away is kind of a no-brainer, but the biggest thing you can do is write a review. If you enjoyed *Prince from her Past* would you consider doing just that?

I would LOVE to hear from you! My email address is books@candidpublications.com. To stay up-to-date on releases, you can sign up for my newsletter (there's fun stuff - like a super special novella that will be coming FREE later this year!! You'll also get notices of sales, including special preorder pricing! And I won't spam!) or there's always "What's in the Works" or "What I'm Working On Now" on my website :). You can find my website and blog at www.carolmoncado.com. I blog most Sundays and about once more each month at www.InspyRomance.com. And, of course, there's Facebook and my Facebook profile, Author Carol Moncado. If you recently liked my Facebook *page* (Carol Moncado Books)...I hope you'll "follow" the profile as well. Facebook recently changed the rules again which means very few people (often 1-5% of "likes") will see anything I post there. Following the profile will show you my book updates, updates about books from authors I love, funny cat (or dog or dinosaur!) memes, inspirational quotes, and all sorts of fun stuff!! I hope to see you there soon!

Thanks again!

Until next time,
Carol

ACKNOWLEDGMENTS

They say writing is a solitary endeavor and it absolutely can be. Sitting in front of the computer for hours on end, talking to imaginary people.

And having them talk back ;).

But the reality is no one walks alone. Since I began this writing journey nearly six years ago, I can't begin to name all of those who've helped me along the way. My husband, Matt, who has always, *always* believed in me. All of the rest of my family and in-loves who never once looked at me like I was nuts for wanting to be a writer. Jan Christiansen (my "other mother") has always believed in me and Stacy Christiansen Spangler who has been my dearest friend for longer than I can remember.

For *Prince from her Past* specifically - I can't begin to count the number of text messages Emily N. and Ginger V. put up with trying to sort things out. Ginger Solomon, author of *One Choice*, has been invaluable with her proofreading services.

And Jerenda F. - thank you for letting me borrow your Poppo and Nanny. I appreciate you!

Then there's my writer friends. My NovelSista, Jessica Keller

Koschnitzky, sister of my hear. She is part of my BritCrit gals. Joanna Politano (who has talked me down off more virtual ledges than anyone), Jen Cvelvar (the best case of misidentification *ever*), Kristy Cambron (who is more beautiful inside and out than any one person should be allowed to be), and Stacey Zink (who never, ever fails to have a fabulous encouraging word) are BritCritters, too. We do a lot more living than we do critting, and I wouldn't have it any other way. All five of them are beyond gifted as writers, and I thank God they're in my life. There's my MozArks ACFW peeps who laugh with me, critique, and encourage to no end. And Melanie Dickerson. What would I do without you?

Then there's the InspyRomance crew, the CIA, my Spicy peeps (you know who you are!), and all of the others who've helped me along on this journey. Jennifer Major picked up *Good Enough for a Princess* and demolished the rest of the royalty books in less than a week. She was an invaluable encourager before, but even more since.

I've said it before, but I could go on for days about beloved mentors like Janice Thompson who has poured her time and energy into this newbie, going above and beyond for me. People like one of my spiciest friends, Pepper Basham, who inspires me daily, or Julie Lessman, who has prayed me to this point. All of these and so many more are not only mentors, but *friends* - I am beyond blessed! And, of course, there's Tamela Hancock Murray, agent extraordinaire, who believed in me enough to want to be my agent and encourages me always.

I said I could go on for days, and I could keep going. On and on. I know I've forgotten many people and I hate that. But you, dear reader, would quickly get bored.

So THANK YOU to all of those who have helped me along the way. I couldn't have done this without you and you have my eternal gratitude. To the HUNDREDS of you (I'm gobsmacked!) who pre-ordered and encouraged me without knowing it as that little number continued to climb, you have my eternal gratitude. I hope you stick around for the next one!

And, of course, last but never, *ever*, least, to Jesus Christ, without whom none of this would be possible - or worth it.

DISCOVERING HOME PREVIEW

Movement in the woods to the left of the gate caught Jonathan Langley-Cranston's eye.

Seeing a wild animal there wasn't unusual. He lived in the country. It went with the territory.

But something about this shadow was different.

He moved the gearstick out of first into neutral and set the parking brake.

Moving slowly, he tried to avoid the mud puddles. The shadow skittered to another tree, drawing him further in. He swore under his breath as his foot, in a brand new Bruno Magli shoe, slipped into a puddle just big enough to soak it all.

A few more steps and he found the shadow huddled against a tree. Reaching down, he tried to pick up the animal, but the pile of fur seemed to shrink back even further. Jonathan used his foot to sort of trap the little thing against the tree, blocking its means of escape and finally managing to get his hands on the trembling ball of hair.

He half expected a bark or growl, but instead heard only

whimpering. Caring less about his suit than his shoes, he pulled the small dog closer.

"Hey, little fella," he crooned. "It's okay. I've got you." The black fur was so shaggy Jonathan couldn't see the dog's eyes. "Let's get you inside. It's too wet and cold for you to be out here."

July in the Missouri Ozarks was a study in contrasts. One year hot enough to be mistaken for the Sahara. The next comparatively frigid. This was a frigid year. Though nothing like it would be in a few months, the night before had been jeans and sweatshirt cool.

He wasn't nearly as careful going back to his car. His shoes were already ruined, but the suit could be cleaned. Climbing into the low-slung 2017 Ford Mustang, he gently settled the dog onto the passenger seat, but for all his fear, the animal scampered back over onto Jonathan's lap. He snuggled close even as he practically vibrated in fear.

Pressing the button on his visor, Jonathan put the car back in gear and eased through the gate as it opened. The winding drive didn't take long, and in just a couple minutes, he pulled into the garage. Holding the shaking mass of wet fur close, Jonathan went into the house and set him on a towel on the kitchen counter.

Now what?

"Is there something you need to tell me, sir?"

Jonathan turned to see George, his butler and all-around-right-hand-man, walking into the kitchen. "He was outside the gate."

"He, sir?"

The quivering mass of fur whimpered again. "I guess it could be a she. I haven't looked yet."

"Probably covered in fleas and ticks."

He hadn't thought about that, but it made sense. "Most likely." Options flooded through his mind. "Would you watch him or her for a minute while I change? Then we'll get him a bath and take a picture or two to put online in case someone's missing him."

The look on George's face told Jonathan what he thought the

chances of that were. About the same Jonathan did. Someone had dumped this poor dog in the woods near Serenity Lake. Jonathan toed off his shoes and kicked them into the mud room before stripping his socks off and holding them with one finger and his thumb. "Weigh him on the kitchen scale for me?" Jonathan called as he headed for the stairs. "Can't imagine he'll break it."

George muttered a response, but Jonathan couldn't hear it clearly. He could figure out the gist though. There would be no weighing on the kitchen scale.

It only took a couple minutes to change into an old pair of jeans and a t-shirt that had seen better days. When he made it back downstairs with a giant fluffy towel in his hand, the two hadn't moved at all, though George held his phone.

"You would do well to wash him in Dawn dish detergent, sir. Let it soak for about fifteen minutes to kill the fleas. It may or may not help with the ticks, too."

"And you decided not to do it yourself?" Jonathan kept his chuckle to himself, more or less.

"I didn't want to deprive you of the privilege."

Jonathan scooped the dog up carefully and set him in the deep sink before pulling the dish soap from underneath. Once the water warmed up to a reasonable level, he used the wand to rinse as much of the dirt and mud off as he could. After working the dish soap into the fur, Jonathan wrapped the whole bubbly mess in the towel and held him - definitely a him - close to his chest.

"It's all right, bud. We'll get you taken care of." Jonathan wasn't up on guesstimating weights, but if he had to bet, he'd say this dog weighed maybe four pounds, five tops, and half of that was probably fur. For fifteen minutes, he tried to comfort the little thing before putting him back in the sink and rinsing him again with warm water.

Fleas and ticks both swirled down the drain, along with more dirt, mud, and suds. Jonathan washed him twice more like that before the water seemed to run mostly clear. With the dog wrapped up in a dry towel, Jonathan went into the living room to figure out his plan.

"You are *not* sitting on my couches like that, sir." George appeared out of nowhere.

Jonathan rolled his eyes and headed for the stairs. The dog was clean enough to put on the floor in his room for a few minutes while he changed again.

He texted a couple of friends to see if they could recommend a vet. In just a couple minutes, he heard back from one of them who used one of the top vets in the area - and who happened to be open late. Armed with directions, he took off, this time in his Toyota Tundra. It could handle the dirt better than his Mustang.

He didn't call ahead, just prayed that they would take pity on this poor dog. And him. He didn't know what else to do.

The clinic was across the street from two of the Serenity Landing elementary schools. Only two other cars were in the lot, and when he walked in, he could tell they were wrapping things up.

"Can I help you, sir?"

He held the small guy a little closer. "I found this dog in the woods a couple hours ago. I didn't know you were open, or I would have come straight here. I know I don't have an appointment, but I'd appreciate some help."

The front desk gal came around and reached for the dog. "Come here, sweetheart," she crooned. "Did someone lose you?"

"I don't think so. I've already given him like three baths with Dawn dish soap." He pulled out his phone and showed her a picture. "I know he doesn't look a ton better, but he's cleaner at least. I didn't see him until today, but I'd guess he's been out there a while."

"Probably," she said, using an almost baby voice. "Let's get the vet to take a look at you."

Nearly an hour later, well after closing time, Jonathan left with the still-scared dog in his arms. He also had varied medicines, the knowledge that he didn't have a microchip, and a shopping list. After deliberating on the ninety second drive to Walmart, he decided to look like a dork and carry a blanket in with him. No one would notice the dog inside it. Not something he'd normally do, but desperate times and all.

Once the dog and blanket were snuggled in the seat of the cart, he bee-lined for the back of the store and the pet area. Dry dog food. Wet dog food. A dog bed. A crate. Collar. Leash.

"Hey! I know you!"

Jonathan turned at the sound of a little girl's voice. No more than four or five, the girl practically bounced on her toes. He smiled but didn't say anything.

"You danced with me!"

"Lorelai," her mother reprimanded. "Leave the nice man alone."

"But he danced with me! And let me see at Mrs. Ginger's wedding."

Jonathan glanced up at the mother and remembered. He definitely remembered her, though he'd never known her name. "That's right." He knelt down. "You sat with me for the whole wedding, didn't you? And you let me have your first dance." He winked at her. "I remember it very well."

He also remembered the dance with her mother.

The girl's attention turned to the cart, her eyes wide. "Do you have a doggy in your cart?" she whispered. "Doggies aren't supposed to be in the store."

Jonathan looked over to see the blanket wiggling. "I know. But I found this dog out in the woods a little while ago, and we just left the vet. He's super scared so I didn't want to leave him alone in the truck."

"Can I pet him?"

He winced. "Not right now. He's sick, and I wouldn't want you to catch it. Besides, he doesn't think he looks very handsome at the moment. He needs a haircut but can't get one until he's all better."

"I think he's handsome." Only his nose was showing.

"Lorelai, it's time to go." Her mother pushed the cart toward the food section of the store.

"Are you gonna get him clothes?"

"Should I?" He had never thought to dress a dog. That was a froo-froo girl thing to do. But he wouldn't turn this little girl down.

She reached for an outfit hanging there. "He needs this one." Camouflaged with hunter orange trim. Perfect.

"Let's find his size, then." They looked through until they found an extra-small. "He only weighs about four pounds you know."

Lorelai's eyes went wide. "That's little. I weighed six pounds when I was born."

"That's pretty little, too." Wasn't it? What did he know?

"Six and a half," her mother interjected. "And it's time to go."

"You better listen to your mother." He pulled his wallet out and handed over one of his business cards. "If your mom will email me, I'll send you some pictures after he gets all cleaned up, okay?"

Lorelai took it and nodded eagerly. "Does he have a name yet?"

"Nope."

She cocked her head, blond hair falling over one shoulder. "Mr. Benny Hercules."

"Mr. Benny Hercules?" Not Fido? Rex? And Hercules? Really?

"Yep."

He chuckled. "All right. Mr. Benny Hercules it is."

She held the card in both hands. "Please email him, Mommy?"

Her mom sighed and nodded. "Fine."

Here was his chance. "Can I know your name so I know whose email to expect?"

"Kenzie Ann!" Lorelai practically shouted. "Unless she's in trouble with Papaw. Then he uses her whole name."

Jonathan met Kenzie's gorgeous hazel eyes. "A pleasure to meet you, Kenzie Ann."

"Just Kenzie is fine." She looked at the card in Lorelai's hand. "Jon."

He winced and held out a hand. "Jonathan. My mother was very insistent about that. I should probably get over it, but I haven't yet."

When she didn't take it, he let his arm drop back to his side.

"I'll email you later, Jonathan." She looked down at her daughter. "We've got to get going, Lorelai."

The two walked off, but Lorelai turned back and waved. "Bye, Mr. Jonathan! I can't wait for pictures of Mr. Benny Hercules!"

He watched them walk off, then picked up a couple other things he thought he might need and headed home.

⁂

If MacKenzie Annette Davidson heard one more word about Mr. Jonathan and Mr. Benny Hercules, she'd snap.

"Lorelai, honey, I think it's time to talk about something else." Anything else. Anyone else.

Because when her daughter mentioned Jonathan William Langley-Cranston IV, all Kenzie could do was remember the breathless feeling of dancing in his arms. She'd known who he was even then and couldn't help but refer to him by his full name like the media tended to do. She'd nearly choked calling him Jon.

"But you'll email him, right?"

"Yes." She had no choice. Her daughter wouldn't leave her alone if she didn't.

Rain pelted her windshield, but no matter how fast the wipers went, they couldn't quite keep up. Not when they desperately needed replacing. She'd hoped to beat the rain home, but no such luck. Her weak high beams barely sliced through the darkness of the back country road that led to home. She took the last turn, still half a mile from her little house and screamed as the wheels lost contact with the pavement. The whole thing couldn't have lasted more than a few seconds, but to Kenzie, it seemed an eternity before the car came to a stop slanted sideways.

In the ditch.

"Are you okay?" Her first movement was to turn on the overhead light and check on her daughter.

Wide eyes met hers as Lorelai nodded.

"Thank you, Jesus," Kenzie whispered. "Okay, stay put, all right, sweetheart?"

Lorelai nodded again. After a few more deep breaths, Kenzie dug her umbrella out of the pocket in the door and opened it, but the water sloshed inside the car as the virtual river ran off the road. She changed her mind and closed the door again.

"Okay, God," she whispered. "Now what?" It was her own fault, because she'd forgotten how the water built up and ran through this particular corner. A list of people who might be able to help sped through her head. She dismissed them all. Her parents were out of town. Friends had cars worse than hers or small kids of their own.

"Mama, could Mr. Jonathan help us?"

"How could he help?"

"He has a truck."

He had said that, hadn't he? "I don't know how to get a hold of him." Could the two of them walk home? It wasn't far, but it was dark and pouring rain.

"His card."

Right. "I don't think it had his phone number on it." She hadn't looked at it that closely.

"It has numbers," Lorelai insisted, as stubborn as her mother.

She pulled her phone out of her purse as Lorelai handed the card to her. Sure enough. A phone number. But did she dare call him? There were so many reasons not to, not the least of which was that she barely knew him.

"Please, Mama."

Kenzie turned to see tears filling her daughter's eyes, fear had to be creeping into her daughter's heart.

"Remember 2 Timothy 1:7?" They'd memorized it. "What shouldn't we have?"

Lorelai took a deep breath, and Kenzie could see her attitude change. "Fear. God's angels are protecting us."

"That's right." And it made her decision for her. Carefully, she punched in the numbers and waited for someone to answer, unsure of what to pray for. An answer or not.

"Hello?" She could hear the puzzle in his voice.

"Can I speak to Jonathan, please?"

"This is him."

"This is Kenzie. My daughter, Lorelai, and I ran into you at the store a little while ago."

"I remember." His voice warmed. "What's up?"

A tear streaked down her cheek. "I need help, and I don't know where else to turn."

"Okay." Caution. Given his identity and the money that went with it, he likely got hit up for "help" all the time.

"My car skidded off the road, and we're stuck in a ditch." She rushed through her explanation. "Home isn't far, but I could really use some help getting there."

"Let me get a few things together, and I'll leave in like three minutes. Where are you?"

She gave him directions.

"I know where that is. It'll probably take me about twenty minutes. Are you safe?"

"I think so. There's not much past this point in the road except our house."

"What about flash flooding?"

"I've never seen the road as bad as it is now." Surely it wouldn't get any worse until he got there, right?

"Okay. I'm calling a friend who may be able to get there more quickly, but I'll be there as soon as I can."

"Thanks." He hung up before she could say anything else. "He's on his way."

"I like Mr. Jonathan."

"I know you do." Probably too much, especially given the little they knew about him.

For the next twenty minutes, they sang songs and did everything she could think of to keep her daughter's mind off the fact that they were stuck in a ditch. Bright lights cut through the darkness as a black SUV drove very slowly through the water, careful to avoid splashing the car. Flashers turned on as he came to a stop a few feet further down the road.

A small, powerful flashlight shown into the car. "Are you all right?" Jonathan called.

Kenzie nodded.

"Do you want to help me get Lorelai out first?" he asked.

She nodded again. The way the car was situated, the back door was higher out of the water.

"Get your stuff together, anything you want to take, just in case, and we'll get it in my car."

He reached for Lorelai and tucked her close as he took a couple large steps up the embankment and settled her in his SUV. It took several more trips to get everything out - paperwork in the glove box, a book of CDs, Lorelai's organizer that fit over the back of Kenzie's seat and held a myriad of indispensable items, and Lorelai's booster seat.

Then, before Kenzie could get out on her own, Jonathan was there, again, holding out a hand to help her. His strong hand gripped her forearm as she held onto his for dear life.

She had underestimated the strength of the current, and therefore, his strength, because he acted like it was nothing. In a minute, they were both in the front seat of his vehicle. Despite the summer month, he had the heat blasting, and she was grateful.

"Now, where to?"

She directed him to their house, but when she turned to tell Lorelai to get ready to run for it, the little girl was already asleep.

"I'll get her. You head on inside." Jonathan's quiet voice reassured her.

"Thank you." What would she have done if he hadn't come to her rescue?

The front door locks stuck worse than usual, and she had to force the door open. Something stopped her in her tracks, even before she turned the light on.

"What is it?"

She glanced back to see Jonathan holding a trash bag of things from her car. He'd thought ahead and brought some bags to keep stuff dry.

"I'm not sure." Kenzie took a step inside, and her heart sank.

Squish.

Another step.

Squish.

She wanted to remain in denial, but she couldn't. Not for much longer. Dread filled her as she pulled her phone out. It took three tries to get the flashlight turned on. The couch looked normal, though she wished Jonathan wasn't about to see their ever-so-humble abode. Or that they slept on bunk beds in the single bedroom. She moved the light, taking a deep breath, and then looked at the floor.

As she suspected, the area around the door was soaking wet, but why?

She looked at the ceiling.

And there it was.

Bubbles full of water, dripping down in several places all over the living area.

Steeling herself, she looked at the floor more closely.

Over an inch of water stood on the other end of the slightly sloping floor.

They wouldn't be able to stay here.

And they had nowhere else to go.

Available Now!

Jonathan William Langley-Cranston IV has come to terms with the idea that he just might remain single and childless for the rest of his life. It's not his first choice, but it seems to be what God has for him, at least for now. Until a chance encounter with a familiar face changes his outlook.

MacKenzie Davidson has been a single mom since before her daughter was born. Just once, she'd love not to worry about losing her job or what will happen if her fledgling yarn dyeing business doesn't take off. A stormy night and flooded road bring the straws that finally break the back of her independent streak.

Her knight-in-shining-SUV comes in the form of American royalty. She's read enough of the tabloids to know that's how Jonathan's family is seen and knows she can't begin to measure up.

But when he puts everything aside to help her, her daughter, and her now-floundering business, she begins to wonder. Jonathan quickly comes to believe he's found everything he's looking for. Will they find their way to each other or will they be ripped apart before discovering home?

GRACE TO SAVE PREVIEW

SEPTEMBER 11, 2001

A ringing jolted Travis Harders from a deep sleep. He cursed as the phone knocked to the floor with a clatter. "This better be good," he snapped when he got the handset in place.

A glance at the clock nearly made him groan.

4:07.

"You'll be hearing from the police soon."

He rubbed the sleep out of his eyes with the heel of one hand and tried to process the statement. The words didn't really register as the guy, whoever he was, kept talking until Travis interrupted. "What? Who is this?"

"Mark's dad." Right. Travis's best friend. "You remember us? The ones who treated you like family? Let you live with us?"

Travis's stomach sank. Mark's family had practically adopted him when he moved from southwest Missouri to the Big Apple. They had filled the gap in his life left by parents who disapproved of Travis's choice to move to New York. Mark's parents let him spend holidays and birthdays with them, with Travis making only the obligatory phone calls back home.

But none of that explained why Mark's dad would be calling the police.

"Who is it?" a sleepy Jennifer asked.

Travis covered the mouthpiece and whispered to his girlfriend, "No one." His feet hit the cool floor, and he headed for the other room. At least he had a place to escape to. Being an out-of-work-actor-turned-barista didn't pay much, but he'd lucked into a fabulous apartment. Closing the French door behind him, he tried to focus on the voice yelling from the other end of the line.

But he only caught "my daughter" and "spring break" and "drugged."

If possible, Travis's stomach clenched further as that night flooded back to him. Memories of bringing her back to this very apartment when she was in no condition to go home without risking the wrath of her parents. But after what happened between them...it was only right for him to be on the receiving end of her dad's anger. "I don't know what she told you sir, but..."

"I know all I need to know," he bellowed.

Even though he was in the other room, Travis lowered the volume on the handset. "I take full responsibility for..."

"You're right, you do!" He let loose a string of obscenities. "You'll spend years in prison! Drugging a girl! Sleeping with her!"

"What?" His whole world spun. Travis regretted every minute of that night after they got back to the apartment, but he hadn't drugged her. He didn't even know where to get those kinds of drugs. They weren't in love, never had been, but to place the blame solely on him? The next morning, they'd talked about it enough to know she hadn't blamed him.

What changed? Feeling sucker punched, Travis hung up on the man. What he said didn't matter. Travis would find out when he was on trial for something he didn't do. On autopilot, he dressed for his five a.m. shift. Coffees of the World wasn't the best job, but it had flexible hours and had led to finding this sublet. There was no shortage of interesting characters to populate his imagination. Like the skinny brunette with the shoulder length bob who worked for Morgan Stanley and always ordered a short nonfat mocha, decaf, no foam, no sugar, no whip. She could be the heroine in one of his screenplays even if he never knew her name.

He kissed Jennifer's hair and told her he'd call after work. Five flights of stairs later, the sounds of the city waking up greeted him as he walked toward the train that would take him to the Trade Center. Standing at the top of the subway steps, he changed his mind. Travis headed for his car parked a couple streets over and called in.

Two hours later, he stopped in McLean for gas about seven thirty, filling up the tank of his Toyota Corolla hatchback. Three hours after that, he could still drive for a while longer before he'd need to stop again. He contemplated leaving the state, but decided not to, instead turning northward before leaving Allegany County.

He'd gone through more emotions than he knew he had, none of them good. Anger. Fear. Frustration. Blame. Worry. Intimidation. In western New York, things were more peaceful than they ever were in downtown Manhattan, but his insides were in utter turmoil at the thought of an arrest and trial.

His favorite heavy metal CD blared from the speakers. During the lull between songs, Travis could hear his cell phone vibrating on the passenger seat where he'd tossed it. After an hour and a half of the stupid thing ringing nearly nonstop, he finally snatched it up.

"What?" Travis growled.

"Are you okay?" Though he only talked to her twice a year, there was no mistaking his mother's voice.

Or the panic in it.

The tremor set him on edge. "Yeah. Why?"

"Thank you, Jesus," she whispered, though Travis couldn't

figure out what she was thanking Him for. "Where are you? You got out okay? Were you working? There was no answer at your apartment."

Why was Mom calling just to ask if he was okay? Why was she frantic? "I'm in western New York State. Out for a drive. Get out of where?" Could Mark's dad have called already?

"You don't know?" Frenzy changed to disbelief.

"Know what?" Travis held the phone against his shoulder as he downshifted into a turn.

He could hear the tears over the static-filled line. "Two planes, Trav. They hit the Towers. Both of the buildings are on fire."

His heart thudded to a stop. "What?" Hadn't a bomber hit the Empire State Building in WWII? But two planes? On a brilliantly clear day? No weather in sight. "How bad is it?" he croaked.

"They're saying it's a terror attack. The Pentagon is on fire. There's another plane out there somewhere. Big jets, Travis. I saw the second one hit. The explosion. Papers flying everywhere. The people..." Her voice broke. "You really weren't there?" she confirmed.

"No, Mom. I'm not anywhere near there." But he needed to find a place to stop. A television. He had to see for himself. Tens of thousands of people would be dead and dying. Did he know any of them?

"There are people jumping, falling, out of the upper stories. I can't imagine." He could almost see her pacing around the kitchen alternately running her hands through her hair and wringing them together. "They're jumping from a hundred stories up. What could be so bad to make that the better option?" Her voice caught. "I don't know how I can watch this, Trav, but I can't turn away. All I can do is pray."

Pray. Right. A face flashed before Travis. The uptight former-football-player-turned-businessman from the 102nd floor of the North Tower with his caramel macchiato and corny joke of the day. Was he one of those jumping?

She gasped then whispered. "Dear God, no. No!" Her scream made him move the phone even as his stomach sank.

He pulled into a café parking lot near Danville. "What?"

"The tower. It's gone. Just gone. The south one, I think." Her voice trailed off in prayer.

The shock he'd felt after the phone call from Mark's dad paled compared to what he felt now. "Mom, I gotta go." Jen. His friends. His coworkers. He needed to make calls of his own. Find out if they were okay. And Mark. His best friend had been a firefighter for a year. He'd be down there. Inside one of the Towers. Travis hadn't talked to him since that night, the Match before, but part of him, the part that still believed there was a God in heaven, whispered a prayer that Mark was somewhere safe as faces of customers and friends flashed through Travis's mind.

The blonde. The cute, petite one who ordered a crunchy, cinnamon pastry and half caf, double tall, easy hazelnut, non-fat, no foam with whip extra hot latte on Tuesdays. She flirted shamelessly, though he knew she was recently and happily engaged to some guy in Tower Seven. Her family lived near his in Serenity Landing, Missouri, and she worked at the Marriot World Trade Center in the shadow of the Towers. Could it have survived the collapse? Was Joanna now buried underneath the rubble?

"Be safe, Travis. Do you have somewhere you can go? They're evacuating Manhattan."

"I'll be okay." He hesitated. "I love you, Mom. You, Dad, Jay. I love all of you. I'll call when I can, but I have to try to find out about my friends, about my girlfriend. I'll talk to you soon."

His mom's "I love you," came through the line as he clicked his phone off.

He started his first call as he walked into the café. Call after call failed as he stood with others, watching the screen in horror as the second tower crashed down. His problems. Mark's dad. Mark's sister. All of it fled as the enormity of what was happening sunk in.

The whole world had changed.

December 18, 2001
"It's a girl."

Abi Connealy collapsed back onto the bed, tears streaming down her cheeks as a newborn squawk filled the delivery room.

A girl.

A million thoughts flew through her mind, few of them happy, as a nurse laid the baby on her chest. So small. So scrunched up and red. Dark hair. Abi couldn't see her eyes as she wrapped her arms around the tiny bundle. "Hi, baby," she whispered. "I'm so glad you're here."

"How are you?"

Abi looked up at Brenda Wardman. Her brother's girlfriend had been a rock the last few months. She didn't need to clarify, because Abi knew what she meant. "I don't know." The voice mail she'd left her parents on the way to the hospital remained unanswered unless Brenda knew something she didn't.

Her fingers brushed over the cheek of the tiny girl. "She's perfect, Bren." Another tear fell, this one landing on her new daughter's face as Abi closed her eyes.

The nurse took the baby to the warmer and did whatever it was nurses did, but Abi didn't see any of it. Her eyes remained closed, and she clasped Brenda's hand as more hot tears streaked into her ears. Just under twenty-four hours of labor meant she didn't have the energy to wipe them away. She knew she didn't have the will to do so even if she could have.

"Do you know what you're going to do?"

Abi wanted to yell at her friend for bringing up the most difficult decision of her life just moments after the birth of her daughter. But since Abi hadn't made up her mind beforehand, Brenda needed to know to help make the arrangements.

Except Abi didn't know.

Not for sure. She knew what the smart decision was, though her head and her heart didn't agree. But she had to put her baby first. "I'll have them call."

"It's going to be fine," Brenda tried to reassure her, but Abi heard the doubt in her friend's voice.

Right.

Fine.

Once the social worker arrived, she'd never be fine again.

Somehow, Abi managed to doze for several hours during the afternoon, but after listening to the message from her parents, the one that told her all she needed to know without really saying anything, her eyes refused to close. Instead, she stared at the bracelet encircling her wrist, rotating it around time and time again.

A knock sounded half a second before the door pushed open. "Hi, there, Abi. Someone's looking for her mama." The nurse compared the baby's bracelet to Abi's before lifting the blanketed bundle out of the clear bassinet. "The card says you're giving her formula?"

There was no judgment in the woman's voice, but Abi felt her own condemnation eating away at her. All she could do was nod.

After a few minutes of helping them get situated, the nurse started to leave, but stopped before walking out the door. "The emotions are normal, honey. They get everyone at one point or another."

Abi nodded but didn't take her eyes off the little cheeks sucking in and out. She memorized the sounds, the smells, the essence of the tiny bundle in her arms. Or tried to. Even as she did, she knew it would never work. In the morning, a social worker would come and Abi would sign the papers put in front of her.

And she'd never see her daughter again.

But when the social worker sat in the chair by the window, asking the questions, one tripped Abi up.

"Do you know who her father is?"

The night was burned in Abi's memory banks. Part of it anyway. When she hesitated too long, the worker prompted her again. Abi nodded. "Yes. I know who the father is."

"Then we'll need his signature, too."

"He doesn't know," she whispered. "I haven't talked to him since. I was going to, but then 9/11..." Her voice trailed off.

"Was he in the Towers?" the social worker asked as gently as she could.

Abi shook her head. "I don't he was. I mean, I know he wasn't one of the three thousand, but I don't know if he was there or not." She'd called his apartment from a pay phone a few weeks later. When he answered, she hung up.

"If you know who he is, we have to have him sign away his parental rights, sweetie."

Something she hadn't considered when she made this plan.

The nurse walked in, once again pushing the bassinet. Her face fell when she saw the social worker. "I'm sorry. I didn't realize you were..."

With a swipe of the overused Kleenex, Abi wiped her face. "I wasn't sure, but now I can't anyway."

The social worker left a couple of fliers and walked out with a sympathetic smile. The nurse awkwardly helped Abi get situated to feed her daughter one more time.

"Do you have a name you like?" The woman sat on the edge of the bed holding Abi's empty water bottle.

"Cassandra."

"That's beautiful."

"It was my grandmother's name. She died this past summer." The grandmother who would have adored meeting her great-granddaughter, who would have taken Abi and the baby in when she needed somewhere to turn. Had given Abi hope she'd do just that before succumbing to a sudden, massive stroke.

Abi didn't have anyone else like that in her life. Brenda would if she could, but there was no way. Abi had no other family. No one else in her life who would support her no matter what.

Darkness descended, but Abi refused to send little Cassie back to the nursery. She didn't know what she planned to do about adoption, but she wouldn't give up another minute with her baby.

Yet another round of tears leaked down her face as Abi cuddled the tiny bundle against her chest. With all but one light turned out, the desperate whisper ripped from her throat. "God? Are you there?" She'd never prayed before, but this seemed like the time to start if there ever was one. "I don't know what to do."

Baby Cassandra yawned and blinked her eyes open, staring up at her mother. The light caught them just right and struck Abi with the bright blue.

Then it hit her.

The one place she could take her daughter where she'd be safe. And loved.

December 23, 2001

Two days before Christmas, Abi sat in a coffee shop on Long Island and waited. Calling him had taken every ounce of courage she had. Leaving the voicemail took more.

Sitting there, Abi didn't know if she could go through with it. The stroller with her little girl sat to her right. On the other side of it, Brenda sat with her back to the door. Diners nearby sipped on gourmet coffee, but Abi focused on the stationary in front of her. She arrived early so she could write the note, but the paper remained nearly blank.

When she'd arrived at her parents' Long Island home after

leaving the hospital, a note reiterated her father's threat. Since then, Abi had planned what to say, but realized she'd never make it through even the shortest speech. She'd planned the words to write, but now the time had come to put pen to paper, and she only managed his name. A glance at her watch told her she didn't have much time. If she didn't write it now, she'd have to make the speech. No way could she do that.

She picked up the Mont Blanc knock-off she'd received for graduation from her grandmother and scribbled a few lines. Her heart squeezed as she reread the note. She couldn't be a student and a mom. But *this*? Abi had her suitcase packed. She wouldn't return to her parents' home but would crash at Brenda's for a few days while her friend went out of town. Brenda knew most of what happened, but not everything. Abi's fingers furrowed through her hair, and she turned to stare out the window. There he stood. His six-foot frame seemed shorter with his shoulders slumped and hands shoved deep in the pockets of his coat. He looked at his watch and trudged across the street.

The bell over the door jangled. Abi crossed through the unfinished sentence, scribbled a last sentiment and her name, and shoved the note in her purse as he sat down across from her.

"Hi." At the sound of his voice, the knots in her gut tightened.

Abi looked up, knowing he'd see the remnants of her tears. She twisted the napkin in her hands and tried not the think about the weight she'd gained. And if he'd notice.

"Thanks for coming. I wanted to try to explain, but..." Abi shrugged. "After 9/11, after Mark..." The thoughts of her brother nearly overwhelmed her already overwrought emotions. "Daddy isn't going to pursue anything. I tried to tell him you weren't guilty, but he didn't believe me at first. He found your name in my journal on 9/11-before it was '9/11.' I'd left it lying out by acci-dent." This time the shrug was a mere halfhearted lift of one shoulder.

"Mark?" he interrupted. "I read the list of firefighters a bunch of times to make sure he wasn't there."

"He wasn't on the lists. He was killed at a fire on 9/11. Not at the Trade Center. Another fire where they didn't have enough manpower because of everything else. They think he died right around the time the first tower fell."

Were those tears in his eyes? He and Mark hadn't spoken in months. "I'm so sorry."

Cassandra let out a cry. The disguised Brenda made a shushing sound, but Abi didn't look. She couldn't. It was too much. She had to get out. "Can you excuse me for a minute?"

She didn't wait for a reply but motioned toward the back, leaving before he had a chance to stop her. Brenda went out the front door. Abi dug the paper out and waved the barista over. "Can you give this to that guy?"

The woman nodded. Abi fled to the other side of the street and collapsed in Brenda's arms.

Travis read the note three times before it began to sink in.

Dear Travis,

She had to have written it earlier. There hadn't been time since she excused herself.

I hate doing this to you, especially like this. I tried to handle it on my own. I thought I could, but this semester was so hard. Even more than just everything on 9/11 and Mark. I can't do it. I can't be a college student and a mom.

It took several minutes for that to really register.

A mom?

He read on, his disbelief growing with each word.

The baby in the stroller is yours. From that night. I hate that I haven't told you sooner, but I didn't know how. I couldn't tell my parents what happened, not all of it. They would blame you, and it wasn't your fault. I know this is the coward's way out, but I can't tell you to your face. Everything you need for a couple of days is in the diaper bag and the duffel on the bottom of the stroller. So is her birth certificate.

Her name is Cassandra. She's only a few days old. Please take good care of her for me. I won't be home for a while so you can't reach me. My parents left for vacation out of the country, so they wouldn't be here when she was born.

I wish things had worked out the way we planned. The way we talked about all those times. ~~I wish~~

Whatever she wished, she didn't finish the thought before scribbling through it. About like their relationship had been. A wish that was never finished. He went back to the letter.

Tell Cassandra I love her.

I'm sorry.

Abi

He read it two more times, starting to come to grips with what it meant.

And then the baby began to fuss.

Taking a deep, steadying breath to fortify himself, he turned to the blanket tented over the handle of the car seat. Lifting up one corner, he saw pink. Fuzzy bunnies on the toes of a sleeper. A tiny foot kicking those bunnies in the air. He looked further and saw the bluest eyes he'd ever seen staring back at him, almost as though she knew who he was.

Her father.

Her daddy.

The one responsible for her from here on out.

And in that moment, he fell helplessly in love.

December 25, 2001

Christmas night, the little gray Toyota turned off I-44, south towards Serenity Landing, as the wailing in the backseat reached a new level.

"I'm sorry, Cassandra. We're almost there. I'll get you something to eat in a ten minutes, I promise." Jennifer kicked him out the moment he tried to explain his arrival at the apartment with a baby. Instead, he'd boxed up all his worldly belongings along with the things Abi had left for the baby and packed it in his car. They headed for the only place he knew he could get the help he needed until he had a better handle on things.

Over twelve hundred miles. Stopping every two or three hours to feed his daughter or change her diaper. Sometimes more often than that. Always taking much longer than it should. Failing to take into account how many things would be closed on Christmas Day, he ran out of the bottled water when he needed to make one more meal for his daughter. He pressed the pedal a little closer to the floor in an effort to reach Serenity Landing a little faster.

The newborn squalling had quieted a bit when Travis finally pulled to a stop in front of the house where he'd grown up. In the front window, a Christmas tree stood, multi-colored lights twinkling. In the window next to it, he could see Mom and Dad sitting at the dining room table, though he knew they wouldn't be able to see him. His brother walked in with a platter, piled high with a turkey way too big for the three of them. They'd be eating leftovers for a month.

Another squeak came from the back. "Okay, baby. We're here."

Somehow, Travis managed to get the diaper bag and the baby seat out of the car and headed toward the door, snow crunching under his boots with each step. The smell of oak burning in the fireplace both comforted him and heightened his anxiety. What if they turned him away? Then what?

Should he knock?

He hadn't been home in two and a half years. Did he just walk in?

Even with his hands full, Travis managed to press the doorbell. He took a deep breath and blew it out slowly, finishing as the door opened.

Mom stood there, her jaw hanging down for a second before her hands covered her mouth. "Travis!"

He tried to smile but failed miserably. "Hi, Mom." In the space of a heartbeat, he saw what he needed to in her eyes. Forgiveness. Acceptance. Love. Grace. With a prayer tossed heavenward, he tried again to smile, this time successfully. "There's someone I want you to meet."

Grace to Save
Serenity Landing Tuesdays of Grace

Available Now!

Travis Harders has been a single dad since the day he learned he had a daughter with his only one-night stand. Fifteen years later, he and Cassie are getting along just fine and he's even fallen in love. The last thing he expects to find on his doorstep one Tuesday morning is Cassie's mom - the one person he thought he'd never see again - and she's asking the impossible.

Circumstances, including her firefighter brother's death on 9/11, forced Abi Connealy into a decision she's spent years regretting and her daughter grew up without her. But now, a family crisis compels her to do the one thing she swore she never would: find the daughter she'd abandoned just a few days after birth.

Shocked when Travis doesn't send her packing, Abi prays to a God she doesn't believe in that her relationship with her daughter will be restored.

Travis plans to propose to his girlfriend, but their relationship hits the rocks as he and Abi both struggle with the long-dormant feelings that never had the chance to develop.

When Cassie demonstrates incredible grace toward the grandfather who refuses to acknowledge her existence, Abi begins to learn the love of a Savior - a Savior who has more than enough Grace to Save.

ABOUT THE AUTHOR

When she's not writing about her imaginary friends, USA Today Bestselling Author Carol Moncado prefers binge watching pretty much anything to working out. She believes peanut butter M&Ms are the perfect food and Dr. Pepper should come in an IV. When not hanging out with her hubby, four kids, and two dogs who weigh less than most hard cover books, she's probably reading in her Southwest Missouri home.

Summers find her at the local aquatic center with her four fish, er, kids. Fall finds her doing the band mom thing. Winters find her snuggled into a blanket in front of a fire with the dogs. Spring finds her sneezing and recovering from the rest of the year.

She used to teach American Government at a community college, but her indie career, with over twenty titles released, has allowed her to write full time. She's a founding member and former President of MozArks ACFW, blogger at InspyRomance, and is represented by Tamela Hancock Murray of the Steve Laube Agency.

www.carolmoncado.com
books@candidpublications.com

The CANDID Romance Series

Finding Mr. Write
Finally Mr. Write
Falling for Mr. Write

The Monarchies of Belles Montagnes Series
(Previously titled The Montevaro Monarchy
and The Brides of Belles Montagnes series)

Good Enough for a Princess
Along Came a Prince
More than a Princess
Hand-Me-Down Princess
Winning the Queen's Heart
Protecting the Prince (Novella)
Prince from her Past

Serenity Landing Second Chances

Discovering Home
Glimpsing Hope
Reclaiming Hearts

Crowns & Courtships

Heart of a Prince
The Inadvertent Princess
A Royally Beautiful Mess

Crowns & Courtships Novellas

Dare You

A Kaerasti for Clari

Serenity Landing Tuesdays of Grace
9/11 Tribute Series

Grace to Save

Serenity Landing Lifeguards
Summer Novellas

The Lifeguard, the New Guy, & Frozen Custard
(previously titled: The Lifeguards, the Swim Team, & Frozen Custard)
The Lifeguard, the Abandoned Heiress, & Frozen Custard

Serenity Landing Teachers
Christmas Novellas

Gifts of Love
Manuscripts & Mistletoe
Premieres & Paparazzi

Mallard Lake Township

Ballots, Bargains, & the Bakery (novella)

Timeline/Order for Crowns & Courtships and Novellas
1. *A Kaerasti for Clari*
2. *Dare You*
(the first two can be read in either order, but technically this is the timeline)
3. *Heart of a Prince*
4. *The Inadvertent Princess*
5. *A Royally Beautiful Mess*

Made in United States
Orlando, FL
25 March 2022

16149472R00221

Prince from her Past

Carol Moncado

USA Today Bestselling Author

CANDID
Publications